PRIMARY THREAT

Primary Threat

The Forging of Luke Stone—Book #3 (an Action Thriller)

Jack Mars

JACK MARS

Jack Mars is the USA Today bestselling author of the LUKE STONE thriller series, which includes seven books. He is also the author of the new FORGING OF LUKE STONE prequel series, comprising three books (and counting); and of the AGENT ZERO spy thriller series, comprising seven books (and counting).

ANY MEANS NECESSARY (book #1), which has over 800 five star reviews, is available as a free download on Amazon!

Jack loves to hear from you, so please feel free to visit www. Jackmarsauthor.com to join the email list, receive a free book, receive free giveaways, connect on Facebook and Twitter, and stay in touch!

TABLE OF CONTENTS

CHAPTER ONE

September 4, 2005
5:15 p.m. Alaska Daylight Time (9:15 p.m. Eastern
Daylight Time)
Martin Frobisher Oil Platform
Six Miles North of the Arctic National Wildlife
Refuge
The Beaufort Sea
The Arctic Ocean

No one was ready when the killing started.

Moments before, the man they called Big Dog stood at the rail in quilt-lined coveralls, steel-toed boots, thick leather gloves, and a faded yellow baseball cap that said *Hunt Hard* across the front.

It was cold out, but Big Dog didn't feel the cold anymore. And it was nowhere near as cold as it was going to be. All around him was the vastness of the Arctic—gray sky, dark water punctuated with bright white ice, as far as the eye could see.

He smoked a cigarette and watched a double-hulled personnel boat working its way through the ice floes in the bleak light of late afternoon. You couldn't call it sunlight. The cloud cover was constant now, like a heavy blanket, and Big Dog hadn't seen a speck of sunlight in at least a week. It was easy to lose track of the sun. It was easy to lose track of everything.

"They're early," Big Dog said out loud to himself.

That boat didn't sit quite right with him. It gave him an uncertain feeling in his gut. It looked a lot like a boat that would bring crew members out to the rig after a break. In fact, from here he could make out at least a dozen men on the deck of the boat, preparing to disembark when they reached the dock.

But shift changes didn't happen early, and boats didn't appear unscheduled and unannounced. Not out here. He tried to run through the possible reasons for that boat in his mind. But he was hung over again, and the jackhammer pain in his head, combined with the brain fog from lack of sleep, made it hard to think.

No matter. It would all get worked out when they got here. It was just barely possible that someone made a mistake. A lot of people in the Arctic had no idea what day it was. No one here spoke of Monday or Tuesday or Wednesday or Thursday. What would be the point? Every twelve hours was the same, working or sleeping, working or sleeping. Time blended, blurred, faded into hard steel and cold white oblivion.

Whoever they were, no matter what they were doing, they would have to come talk to Big Dog. Big Dog wasn't as mean as he once had been. He had grown up on the reservation, what he called half Blackfeet Indian, and half "American." And once upon a time, he'd been as mean as they came.

Six feet, seven inches tall, 250 pounds when he was light, 275 when he was carrying beer muscle. Past fifty years old now, he was easier, less quick to anger, possibly even a little bit compassionate. Still, he was the biggest man out this way, maybe the biggest man in the Arctic, and this was his oil rig.

Big Dog had been on the crew that built this thing. For five years, he had been the crew foreman. He was not a geologist, he was not the driller, and he was not a college-educated company man, but make no mistake. There were more than ninety men on this rig at any given time, and every single one of them, even the bosses, reported to him.

It was a half-billion-dollar hunk of steel, the *Martin Frobisher*—"The Bish," as the roughnecks who worked it, and lived on it for two weeks at a time, tended to call it. The Bish was a royal blue and yellow tower, platforms and blocks of machinery stacked high over the hole where the drill entered the ocean floor. The top of this tower stood forty stories above the water. It was positioned more than 250 miles above the Arctic Circle, on a six-acre man-made island just offshore from the Arctic National Wildlife Refuge.

The Bish was owned by a small company called Innovate Natural Resources. Innovate had contracts with all the biggies—BP, ExxonMobil, ConocoPhillips—but this was Innovate's own rig. Big Dog often thought the heavy hitters let Innovate operate out here because it gave them plausible deniability about what was going on. Innovate did the dirty work, and if anyone found out about it, Innovate would take the fall.

The island was reachable by ice road over the frozen sea most of the year. But not in summer, and not even in September. Not anymore. The permanent ice was gone—melted—and the water was open all summer. With summer over, the seasonal ice was starting to fill in.

As Big Dog watched, the boat pushed through the last of it and pulled up to the dock. A couple of Bish dockworkers began to tie the boat's lines when a strange thing happened. It was so strange that several seconds passed before Big Dog's mind could grasp it.

Men jumped off the boat and shot the dock hands.

CRACK! came the sharp report of gunfire, echoing across the distance in the still, cold air. In the fading light, miniature men fell dead with each shot.

CRACK!

CRACK!

Suddenly Big Dog was running. His heavy boots pounded across the iron rails of the deck, and he burst through the doors of the doghouse, the command center. It was like the pilot house of a ship, only instead of watching the open sea, men watched the drill all day. There were three men inside this time of day. As Big Dog came in, the men were already up and moving, breaking into the cabinet where the rifles were stored. The rifles were meant for polar bears, not invasions.

"What the hell is going on?" Big Dog said.

A heavyset man with glasses, Aaron, a company man, tossed a heavy rifle to Big Dog. It had a banana magazine poking from the bottom of it, and a scope up top.

Big Dog chambered a round.

Aaron shook his head. "No idea. We tried to raise them on the radio, but no answer. We figured we'd wait until they got here. Then they got here and started shooting."

He gestured at the closed circuit security screens.

On one screen, a group of men moved up the docks. They were dressed in black, for cold weather, faces covered except for the eyes, and draped with guns and ammunition belts. As Big Dog watched, one of them approached a man writhing on the dock, pulled a pistol, and shot the man in the head.

"Aw no," Big Dog said.

It hurt him. It hurt him to his core. And it made him angry. This was his rig, and those were his men being killed out there. During his decades in the Arctic oil industry, nothing like this had ever happened. Were there fights? Sure. Fist fights, knife fights, fights with pool cues and iron pipes. Gunfights, even? Yes, once in a rare while, someone pulled a gun.

But this?

No way.

And it wouldn't stand.

The men in the control room stared at Big Dog.

The first thing Big Dog did when he left the reservation at the age of seventeen, he joined the Marine Corps. They spotted his eye right away, and they made him a sniper.

"The sons of bitches," he said.

He didn't care who they were or what they thought they were doing, it wasn't going to stand. He went back out onto the deck, rifle cradled in his thick hands.

Below him, the group of men was running through the compound now, running for the Quonset huts that served as housing, the rec hall, the mess hall. Clarion alarms were screeching, and men were starting to emerge from everywhere, running. There was confusion, and there was fear.

Shooting came easy to Big Dog. Men had their skills, he supposed, the things that came easy. This was one of his. He sighted through the scope and put one of the black-jacketed invaders in the middle of the circle. The man was RIGHT THERE, so close Big Dog could reach out and touch him. Big Dog squeezed the trigger. The rifle bucked in his hands and pushed against his shoulder.

BANG!

The sound echoed far away across the ice and water.

It was a center mass hit, chest high. The man threw up his arms and dropped his gun. He was knocked backward, off his feet, and he tumbled across the frozen ground.

Not good. That told Big Dog the man was wearing body armor. The bullet didn't pierce him—it knocked him backward. He was going to feel that thing for a while, and he was going to be sore as hell tomorrow, but he wasn't going to be dead.

Not yet, anyway.

Big Dog ejected the spent shell and chambered another round. He sighted again and found his man crawling along the ground.

He put the circle around the man's head.

BANG.

The echo drifted away across the vast, empty wastes. Blood sprayed where the man's head had just been. Automatically, without thought, Big Dog ejected the shell and chambered a new round.

Next.

Another black-jacketed bastard kneeled by the dead guy. He seemed to be checking vital signs. Checking them for what? Half the man's head was gone.

Big Dog smiled and put the new guy's head in the circle, dead center. The guy was an idiot.

BANG.

But not anymore.

The second man's head exploded just as the first had done, a spray of red in the air, like the white spray from the blowhole of a humpback whale just below the surface. The two dead men slumped together now, black mounds on white ground.

Big Dog pulled the gun down to get a wider view of the field. The scene was chaos. Men were running everywhere. Men were shooting. Men were falling dead.

Too late, he saw two men in black, both taking a knee. They pointed guns up at him. From this distance, he couldn't tell what the men were carrying. They were small submachine guns, compact, Uzis maybe, or MP5s.

Less than a second passed.

Big Dog pushed away from the iron railing just as the first spray of bullets hit. They went right through him and he felt himself doing a spastic, jittering dance. Then the pain came, as if on time delay.

His feet slipped backward, out from under him, and he fell forward onto the railing. He thought he might vomit over the side.

But his height, and his momentum, carried his whole body forward. There was an awkward moment when it seemed he was perched on the rail, all the weight on his stomach. Then he was falling. He scrabbled madly for the iron slats behind him, but it was no use.

A second or two passed. Then IMPACT.

Time stopped. He drifted. When he opened his eyes again, it seemed he was gazing up at a dark sky. The last of the bleak day had passed, and the cold stars in their millions were coming out, playing hide and seek behind skittering clouds. He blinked and it turned to daylight again.

He knew what had happened. He had fallen to the iron deck two stories below the doghouse level. He had hit hard. His whole body must be broken. His skull must be cracked.

Also, when the memory came, it was like the bullets were piercing him again. His body jerked convulsively. He had been shot with machine guns.

There was no telling how much time had passed. It could have been minutes. It could have been hours. He tried to move. It hurt to do anything. That was a good sign—he could still feel. There was a lot of dark liquid around him on the deck—his blood. He wheezed as he breathed, like a hydraulic lift going bad, fluid bubbling from his mouth.

Somewhere, not far, gunshots were still ringing out. Men were shouting. Men were screaming in pain, or in terror.

Shadows moved across him.

Two men stood there, looking down. They both wore heavy black jackets with white patches. The image on the patches seemed to be an eagle or another bird of prey. They wore green camouflage pants, like an army would wear on land, someplace where the world wasn't covered in white. And they wore heavy black boots.

The men's faces were covered in black balaclavas. Only their eyes showed. Their eyes were hard, without sympathy.

What did these guys think they were doing?

"Who …?" Big Dog said.

It was hard to speak. He was dying. He knew that. But he wasn't someone who threw in the towel. Never before, and not now.

"Who are you?" he managed to say.

One of the men said something in a language Big Dog didn't understand.

He raised a pistol and pointed it down at Big Dog. The hole at the end of the barrel was there, like a cave. It seemed to loom larger and larger.

The other man said something. It was a serious thing. Neither of them laughed. Their flat expressions didn't change. They probably thought they were doing Big Dog a favor, putting him out of his misery.

Big Dog didn't mind a little pain. He didn't believe in heaven, or hell. When he was young, he had prayed to his ancestors. But if his ancestors were out there, they hadn't seen fit to respond.

Maybe there was life after death, maybe there wasn't.

Big Dog would rather take his chances here on Earth. The rig doctor might be able to patch him up. A medevac helicopter might come and bring him to the small trauma center in Deadhorse. An Apache helicopter might come and wipe these guys out.

Anything could happen. As long as he was breathing he was still in the game. He raised a bloody hand. Amazing he could still move his arm.

"Wait," he said.

I don't want to die now.

Big Dog. For decades, that's what practically everyone had called him. His ex-wife called him Big Dog. His bosses called him Big Dog. The president of the company had flown in here one time, shook his hand, and called him Big Dog. He grunted at the thought of it. His real name was Warren.

A small flash of light and flame appeared from the black maw at the end of the man's gun. The darkness came and Big Dog didn't know if he'd really seen that light, or if this whole thing had been a dream all along.

CHAPTER TWO

9:45 p.m. Eastern Daylight Time
The Situation Room
The White House
Washington, DC

"Mr. President, your thoughts?"

Clement Dixon was too old for this. That was his major thought.

He sat at the head of the table, and all eyes were on him. Over a long career in politics, he had learned to read eyes, and facial expressions, with the best of them. And what his face reading told him was this: the high-powered people looking at the white-haired gentleman presiding over this emergency meeting had all reached the same conclusion as Dixon himself.

He was too old.

He had been a Freedom Rider since the very first ride, May 1961, risking his life to help desegregate the South. He had been one of the young speakers on the streets during the Chicago Police Riot of August 1968, and had been tear-gassed in the face. He had spent thirty-three years in the House of Representatives, first sent there by the good people of Connecticut in 1972. He had served as Speaker of the House twice, once during the 1980s, then again up until just a couple of months ago.

Now, at the age of seventy-four, he suddenly found himself President of the United States. It was a role he had never wanted or imagined for himself. No, wait. Scratch that—when he was young, a teenager, early twenties, he had pictured himself one day as President.

But the America he had imagined himself President of was not *this* America. This was a divided place, embroiled in two publicly acknowledged foreign wars, as well as half a dozen clandestine "black operations"—operations so black, apparently, that the people overseeing them were reluctant to describe them to their superiors.

"Mr. President?"

In his youth, he had never imagined himself President of an America still utterly dependent on fossil fuels for its energy needs, where twenty percent of the population lived in poverty, and another thirty percent teetered on the verge of it, where millions of children went hungry every night, and more than a million people had nowhere to live. A place where racism was still alive and well. A place where millions of people could not afford to get sick, and people often had to decide between taking their prescription medications and eating. This was not the America he had dreamed of leading.

This was a nightmare America, and suddenly he was in charge of it. A man who had spent his whole life standing up for what he believed was right, and fighting for the highest ideals, now found himself crawling through the muck. This job offered nothing but trade-offs and gray areas, and Clement Dixon was right in the middle of it all.

He had always been a religious man. And these days he found himself thinking of how Christ had asked God to let the cup pass him by. Unlike Christ, however, his place on this cross was not pre-ordained. A series of mishaps and bad decisions had brought Clement Dixon to this place.

If President David Barrett, a good man whom Dixon had known for many years, hadn't been murdered, then no one would have looked to Vice President Mark Baylor to take his place.

And if Baylor hadn't been implicated by a mountain of circumstantial evidence in that murder (not enough to charge him, but more than enough to see him disgraced and banished from public life), then he wouldn't have resigned, leaving the Presidency to the Speaker of the House.

And if Dixon himself hadn't agreed last year to spend just one more term as Speaker, despite his advanced age...

Then he wouldn't have found himself in this position.

Even if he'd just had the strength of will to *turn the damn thing down*...Just because the Line of Succession dictated that the Speaker assume the job, didn't mean he had to *accept the job*. But too many people had fought for too long to see a man like Clement Dixon, the fiery standard bearer of classical liberal ideals, become President. As a practical matter, he could not walk away.

So here he was—tired, old, limping through the hallways of the West Wing (yes, *limping*—the new President of the United States had arthritis in his knees and a pronounced limp), overwhelmed by the sheer weight of the thing entrusted to him, and compromising his ideals at every turn.

"Mr. President? Sir?"

President Dixon was sitting in the egg-shaped Situation Room. Somehow, the room reminded him of a TV show from the 1960s— the show was called *Space: 1999*. It was a silly Hollywood producer's idea of what the future must look like. Stark, empty, inhuman, and designed for maximum use of space. Everything was sleek and sterile, and exuded zero charm.

Large video screens were embedded in the walls, with a giant screen at the far end of the oblong table. The chairs were tall leather recliners like the captain on the control deck of a starship might have.

This meeting had been called at short notice—as usual, there was a crisis on. Outside of every seat at the table being taken, and a few along the walls, the room was mostly empty. The usual suspects were here, including a few overweight men in suits, along with thin and ramrod-straight military men in uniform.

Thomas Hayes, Dixon's new Vice President, was also here, and thank heavens for that. Having come aboard straight from being

governor of Pennsylvania, Thomas was accustomed to making exec-
utive decisions. He was also on the same page with Dixon about
many things. Thomas helped Dixon form a unified front.

Everyone knew that Thomas Hayes had designs on the presidency himself, and that was fine. He could have it, as far as Clement
Dixon was concerned. Thomas was tall, and handsome, and smart,
and he projected an air of authority. Yet the most prominent thing
about him was his very large nose. The national press had already
started to tweak him about it.

Just wait, Thomas, Dixon thought. *Wait until you're President.* The
political cartoonists were drawing Clement Dixon as the absent-
minded professor, a cross between Mark Twain and Albert Einstein
with their shoes untied, and minus the homespun humor or penetrating intelligence.

Boy, they would sure have fun with that Hayes nose.

A tall man in a green dress uniform stood at the far head
of the table, a four-star general named Richard Stark. He was
thin and very fit, like the marathoner he surely was, and his face
appeared to be chiseled from stone. He had the eyes of a hunter,
like a lion, or a hawk. He spoke with utter confidence—in his
impressions, in the information given him by his underlings, in
the ability of the United States military to hammer any problem
into submission, no matter how thorny or complicated. Stark was
practically a caricature of himself. He seemed as if he'd never
experienced a moment of uncertainty in his lifetime. What was
the old saying?

Often incorrect, but never in doubt.

"Explain it again," President Dixon said.

He could almost hear the silent groans from around the room.
Dixon hated to have to hear it again. He hated the information as
he understood it, and he hated that one more try ought to make
him understand it completely. He didn't want to understand it.

Stark nodded. "Yes, sir."

He pointed with a long wooden pointer at the map on the large
screen. The map showed the North Slope borough of Alaska, a vast

territory at the northern edge of the state, inside the Arctic Circle, and bordering on the Arctic Ocean.

There was a red dot in the ocean just north of land's end. The land there was marked ANWR, which Dixon well knew stood for the Arctic National Wildlife Refuge—he was one of the people who had fought for decades to have that sensitive region protected from oil exploration and drilling.

Stark spoke:

"The Martin Frobisher drilling platform, owned by Innovate Natural Resources, is located here, in the ocean six miles north of the Arctic Wildlife Refuge. We don't have an exact census at the time of the attack, but an estimated ninety men live and work on that platform, and a small surrounding artificial island, at any given time. The platform operates twenty-four hours a day, three hundred sixty-five days a year, in all but the most severe weather."

Stark paused and stared at Dixon.

Dixon made a hand motion like a wheel spinning.

"I got it. Please continue."

Stark nodded. "A little over thirty minutes ago, a group of heavily armed, unidentified men attacked the platform and the encampment. They arrived by boat, on a vessel made to appear as a personnel tender bringing workers to the island. An unknown number of workers have been killed or taken hostage. Preliminary reports, gleaned from video and audio feeds, suggest that the invaders are of foreign, but still unknown, origin."

"What suggests this?" Dixon said.

Stark shrugged. "They don't seem to be speaking English. Although we have no clear audio yet, our language experts believe they are speaking an eastern European, likely a Slavic, language."

Dixon sighed. "Russian?"

The day he took over this thankless job, indeed moments after he took the Oath of Office, he had unilaterally stood American forces down from a confrontation with the Russians. The Russians had done him a favor and responded in kind. And Dixon had then been subjected to merciless and scathing criticism from the warmongering quarters of American society. If the Russians turned around and attacked now…

Stark shook his head the slightest amount. "Not sure yet, but we think not."

"That narrows it down," Thomas Hayes said.

"Do we have any idea what they want?" Dixon said.

Now Stark shook his head completely. "They haven't contacted us, and refuse to answer our attempts at contact. We have flown over the complex with helicopter gunships, but except for a few fires, the place currently seems deserted. The terrorists, and the prisoners, are either inside the rig itself, or inside complex buildings, away from our prying eyes."

He paused.

"I imagine you want to go in with force and take the rig back," Dixon said.

Stark shook his head again. "Unfortunately, no. As much as we are one hundred percent certain we can take back the facility through sheer force, doing so will put the lives of any men being held prisoner at risk. Also, the facility is of a sensitive nature, and if we make a large-scale counterattack, we risk calling attention to it."

A few people in the room began murmuring together.

"Order," Stark said, without raising his voice. "Order, please."

"Okay," Dixon said. "I'll bite. What's sensitive about it?"

Stark looked at a bespectacled man sitting halfway down the table from the President. The man was probably in his late thirties, but he carried some extra weight that made him look almost like an angelic child. The man's face was serious. Heck, he was in a meeting with the President of the United States.

"Mr. President, I'm Dr. Fagen of the Department of the Interior."

"Okay, Dr. Fagen," Dixon said. "Just give it to me."

"Mr. President, the Frobisher platform, although owned by Innovate Natural Resources, is a joint venture between Innovate, ExxonMobil, ConocoPhillips, and the United States Bureau of Land Management. We have extended them a license to do what is known as horizontal drilling."

On the screen, the image changed. It showed an animated drawing of an oil platform. As Dixon watched, a drill extended downward from the platform, below the surface of the ocean, and into the sea floor. Once underground, the drill changed direction, making a ninety-degree turn and now moving horizontally beneath the bedrock. After a time, it encountered a black puddle beneath the ground, and oil from the puddle began to flow sideways from the drillhead into the pipe following behind it.

"Instead of drilling vertically, which is how the vast majority of drilling was done in the twentieth century, we are now mastering the science of horizontal drilling. What this means is that an oil platform can be many miles from an oil deposit, perhaps a deposit in an environmentally sensitive location ..."

Dixon held up a hand. The hand meant STOP.

Dr. Fagen knew what the hand meant without having to ask. Instantly, he stopped speaking.

"Dr. Fagen, are you telling me that the Martin Frobisher, out at sea six miles north of the Arctic National Wildlife Refuge, is in fact drilling inside the Wildlife Refuge?"

Fagen was staring down at the conference table. His body language alone told Clement Dixon all he needed to know.

"Sir, with the newest technologies, oil platforms can exploit important underground deposits without endangering sensitive flora or fauna, which I know you have previously expressed your concern ..."

Dixon rolled his eyes and threw his hands up in the air.

"Aw, hell."

He looked at the general.

"Sir," Stark said. "The decision to grant that license was made two administrations ago. It was just a matter of perfecting the technology. Granted, it's controversial. Granted, neither you nor I may agree with it. But I believe that's a fish to fry at another time. At this moment, we have a terrorist operation underway, with an unknown number of American civilians already dead, and even more American lives at risk. Time is of the essence. And as much as is possible, I think we need to keep this incident, and the nature of that facility, out of the public eye. At least for now. Later, after we rescue our people and the smoke clears, there will be plenty of time for debate."

Dixon hated that Stark was right. He hated these…

…*compromises.*

"What do you suggest?" he said.

Stark nodded. On the screen, the image changed and showed a graphic of what appeared to be a group of cartoon scuba divers swimming toward an island.

"We strongly suggest a covert group of highly trained special operators, Navy SEALs, infiltrate the facility, discover the nature of the terrorists and their numbers, decapitate their leadership, and, if at all possible, take back the rig with as little loss of civilian life as circumstances will allow."

"How many and how soon?" Dixon said.

Stark nodded again. "Sixteen, perhaps twenty. Tonight, within the next several hours, before first light."

"The men are ready?" Dixon said.

"Yes, sir."

Dixon shook his head. It was a slippery slope when you were President. That's what he, despite all his years of experience, had never understood. All his fiery stump speeches, his podium thumping, his demands for a fairer, cleaner world…for what? Everything had been sold down the river before you even started.

The Arctic National Wildlife Refuge was off limits to drilling. From the surface. So they parked themselves at sea and drilled from beneath it. Of course they did. They were like termites, always biting, gnawing, and turning the sturdiest construction into a house of cards.

And then the men doing the drilling were attacked and held hostage. And as President, what were you supposed to say—"Let them eat cake"?

Not a chance. They were Americans, and on some hard-to-understand level, they were innocents. *Just doing my job, ma'am.*

Dixon looked at Thomas Hayes. Of all the men in this room, Hayes would be the closest to his own thoughts on this. Hayes would probably be feeling boxed in, betrayed, frustrated, and flabbergasted, just like Clement Dixon.

"Thomas?" Dixon said. "Thoughts?"

Hayes didn't even hesitate. "I understand it's a discussion for another time, but I'm shocked to hear that we're drilling in a natural environment that needs to be cherished and protected. I'm shocked, but not surprised, and that's the worst part."

He paused. "After these men are rescued, and as you say the smoke clears, I think we need to revisit the moratorium on drilling, and make it crystal clear that no drilling means no drilling, whether from the surface or from under the sea.

"Further, if there is going to be a military action here, I think we need to make sure there's civilian oversight of the entire operation from beginning to end. No offense, General, but you guys at the Pentagon have a tendency to swing at mosquitoes with sledgehammers. I think we've heard about one too many wedding receptions in the Middle East being annihilated by drone strikes."

General Stark looked like he was about to say something in reply, then stopped himself.

"Can you do that, General Stark?" Dixon said. "No matter how many military assets are involved, can you guarantee me civilian oversight and participation during the entire operation?"

The general nodded. "Yes, sir. I know the exact civilian agency for the job."

"Then do it," Dixon said. "And save those men on the rig if you can."

CHAPTER THREE

10:01 p.m. Eastern Daylight Time
Ivy City
Northeast Washington, DC

A large man sat on a metal folding chair, in a quiet corner of an empty warehouse. He shook his head and moaned.

"Don't do this," he said. "Don't do this thing."

He was blindfolded, but even with the rag obscuring part of his face, it was easy to see that he was bruised and beaten. His mouth was swollen. His face was covered by sweat and some blood, and the back of his white T-shirt was stained with perspiration. There was a dark stain across the crotch of his blue jeans, where he had wet himself moments ago.

From the ends of his shirtsleeves to his wrists was a dense tangle of tattoos. The man looked strong, but his wrists were manacled behind his back, and his arms were secured to the chair with heavy chains.

His feet were bare, and his ankles were also cuffed with steel manacles—they were cuffed so close together that if he managed to stand up and tried to walk, he would have to bounce instead.

"Do what thing?" Kevin Murphy said.

Murphy was tall, slim, very fit. His eyes were hard, and there was a small scar across his chin. He wore a blue dress shirt, dark dress pants, and polished black Italian leather shoes. His sleeves were rolled just a couple of turns up his forearms. There was nothing rumpled, sweaty, or bloody about him. He did not appear to have made any sort of strenuous exertion. Indeed, he could be on his way to a late dinner at a nice restaurant. The only things that didn't quite fit his look were the black leather driving gloves he wore on his hands.

For a few seconds, Murphy and the man in the chair were like statues, standing stones at some medieval burial site. Their shadows slanted away diagonally in the bleak yellow half-light illuminating this small corner of the vast warehouse.

Murphy took a few steps away across the stone floor, his footfalls echoing in the cavernous space.

He was dealing with an odd combination of feelings right now. For one, he felt relaxed and calm. He was just settling in to the interview, and he had the next few hours if he needed them. No one was coming here.

Outside of the gates to this warehouse was a slum. It was a concrete wasteland, dismal shops all crammed together, liquor stores, check cashing, and payday loan places. Crowds of women carrying plastic bags waited at bus kiosks in the daytime, drunken men on street corners held beer cans and cheap wine in brown paper bags all day and into the night.

Right now, Murphy could hear the sounds of the neighborhood: passing cars, music, shouts and laughter. But it was getting late, and things were beginning to quiet down. Even this neighborhood eventually went to sleep.

So yes, in the near term, Murphy had time. But in the larger sense, time was not his friend. He was a former Delta Force operator and a probationary employee of the FBI Special Response Team. He had performed well so far, including what was considered a brilliant performance in a smoking hot gunfight up in Montreal during his very first assignment.

What no one understood was how brilliant that performance really was. He had played both sides, and before the battle, convinced former CIA operative Wallace Speck, the so-called "Dark Lord" himself, to wire two and a half millions dollars to Murphy's anonymous account on Grand Cayman.

Now Speck was in federal prison and facing the death penalty. That left a question looming large in Murphy's life: Was Speck talking to his captors? And if so, what was he saying?

Did Speck even know who Kevin Murphy was?

"Don't kill me," the man in the chair said.

Murphy smiled. Nearby to the man was another chair. Murphy's sports jacket was draped over it. Underneath the jacket were his holster and his gun. In the pocket of his pants was the large sound suppressor that fit the gun like a hand fits a glove.

Made for each other. How did that old TV ad go? *Perfect together.*

"Kill you? Why would I do that?"

The man shook his head and began to cry. His big upper body heaved with sobs. "Because that's what you do."

Murphy nodded. True enough.

He stared at the man. Sniveling bastard. He hated guys like this. Vermin. The guy was a cold-hearted murderer. A bully. A wannabe tough guy. A man with the words BANG and POW! tattooed across his knuckles.

This was the type of guy who killed helpless innocent people—partly because that's what he was paid to do, but also partly because it was easy, and because he liked doing it. Then, when he ran across someone like Murphy, he fell all to pieces and started to beg. Murphy himself had certainly killed a lot of people, but as far as he knew, he had never once killed a noncombatant or an innocent party. Murphy specialized in killing men who were hard to kill.

But this guy?

Murphy sighed. He had no doubt he could make this guy crawl across the floor like a worm, if he wanted.

He shook his head. It didn't interest him. All he really wanted was information.

"Some weeks ago, right around the time our dear departed President first disappeared, you killed a young woman named Nisa Kuar Brar. Don't deny it. You also killed her two children, a four-year-old girl and a babe in arms. The four-year-old was wearing Barney the Purple Dinosaur pajamas at the time. Yeah, I saw pictures of the crime scene. These people you killed were the wife and daughters of a cab driver named Jahjeet Singh Brar. The whole family were Sikhs, from the Punjab region of India. You bluffed your way into their apartment in Columbia Heights by claiming you were a DC Metro cop named Michael Dell. That's pretty funny. Michael Dell. Did you think that was funny?"

The man shook his head. "No. Absolutely not. None of that's true. Whoever told you all that was a liar. They lied to you."

Murphy's smile broadened. He shrugged. He almost laughed.

This guy...

"Your accomplice told me. A guy who was calling himself Roger Stevens, but whose real name was Delroy Rose." Murphy paused and took another deep breath. Sometimes he got worked up in situations like this. It was important he stay calm. This meeting was about information, and nothing else.

"Any of this starting to ring a bell with you now?"

The man's shoulders slumped. He sobbed quietly, his body shaking.

"No. I don't know who that..."

"Shut up and listen to me," Murphy said. "Okay?"

He didn't touch the man or move closer to him, but the man nodded and didn't say another word.

"Now...I already interviewed Delroy at length. He was helpful, but only up to a point. Things got a little messy, so at the end of the day, I'm willing to believe he told me everything he knew. I mean, who would go through all that suffering just to...what? Protect *you*? Protect someone else like you? No. I think he probably gave me everything he had. But it wasn't enough."

"Please," the man said. "I'll tell you everything I know."

"Yes, you will," Murphy said. "And hopefully without a lot of foolishness."

The man shook his head, emphatically, energetically. For a moment, he was like a mechanical doll, one that you wind up and its head shakes until the key in the back winds down again.

"No. No foolishness."

"Good," Murphy said. He walked to the man and lifted the bloody rag from his eyes. The man's eyes gaped and rolled in their sockets, then settled on Murphy.

"You can see me, right?"

The man nodded, very helpful. "Yes."

"Do you know who I am?" Murphy said. "Yes or no. Don't lie."

The man nodded again. "Yes."

"What do you know about me?"

"You're some kind of Special Forces dude. CIA. Navy SEAL. Black ops. Something like that."

"Do you know my name?"

The man stared straight at him. "No."

Murphy wasn't sure he believed him. He threw out a softball to test the guy.

"Did you kill Nisa Kuar Brar and her two children? There's no sense lying now. You've seen me. All the cards are on the table."

"I killed the woman," the man said without hesitating. "The other guy killed the kids. I had nothing to do with that."

"How did you do the woman?"

"I pulled her into the bedroom and strangled her with a length of computer cable. Ethernet Cat 5. It's strong, but not sharp. It does the job without a lot of blood."

Murphy nodded. That was exactly how it was done. No one without inside information about the crime scene would know that. This guy was the killer. Murphy had his man.

"What about Wallace Speck?"

The man shrugged. "What about him?"

Now Murphy's shoulders slumped.

"What do you think we're doing here, you moron?" he said. His voice echoed through the darkness. "You think I'm out here in this concrete shoebox with you, in the middle of the night, for my health? I don't like you that much. Did Speck hire you to kill that woman?"

"Yes."

"And what does Speck know about me?"

The man shook his head. "I don't know."

Murphy's fist pistoned out and connected with the man's face. He felt the bone across the bridge of the man's nose break. The man's head snapped back. Two seconds later, blood began to flow from one nostril, down the man's face and across his chin.

Murphy took a step back. He didn't want to get any blood on his shoes.

"Try again."

"Speck said there was a black ops guy, special ops. He had an inside track on the whereabouts of the President's Chief of Staff. Lawrence Keller. The special ops guy was going up to Montreal, he was part of the team that was supposed to rescue Keller. Maybe he was the driver. He wanted money. After that…"

The man shook his head.

"You think I'm that guy?" Murphy said.

The guy nodded, abject, in despair.

"Why do you think that?"

The man said something in a quiet voice.

"What? I didn't hear you."

"I was there," the man said.

"In Montreal?"

"Yes."

Murphy shook his head. He smiled. He laughed this time, just a bit.

"Oh, buddy."

The guy nodded.

"What did you do, ditch when it got hot?"

"I saw where it was going."

"And you saw me."

It wasn't a question, but the guy answered it anyway.

"Yeah."

"Did you tell Speck what I looked like?"

The guy shrugged. He was staring at the concrete floor.

"Talk!" Murphy said. "I don't have all night."

"I never spoke to him after that. He was in jail before the sun came up."

"Look at me," Murphy said.

The guy looked up.

"Tell me again, but don't look away this time."

The man looked directly into Murphy's eyes. "I haven't talked to Speck. I don't know where they're holding him. I don't know if he's talking or not. I have no idea if he knows who you are, but if he does, he obviously hasn't given you up yet."

"Why didn't you run?" Murphy said.

It wasn't an idle question. Murphy was facing the same choice himself. He could disappear. Now, tonight. Or tomorrow morning. Sometime soon. He had two and a half million dollars in cash. That would last a man like him a long time, and with his...unique skills...he could top it up once in a while.

But he would spend the rest of his life looking over his shoulder. And if he ran, one person who might creep up behind him was Luke Stone. That wasn't a pleasant thought.

The guy shrugged again. "I like it here. I like my life. I have a little son that I see sometimes."

Murphy didn't like that, the way the guy slipped his son into the conversation. This cold-blooded killer, a man who had just admitted to murdering a young mother, and who was an accessory to the murder of two small children and only God knew what else, was trying to play the sympathy card.

Murphy went to the chair and pulled his gun out of the holster. He screwed the sound suppressor onto the barrel of the gun. It was a good one. This wasn't going to make a lot of noise. Murphy often thought it sounded like an office stapler punching through stacks of paper. Clack, clack, clack.

"You have no reason to kill me," the man said from behind him. "I haven't told anybody anything. I'm not going to talk to anybody."

Murphy hadn't turned around yet. "You ever hear of tying up loose ends? I mean, you do work in this business, don't you? Speck might know who I am, he might not. But you definitely do."

"You know how many secrets I'm sitting on?" the guy said. "If I ever got taken in, believe me, you would be the least of what interests them. I don't even know who you are. I don't know your name. I saw a guy that night. Dark hair, maybe. Short. Five foot nine. Could have been anybody."

Murphy turned and faced him now. The man was sweating, the perspiration popping out on his face. It wasn't that hot in here.

Murphy took the gun and pointed it at the center of the man's forehead. No hesitation. No sound. He didn't say a word. Every line was etched clean, and the man seemed to be bathed in a circle of bright white light.

The guy was talking fast now. "Look, don't do it," he said. "I have cash. A lot of cash. I'm the only one who knows where it is."

Murphy nodded. "Yeah, me too."

He pulled the trigger and...

CLACK.

It was a little louder than normal. He hadn't figured on the echo in the big empty space. He shrugged. Didn't matter.

He left without looking twice at the mess on the floor.

Ten minutes later, he was in his car, driving on the Beltway. His cell phone rang. The number was blocked. It didn't mean anything. It could be good, it could be bad. He picked it up.

"Yes?"

A female voice: "Murph?"

Murphy smiled. He recognized the voice instantly.

"Trudy Wellington," he said. "What a lovely time of night to hear from you. If you tell me where you're calling from, I'll be right over."

She almost laughed. He heard it in her voice. Get them laughing. That was the way into their heart, and into their bedroom.

"Ah...Yeah. Get your mind out of the gutter, Murph. I'm calling from the SRT offices. There's a crisis and we've been pulled in. Don wants a bunch of people in here now, as fast as possible. You're one of them."

Chapter Four

10:20 p.m. Eastern Daylight Time
Fairfax County, Virginia
Suburbs of Washington, DC

"What do you think, baby?"

Luke Stone whispered the words. Probably no one could hear them but him.

He sat on the long white sofa in his new living room, holding his four-month-old baby boy, Gunner, in his lap. Gunner was a big, heavy baby. He wore a diaper and a blue T-shirt that said *World's Best Baby.*

He had drifted off to sleep in Luke's arms some time ago. His little tummy rose up and down, and he snored softly as he slept. Were babies supposed to snore? Luke didn't know, but somehow the sound was comforting. More, it was beautiful.

Now Luke just held Gunner in the semi-darkness and gazed around the room, trying to make sense of the house.

The place was a gift from Becca's parents, Audrey and Lance. That, all by itself, was hard to swallow. He could never afford this place on his government salary, which was a big upgrade from what he'd been making in the Army. Becca wasn't working at all. The two of them together, even if Becca had been working, couldn't afford this house. And that finally brought home to Luke just how much money Becca's family really had.

He had known they were rich. But Luke had grown up without money. He didn't know what rich was. He and Becca had been living at her family's cabin, which fronted Chesapeake Bay on the Eastern Shore. To Luke, that one-hundred-year-old cabin, even though it was an hour-and-a-half commute from his job, had been a spectacular living arrangement. Luke was accustomed to sleeping on the hard ground, or not sleeping at all.

But this place?

He glanced around the house. It was a modern home, with floor to ceiling windows, like something out of an architectural magazine. It was like a glass box. When winter came, when it snowed, he could picture how it might be like one of those old snow globes people used to have when he was a kid. He pictured this coming Christmastime—just sitting in this stunning sunken living room, the tree in the corner, the fireplace lit, the snow coming down all around.

And that was just the living room. Never mind the oversized country kitchen with the island in the middle and the giant double-door refrigerator, freezer on the bottom. Never mind the master bed and master bath. Never mind the rest of the place. And never mind that this house was about a twelve-minute drive from the office.

From Luke's spot on the sofa, he could see out the big south- and west-facing windows. The house sat up on a little rolling hillock of grass. The height extended his vantage point. The house was in a quiet neighborhood of other large houses, set back from the street. There was no parking on the street. In this neighborhood, people parked in their own driveways or garages.

They hadn't met many of their neighbors yet, but Luke imagined they were lawyers, maybe doctors, maybe people with high-level jobs at corporations. He had mixed feelings about it. Not the people, but the place.

For one, he didn't trust Audrey and Lance.

Becca's parents had never liked him. They had always made this clear. Even after Gunner was born, they were grudging at best about letting him and Becca use the cabin. Audrey especially was a master at the snide comment and the undermining maneuver.

He pictured her in his mind—there was something about her that reminded him of a crow. She had deep-set eyes with irises so dark, they seemed almost black. She had a sharp nose, like a beak. She had tiny bones and a thin frame. And she tended to hover nearby, like a harbinger of bad tidings.

But then the Special Response Team had taken on a couple of high-profile operations, and Audrey and Lance had met the legendary Don Morris, pioneer of special operations and the director of the SRT.

Suddenly, they felt that he and Becca needed a better house, and one closer to his work. And just like that, here they were.

He shook his head at the speed of it. He had been known in his career for his sudden reflexes and his fast response time, but this house purchase had happened so fast it nearly made his head spin off his neck.

Two people who had disliked him intensely for years had now just presented him with the greatest gift anyone had ever given him.

He stopped and listened to the quiet. He took a deep breath, almost in tandem with his young son. No. That was wrong. This little boy was the greatest gift he had ever been given. The house was nothing compared to this.

On the table in front of him, his telephone lit up. He stared at it, the blue light throwing crazy shadows in the semi-darkness. The phone was silent because the ringer was off. He hadn't wanted to disturb the baby, or the baby's mama, who was getting some well-deserved and much needed sleep in the bedroom.

He glanced at the time—after ten o'clock. That could only mean a small handful of things. Either an old military buddy was drunk dialing, it was a wrong number, or…He let the phone go until it stopped and went dark.

A moment later, it started up again.

He sighed and glanced at the number. Of course it was work.

He picked up the phone.

"H'lo?"

He said it in the quietest, *I'm asleep why are you bothering me* voice he could muster.

A female voice spoke. Trudy Wellington. He pictured her—young, beautiful, smart, with brown hair cascading over her shoulders.

"Luke?"

"Yes."

She was all business. The thing that had almost happened between them, and which they never talked about, seemed to be dwindling in her rearview mirror. That was probably for the best.

"Luke, we have a crisis. Don is rounding up the usual suspects. I'm already here. Swann, Murphy, and Ed Newsam are on their way."

"Now?" He asked the question even though he knew the answer.

"Yes. Now."

"Can it wait?" Luke said.

"Not really."

"Hmmm."

"And Luke? Bring a bug-out bag."

He rolled his eyes. The job and family life were having trouble meshing. Not for the first time, he wondered if what he did for a living was not compatible with the happy home he and Becca were trying to build for themselves.

"Where are we going?" he said.

"Classified. You'll find out at the briefing."

He nodded. "Okay."

He hung up the phone and took a deep breath.

He hoisted the baby in his arms, stood, and padded down the hall to the master bedroom. It was dark, but he could see well enough. Becca was dozing in the big king-sized bed. He reached down and placed the baby next to her, just touching her skin. In her half-sleep, she made a little sound of pleasure. She put a hand softly on the baby.

He stared down at the two of them for a bit. Mom and baby. A wave of love so intense he would never be able to describe it washed over him. He could barely grasp it himself, never mind express it to another person. It was beyond words.

They were his life.

But he also had to go.

CHAPTER FIVE

11:05 p.m. Eastern Daylight Time
Headquarters of the Special Response Team
McLean, Virginia

"Why are we here?" Kevin Murphy said.

He was dressed in business casual, as though he had just come from a mixer of young professionals.

Mark Swann, dressed in anything but business attire, smirked. He wore a black Ramones T-shirt and ripped jeans. His hair was in a ponytail.

"In the existential sense?" he said.

Murphy shook his head. "No. In the sense of why are we all in this room together in the middle of the night?"

The conference room, what Don Morris sometimes optimistically referred to as the Command Center, was a long rectangular table with a speakerphone device mounted in the center. There were data ports where people could plug in their laptops, spaced every few feet. There were two large video monitors on the wall.

The room was somewhat small, and Luke had been to meetings in here with as many as twenty people. Twenty people made the room look like a crowded train car in the Tokyo subway at rush hour.

"Okay, people," Don Morris said. Don wore a tight-fitting dress shirt, sleeves halfway up his forearms. He had a cup of coffee in a thick paper cup in front of him. His white hair was cropped very close to his head—as if he'd just gone to the barber this afternoon. His body language was relaxed, but his eyes were as hard as steel.

"Thanks for coming in, and so quickly. But let's shut up with the banter now, if you don't mind."

Around the room, people murmured their assent. Besides Don Morris, Swann, Murphy, and Luke, Ed Newsam was here, slouched low in his chair, wearing a black long-sleeved shirt that hugged his muscular upper body. He wore jeans and yellow Timberland work boots, with the shoelaces untied. He looked like this meeting had awakened him from a deep sleep.

Also here was Trudy Wellington. She was in a blouse and dress pants, as though she had never gone home after work. Her red glasses were pushed up onto her head. She seemed alert, also drinking coffee, and she had already begun tapping information into the laptop in front of her. Whatever was going on, she had been privy to it first.

At the far end of the table, near the video screens, was a tall and thin four-star general, in impeccable dress greens. His gray hair was trimmed to the scalp. His face was devoid of whiskers, as if he had just shaved before he walked in here. Despite the lateness of the hour, the guy looked fresh and ready to go another twenty-four, or forty-eight, or however long it took.

Luke had met him once before, but even if he hadn't, he already knew the man in his bones. When he woke each morning, he made his bed before doing anything else—that was the first achievement of the day, and set the table for more. Before the sun peeked into the sky, the guy had probably already run ten miles and scarfed down a meal of cold gruel and high octane coffee. He had West Point go-getter written all over him.

Seated at the table near him was a colonel with a laptop in front of him, as well as a stack of paper. The colonel hadn't looked up from the computer yet.

"Folks," Don Morris said. "I'd like to introduce you to General Richard Stark of the Joint Chiefs of Staff, and his aide, Colonel Pat Wiggins."

Don looked at the general.

"Dick, the brain trust of the Special Response Team is at your disposal."

"Such as it is," Mark Swann said.

Don Morris scowled at Swann, a look one might give a teenage son with a big mouth. But he said nothing.

"Gentlemen," Stark said, then bowed to Trudy. "And lady. I'll get right to the point. There is an unfolding hostage crisis in the Alaskan Arctic, and the President of the United States has authorized a rescue. He has stipulated that the rescue involve the oversight and participation of a civilian agency. That's where you come in.

"When talking with the President, it occurred to me that you give us the best of the both worlds—the Special Response Team is a civilian law enforcement agency, but is loaded with former military special operators. The FBI Director has green-lighted your participation, and Don was kind enough to call this meeting at short notice."

He looked at the group. "With me so far?"

There was a general murmur of agreement.

The colonel was controlling the video screen from his laptop. A map of northern Alaska appeared, along with a sliver of the Arctic Ocean. A small dot out at sea was circled in red.

"This is a rapidly developing situation. What I can tell you is that an hour and a half ago, an oil rig in the Arctic Ocean was attacked and overwhelmed by a group of heavily armed men. There were approximately ninety men stationed on that rig and the artificial island that surrounds it, and an unknown number of those men were killed in the initial attack. A number were also taken hostage, though we do not know how many."

"Who attacked the rig?" Luke said.

The general shook his head. "We don't know. They have refused our attempts at contact, though they have sent video of oil workers gathered in a room and held at gunpoint by men in black masks. Audio from monitoring equipment at the rig has been made available to us by the company that owns the rig. The sound is poor quality, but it does pick up some voices. Besides the English spoken by the oil workers, there appear to be men speaking an Eastern European, possibly Slavic language, though we have no real evidence to back that up."

On the screen, the map changed to aerial imagery of the rig and the camp surrounding it. The oil rig, probably thirty or forty stories high, dominated the first image. Below the rig were numerous Quonset hut–type buildings, as well as walkways between them. Surrounding the tiny compound was a vast, icy sea.

A blown-up image appeared. It showed the compound and the buildings in close detail. There were no people standing upright anywhere. There were at least a dozen bodies lying on the ground, some with halos of blood around them.

Another image appeared. Stretched across the ground was a large white banner with hand-painted black lettering.

AMERICA LIARS + HYPOCRITES.

"That's quite a message," Swann said.

"Admittedly, we have very little to go on. The banner you see certainly suggests an attack by foreign nationals. All of our drone footage shows us a compound devoid of personnel. The attackers appear to have taken all of the surviving workers indoors. Whether that is inside these buildings you see, or aboard the rig itself, we don't know."

For a moment, the screen went blank.

"We have a plan to take back the facility, neutralize the terrorists, and rescue however many civilian personnel are still alive. The plan involves an infiltration and assault, primarily using active-service Navy SEALs, but also yourselves. To carry out that plan, we need to get you to the Alaskan Arctic. Which means we need to hurry."

Ed Newsam raised a hand. "When do you intend to carry out this plan?"

The general nodded. "Tonight. Before first light. Every experience we've had with terrorists over the years suggests that allowing a situation to become protracted is a recipe for failure, and even disaster. The public becomes involved, as do the politicians. The media puts it on the twenty-four-hour television doom loop. Second-guessing the government response becomes a national pastime. A long standoff excites and inspires terrorist fellow travelers in other places. Images of blindfolded hostages held at gunpoint…"

He shook his head.

"Let's not explore that path. The group in question attacked without warning, and so will we. Hitting them before sunrise, under cover of darkness just hours after their own assault, allows us to take back the initiative. A successful incursion, and I have every confidence in its success, will demonstrate to other terror groups that we mean business."

Stark must have seen the stares coming from the SRT personnel.

"We believe the Special Response Team is the right civilian agency to participate in this operation. If you don't agree…" He let that hang there.

Luke had to admit he didn't like where this was going. He had just left his wife and baby son in bed. Now he was supposed to go to the Arctic?

"The Alaskan Arctic has to be four thousand miles from here," Swann said. "How are we supposed to get our people there before first light?"

Stark nodded again. "Closer to forty-five hundred miles. You're right, it's a long way. But we're four hours ahead of them. At the oil rig, it's not quite seven thirty p.m. We'll take advantage of the time difference."

He paused.

"And we have the technology to get you there faster than you might imagine."

"What is he not telling us?" Luke said.

He was sitting in Don's office, across the wide expanse of desk from the man himself.

Don shrugged. "You know they always hold something back. There's something classified about the oil rig, perhaps. Or they know more about the perpetrators than they're letting on. Could be anything."

"Why us?" Luke said.

"You heard the man," Don said. "They need civilian participation and oversight. That comes straight from the President. The man is a long-time liberal. He thinks the military is a big scary bogeyman. Little does he know that the civilian agencies are all packed with ex-military."

"But look at how small we are," Luke said. "No offense, Don. But NSA is a civilian agency. The FBI is, too. Both have a much longer reach than we do."

"Luke, we *are* the FBI."

Luke nodded. "Yes, but the Bureau proper has field offices close to the action out there. Instead, they want to fly us across the continent."

Don stared at Luke for a long moment. For the first time, it really hit Luke how ambitious Don was. The President wanted the SRT for this gig. But Don wanted it just as badly, if not more so. These missions were feathers in Don's cap. Don Morris had put together a team of world-beaters, and he wanted the world to know it.

"As you know," Don said, "the field offices are full of field agents. Investigators and police officers, basically. We are special operations. That's what we're designed for, and that's what we do. We are fast and light, we hit hard, and we've earned a reputation, not only for success in difficult circumstances, but also for total discretion."

Luke and Don looked across the vast desk at one another.

Don shook his head. "Are you having cold feet, son? It's okay if you are. You don't have to prove anything to anyone, least of all me. But at this moment, your team is out there gearing up."

Luke shrugged. "I'm already packed."

Don's broad smile suddenly appeared. "Good. I'm sure you'll all do fine, and you'll be back here for breakfast."

❖ ❖ ❖

"Let's go, man," Ed Newsam said. "This mission ain't gonna happen by itself."

Ed was at Luke's door. He stood there, shouldering a heavy pack. He did not look gung-ho. He did not look excited. If Luke could use one word to describe how Ed looked, he would say it was *resigned.*

Luke sat at his desk staring at the telephone.

"Chopper's on the pad."

Luke nodded. "Gotcha. I'll be right there."

They were about to leave. Meanwhile, Luke was suffering from an ailment he called thousand-pound telephone syndrome. He was physically unable to pick up the receiver and make a call.

"Dammit," he whispered under his breath.

He had checked and rechecked his bags. He had his standard gear for an overnight trip. He had his Glock nine-millimeter, in its leather shoulder holster. He had a few extra magazines loaded for the Glock.

A garment bag with two days of clothing changes was draped over the desk. A small bug-out bag packed with travel-size toiletries, a stack of energy bars, and half a dozen Dexedrine pills sat next to the garment bag.

The Dexies were amphetamines—speed. They were practically in the instruction manual for special operators. They would keep you awake and alert for hours on end. Ed sometimes called them "the quicker picker-uppers."

These were generic supplies, but there was no sense trying to get more specific. They were going to the Arctic, the operation was going to require specialized gear, and that gear would be provided when they landed. Trudy had already sent everyone's measurements on ahead.

So now he stared at the phone.

He had left the house with barely a word of explanation to her. Of course, she had been asleep. But that didn't change anything.

And the note on the dining room table didn't explain anything.

Got called in for a late meeting. May need to pull an all-nighter. Luv you, L

An "all-nighter." That was rich. It sounded like a college kid cramming for the final exam. He had gotten into the habit of lying to her about the job, and it was becoming a hard habit to break.

What good would it do to tell the truth? He could call her right now, wake her out of a sound sleep, wake the baby and get him to start crying, all to tell her what?

"Hi, honey, I'm heading up to the Arctic Circle to take out some terrorists who attacked an oil rig. There are dead bodies all over the ground. Yeah, looks like I could be walking into another blood-bath. Actually, I might never see you again. Okay, sleep tight. Give Gunner a kiss for me."

No. Better to just take his chances, do the operation, and trust that between the Navy SEALS and the SRT, they had the best people to get the job done. Call her in the morning, after it was over. If all went well and everyone was in one piece, tell her they had to fly out to Chicago to interview a witness. Keep the fiction rolling along that working for the SRT was mostly some kind of detective job, marred by the occasional outburst of violence.

Okay. That's what he would do.

"You ready?" a voice said. "Everybody else is boarding the chopper."

Luke looked up. Mark Swann was standing in the doorway. It was always a little startling to see Swann. With his ponytail, his avia-tor glasses, the wisp of scraggly beard on his chin, and the rock-n-roll T-shirts he always seemed to wear…he could practically be wearing a sign around his neck: NOT MILITARY.

Luke nodded. "Yeah. I'm ready."

Swann was smiling. No, cancel that. He was positively beaming, like a kid at Christmas. It was an odd thing to be doing when faced with a tedious flight across North America, followed by a nerve-wracking shoot 'em up against an unknown enemy.

"I just found out how they're getting us there," Swann said. "You won't believe it. Absolutely incredible."

"I didn't realize you were even coming on this trip," Luke said.

If anything, Swann's smile grew even broader.

"I am now."

CHAPTER SIX

September 5, 2005
8:30 a.m. Moscow Daylight Time (12:30 a.m. Eastern
Daylight Time)
The "Aquarium"
Headquarters of the Main Intelligence Directorate
(GRU)
Khodynka Airfield
Moscow, Russia

"What news from our friend?" the man named Marmilov said. He sat at his desk in a windowless basement office, smoking a cigarette. A ceramic ashtray was on the green steel desk in front of him. Although it was early in the morning, there were already five spent cigarette butts in the ashtray. A cup of coffee (with a splash of whiskey—Jameson, imported from Ireland) was also on the desk.

In the morning, the man smoked and drank black coffee. It was how he started his day. He wore a dark suit and his thinning hair was swooped over the top of his head, hardened and held in place by hairspray. Everything about the man was harsh angles and jutting bones. He seemed almost like a scarecrow. But his eyes were sharp and aware.

He had been around a long time, and had seen many things. He had survived the purges of the 1980s, and when the change came, in the 1990s, he had survived that as well. The GRU itself had come through largely intact, unlike its poor little sister,

39

the KGB. The KGB had been broken apart and scattered to the winds.

The GRU was as large and as powerful as it ever was, perhaps more so. And Oleg Marmilov, fifty-eight years old, had played an integral role in it for a long time. The GRU was an octopus, the largest Russian intelligence agency, with its tentacles in special operations, spy networks around the globe, communications interception, political assassinations, destabilizing governments, drug trafficking, misinformation, psychological warfare, and false flag operations, not to mention the deployment of 25,000 elite Spetsnaz troops.

Marmilov was an octopus living inside the octopus. His tentacles were in so many places, sometimes a subordinate would come to him with a report, and he would draw a blank for a moment before thinking:

"Oh yes. *That thing.* How is it going?"

But some of his activities were right on the top of his mind.

Bolted to the top of his desk was a television monitor. To an American of the right age, the monitor would seem similar to the coin-operated TVs that once graced intercity bus stations across the country.

On the screen, live footage from security cameras cycled through. The man assumed there was a delay in the feed, possibly as much as half a minute. Otherwise, the footage was up to the moment.

It was dark in the footage, night had fallen, but Marmilov could see well enough. An iron stairwell climbing the side of an oil rig. A cluster of battered, corrugated aluminum huts on a cold and barren plot of land. A tiny port facility on a frozen sea, with a small, rugged ice cutter ship docked. There didn't appear to be any people in the footage.

Marmilov looked up at the man standing in front of his desk.

"Well? Any news?"

The visitor was a younger man, who, while wearing a drab, ill-fitting civilian business suit, also seemed to stand at military attention.

He stared at something in a far imaginary distance, instead of at the man sitting just a few feet before him.

"Yes, sir. Our contact has relayed the message that a group of commandos has been chosen. Most of them are already amassing at the airfield in Deadhorse, Alaska. Several more, who represent the civilian oversight of the project, are en route by supersonic airplane and will arrive within the next few hours."

The man paused. "From then, it will likely be a very short time before the assault force is deployed."

"How reliable is this intelligence?" Marmilov said.

The man shrugged. "It comes from a secret meeting held at the White House itself. The meeting could of course be a ruse, but we don't think so. The President was in attendance, as were members of the military command."

"Do we know the method of attack?"

The man nodded. "We believe they will deploy frogmen who will swim to the artificial island, emerge from beneath the ice, and mount the attack."

Marmilov thought about that. "The water must be quite cold."

The man nodded. "Yes."

"It sounds like quite a difficult assignment."

Now the young man showed the ghost of a smile. "The frogmen will be wearing cumbersome underwater gear designed to shield them from the cold, and our intelligence suggests they will carry their weapons in sealed packages. They are hoping for the element of surprise, a sneak attack by highly trained elite divers. The weather is forecast to be very poor, and flying will become difficult. As far as we understand, no simultaneous attack by sea or by air is planned."

"Can our friends repulse them?" Marmilov said.

"Given advance warning of their approach, and knowing the method of attack, it's possible that our friends can be waiting for them, and kill them all. After that..."

The man shrugged. "Of course the Americans will bring the hammer down. But that won't be our concern."

Oleg Marmilov returned the young man's smile. He took another deep drag on his cigarette.

"Exceptional," he said. "Keep me informed of developments."

"Of course."

Marmilov gestured at the monitor on his desk. "And naturally, I am a great fan of sport. When the action starts, I will watch every moment of it on the TV."

CHAPTER SEVEN

12:45 a.m. Eastern Daylight Time (8:45 p.m. Alaska Daylight Time, September 4)
The skies above the Upper Peninsula
Michigan

The experimental airplane rocketed across the black sky.

Luke had never been in a plane quite like it. Everything about it was unusual. As the SRT team had approached it on the tarmac, the lights had been out. Not just the lights on the plane itself, but any nearby runway or airport lights. The plane was just sitting there in something close to total darkness.

Its airframe had an odd shape. It was very narrow, with a drooped nose like a bird dipping its beak into the water. The rear stabilizers had an odd triangular shape that Luke hadn't seen before, and couldn't quite make out.

Inside, the cabin layout was also unusual. Instead of being set up like a typical corporate or Pentagon jet, or even the SRT jet, with bucket-type seats and pull-out tables, the thing was configured like someone's living room.

There was a long sectional couch along one wall, its high back blocking where there would normally be small oval windows. There were two recliners facing it, and between the couch and the chairs, a heavy wooden table, like a coffee table, bolted to the floor. Even stranger, directly across from the sofa was a large flat-panel television, blocking where the other row of windows should be.

Stranger than that, from where Luke was sitting on the couch, to his left was a thick glass partition. A glass door was carved into the middle of it. On the other side of the partition was another passenger cabin, this one with seating more typical of a small passenger jet. And strangest of all, two men were seated inside the cabin, discussing something and looking at the screen of a laptop.

The glass partition was apparently soundproof, because the men seemed to be speaking normally, and Luke couldn't hear anything they were saying. The men were both crew-cutted and of military bearing, one wearing a jacket and tie, and one wearing a T-shirt and jeans. The man in the T-shirt was big and well-muscled.

"It's an SST," Swann said. He was sitting on the couch with Luke, just on the other side of Trudy Wellington, who sat between them, poring over documents on her laptop. The plane's very existence seemed to excite Swann in a way that Luke didn't quite understand.

"Supersonic, but not a fighter plane. A passenger jet. Since the French gave up on the Concorde and the Russians gave up on the Tupolev, no one on Earth will even acknowledge working on supersonic passenger jets."

"I guess someone's been working on this one," Luke said.

Murphy, sitting in one of the recliners, gestured with his head at the glass partition.

"I'm wondering who the monkeys are behind door number three."

Big Ed Newsam, slouched like a large mountain in the other recliner, nodded slowly. "You and me both, man."

"Never mind about that," Swann said. He pointed at the TV screen across from the couch. The screen was currently showing an image of an airplane, skirting the northern border of the United States above the state of Michigan. Data along the bottom showed altitude, equivalent groundspeed, and time to destination.

"Look at those numbers. Altitude 58,000 feet. Groundspeed 1,554 miles per hour, roughly Mach 2, twice the speed of sound. We're in the air a little more than thirty minutes, and we've got only two and a half more hours to go. Absolutely mind-blowing for a jet this size, which I'd guess is about the same profile as a typical Gulfstream. Can you imagine the thrust this thing must put out to overcome the drag? I didn't even hear a sonic boom."

He stopped for a second and looked around.

"Did you hear anything?"

Nobody answered him. Everyone else seemed to have their minds on the destination, the mission, and the mysterious nature of the two men in the other room. How they were getting to the mission was beside the point. To Luke, the plane was just another big boy toy, probably overpriced.

But Swann loved his toys. "Notice something about our flight path. We're on our way to the Alaskan Arctic, and by far the most efficient way to get there is by crossing into Canada and moving diagonally north and west across their heartland. But we hug the border instead. Why?"

"Because we like inefficiency?" Ed Newsam said, and smiled.

Swann didn't even catch the joke. He shook his head. "No. Because if we cross into Canada, we have to explain to them what this thing is that's moving twice the speed of sound above their airspace. They might be one of our closest allies, but we don't want to tell them about this plane. That tells me it's classified."

"As a practical matter," Trudy said, without glancing up from her computer, "we'll have to cross into Canada at some point. Alaska isn't attached to the rest of the United States."

Swann stared at Trudy.

"Ouch," Ed said. "Geography lesson. That had to hurt."

"Can we talk about something else?" Murphy said. "Please?"

Luke looked at Trudy Wellington, sitting next to him. She was curled up on the sofa in a customary pose for her, legs curled under her. She could be sitting on her couch at home, eating popcorn and about to watch a movie. Her curly hair was hanging down, and her red glasses were at the end of her nose. She was scrolling through a screen.

"Trudy?" Luke said.

She glanced up. "Yes?"

"What are we doing here?"

She stared at him. Her owlish eyes went wide in surprise.

"Best guess," he said. "Who are the terrorists, what do they want, why did they hit an oil rig, and why now?"

"Is that going to help you?" she said. "I mean, with the mission?"

Luke shrugged. "It could. We seem to be in the dark about everything, and no one seems interested in enlightening us even a little bit."

"Or talking to us, for that matter," Murphy said. He was still staring at the men on the other side of the glass.

"Okay," Trudy said. "I'll give you the easy part first. Why hit an oil rig and why now. Then I'll do a very hazy guess about who they are and what they want."

Luke nodded. "We're all ears."

"I'm going to assume no prior knowledge," Trudy said.

Ed Newsam was slouched so low in his chair he looked like he might slide off onto the floor. "That's probably the safest assumption I've heard all day."

Trudy smiled. "The Arctic Ocean is melting," she said. "People, countries, the media, large corporations, they're all debating the long-term effects of global warming, or whether it even exists. The consensus among the vast majority of scientists is that it's happening. No one has to agree with them. But what can't be denied is that the polar ice caps, which have largely been frozen since the beginning of recorded human history, are now melting, they're doing it quickly, and at an accelerating pace."

"Scary," Mark Swann said. "The end of the world as we know it."

"And I feel fine," Murphy added.

Trudy shrugged. "Let's not go there. Let's just stick with what we know. And what we know is that each year, the Arctic Ocean has less ice on top of it than the year before. Soon, possibly within our lifetimes, it's not going to freeze over anymore at all. Already, the ice cover is thinner, and covers less of an area, for less of the year, than at any time we know of."

"And this means…" Luke said.

"It means the Arctic is opening up. Shipping lanes that never existed before are going to open for traffic. On this side of the world, we're talking about the Northwest Passage that runs between Canadian islands, and which Canada considers inside its sovereign territory. On the other side of the Arctic, we're talking about the Northeast Passage, which hugs the northern coastline of Russia, and which Russia considers its territorial waters. In particular, when the ice opens for good, the Russian Northeast Passage will become the shortest and fastest shipping route between factories in Asia and consumer markets in Europe."

"And if the Russians control it..." Murphy began.

Trudy nodded. "Correct. They will control much of the world's trade. They can tax it, charge tariffs, and Russian ports that have been mostly frozen outposts for hundreds of years may suddenly become bustling ports of call."

"And if they so desired, they could..."

Trudy was still nodding. "Yes. They could shut it down. Meanwhile, the Northwest Passage is a little dicey. If you look at a map, it really is part of Canada. But the United States wants to lay claim to it, potentially setting up strife between two neighboring countries, long-term allies, and trading partners."

"So you think the Russians..." Ed began.

Trudy held up a hand. "But that's not all. There are eight countries that ring the Arctic Ocean. The United States, Canada, and Russia of course, but also Sweden, Norway, Iceland, Finland, and Denmark. Denmark's claim is from owning the territory of Greenland. And the much bigger issue here is that up to one-third of the world's untapped oil and natural gas reserves are thought to be under the ice in the Arctic."

They all watched her.

"Everybody wants those fossil fuels. Countries that have no valid land claims in the Arctic, like Britain and China, are also getting in on the action, seeking to build alliances and obtain drilling rights. China has started referring to itself as a near-Arctic country. Britain has begun talking a lot about their Arctic partners."

"That doesn't explain who did it," Luke said.

Trudy shook her head and her curls bounced the slightest bit. "No. As I said, I was giving you the easy part first. Why attack an oil rig in the Arctic, and why now. The answer is the race is on for Arctic natural resources, and it's going to be a death race. People are going to get killed, in the same way they've been getting killed since oil was discovered in the Middle East in the early part of the twentieth century. The Arctic is an emerging flashpoint for competition among the major powers, and as a result, for violence and even war. It's coming."

Luke smiled. Trudy always seemed to have the answers, but sometimes she needed to be drawn out a little bit to share her conclusions.

"So…who was it?"

But she wasn't ready to play that game. She just shook her head again.

"Impossible to say with any certainty. There are more actors than just those countries involved. There are indigenous groups spread throughout the Arctic, such as Eskimos, Aleut, Inuit, and many others. All of these groups are worried about the new interest in the Arctic. They're concerned about losing their lands, their cultures, and their traditional hunting rights. They're concerned about oil spills and other environmental disasters. In general, indigenous peoples do not have a history of good experiences with powerful countries and large corporations. They're very leery of what's coming, and some of the groups are already radicalized."

"But are they big enough, and well-trained…"

"Of course not," Trudy said. "Not on their own. But we can't assume anyone is acting by themselves. There are dozens of environmental groups, several of which are also radicalized. There are major corporations, especially oil companies, jockeying for position. There are Middle Eastern countries wondering if oil exploration in the Arctic is about to leave them in the lurch. And of course, there's Russia and China."

"The banner," Luke said.

"Yes. The banner calls America hypocrites and liars. That doesn't tell us much, but the simplicity and garbled syntax of it suggests that the people who made the banner are not native English speakers. Meanwhile, the apparent professionalism of the attack suggests at least a high level of training, including cold-weather training, and probably combat experience."

Luke could see where she was headed with this.

"Most of the Arctic countries are either close allies of ours, like Canada, Norway, and Sweden, or have friendly to neutral relations with us, like Iceland, Denmark, and Finland. And I don't think the Russians or Chinese would attack us directly, especially not after all the recent trouble. But would they fund and train a cat's paw, a group that either feels disenfranchised by us, or expects they are about to become disenfranchised?"

She paused.

"Of course they would," Swann said.

Trudy nodded. "They might just."

"So a new, radical anti-American group, kind of like an Al Qaeda of the Arctic?"

Trudy shrugged. "I can't say that for sure. Could be an armed and trained indigenous group or groups. Could be white supremacists from the old Viking world, who are hoping to see the glory of the Scandinavian countries restored. Heck, it could be Quebec separatists. I don't know."

To Luke's left, the glass door to the other passenger cabin slid open. The two men came in. "Good guesses, Ms. Wellington," the older of the two men said. "Probably wrong, but as scenario spinning goes, pretty good nonetheless."

The younger guy wore jeans and a T-shirt. The jeans hugged his muscular legs. The T-shirt hugged his muscular chest. The shirt had two words across the front, very small, white on a black background.

GET HARD.

"Guys, I'm Captain Brooks Donaldson, of the United States Naval Special Warfare Development Group, sometimes called DEVGRU, often called SEAL Team Six."

He was holding up a thick orange wetsuit, complete with hood, gloved hands, and boots. Odd for a Navy SEAL, he had just put down a soft drink can on the table. Luke stared at it. Dr. Peck's ginger beer.

"I want to talk to you all a little bit about hypothermia. It's important for us to think about. For all we know of freezing and its physiology, no one can predict exactly how quickly and in whom hypothermia will strike—and whether it will kill when it does. We do know that it's more likely to kill men than women, and it's more lethal to the thin and well-muscled—and that pretty well describes everyone in this room—than it is to people with a lot of body fat. It's least forgiving to people who are ignorant about its effects. In other words, if you're not prepared for it, and you don't know what to do about it, it can easily kill you."

Already, Luke didn't like where this was going. Nobody had told him to expect anything about wetsuits or hypothermia or Navy SEALs who drank soda pop. The man, Donaldson, indicated the wetsuit in his hands.

"This suit is your first line of defense out there against hypothermia. The demonstration suit is orange, and your operation suits will be black, but don't let that distract you. Just imagine this one as black. In orange or black, or purple or pink, or any color at all, these are state of the art, probably the best cold-water immersion suits in existence at the current time. It provides both flotation and hypothermia protection. Its features include lifting harness and buddy line, five-fingered insulated gloves for warmth and dexterity, inflatable head pillow, face shield and water-tight face seal, adjustable wrists and ankles, 5mm fire retardant neoprene, hailing whistle, light pocket, and non-slip thick-soled booties. But it's a little bit of work to put on and take off in stormy conditions. And I'm going to show you how to do that."

Everyone in the cabin was staring at him.

"Any questions before I begin?"

Murphy raised a hand.

"Yes, Agent…"

"Murphy."

"Yes, Agent Murphy. Shoot."

Murphy glanced at the ginger beer can on the table. He scowled, just a little bit. Murphy was an Irishman from the Bronx. It wasn't clear to Luke what Murphy's exact thoughts were about that ginger beer, but it sure seemed like he didn't approve.

"What are we talking about here?"

Donaldson seemed confused. "What are we talking about?"

Murphy nodded. He gestured at the orange wetsuit. "Yeah. That. Why are you telling us about it? We're not SEALs. We're not really water people at all. Newsam, Stone, and I are all former Delta Force. Airborne assault. I was 75th Rangers before Delta, Stone was 75th Rangers, Newsam was…"

He paused and looked at Ed. Ed was slumped very low in his chair. Any lower, and he would ooze out onto the floor.

"82nd Airborne," Ed said.

"Airborne," Murphy said. "There's that word again. You can show us that suit from now until we land, and all next week, but that's not going to suddenly make us into divers."

"I've done some diving," Ed said.

Murphy stared at him. Luke wasn't sure, but he didn't think he'd ever seen someone stare at Ed that way. Murphy was a vehicle that didn't have reverse.

"Thanks," he said. "You diving wrecks in Aruba really helps my argument."

Ed smiled and shrugged.

The SEAL nodded. "I get your point. But this is an underwater operation. We will drop into the water at a temporary camp being constructed right now on a floating ice sheet about a mile and a half from the oil rig. I thought you knew that."

Luke shook his head. "This is the first we're hearing of it."

"There's no way to go in there by boat," Donaldson said. "We have to assume that our opponents will have all the approach points covered. They appear to have heavy weaponry available to them. Any boat slogging its way through the ice to that oil rig is going to get hit, and hit hard."

"Can we come in from the sky?" Luke said.

Donaldson shook his head. "Even worse. They're expecting a storm to pass through that area in the next few hours. You do not want to be falling from the sky during an Arctic storm, I promise you that. And even if things clear, then they have a clean shot at you as you come down. It'll be like shooting ducks. There's only one way in, and that's to come out from under the ice and take them by surprise."

He paused. "And we're going to need all the surprise we can get. As much as we're going in hard, we need to keep at least one of the attackers alive."

"Why's that?" Ed said.

Donaldson shrugged. "We need to know what these men wanted, what their plan was, and whether they acted alone. We want to know everything about them. Assuming they don't leave us some kind of manifesto, and since no one has claimed responsibility for the attack so far, we have to assume the only way to get that information is to capture at least one of them, and preferably more than one."

Now Luke really didn't like it. They were going in under the ice, and when they came up, they were supposed to capture someone. What if they were jihadis who didn't give up? What if they fought until their last breath?

The whole operation seemed hastily organized and poorly thought through. But of course it was. How could it not be when the plan was to take back the oil rig the same night it was attacked, and in fact, mere hours later?

They had no intel on the attackers. There had been no communication. They didn't know where they were from, what they wanted, what weapons they had, or what other skills. They didn't know what the attackers would do if they themselves were attacked. Would they kill all the hostages? Commit suicide by blowing up the rig? No one knew.

So instead, the whole group was going in blind. Worse, Luke's team was supposed to be the civilian oversight, but they were participating in a mission that was underwater—ice water—something they had no training for. Precious few American soldiers had training for ice water immersion.

"This whole thing," Murphy said, "strikes me as FUBAR."

Luke wasn't sure if he agreed completely. But he was sensitive to the fact that Murphy still probably thought Luke's poor decisions had led to the deaths of their entire assault team in Afghanistan.

If Murphy, or Ed, or even Swann or Trudy decided they wanted out of this mission, it was fine with Luke. People had to make their own decisions—he couldn't decide for them.

Suddenly, he wished he had talked to Becca before leaving on this trip. Now it was too late.

"We've got less than two hours until our ETA," the older man said, glancing at his watch. He looked at Donaldson, who was still holding the thick orange bodysuit. Then he made a spinning motion with his hand, like the arms on a clock moving rapidly.

"I suggest you get this demonstration underway."

CHAPTER EIGHT

**9:15 a.m. Moscow Daylight Time (10:15 p.m. Alaska
Daylight Time, September 4)
The "Aquarium"
Headquarters of the Main Intelligence Directorate
(GRU)
Khodynka Airfield
Moscow, Russia**

Blue smoke rose toward the ceiling.

"There is a great deal of movement," the latest visitor, a pot-bellied man in the uniform of the Interior Ministry, said. His voice belied a certain anxiety. It was nothing in the timbre of the voice. It didn't tremble or crack. You had to have the right ears to hear it. The man was afraid.

"Yes," Marmilov said. "Would you expect anything less from them?"

Although the office had no windows, the light had changed as the morning progressed. Marmilov's swooping, hardened hair now resembled a type of dark plastic helmet. The overhead lights seemed so bright it was as if Marmilov and his guest were sitting in the desert at midday, the sun casting deep shadows into the fissures carved into the ancient stone of Marmilov's face.

People sometimes wondered why a man with such influence chose to run his empire from this tomb, underneath this bleak, crumbling, run-down building well outside Central Moscow. Marmilov knew about this wonder because men, especially powerful men, or those aspiring to be powerful, often asked him this very question.

"Why not a corner office upstairs, Marmilov? Or a man like yourself, whose mandate far surpasses just the GRU, why not get yourself transferred to the Kremlin, with a wide view of Red Square and the opportunity to contemplate the deeds of our history, and the great men who have come before? Or perhaps just watch the pretty girls passing by? Or at the very least, a chance to see the sun?"

Marmilov would smile and say, "I do not like the sun."

"And pretty girls?" his friendly tormentors might say.

To this Marmilov would shake his head. "I'm an old man. My wife is good enough for me."

None of this was true. Marmilov's wife lived fifty kilometers outside the city, in a country estate dating to before the Revolution. He barely ever saw her and neither she nor he had a problem with this arrangement. Instead of spending time with his wife, he stayed in a modern hotel suite at the Moscow Ritz Carlton, and he feasted on a steady diet of young women brought directly to his door. He ordered them up like room service.

He had heard that the girls, and for all he knew, their pimps as well, referred to him as Count Dracula. The nickname made him smile. He couldn't have chosen a more fitting one himself.

The reason he stayed in the basement of this building, and didn't move to the Kremlin, was because he didn't want to see Red Square. Although he loved Russian culture more than anything, during his workday, he didn't want his actions tainted by dreams of the past. And he especially didn't want them handicapped by the unfortunate realities and half-measures of the present.

Marmilov's focus was on the future. He was hell bent on it.

There was greatness in the future. There was glory in the future. The Russian future would surpass, and then dwarf, the pathetic disasters of the present, and perhaps even the victories of the past.

The future was coming, and he was its creator. He was its father, and also its midwife. To imagine it fully, he couldn't allow himself to become distracted by conflicting messages and ideas. He needed a pure vision, and to achieve this, it was better to stare at a blank wall than out the window.

"No, I wouldn't," the fat man, Viktor Ulyanov, said. "But I believe there are some in our circle who are concerned by the activity."

Marmilov shrugged. "Of course."

There were always those who were more concerned about the skin on their own necks than on leading the people to a brighter day.

"And there are some who believe that when the President…"

The President!

Marmilov nearly laughed. The President was a speed bump on this country's path to greatness. He was an impediment, and a minor one at that. Ever since this President had taken the reins from his alcoholic mentor Yelstin, Russia's comedy of errors had worsened, not improved.

President of what? President of garbage!

The President needed to watch his back, as the saying went. Or he might soon find a knife protruding from it.

"Yes?" Marmilov said. "Concerned that when the President… what?"

"Finds out," Ulyanov said.

Marmilov nodded and smiled. "Yes? Finds out… What will happen then?"

"There will be a purge," Ulyanov said.

Marmilov squinted at Ulyanov in the haze of smoke. Could the man be joking? The jest wouldn't be that Putin finding out would lead to a purge. If handled incorrectly, of course it would. The jest would be that at this late date in the preparations, Ulyanov and unnamed others would suddenly be thinking about such a thing.

"The President will find out after it is too late," Marmilov declared simply. "The President himself will be the one who is purged." Ulyanov, and any others he was speaking for, must know this. It had been the plan all along.

"There is concern that we are arranging a bloodbath," Ulyanov said.

Marmilov blew smoke into the air. "My dear friend, we are not arranging anything. The bloodbath is already arranged. It was arranged years ago."

Here in Marmilov's lair, a laptop computer had sprouted like a mushroom next to the small TV screen on his desk. The TV still showed closed circuit footage from security cameras at the oil rig. The laptop showed transcripts of intercepted American communications translated into Russian.

The Americans were tightening a noose around the captured oil rig. A ring of temporary forward bases were appearing on floating ice within a few miles of the rig. Black operations teams were on high alert, preparing to strike. An experimental supersonic jet had received clearance, and landed at Deadhorse perhaps thirty minutes ago.

The Americans were set to strike.

"It was never the intention to hold the rig for very long," Marmilov said. "This is why we used a proxy. We knew that the Americans would take back their property."

"Yes," Ulyanov said. "But the very same night?"

Marmilov shrugged. "Sooner than we expected, but the result will be the same. Their initial assault teams will meet with disaster. A bloodbath, as you say. The bigger, the better. Their hypocrisy regarding the environment will be exposed. And the world will have occasion to remember their war crimes of the not too distant past."

"And how much of this will blow back to us?" Ulyanov said.

Marmilov took another deep inhale from his cigarette. It was like the breath of life itself. Yes, even here in Russia, even here in Marmilov's inner sanctum, you could no longer hide from the facts. Cigarettes were bad for you. Vodka was bad for you. Whiskey was bad for you. But if so, why had God made them all so pleasurable?

He breathed out.

"It remains to be seen, of course. And it will depend on the media outlets covering it in each country. But the first dispatches will of course be in our favor. In general, I suspect that events will reflect rather poorly on the Americans, and then, a bit later, they will reflect poorly on our beloved President."

He paused, and thought about it just a bit more. "The truth, and events will confirm this as they unfold, is the worse the disaster, the better our position."

Chapter Nine

11:05 p.m. Alaska Daylight Time (September 4)
US Navy Ice Camp ReadyGo
Six Miles North of the Arctic National Wildlife
Refuge
Two Miles West of the Martin Frobisher Oil
Platform
The Beaufort Sea
The Arctic Ocean

"No way, man. I can't do this."

The night was black. Outside the small modular dome, the wind howled. A frozen rain was falling out there. Visibility was deteriorating. In a little while, it was going to be near zero.

Luke was tired. He had taken a Dexie when the plane landed, and another a few moments ago, but neither one had kicked in.

The whole thing seemed like a mistake. They had traveled across the continent in a mad dash, at supersonic speeds, the mission was about to get underway, and now one of his men was backing out.

"This does not look right at all."

It was Murphy talking. Of course it was.

Murphy did not want to go on this thrill ride.

The temporary ice camp, basically a dozen modular weatherproof domes on a floating ice sheet, had sprung up like so many mushrooms after a spring rain, apparently in the past two hours. It was one of several camps just like it, ringing the oil rig a safe distance away. The establishment of several camps out here on the periphery was in case the terrorists were watching. The activity was designed to make it hard for them to know where the counterattack was coming from.

Inside each of the domes, a rectangular hole had been cut through the ice, roughly the size and shape of a coffin. The ice here was two or three feet thick. A deck made of some wood-like synthetic material had been snapped into place around each hole. Diving lights had been affixed underwater, giving the hole an eerie blue color. New ice was already forming on the surface of the water.

Luke and Ed were in their neoprene dry suits, sitting in chairs near the hole. Brooks Donaldson was doing the same. Each man was being worked on by two assistants, men in US Navy fleece jackets, who busied themselves putting on the men's equipment. Luke sat still as a man mounted his buoyancy compensator around his torso.

"How's it feel?" the guy said.

"Bulky, to be honest."

"Good. It is bulky."

Luke's hands weren't in his gloves yet. They kept straying to the waterproof zipper across his chest. It was tight and hard to pull. As it should be. It was cold water down there. The zipper made a firm seal. But that meant it was going to be hard to open when they reached the destination.

"How am I supposed to open this thing?" he said.

"Adrenaline," one of the assistants said. "When the shit starts flying, guys practically rip these suits off with their bare hands."

Ed laughed. He looked at Luke. His eyes said it wasn't that funny.

"Oh, man," he said.

Murphy wasn't laughing at all. He had come here with them from Deadhorse, but he never even began the process of suiting up.

"This is a death trap, Stone," he said. "Just like last time."

"You have nothing to prove to me," Luke said. "Or anyone. No one has to go. It's not like last time at all."

Last time.

The time when they were both in Delta, back in eastern Afghanistan. Luke was the squad leader, and he had failed to

overrule a glory hound lieutenant colonel who had led everyone—
everyone except Luke and Murphy—to their deaths.

It was true. He could have aborted the mission. Those were his
guys—they had no allegiance to the lieutenant colonel at all. If
Luke had said stop, the mission would have stopped. But he would
have risked a court martial for insubordination. He would have
risked his entire military career—a career, oddly enough, which
ended that night anyway.

Murphy looked at Ed. "Why are you going?"

Ed shrugged. "I like excitement."

Murphy shook his head. "Look at that hole, man. It's like someone dug your grave. Drop a coffin in there and you're all set."

Murphy wasn't a coward. Luke knew that. Luke had been in at
least a dozen firefights with him in Delta. He'd been in the shootout with him in Montreal, the one that saved Lawrence Keller's life
and brought President David Barrett's killers to justice. He'd even
had a fistfight with Murphy on top of John F. Kennedy's eternal
flame. Murphy was a tough customer.

But Murphy didn't want to go. Luke could see he was scared.
That might be because Murphy didn't have the training for this.
But it just might be because …

"Okay, guys, listen up!"

A burly man in a Navy fleece had come into the dome. For a split
second, as he pushed through the heavy vinyl drapes that formed
the airlock to the outside, the wind shrieked. The man's face was
bright red from the cold.

"As I understand it, you were all briefed in Deadhorse."

The guy stopped. He looked at the empty seat where Murphy
should be sitting. Then he looked at Murphy.

Murphy shook his head.

"I ain't going."

The guy shrugged. "Suit yourself. But this is a classified operation. If you're not going, you're not going to hear what I'm about
to say."

"I'm part of the civilian oversight team," Murphy said.

The guy shook his head. "My orders are that two members of the civilian oversight team are at the command center in Deadhorse, and the rest of the team is suited up and going in with the SEALs."

He raised his empty hands as if to say: *That's all I got.*

"If you're not at the command center and you're not suited up, I don't think you're on the team."

Murphy shook his head and sighed. "Ah, hell."

He shrugged a heavy green parka over his thick coveralls.

"Murph," Luke said. "Call Swann and Trudy. They'll get you on a chopper."

The new guy shook his head. "Choppers are grounded. The storm is coming in hard. We don't want any accidents out there. The mission is bad enough."

Murphy cursed under his breath and went out the way the man had just come in. The vinyl flapped and the wind shrieked again. The man watched Murphy leave, then looked at the three divers remaining.

"Okay," he said. "This is an ice dive, at night, in a storm, in an overhead environment. I almost can't think of a more challenging assignment. A year ago, we lost two experienced divers in a similar overhead ice environment, but it was a daytime training dive, there was no storm, and they were tethered to their home base. Okay? You should know that."

"Were they swimming toward a firefight?" Ed said.

The man just looked at him. He was in no mood for humor. Luke felt much the same way. There was nothing funny about this.

"As you probably realize, this is not a tethered dive. For much of the swim, the ice above your heads will be frozen solid. You do not want to make contact with it. You want to drop five meters below it, then maintain neutral buoyancy, and good level trim."

There were four swimmer delivery vehicles at his feet. They were basically small, battery-powered electric torpedoes. Each diver would hold the handle on a vehicle with one hand, and the propulsion would carry him to the destination much faster, and with much less effort, than he could swim by himself.

The man picked one up in both arms. "Who here has used one of these?"

All three hands went up.

The man nodded. "Good. Normally, we would use Mark 8 submarine delivery vehicles, each carrying two to four men, but we couldn't get them here in time, and the environment is a difficult one in which to deploy them. So we're going with the handhelds. All right?"

He paused. But no one said a word. It was what it was. It didn't matter if it was all right or not.

"Watch your compass. You are headed due east. You've got seventeen other guys…" He looked at Murphy's empty chair again. "Sixteen other guys down there. Move with the flow of traffic. This group is the oversight group, so you are taking the rear. If you get confused, you get lost, the way back is due west. This camp is lit up like a Christmas tree down there, so just head for the lights."

He held up a waterproof helmet, with visor and mask.

"Your head gear has two-way radio communications. Keep chatter to a minimum. Listen for the leaders up ahead. Visibility is going to be low. Your ears might save you. Your mouth might kill you."

He stared hard at them all.

"No air support. No amphibious support. It could get hot. Keep an eye above you. When you notice open air, you are almost there. As you reach the overhead ice's edge, turn off your headlamps. The idea, gentlemen, is to take them by surprise."

The man held up an MP5 machine gun with a pre-mounted magazine. The gun was shrink-wrapped in thick, translucent plastic. He held up a three-pack of grenades, wrapped the same way.

"These things are out of the elements right now. This is one hundred percent waterproof packaging. When you get onto land, use your knives to cut it open."

He smiled, then shook his head. "If you need to, use your knives to cut yourselves out of those suits, too."

Luke glanced at Ed. Ed made a grimace, a funny facial expression that Luke had never seen him make before. He looked like a kid in elementary school when the teacher suggested the class should sing some Christmas carols.

The assistants behind Ed lifted his helmet, and then let it settle into place on his head. His breath fogged up the visor.

The assistants behind Luke were about to do the same.

"Any questions?" the man at the front said.

What are we doing? came to mind.

"Good. Then let's hit it."

Murphy was in a bad mood.

"I'm sick of this mission, Swann. I never liked Navy people, and now I really don't like them."

The communications here were okay, despite the storm. Swann had explained it to him, but Murphy hadn't listened to the whole thing. Something about antennas built into these domes, plus satellite signals that penetrated fast moving cloud cover and precipitation, plus the unbreakable encryption Swann was known for...

Whatever.

He waited through the delay as the signal bounced around so the terrorists couldn't trace and listen in.

Murphy was fed up, irritated. He wasn't a diver. Stone and Newsam weren't divers either. The SEALs had been training with elite cold-water dive teams from Norway and Sweden for the past several years. Meanwhile, the unprepared SRT had been tacked onto this mission like some kind of garish hood ornament.

The way that big guy had looked at the empty chair... then at Murphy... then back at the chair. He was lucky they were both on the same team. Murphy would gladly remodel the guy's face with that chair.

"Yeah, I don't get it," Swann said finally. "We're pretty much window dressing back here at mission control. Nobody wants civilian oversight on this thing. They want a rubber stamp. They put us in our own office, away from everybody else, with a couple of computers and a coffee machine."

Murphy smiled. He could picture hardened SEAL and JSOC officers getting a load of the tall, gangly, long-haired, bespectacled computer freak Swann, and the tender young morsel Trudy Wellington, and thinking...

Nothing. The engines powering the typical military brain would grind to a halt. The sight of Swann alone was enough to pour sugar in the gas tank.

Put them in another room, somewhere out of sight.

"Those guys are gonna get themselves killed down there. I tried to tell Stone, but then some Navy chump kicked me out because the briefing was classified."

"Where are you now?" Swann said.

Murphy looked around. He was inside an empty dome, sitting on a chair that until recently must have held a Navy SEAL. The hole in the ice glowed blue. There was a command dome around here somewhere, and after the SEALs went in, the support staff must have gone there to watch the radar blips moving under the ice sheet.

"I'm in hell," Murphy said. "A frozen hell."

Trudy's voice came on. It was musical, like fingers lightly tinkling the piano keys.

"What do you want to do?" she said.

The answer to that was easy enough. Murphy wanted to disappear. He wanted to leave this Arctic wasteland, this pointless terrorist atrocity, whatever it was, go down to Grand Cayman, grab his $2.5 million in cash, and just evaporate.

It was easier said than done, however. It was going to take planning, and time to engineer a disappearance like that. Time he didn't have. Don still wanted him to do six months in Leavenworth in exchange for an honorable discharge. Meanwhile, Wallace Speck was in custody, out of Murphy's reach, and could start saying unfortunate things at any moment.

The worst-case scenario was Murphy arriving in Leavenworth at the exact moment Speck mentioned his name.

Naturally, these were not things Murphy could talk about with Mark Swann and Trudy Wellington. But there were things he could talk about. Swann and Trudy could help him, not to get out of here, but to get further in.

Stone was wrong. Murphy had something to prove. He always had something to prove. Maybe not to Stone, and maybe not to that Cro-Magnon-skulled SEAL trainer, but to himself. This mission had rubbed him the wrong way. They had catapulted across the country at warp speed, for what? A half-baked operation that was FUBAR before it even got underway. Who dreamed this up, Wile E. Coyote? It was the Iran embassy rescue operation part two, with ice this time instead of sand.

That it seemed so poorly and hastily designed irritated Murphy. The fact that Stone went along with it irritated him more. The fact that Newsam went along with it piled the irritation sky high.

The fact that he, Murphy, couldn't bring himself to squeeze into that claustrophobic diving suit and climb through that grave hole in the ice added a little bit of humiliation to the mix. And the way that mindless drone looked at that chair…

Murphy's hands clenched and unclenched. He had come to terms long ago that part of why he had joined the military, and then Delta Force, was to do something constructive with his anger.

He knew his history. He had studied skilled, prolific killers from past wars. Audie Murphy in World War II. Bloody Bill Anderson during the American Civil War. Much of what drove those guys was rage.

In his mind's eye, he could see Audie Murphy at Colmar, standing alone atop a burning tank killer, mowing down dozens of Germans with a .50 caliber machine gun, while taking enemy fire the entire time.

Murphy, Newsam, and Stone had all taken Dexies earlier. Murphy had been tired and taken two. They were kicking in hard right now. He could feel his heart beginning to pound and his breathing pick up. Items inside this dome began to jump out at him in exquisite detail. He stifled an urge to stand up and do a bunch of jumping jacks.

He could kill someone right now, a lot of someones. And Cayman Island was far away, out of reach for the moment. Stone and Newsam had just sent themselves off with the underwater version of the Donner Party, a frozen suicide mission that could only end in disaster. And there were a bunch of terrorists out there who had already killed innocent people. The men holding that oil rig were bad guys, and no one was going to be bothered all that much if they died.

Murphy's mind began to race along. Swann and Trudy had been banished to their own office, and that was not necessarily a bad thing. They were both wizards with technology. If their communications weren't quarantined ... a big if, but ...

"Murph? What do you want to do?"

Murphy's eyes were shooting laser beams. His hands could throw flaming fireballs. He was unstoppable right now, the way he'd always been. All these years in combat, and he'd hardly ever seen a scratch. It was amazing how things came together.

"I want a boat," he said, without realizing he would say that. "I want weapons, I want drone support, and I want guidance across the storm to that oil rig."

He paused, his mind moving so fast now, pure images, that he could barely articulate the thoughts in words.

"I want to get in the game."

Luke jumped into the dark hole.

He dropped through a thin sheen of ice into a surreal underwater world. In an instant, the utilitarian, almost locker-room like environment of the dome was gone, replaced by *this* ...

The sea was dark blue, disappearing into the black void below him. Above his head, the ice was a stark bluish white, with glowing rectangles of bright white light marking where the domes were, where the holes had been cut through the ice.

It was an alien place.

He could be an astronaut sailing weightless through deep space.

The most pressing thing he noticed was the cold. It wasn't the frigid cold of jumping into the ocean during late autumn. It didn't penetrate him. The dry suit was perfectly effective at keeping out the ice water that would kill him in moments.

In that sense, he wasn't cold. But he could feel the cold all around him, against the outside of the thick neoprene. His skin felt cold. It was if the cold was alive, and trying to burrow its way in to reach him. If it found a way, he would die down here. It was just that simple.

The only sound he could hear was his own breathing, loud in his ears. He noticed it was fast and shallow, and he concentrated on slowing it down and deepening it. Shallow breathing was the beginning of panic. Panic made you lose your head. In a place like this, it would make you lose your life.

Relax.

Luke put his cylindrical, torpedo-like delivery vehicle into gear, and surged gently forward.

Ahead, the group of divers moved, their headlamps lighting up the dark, casting eerie shadows. Luke half expected a giant shark, a prehistoric megalodon, to suddenly appear out of the darkness in front of them.

As they left the camp behind, he noticed the sea was moving, roiling, and the thick ice ceiling above their heads rippled and surged like land under the effect of a powerful earthquake. He and Ed moved side by side, traveling through the heavy currents, the diver delivery vehicles in their hands doing most of the work.

Luke felt himself being pushed around, he felt the water's attempts to turn him upside down, or send him reeling into Ed, but he rolled with it and pushed on.

He glanced at Ed. Ed had good trim, his body nearly horizontal, pitched forward just a touch, his head up. Luke could not see Ed's face beneath his helmet. The effect was alienating. Ed could be an imposter, or a machine.

Murmured voices started to come through the helmet radio. Luke could barely hear them, and couldn't make out what they said.

The sound of his breathing apparatus was much louder than the radio. It was going to be hard to communicate.

He glanced back. The lights penetrating into the darkness from above were fading into the distance. They had already left the base camp behind.

Time entered a strange sort of fugue state. He glanced at his watch. He had set the mission timer just before he had dropped into the water. It had clocked a little over ten minutes since that moment.

They passed the edge of the ice sheet and the ceiling above them became dark, even black, punctuated with moving blocks of ice. Everything went dark now, lit only by their headlamps, and the headlamps ahead of them.

They were already close, and it had happened much faster than he expected.

Steady... steady.

He passed a small device, glowing green in the darkness. It was a metal box, perhaps ten meters to his right. At a guess, it was a meter tall and half a meter wide. There were controls of various kinds along one side. It was small enough and far away enough that he almost didn't see it at all.

It was a robot, what Luke knew as a remotely operated underwater vehicle, or ROV. It was attached to a thick yellow tether that disappeared into the black distance to the north. The tether was probably its primary electricity source. It probably also contained the wires that controlled it, and through which it sent data back to ... where?

It had a large round eye, likely the lens of a camera.

Hadn't anyone else noticed this thing?

He tried to make a turn in that direction, but his momentum carried him past before he could get anywhere near it. Ed turned to look at him. Luke tried to point to the ROV, but it was well behind him now, and the suit and the equipment were too bulky.

They should go back, grab that thing, and at least inspect it. No one said anything about remote controlled cameras being deployed on this mission. It was sending images to someone.

They needed to cut that tether.

The murmuring inside his helmet grew louder now, but somehow he still couldn't make out the words. One by one, the headlamps ahead of him winked out, ushering in total darkness.

The first commandos were reaching the shoreline.

Luke glanced back one last time. The lights of the camp were far away, like stars in the night sky. If you got lost, you were supposed to make for those.

The green robot drifted, already far behind, watching him. At this distance, it could be a nothing more than a piece of green bioluminescence.

He reached up to turn off his headlamp. To his left, Ed's light winked out.

And that's when the screaming started.

Murphy hated everyone.

He realized the truth of it, he was raging, and he let that rage take him. It was a cold, sick world, and it deserved nothing less than his complete disdain. Disdain and hate. Hate guided him. Hate nourished and sustained him. Hate protected him from harm.

You couldn't kill officious military dinks that kicked you out of meetings and mocked you with their eyes. That was against the rules. That would land you in jail. But you *could* kill the enemy.

He steered the small Navy riverine boat through the storm. The boat was not built for Arctic waters, but it would do for one mad kamikaze run.

It was powered by two big 440 brake horsepower twin diesel engines. The hull was aluminum with plate armor. The collars were high-strength solid cell foam. The icy swells here were huge, crashing over the bow. He rammed the boat through chunks of ice, making vicious ripping sounds every time he did. The wind screamed in his ears.

He was in the cockpit, behind an armored wall. A smoke grenade launcher and a big .50 caliber chain gun were mounted up in the bow, ten feet in front of him. The chain gun would rip an armored vehicle to shreds, but he had no idea if it was going to work—it was freezing out here, and salty, frozen water was spraying all over the place. Moreover, this was not a one-man boat—he'd have to ditch the cockpit to get to the gun.

The boat's running lights were off, and he raced through absolute darkness. He wore night-vision goggles, but the green world they showed gave him nothing. Monster waves, icy black water, and white foam against black sky. He was running blind into the fury of the storm.

He slid down the face of a swell, the boat crashing into the water at the bottom as if he was on a log flume ride. Boats sometimes came down steep swells and dove straight underwater, never seen again. He knew that. He didn't want to think about it.

"Swann!" he screamed into the darkness. "Where am I?"

This thing was outfitted with radar, depth sounder, GPS, VHF tactical radio, and a host of other sensors and processing systems, but Murphy could barely steer the boat, never mind make sense of all the data coming in. Swann was supposedly tracking him and his relationship to the oil rig.

A voice crackled in his headset.

"Swann!"

"Go north!" he heard the voice shout. "North by northeast. You're being pushed to the south."

Murphy checked the compass. He could barely see it. He turned the boat's wheel to the left a bit, aligning himself more to the north. He had no idea where he was going. Something could loom up right in front of him, he could crash into it, and never see it.

He had no plan. No one knew he was coming, not even his own guys. Swann and Trudy were the only ones who knew he had taken this boat. They were the only ones who knew he had quickly shrugged into body armor, and loaded the boat with weapons and ammo. They were the only ones who knew where he was at all. He didn't even know where he was.

And he almost didn't care.

He didn't care whose side he was on.

He was empty, hollowed out.

He was the Dexedrine speaking, and the adrenaline.

There were terrorists out there, bad guys, and he was the good guy. He was the cowboy and they were the Indians. He was the cop, and they were the robbers. They were the FBI, and he was John Dillinger. They were Batman and he was the Joker. He was Superman and they were … whoever.

It didn't matter who was who and what was what.

They were the other team, and he was going to ram this boat right down their throats. If he lived, he lived. If he died, he died. This is how he had always gone into combat, and he had always come out the other side. Total confidence.

He didn't care about life very much, his or anyone else's.

He was dead inside.

This. These moments. This was when he was alive.

"East!" Swann shouted. "Straight east!"

Murphy gently steered to the right.

"How far?" he shouted.

"One minute!"

A strange shiver ran through Murphy. He was freezing. Hell, he was practically frozen solid. Even in coveralls, a big parka, thick gloves, a hat, and his face covered, he was frozen. His clothes were drenched. He was shivering, maybe from the cold, maybe from the newest surge of adrenaline.

This was the game. This was it.

Right here. It was coming.

He gave the boat even more throttle. He peered into the gloom. The storm surged around him. He steadied his legs and gripped the wheel as the boat got knocked from side to side.

Now, he could just see some lights out there. And he could hear something.

Pop! Pop! Pop!

It was shooting.

"Slow down!" Swann screamed. "You're about to hit land!"

In front of Murphy, bright lights suddenly appeared.

He was moving fast. Too fast. Swann was right. The shoreline was RIGHT THERE.

But the boat was designed for beach landings.

There was no way to stop anyway. Murphy gave the throttle everything and braced for impact.

A dead man floated in the water above Luke's head.

Luke stared at the man. He was a Navy SEAL in full gear, shot as he tried to climb out of the water. He drifted this way and that, turning over like seaweed in the surging currents. His arms and legs waved randomly, like overcooked spaghetti.

He sank toward Luke.

Blood drifted out from multiple holes in the man's body and stained the water near him red. Luke knew the bleeding wouldn't last long—now that the man's dry suit was cut open and he was exposed to the cold, he was going to freeze very quickly.

Blinding white light shone down from above. A moment ago, land-based klieg lights had come on, illuminating the water. The SEALs were exposed, and it didn't look like anyone had made it up out of the water yet.

Forget about getting the dry suits off. Forget about getting the weapons out of their weather-proof bags. Forget about getting oriented and taking the initiative. Forget about a surprise attack.

The enemy wasn't surprised at all. They were positioned up there, firing down into the water.

They knew the SEALs were coming. They had anticipated an underwater assault. The image flashed through Luke's mind again—that robot, with an embedded camera, glowing green in the dark water.

It was an ambush. It was going to be like shooting fish in a barrel.

Luke, twenty meters below the surface, saw bullets penetrate the icy water above his head, then lose momentum as they approached.

Inside Luke's headset, someone shrieked.

Ed was still beside him. He pushed Ed hard. Ed turned to look, and Luke pointed backwards and down. Deeper. They needed to retreat and go deeper. In a moment, those guys up top were going to notice the bullets weren't reaching their targets, and they were going to start firing heavier, more powerful guns.

"Abort!" someone else shouted in Luke's helmet. It was the first time a message came through clearly. "Abort!"

The boat slid up onto the island and across the icy ground.

The deceleration was instant. The sound of metal scraping rock was awful. Murphy was thrown like a rag doll. He flew over the control console and out of the cockpit. His legs caught on the console and flipped him upside down.

He went head over heels and landed on his back in the bow of the boat. His head banged off the aluminum flooring. BONG. His ears started ringing instantly. Tubular bells. His night-vision goggles were gone.

He gasped for air. The impact had knocked the wind out of him. *No time for that.*

He groaned, pushed himself up and lurched like Frankenstein for the chain gun.

He stood, taking in a view of the battlefield.

At least twenty men were across from him, dressed in dark clothes and wearing black headgear and masks against the cold. Giant spotlights were shining down from ten-foot-high mounts. The men in black stood and kneeled in the freezing rain, firing guns into the water—the water where the Navy SEALs probably were.

That's what the big spotlights were for—to give them targets in the water. The lights probably also served to blind the swimmers and deny them targets, if any of them could even get their guns out.

The men in black began to turn toward Murphy. They almost seemed to be moving in slow motion. In another second, they were going to start shooting him full of holes.

Murphy gripped the heavy gun in front of him with both hands.

His finger found the trigger mechanism.

Please work.

He opened up. DUH-DUH-DUH-DUH-DUH-DUH came the metallic sound of bullets firing. He easily rode the recoil of the mounted gun. Spent shells fell to the bottom of the boat, tinkling like jingle bells.

Murphy hosed the men down. He hit four or five with his first burst.

They didn't fall as they were shot. They came apart like rag dolls, the bullets ripping through them. Now the others were running, seeking cover.

"Run, you monkeys," he said.

A sound came.

WHOOOOOOOOOSSSSHH.

A rocket flew past him. His entire body jerked in response.

Just missed. He hadn't even seen it coming. It hit somewhere in the water behind him. He didn't hear an explosion, but he saw an orange and yellow flash go up.

How did he see that out of the corner of his eye?

No. He must have eyes in the back of his head.

His ammunition belt was already running down. He didn't have a backup.

Running out of ammo was a problem. That RPG was also a problem—there were going to be more. Already, the men were regrouping out there and taking up firing positions facing Murphy. He reached with his left hand and fired a smoke grenade.

Then he dropped to the floor of the boat.

A second later, rounds started hitting the armored plating of the boat. Thunk, thunk, thunk, thunk...

Bullets whistled overhead.

He looked up at the trigger of the chain gun. He still had some rounds left, but if he tried to reach his hand up....

WHOOOOSSSHHH.

Another rocket went by. Whoever had the rocket launcher was a lousy shot.

Thank God.

Murphy had a pistol on him. He pulled it from the holster. He crouched below the lip of the bow. The first man who appeared there was going to take a bullet in the head. After that...

But they weren't that dumb. A grenade suddenly appeared, bouncing around inside the front of the boat like a rubber ball. It made solid metallic BONKS as it bounced. Murphy picked it up, waited half a beat, and threw it back.

An instant later: BOOOOM.

Someone out there screamed. Dirt and ice and blood and meat rained down.

They were *right there*, creeping up.

Murphy's breaths came in harsh rasps. He wasn't gonna last. He was outmanned. He was outgunned. He couldn't seem them—if he peeked over the side, they would take his head off. He couldn't throw back every single grenade that came. The guy with the rocket launcher wasn't gonna miss all night.

Murphy was gonna die right here in this boat.

His mind raced, looking for options.

"Oh God," he said.

This might have been a mistake.

Something had changed.

At one moment, they had seemed like they were all doomed, trapped in the water, the enemy above them and firing down, machine gunning them. Now they were on the offensive again, moving forward.

Luke came bursting out of the water.

He pulled himself up onto a low frozen seawall, an icy wave breaking over him, washing him further onto land. He reached down and wrenched his flippers off, tossing them aside. It was dark. All around him, men were surging out of the water.

A few of the SEALs already had their guns out. There was firing up and down the beach. DUH-DUH-DUH-DUH-DUH.

Bodies were strewn all over the ground.

Where was the enemy? Luke couldn't spot them.

Nearby, two Navy SEALs dragged their fallen comrade up onto land. He was shot full of holes, blood all over him. The man was not moving.

"Medic!" one of the men shouted.

Another wave crashed, spraying Luke with icy foam. A cold rain came down in sheets. It took his breath away.

There was no way around it. They were going to be wet, and cold. Luke unhooked his scuba tanks and let them drop. He pulled out his knife, opened it, and cut off the straps of his buoyancy compensator. He let that drop, too. Now he had to get out of this dry suit. It had taken him fifteen minutes to get into the damn thing.

Whoever thought all this was somehow a good idea must have been out of their minds. Either that or they knew nothing about combat. Luke glanced around. All around him were men fighting to get out from under their scuba gear.

An odd thought occurred to Luke, one he had never had before…

Just wait until I file my report.

He looked at the six-inch serrated blade of his knife. He shook his head. *The hell with it.* He unlocked the seal on his gloves and pulled them off. His hands would go numb quickly, he knew. He grabbed a hunk of his dry suit and pulled it away from his body. Then he slipped the knife in and started cutting.

✣ ✣ ✣

Nothing happened.

No more grenades came. The firing stopped—at least, the firing directed at him.

Murphy still had his gun. He was still crouched in the icy rain, waiting for the enemy.

But no one came.

He peeked over the top of the armor plate, his mind recoiling from the task, fully expecting to take a sniper's round in the head.

Nope. Nearby, there was nothing but a bunch of dead and dying men, two or three crawling across the ground, leaving a trail of blood like snails. The rest were lumps of raw, steaming meat.

Up the shoreline, men in dark scuba suits were appearing on the beach. A few of them had already taken up positions, their scuba gear still on their backs, and were lying down, suppressing fire. Murphy's attack must have given them just enough time to come ashore. And face-to-face with Navy SEALs, the bad guys had fallen back.

In the distance, the gigantic oil rig itself loomed against the dark sky.

The SEALs were firing in that direction.

As Murphy watched, another dark scuba diver crawled up out of the icy, raging water. The man wriggled up the beach about ten feet, rolled onto his back, and began to rip himself out of his diving suit.

Another one crawled out of the ocean like a sea monster and did the same thing. As he did, a rocket came down from the rig and exploded on the beach.

BOOOOM!

It was the lights. The bad guys had evidently retreated, but those spotlights were still giving them something to shoot at.

Murphy went to the chain gun and pointed it up at the big spotlights. With a couple of brief bursts, he took them out. The SEALs flinched as the lights shattered, sparked, burst into flames, and went out. But now they were safely in darkness again.

Murphy sighed. He clambered to the back of the boat, opened the gear chest, and grabbed a shrink-wrapped MP5 from inside. His hands shook as he picked it up. The gun was heavy. Murphy's shoulders slumped—he almost couldn't lift the damn thing.

His whole body started to tremble.

He suppressed a sudden urge to start crying.

"Almost bought it this time," he said. The words didn't sound like anything. His teeth were chattering. He was very cold now, and he had almost been dead. The energy seemed to be flowing out of his body. He'd never felt quite like this before.

He looked down at himself, doing a body check. Was he hit?

No. He was just...wiped out.

He climbed over the gunwale, got low, and moved across the ice toward where the men were. He stared up at the giant oil rig, rising dozens of stories into the sky. He could see the muzzle flashes of enemy guns up there. They were shooting at them.

Just in front of Murphy, a SEAL managed to rip open his dry suit across the chest. He pulled a small handgun from inside it. He ripped the gun out of its wrapper, then turned and pointed the gun at Murphy. It was almost laughable. The whole operation had taken the guy at least ten seconds. Murphy could have killed him twenty times by now.

"Who are you?" the man said.

Murphy smiled and raised his hands in mock alarm. He was still trembling, but already beginning to feel a little better. He was cold, he was soaked to the bone, he was shaking uncontrollably, and his body hurt from the impact of crashing into land.

Admit it. You almost got killed out here.

Yeah, he admitted it. And it brought back bad memories. He had almost died before, many times, but this one had seemed especially bad. He might even have been *traumatized* by it. For a second, he had really thought he was a goner. He wasn't sure if he'd ever felt that way before, not even with Stone that time in...

He shook that thought away. It had all been worth it tonight. These guys would have been Swiss cheese if it wasn't for him.

"I'm an American," he said.

"Stone!" a voice shouted.

Luke was still struggling to cut himself out of his dry suit. It was aggravating. The bad guys had pulled back, but if they hadn't, he would have been a sitting duck in this thing. He would have practically been a baby seal, waiting to be clubbed.

"Stone!"

Luke looked up this time.

Here came ... Murphy?

Murphy limped up the beach, cradling an MP5 in two gloved hands. He wore a heavy parka, black coveralls underneath. His hood was down, and he wore a thick hat of some synthetic wool-type material. His face was red and raw and exposed to the elements. But his eyes were sharp.

"What are you doing here?" Stone said.

Murphy smiled. "What do you think I'm doing here? I came here to save your asses." He gestured at the corpses of terrorists strewn on the ground behind him.

"See all the dead guys? Who do you think deaded them?"

Luke smiled and shook his head. The picture came together with an almost audible click. The reason why the battle turned was Murphy. Luke looked down the shoreline and spotted the silhouette of the Navy patrol boat on the beach.

The guy was truly one of a kind.

"Murph, I can't tell you how happy I am to see you. Now cut me out of this thing, will you?"

Chapter Ten

12:01 p.m. Moscow Standard Time (12:01 a.m. Alaska Daylight Time)
The "Aquarium"
Headquarters of the Main Intelligence Directorate (GRU)
Khodynka Airfield
Moscow, Russia

"All is not yet lost," the young man said.

Marmilov took a long drag on his latest cigarette. The ceramic ashtray on his desk was already piled high with the dead ends of the others.

"No," he said. "But nearly so."

"Yes, sir," the man said. "Nearly so."

He was back again, this young man, with his military bearing and his ill-fitting business suit. He was bright enough, Marmilov thought, and he might have a decent career if he learned to dress well. But good clothes cost money, and money was likely the man's problem. He was on a government salary. And perhaps he hadn't yet learned that his position would afford him easy access to money, if he were just a little bit daring. The criminals, from the street pimps up to the corporation directors, were all terrified of the intelligence agencies.

Marmilov sighed and shook his head. That was a lesson for another time.

He had watched the American assault on the artificial island in the Arctic Ocean. He'd had a very good view, as a surveillance camera had long ago been set up along the waterfront where the frogmen came ashore. The imagery was grainy and in black-and-white, but the perspective couldn't have been better.

Moments ago, he had shut it off. He had also shut off the laptop computer that was scrolling Russian translations of intercepted American intelligence. There was very little to learn from either thing.

The fight on the beach had been a rout. This was not because the defenders had been driven back by the frogmen. It was because an amphibious assault had occurred simultaneously. The defenders had been ill prepared for this, and in the first seconds of the assault, numerous men had been mowed down like so much tall grass. They had been drive into confusion, and by the time they regained their composure and counterattacked, the first frogmen were already on land.

The remnants of the beach party had fallen back to the oil rig, but it was unlikely they would hold it for long. At this juncture, there couldn't be more than a dozen men left alive.

"There was no indication the amphibious assault was coming?" Marmilov said.

The young man stood tall, his shoulders back, his chest out. Once again, despite being in a small underground office with no windows, he seemed to be staring off into the distance, a thousand meters away.

"We had no indication," the man said. "Our source in their White House described only an attack by swimmers. Our own listening stations…"

Marmilov suddenly pounded the desk with his fist.

"Do our listening stations ever hear anything worth knowing?"

The young man said nothing.

Marmilov cleared his throat. Outbursts of emotion were rare with him. He did not make them lightly. This one came with no forethought at all. His frustration had simply boiled over.

"It was a failure of intelligence, wouldn't you say?"

The man nodded. "Yes, sir."

Marmilov took another drag from his cigarette. He felt peevish. The Americans would take their island back, and their oil rig perhaps, but he would deny them victory, if he could.

"Are we in touch with the men in the oil rig?" he said.

"Difficult."

Marmilov shrugged. "Difficult, but still possible?"

The man nodded. "Yes. But at this point, we don't know who is alive and who is dead. We don't know if they are monitoring their communications equipment. We don't know who is now in command, if anyone. Also, given the collapsing nature of the situation and the widespread monitoring that must be taking place in many quarters, it will now be dangerous to be in contact with them for more than a few seconds."

"What do you recommend?" Marmilov said.

He was aware that time was growing short, and he would like to get directly to the point, before it was too late.

"Sir, in my opinion, now it is best to speak briefly, in one- or two-word codes, via shortwave radio, broadcast from a location far outside Russia. A word will leave no impression on anyone, except the person designated to receive that word."

Marmilov nodded. "Good. Do we have a code word for killing the hostages?"

"Sir?"

"I think you heard me perfectly well. The American hostages that remain. I want them dead. Is there a code word for this?"

"All of them, sir?"

Marmilov clapped his hands once. The sound was like a gunshot. The young man's strong body jerked as if Marmilov had suddenly put a bullet through his heart.

"Yes, all of them."

The man hesitated for a long second. Marmilov hoped he wouldn't have to clap his hands a second time.

"The code for that is *bela rada*."

Marmilov nodded. "Excellent."

An excellent code for an exceptional task. *Bela rada* was the Serbian phrase for the white, or common, daisy. In earlier times, before modern burial vaults, daisies would often grow by the thousands in the nutrient-rich soil of graveyards. Thus, the command was to turn the remote oil drilling station into a graveyard.

The code pleased Marmilov a great deal.

"Transmit the code," he said.

"Sir?"

"You heard me," Marmilov said. "Send the code. *Bela rada*. Send it immediately, while there is still time."

"What if they don't receive it?" the young man said.

Marmilov sensed the man's reluctance. Of course he did. Marmilov could smell hesitancy in the wind. He raised his hands, palms upward like a supplicant, as if to indicate that would simply be fate.

"If they don't receive it, they don't receive it. These things happen in combat. But God help you if I discover that you didn't send it. Is that understood?"

The man nodded. "Of course."

CHAPTER ELEVEN

12:15 a.m. Alaska Daylight Time (4:15 a.m. Eastern Daylight Time)
Martin Frobisher Oil Platform
Six Miles North of the Arctic National Wildlife Refuge
The Beaufort Sea
The Arctic Ocean

The element of surprise was gone.

Now it was a fight. And they had to move fast. There were hostages here somewhere, and as long as any of the terrorists were still in the game...

Luke didn't want to think about it.

He and Murphy found Ed and moved through the darkness, headed for the towering oil rig. It loomed above them like some mysterious ancient ruin.

The storm beat down, a cold salty rain blowing in sheets, freezing everything over. Shots rang out. Constant gunfire. SEAL teams were searching the Quonset huts, but they were empty. Everyone was on that rig.

"How many SEALs got hit?" Luke shouted to Ed.

Ed held up three fingers. "I saw three. Three dead on the beach. They were working on them, but..." He shook his head.

Up ahead, on the path between outbuildings, a man in black jumped out. He fired his gun, short automatic bursts, probably an Uzi. Two SEALs shot him at the same time, both head shots, from different directions. His head came apart, a piece going this way, a piece going that way. His body spun like a ballerina.

Murphy laughed. "They triangulated that bastard's skull."

Luke glanced at him. Murphy was utterly bedraggled. He looked like a cat that had fallen into a swimming pool.

"You all right?" Luke said.

Murphy nodded. "Yeah. But let's finish this up, all right?"

"You got it."

The rig was right above them now. They reached the base of it.

SEALs pounded up the iron stairs ahead of them. More gunshots rang out. A man in black, his face covered by a black balaclava, tumbled down the stairs. Luke looked at him. There was a white patch on his coat, with an image of a hawk or an eagle.

Who were these guys?

Whoever they were, they were in total disarray now. Command and control had collapsed. The leaders must be dead. There was no plan, no coordination, just random guys popping out, taking their best shot, and getting cut down.

Luke reached a landing.

A group of SEALs stood near a heavy iron door, staring at it.

Luke stopped. He signaled to Murphy and Ed, who were just ahead, moving up the next flight of stairs: *Keep going.*

The SEALs looked at Luke. They were young guys. They looked like they were just out of BUD/S training.

"What's up, guys?"

None of the SEALs moved or said a word.

"I'm Agent Stone," Luke said. "FBI Special Response Team. Supposedly I'm the civilian oversight on this operation. That means I'm in charge. What's up?"

One of the SEALs gestured at the door. "We heard shots fired from in there, but there's no way to engage the enemy. The door is sealed. There doesn't seem to be any other way in. It's like someone locked themselves in there, and then..."

"Blow it," Luke said.

The kid raised a hand. "Yes sir, that's what we're thinking. But given the circumstances, and the possibility of the presence of non-combatants, we're just waiting for authori…"

"I'm your authorization," Luke said.

That thick sealed door gave him a bad feeling. The kid had the same feeling—Luke could see it in his eyes.

"Blow it now. I take full responsibility."

The kid nodded. Two SEALs kneeled by the door and affixed plastic explosive charges near the bottom hinge, and near the lock mechanism. Another affixed an explosive near the top hinge. Luke backed up the stairs, as did the soldiers. Everyone got low and covered up.

"Fire in the hole!"

BOOOM.

The door fell off its hinges. The lock survived, and the door leaned diagonally to the right. Two SEALS went up to it, wrenched it away from the lock mechanism, and let it fall to the deck. It fell with a heavy CLANG.

Two more burst in, weapons drawn. Then two more.

No sound came. Then a SEAL came stumbling out of the open hole.

"Oh, God," he said. He bent over and vomited.

"Medic!" another SEAL screamed from inside. "Corpsman!"

Luke went to the door. Inside there was a pile of bodies, impossible to say how many. They were bound, zip-tied with their hands behind their backs. There was blood all over the floor, and all over the corpses. They looked like bags of garbage, left behind and forgotten. The room was deep, maybe twenty meters across. The bodies were like wall-to-wall carpeting.

Tied up and executed. All of them.

Luke spotted two men in the black uniforms of the terrorists. They were not tied, but they lay among the dead. It was easy to see what had happened here. They had killed the hostages, then themselves.

Luke grabbed the arm of the SEAL he had talked to.

"See if anyone's alive in there. If not, pull your medics back and secure the scene. No one goes in or out. No one touches anything.

We're going to want a forensics team in here. This is evidence of a crime against humanity. The more your men step on it, the harder it becomes to prove anything."

The kid stared at him.

"Got it?"

The kid nodded. His eyes said he had never seen anything like this before. His eyes said his mind was going blank.

"Yes sir," he said, but there wasn't much in it.

"I'll be right back," Luke said. He smacked the kid on the side of the head. "Sharpen up and secure this crime scene. Now."

The kid shook his head. His eyes watered for a second, then cleared.

"Yes sir!"

Luke continued on. He tried to shake off the image of the dead men, but this mission just kept getting worse and worse. What was next?

Three stories further up, he reached the control deck. A shootout had just happened here. The thick glass of the control room was shattered. SEALs had taken it over. Ed and Murphy were in there, too.

One terrorist was left, standing by an open laptop computer, with his hands up. His black jacket had two grenades hanging from it. The Americans surrounded him, guns drawn. Luke moved into the room.

"Careful," he said. "The brass wants someone to interview."

"That's why we saved this one for you," one of the SEALs said.

"Any others alive besides him?" Luke said.

The SEAL gestured at the three dead men on the floor.

"We haven't found any."

The last man standing was short, with close-cropped dark hair. He wore the same black jumpsuit as the others. He had the same white patch on his jacket. His face was weathered. His eyes were hard. His hair had a touch of gray in it.

This was a man who had seen and done a lot of things. He stared at Luke.

"Speak English?" Luke said.

The man made a gesture with his hand, holding two fingers about an inch apart. Now he smiled.

"Little."

Suddenly his hand strayed to a grenade on his chest. He pulled at it.

"Don't do that!" Luke shouted.

BANG!

One shot rang out. The man's head snapped back. A chunk of skull and brain flew backward. The man stood still for half a second, as if he didn't know he was dead, and then slithered to the floor.

Luke turned to the source of the gunshot.

Murphy stood there, his arm outstretched, pistol in hand.

He shook his head. "I ain't getting blown up over this. Sorry."

Luke's shoulders slumped. He looked at big Ed Newsam.

Ed shook his head and smiled. Then he laughed. It was if Ed was saying, *Murphy's a loose cannon, but he's our loose cannon.* Ed was free to laugh. He hadn't seen the room with the hostages yet.

Even so…

Luke laughed too. It felt good to laugh. What a nightmare this had been. What an absolute nightmare. The sheer absurd horror of it somehow made it funny.

"Holy hell, Murph."

A second later, everyone in the room seemed to be laughing.

"It's been a long night," Murphy said. "My patience with these people is wearing thin."

Luke stepped over the body and went to the laptop. He looked at the screen. The characters were Cyrillic, nothing he could read. He closed the cover and tucked the computer under his arm. He was taking it with him. Whatever the hell had happened here, some clue to it must be inside this machine.

He looked at Murphy and Ed. He looked at the gathered SEALs. They were all still smiling. Nothing was funny. But everything was funny.

Luke shrugged. "Well, I guess that's the end of the interview."

CHAPTER TWELVE

9:45 a.m. Eastern Daylight Time
Headquarters of the Special Response Team
McLean, Virginia

"They are cleared to land."

The windsock indicated a slight breeze out of the south. The sleek black helicopter hovered and slowly lowered itself to the tarmac.

From outside the security fence surrounding the helipad, Don Morris watched his team arrive. The doors of the chopper slid open, and a group of tired-looking people climbed out.

The mission had been a disaster. It had been a highly classified covert operation. No one knew anything about it yet, but it was going to be impossible to keep it that way for long. Three Navy SEALs were dead, but the bigger issue was the dead hostages. The men on that oil rig had friends and family—family that were going to wonder what happened to their fathers, sons, husbands, and brothers.

And that meant the SRT needed to have its ducks in a row before the explosion of publicity came.

As Don stood there, the team filed past like a line of zombies.

"Good job, guys," Don said. He clapped his hands. "I'm proud of you all."

Don took his role as head cheerleader seriously. Especially when a mission went wrong, but your people performed well, it was important to remind them of that. These people were the best, but even the best could use a little boost sometimes.

Luke Stone was last in line. He crossed the tarmac carrying an overnight bag on his shoulder and a laptop computer tucked under his arm.

"How are you doing, son?" Don said to him.

Luke shook his head. He looked more than tired—he looked angry.

"I don't think we should really talk about it here," he said in a low voice. "But suffice to say it was one of the most poorly planned operations I've ever seen. It was like someone had a daydream, and then put it in motion. The enemy knew we were coming, and from where—they were waiting for us. They either had great intel, or they anticipated us every step of the way. If Murphy hadn't gone rogue and saved our necks, I think we'd have had fifteen dead SEALs instead of three. Maybe all of them would have died, along with me and Ed as well. As a country, if that's the best we can do…"

He trailed off and shook his head. "I don't know, Don."

Don nodded at the laptop.

"I heard you took something that didn't belong to you."

Luke nodded. "After what I saw out there, I didn't think it was a good idea to trust this thing to anybody but us. Whatever it says, it's in Cyrillic, which suggests to me the Russians were involved. But now that we're home, we can break it open, decode it, and find out for sure."

"Just as long you know," Don said. "There are other people around who want to take a look inside there."

Luke shrugged. "They can wait. It was their mission, and it was a mess. We had no business being involved. But since they invited us, and since they nearly got us all killed, I took a souvenir. It seems like a fair trade to me."

He began to head inside.

"You saw it?" Don said. "The bodies?"

Luke stopped. He stared into Don's eyes. Don could feel the heat coming from there. Luke was a good man, a true American, and one of the best special operators Don had ever seen. And he was young. He had the potential to become more than just a great soldier in the field, but a great strategist and leader.

But he was still a bit of a hothead. He had killed a lot of men in his time. He had seen a lot of death. And he had a tendency to become emotional about it. He could get his feelings hurt. That didn't make him weak—it made him human. But at some point, he was going to have to grow past it and learn to see the bigger picture.

"The massacre?" Luke said. "Yeah, I saw what was left. It was fresh. They probably did it right after we took the beach. I saw the bodies. I saw men who had been bound hand and foot, and shot while they were sitting on the ground."

"And?"

"It makes it personal," Luke said. "Whoever organized this, wherever they are, I'm going to get them."

"Okay, let's hear it."

Luke was exhausted. An hour had passed since they got in.

He was sitting in the conference room with Don Morris, Swann, Trudy, and a young guy he'd never seen before. Luke assumed he was a technician or expert on some thing or another.

Murphy and Ed Newsam had already gone home. That was next on Luke's agenda. If he was sane, he would have left, too. But those killings had stuck in his craw. He didn't want the SRT's response to get out ahead of him. And he didn't want what they found out being passed around.

Also, before he could go home, he needed to call Becca and sound her out. He dreaded making that call.

It was a little bit astonishing to him that he had traveled to the Arctic Circle, engaged in an underwater operation and a gun battle, nearly got killed, then came all the way back here, and Becca still didn't know a thing about it. It was possible the whole thing might be filed under *Late Night at the Office* and forgotten.

He welcomed that, but it also worried him. He couldn't keep lying to her like this. It wasn't fair to her, and it wasn't fair to him. His career couldn't be based on lies. She had to be an equal partner. She had to know what he was doing, and why.

As a practical matter, she was bound to find out sooner or later. She attended SRT functions. People talked. He could see it unfolding, months from now, people standing around, shoveling catered food into their mouths:

"Stone, remember that FUBAR Arctic Circle op?"

"Oh, which one was that?" Becca might say.

"You should have seen it. Scuba swim under the ice, in a storm. Everybody nearly got murdered coming out of the water. A bunch of civilians got massacred. A guy tried to blow himself up, but Murphy shot him in the head at the last second."

Becca turning to Luke: "I've never heard of this. Were you there, honey?"

"Ha, ha, he was there, all right."

Right now, Luke's skin was red from exposure to the cold. He looked a little like a lobster that had been boiled in its tank. His face was red. His hands were red. His fingers were even still a little numb. The feeling, and the coloration, were both starting to fade, but they were going to be around a while longer, and they were going to be hard to explain. It was early September. The weather was still warm. Maybe he had gotten too much sun on his motorboat.

Trudy sat in front of a laptop, the one that Luke had taken from the oil rig. She looked tired too, like she might fall asleep in her chair. The laptop was a Toughbook style, made of heavy metal and surrounded by shockproof rubber.

"We've confirmed that the language used on the laptop is Serbian," Trudy said.

"Serbian?" Luke said. "Not Russian?"

Trudy gestured to the young guy. The guy smiled. "Hi Agent Stone, I'm Saul Leishman. I'm a language analyst. My specialty is Eastern Europe. I'm fluent in Russian, Serbian, Hungarian, and I have a bit of Greek, Romanian, and Czech as well."

Luke nodded to the man, who looked like he had graduated high school about eight minutes ago. Something about his perky demeanor aggravated Luke.

"Do you even have security clearance to look inside that computer?"

"Stone," Don said. "You're overtired."

"No, it's okay," Leishman said. "I'm a freelancer, but I hold security clearances with the Bureau proper, as well as the NSA and the CIA. I've also worked with Treasury and the State Department. I've actually done a lot of government work, and I'm pretty good, if I do say so myself."

The thought flashed through Luke's mind: if Don had brought in a language expert who worked for the other intelligence agencies, that meant by now *everybody* knew Luke had taken the laptop.

"I'm not worried that you can't translate the material," Luke said. "I'm worried who you're going to talk to about it. We went in there last night, and we nearly walked into a buzz saw."

For the first time, it hit Luke what was so wrong about the mission—the terrorists had deployed an underwater camera and were waiting for the SEALs to come up out of the sea, *as if someone had told them exactly where and when the attack would be.* They had mounted giant spotlights along the waterfront.

"Stone, if you don't stand down, I'm going to send you home."

Luke looked at Don. Don's eyes were ice. He meant it.

"Okay," Luke said. "Okay, I'm sorry. I'd like it noted that I don't feel good about this, but please..." He looked at Leishman. "Continue."

Leishman shook his head. "You don't have to worry about me, Agent Stone."

"Drop it," Don said. "Let's get to the meat of this thing."

Leishman nodded. "All right. Pretty much everything in the laptop is Serbian, including the encryption used to protect it. It was an encryption that the NSA broke back in 1999 during the Kosovo War, which apparently was never updated. Agent Swann already had the decryption key in a database, and he unlocked the computer in minutes."

Swann was slumped in a chair. His eyes were closed. His glasses were on the table. He raised a hand, apparently just to prove he was listening. He didn't say anything.

"That's why we could access the contents so quickly. And once we got in, it was clear immediately who we were dealing with."

Leishman looked at Trudy. "Agent Wellington and I ..."

Luke shook his head. The kid was enamored with Trudy. Of course he was. When did he meet her, half an hour ago?

Trudy nodded. "At this point, the group that seized the Martin Frobisher appears to be the remnants of a paramilitary unit called the White Hawks, which began as a gang of violent Serbian nationalist soccer hooligans in Belgrade during the early 1990s. They were volunteers organized by a mafia don named Zoran Sokic, also known as Sakal, which translates into English as the Jackal. The White Hawks were active during the Yugoslavian Civil Wars and the Kosovo War, and seemed to get most of their funding, and pay their soldiers, through looting and pillaging. They were involved in at least three massacres of Bosnian and Croat civilians, as well as mass rapes and other war crimes. They were believed to have been wiped out, and Sokic himself committed suicide in his cell at the Hague while awaiting trial for war crimes."

"And yet here they are," Luke said, looking at Don. Don's reading glasses were perched at the end of his nose. He busied himself reading some scribblings on a yellow legal pad. It was clear to Luke that he had heard most of this already.

"Still committing massacres."

Leishman raised a hand. "It's possible that most of these guys were merely inspired by the White Hawks, and have resurrected the name. We haven't come across evidence yet that any of the men who attacked the oil rig were original members."

"Then who were they, and what did they want?"

"We don't know. None of them have been identified yet."

"So I guess you don't really have any evidence that they *weren't* original members either."

"The attack was well planned and coordinated," Trudy said. "Clearly some of the perpetrators have formal military experience, and possibly combat experience."

Luke thought back to the fight. Those guys were machine-gunning swimmers in the water. And they murdered a group of defenseless civilians. Newbies usually had a hard time with things like that. The last man standing had gray hair, and he didn't seem afraid to die in the least. If that didn't sound like people who had fought in the Yugoslav Civil Wars, then he didn't know what did.

"Whoever they were, we'll know that soon," Trudy said. "My understanding is photographs, fingerprints, and DNA from the terrorists have already been sent to Interpol. In the meantime, my guess is they wanted revenge for the NATO bombing campaign over Serbia in the spring of 1999.

"As you may recall, that bombing campaign ended the Kosovo War, and destroyed Serbia's military. It also laid waste to Serbia's infrastructure—including their road system, bridges, railways, electrical system, communications, and just about every other aspect of modernity they had. They were humiliated and rendered basically helpless. It was a disaster for them on an epic scale, though most of the world saw it as nothing less than they deserved for the atrocities they committed during those wars.

"In the aftermath, they became completely reliant on the NATO occupation, their sworn enemies, to feed, clothe, heat, house, and provide them with water supplies. Now, the bombing happened six and a half years ago. But there are lingering questions about how NATO and United Nations personnel conducted themselves among the civilian population. Women and children forced into prostitution, trading schemes involving food and heating oil for sex, and things of that nature. There's a lot of anger about that in Serbia, especially among the younger generations."

"Okay," Luke said, beginning to see it now. "So it's a terrorist attack as payback for bombing and occupying them. But it's carried out by a paramilitary group not attached to the government or Serbian military. That way the Serbs can say the terrorists were acting independently, and no one knew anything about it. And there's no one for us to retaliate against."

"Sure," Trudy says. "Sounds reasonable."

"But why attack an oil rig in the middle of the Arctic? Why not set off a bomb at a festival, or attack a subway train in New York?"

Don looked up now. "There was some other reason," he said. "The attack wasn't just an attack."

"We think they plan to use it for propaganda purposes," Trudy said.

"They massacred dozens of unarmed men," Luke said. "Not exactly good public relations."

"That depends on your audience. It shows certain people that America is weak. We're a nation of soft targets, and we're leaving important installations completely undefended. It might inspire others to look for similar soft targets."

Luke shook his head. "But so far, no one even knows any of this happened."

Trudy looked at Swann.

"Swann?"

Swann opened his eyes. He sighed.

"Luke, it's an old computer, but it had been upgraded with improved memory and processing speed—that stuff is dirt cheap nowadays. There was an encrypted high-speed satellite uplink, which was functioning right up until the moment you closed it and put it to sleep. Very good, very new tech. They were feeding live video from around the facility to the computer, which was compiling it and sending it to a satellite. We're talking video from the battlefield, from the command center, even from the room where the massacre happened. It all got sent to a black satellite, very hard to crack, and from there it's anybody's guess where it went and what path it took."

"Is anyone trying to crack that satellite now?" Luke said.

Swann shrugged. "Can't. It went dark. Someone pulled the plug, and it's basically a space rock now. But unless it was a corporate satellite owned by one of the big internet companies, which I highly doubt, then I'm gonna go with Russia or China."

"And with Russia and Serbia's long entwined history of close alliances and cultural affinities…" Trudy said.

Swann nodded. "Yeah. Probably Russians."

"So you think the Russians set this up," Luke said. "But I fail to see how it makes them look good."

"They have their methods," Don said. "I guess we're just going to have to wait and find out what they are."

It didn't take long to find out.

Luke was in his office, at his desk. There was a cup of coffee in front of him. He had stopped tasting the coffee a while ago. It was having no effect. He glanced at the digital clock on the wall. 11:29 a.m.

All he really needed to do was pack up his things, stumble out to the car, and drive about ten or twelve minutes to the house. Traffic might make it fifteen minutes. Somehow, it didn't seem possible. He lived close to the office now, but at this moment, his home seemed far out of reach.

The phone on his desk rang. He glanced at the caller ID.

Becca.

He picked it up. He tried to put on a tone that suggested he was tired, but not nearly as exhausted as he actually felt.

"Hey, babe," he said, his voice almost a singsong. "I'm just finishing up here and…"

Her voice had a tone altogether different from his. He couldn't put his finger on what it was.

"Luke?"

"Yeah. Hi, sweetheart."

"Luke, where were you last night?"

"Where was I?"

Her voice was cold, as cold as the Arctic Ocean itself.

"Yes."

Suddenly he was treading on dangerous ground. Thin ice, as it were. She seemed to know something, something important, and if he lied about this...

He hated it. He hated this whole stupid game. He was continually covering up where he'd been and what he did. No, not because he was having affairs, or drinking too much, or gambling, or anything along those lines. It was because he was out there on the edge, serving his country. He was doing the things he believed in. And, he hoped, making his wife, and one day his son, proud of him.

"You know where I was," he said, copping out completely.

"No, I don't," she said. "I want you to tell me."

"I was at work."

That was true, as far as it went. It didn't exactly tell the whole story, but...

"*Where* were you at work?"

"Becca, what's going on?"

"Tell me where you were."

He hit upon a new tack to take. As he said the words, they seemed right. They felt good coming out of his mouth. They were in a sweet spot, somewhere between a lie and the truth. They were *an obfuscation.*

"Sweetheart, I can't tell you everything. My work is often classified, you know that. I'm not really at liberty..."

"Oh my God, it's true," she said, her voice suddenly shaking. "The whole thing is true, isn't it? Everything, all of it."

"What's true?" he said.

"I can't... I can't talk to you right now. I just... There's no words."

The line went dead.

Instantly, a shadow seemed to loom behind Luke.

He turned, and Swann was standing there. Swann was tall and gangly, and he looked like some strange bird. This might have been the first time Luke had seen him in this way. Exhaustion would do that to you. It gave you insights your alert brain would never even consider. Swann could be a great blue heron, or some kind of sand hill crane. Luke barely even noticed what crazy clothes the man was wearing.

Swann also looked sick, maybe from exhaustion, maybe from something else.

"Have you seen the TV?" he said.

Luke shook his head. "No. Something bad?"

"You should come watch it," Swann said.

A group of people had gathered in the lobby, where a large flat-screen TV was mounted high on the wall near the waiting area.

CNN was on.

A headline ran along the bottom: *Bloodbath off Alaska Coast.*

A pretty thirty-something news anchor sat at a desk. She had dark hair and wore a blue suit. Behind her, hazy darkened scenes of combat were playing out. She held some papers in her hand, stared down at them for a moment, then looked into the camera and read from a teleprompter.

"What you are about to see is graphic, but has been edited for American television. It has already appeared in many parts of the world on the Al Jazeera network, Russia Now, SinoVision, and other outlets. Although edited, it is not for the faint of heart, and viewer discretion is advised."

She looked down at her papers again, then back up. Why did she look at those papers? What was in them? To Luke, she really just seemed to read her lines off a video screen. Was it all an act?

Watching the TV news was a strange assignment for Luke. Everybody at the SRT seemed to watch the news all the time. Keeping up with the news required that you watch television, not Luke's favorite pastime.

The newscaster went on:

"What the video purports to show is an American oil rig in the Arctic Circle, off the coast of Alaska. The Serbian radical environmentalist group Earth Defenders claims that it seized the oil rig, and temporarily took the oil workers prisoner, to demonstrate American hypocrisy. According to a press release from Earth Defenders issued through a designated spokesman, the rig, although out at sea, was actually drilling inside the Arctic National Wildlife Refuge, or ANWR. By law, the ANWR is a nature preserve, off limits to drilling for oil or natural gas."

She stared at the screen. Her voice shook now.

"Earth Defenders claims that the rig was attacked by American commandos last night. They further claim that the commandos killed all of the Earth Defenders activists, and in a false flag operation, executed the oil workers. The claims are beyond words, as is the footage that has been released. We caution you that none of these claims have been verified by authorities."

"Then why repeat them?" someone in the lobby crowd said.

"And again, the footage we're about to show is graphic. Viewer discretion is advised."

The footage started rolling. Men in heavy clothes, on a frozen beach, were being mowed down by machine gun fire. There was a glare from overhead lights. The pouring rain and the foam spray from the waves crashing made it difficult to make anything out. It was hard to say what the men were doing. It was impossible to say what, if anything, the men held in their hands. They could well be unarmed.

Now other men in scuba gear were storming out of the water. It was dark. The men were dropping their gear, cutting themselves out of their dry suits. As Luke watched, a couple of the first divers took guns out and executed wounded men on the beach. They went systematically from one to another, firing a single shot to the head.

The shots echoed hollowly. CRACK! CRACK!

"Oh man," someone said.

It was a very bad look. Luke hadn't seen it happen, but he understood it. There were dead SEALs in the water. And soldiers were trained to kill enemies in combat, even wounded enemies. This was so the wounded enemies wouldn't suddenly turn around and kill you. No one had surrendered. There was no time for surrender.

But it made for terrible TV news.

To someone in the audience, the men on the ground could easily seem helpless. That audience member had no way of knowing that just a moment before, those men were firing machine guns at equally helpless men swimming in the frozen sea.

The scene changed. The camera panned across frightened men on the floor, somewhere indoors. It was dark. The men appeared to be civilians, and they had their hands tied behind their backs. Flashlights shone on them, and along the steel walls. Other men were standing. The standing men were wearing cold-weather fatigues. The fatigues were consistent with United States Army uniforms.

The camera flashed here and there. On the uniforms, Luke saw shoulder patches he recognized instantly—the word AIRBORNE in yellow letters on black, with yellow dagger and lightning flashes on a blue shield below it. It was the insignia of 1st Special Forces Command, and Luke knew its meaning without even thinking. The dagger represented the unconventional nature of Special Forces, and the lightning flashes represented the ability to strike by air, water, or land.

The camera panned away and the image became blurred.

It couldn't be real. There had been no US Army personnel at that site, or involved in the operation.

Suddenly, gunfire erupted and the men on the ground screamed.

The scene went black.

"God," Luke said. He almost didn't realize he was speaking out loud. "They weren't dressed in Special Forces gear when they murdered those men. I saw them. They were dressed all in black. How is this even possible?"

The scene changed again.

Luke recognized this next scene all too well. The scene was shot on the control deck of the oil rig. A group of big Navy SEALs came rushing in. There was a bang and a crashing sound as the windows caved in.

There were shouts back and forth, and a man screamed something in a foreign language, which Luke now gathered was Serbian. It was hard to tell what anyone was saying. But CNN, or someone, had done a helpful job of captioning the footage.

"Keep those hands up!"

"Don't move!"

And then a Serbian voice: "Please! Please don't shoot me!"

"Don't you move!"

"Please! Please! Please! We are scientists! We are unarmed!"

Then the ugly blat of automatic weapons.

The footage skipped, and Luke appeared. He was clearly visible, almost looking directly at the camera. He faced the terrorist who had been standing near the laptop—the last man standing. The camera angle was from behind the man, over his shoulder.

Luke stood there, with three Navy SEALs behind him, and behind them, the shattered windows with the storm raging outside.

The man's hands were raised in the air.

Luke marveled at what he was witnessing. At the time this was going on, the camera footage was being fed into the laptop and sent directly to a satellite. Did the man know he was being filmed? Did he know ahead of time that these were going to be his last moments? Did he volunteer for this duty?

Then Luke's voice: "Speak English?"

"Little."

The man's hand dropped, going for the grenade. But it was impossible to see that from the camera angle. You couldn't tell that the man had grenades pinned to his chest. All you could see was his right hand drop, almost like he was putting his hand across his heart. In fact, if Luke hadn't been there, that's what he would guess the man was doing.

The footage skipped.

A shot rang out.

Suddenly, the man's head became pixilated as it cracked apart. Then the man disappeared.

For an instant, no more than a second or two, Luke's face was very clear. He turned and looked at something off screen. He smiled, and his shoulders slumped in what looked like mock disappointment.

That smile, after an apparently unarmed man had just been killed...

Oh boy.

Now there was the sound of several men laughing. Luke stepped around a wide table, the smile still on his face. He turned his back to the camera, but somehow, his voice was clear and as plain as day:

"I guess that's the end of the interview."

Luke stood among the small crowd in the SRT lobby, staring up at the screen.

"Well, now you're famous," someone said.

Becca saw this.

That thought occurred to him instantly, and very much without warning. This was what she was so upset about. She knew Luke had flown across the continent in the middle of the night. She knew he had risked his life without telling her. And she knew that he had been involved in something that a person on the outside might think of as a summary execution, a war crime, an atrocity.

The film had been cleverly edited. It omitted some very important parts. And the scene where the civilians were killed was an outright lie.

Of course, the truth about the mission would come out eventually, but who was going to believe it?

There were no Army Special Forces personnel on that mission.

Sure, we believe you.

American soldiers did not kill any American civilians.

Yeah, okay.

The men who took over the oil rig were heavily armed members of a paramilitary force known for committing war crimes. They were not a group of environmentalists.

Luke took a deep breath.

People were going to believe what they wanted to believe. That was the simple fact. Al Jazeera and Russia Now (and who knew who else) were out ahead, broadcasting uncensored footage of this in dozens of countries. People predisposed to believe the worst about America were going to believe the worst.

And what was Becca going to believe? What was she going to think about her husband, a man who could watch another man get killed, then apparently smile and tell someone a joke? Would she believe that Luke was part of a death squad who had killed unarmed and tied-up American civilians?

He stood there in a sort of shock. People were beginning to break up, getting back to whatever work they should be doing.

Luke had no work to do. His only job was to go home. But he had no idea if his wife would let him in.

Suddenly a hand was on his shoulder. He turned and Don Morris stood there. His face had no expression, as though he was trying to not to show his emotions. But his eyes looked sad.

"Come in my office for a moment," he said. "We should probably talk."

Luke followed Don down the hall to his office. He stood by the door as Don inserted himself behind the wide expanse of desk. Don made a cradle of his hands and put them on top of his head. He gestured at the chair across from him.

Luke didn't take the bait. He didn't feel like sitting. He didn't feel like having a surrogate dad right now—especially when that dad was the one who had sent him on this ill-fated mission in the first place.

Luke loved Don. He appreciated everything Don had done for him. That much was true. But he was beginning to wonder about some of the decisions Don made.

This most recent decision had put Don's own people in a vulnerable position, up against an enemy whose intentions had been completely misunderstood. Now Luke was left to defend his actions, not just to Don, but to Becca, to the FBI, and possibly to the entire world.

"Don, none of that video is true. I haven't had a chance to write my report yet, but when I do..."

Don shook his head. "It's propaganda. I know that. You know that. We both know there were no Special Forces on the raid, and that will be confirmed by the Pentagon. Obviously, they dressed in American uniforms to make it look like Americans massacred their own. There will be glaring errors in the details. It'll all come out."

"It's not going to matter," Luke said.

Don shrugged. "No, it won't."

"The guys on the beach were armed to the teeth. They had the drop on us. They were about to slaughter us when Murphy showed up."

"I'm sure there's going to be evidence to confirm that as well," Don said.

Luke shook his head. He had a strong feeling inside him, one of futility, and anger, almost rage. He almost felt like he might cry. The video made him out to be an off-hand, cold-blooded killer. It wasn't fair.

"The whole thing was FUBAR on steroids. It was from another galaxy. We were in water that was near freezing, under the ice, in a storm. We had so much gear on it was impossible to get out of it. It was a surprise attack completely without the element of surprise. There was at least one underwater robot filming us as we arrived. All the SEAL training, all the big brains at JSOC doing the planning, and we very nearly got ourselves killed. Then one guy doing improv in a tin can Navy patrol boat—a guy who panicked by the way, and couldn't bring himself to suit up and get under the ice— routs their entire defense?"

Don gestured at the chair again. Luke declined it again. He almost felt that if he sat in that chair, he *would* cry. He felt like a small child. He felt like he needed a hug from someone.

"I agree with everything you're saying," Don said. "From the sounds of it, it was a poorly and hastily planned operation. Which, frankly, is probably why the President wanted civilian oversight. Murphy is SRT, so if the SRT hadn't been there, things would have been a lot worse. And the mission, in one sense, was a success. We killed the enemy and took back the oil rig."

Luke didn't even touch that assessment. There were dozens of dead oil workers, three dead SEALs, illegal drilling in the Arctic Wildlife Refuge had been exposed, and American soldiers looked to many people in the world like psychotic killers. Everything about this situation was a disaster, including Luke's role in it.

"The guy was reaching for a grenade on his chest."

Don nodded. "Okay."

"It looks like we shot him for laughs, but it isn't true. And I didn't shoot him. It was Murphy, and it's a good thing that he did. The guy would have blown the whole control room to hell, with us in it."

"It's all right," Don said. "I'm sure there will be an inquiry, people will give testimony, and all the facts will come out."

"It's not all right," Luke said. "I was home, dozing on the couch with my son, when I got called in for this. Now I look like a maniac."

Don shook his head. "No one can identify you in that video. We know it was you because we know you were there."

"My wife knew right away. I didn't tell her I was there. She just knew."

Don sighed. He took a long pause.

"That's tough."

Luke nodded. "Tell me about it."

"You should go home," Don said. "Take a few days off. Write your report, but otherwise, just relax."

"I can't go home," Luke said. "Becca doesn't want me there."

"Can you go to the cabin?"

"Yeah," Luke said. "I suppose. But I'm so tired I can't bring myself to drive out there right now. I'll fall asleep at the wheel."

Don smiled. "We'll get you a car service. And if you want, I'll talk to Rebecca. This job is all hands on deck. It's just the nature of the beast. You're going to need buy-in from her, or you're never going to make it."

"I feel that," Luke said. "I feel like I'm not going to make it."

"You're just tired," Don said. "Go to the cabin. Relax. Sleep in tomorrow. Things will start to look better when you get a little rest, and a little perspective."

It was a nice thought, one that Luke wasn't overly optimistic about.

"I hope so," he said. "But I doubt it."

CHAPTER THIRTEEN

11:50 a.m. Eastern Daylight Time
The Oval Office
The White House
Washington, DC

"What in the name of God's green Earth is going on?"

If Clement Dixon had been feeling his age yesterday, today was even worse. He might as well be a thousand years old. He had barely slept a wink. And while he was busy tossing and turning, events were busy racing out ahead of him. Caught flat-footed—it was an old saying that seemed to aptly sum up his situation.

He was still trying to get used to the Oval Office. He felt like the ghosts of Lincoln and Roosevelt assessed him every time he walked in here ... and found him lacking.

He was trying to get used to the constant security.

He was trying to get used to the constant questions, the constant press of people, and the information coming from all sides. It was impossible to make sense of it all.

Oh, he'd been the Speaker of the House for many years. And he was accustomed to dealing with people, lots and lots of people. He was accustomed to being the focal point of attention, and he was accustomed to being in charge.

But here's what nobody told you about being President. You weren't actually in charge. The whole thing was a madhouse, completely outside of anyone's control, and you were surrounded by hard chargers jockeying for position. People were pursuing their own agendas, for their own reasons. What happened to the country was someone else's problem. Clement Dixon's problem. There were a thousand tiny sparks surrounding him, and any one of them could suddenly turn into a wildfire.

He, Thomas Hayes, and a few others were in the high-backed chairs in the sitting area at the center of the Oval Office. A lush round carpet adorned with the Seal of the President was at their feet. Three tall windows, with drapes pulled back, looked out on the Rose Garden. Outside, it was a sunny September day. Indian summer—Clement Dixon's favorite time of year.

Not that he was enjoying it.

Outside of the circle, the office was packed with people. Secret Service men stood guard at the doors. Military men from the Pentagon stood at something like attention. Aides and assistants milled around, scribbling notes or tapping their fingers on small electronic toys called BlackBerries.

Dixon had never used a BlackBerry before. He had never even held one. In Congress, the aides called them "Crack-berries," after crack cocaine, apparently because once you started using them, they were so addictive that you could not stop.

Dixon didn't have that problem. He was from another era. The idea of becoming addicted to staring into a tiny screen was about as distant from him as the idea of hunting giant sperm whales, in a large wooden rowboat, with a spear.

A large TV had been brought in on a rolling cart. Everyone in the room had just watched a video that was now playing on television throughout the world. A sanitized version was already being aired on American TV news.

The sanitized version was *not* the version that Clement Dixon had just watched. No, he had watched the graphic version that people in the Middle East, Russia, Asia, Africa and South America were watching. He had watched the version that was popping up on internet sites everywhere. The unedited, unsanitized version. It made for unpleasant viewing.

People who were supposedly unarmed environmental activists, from Serbia of all places, had been mowed down by machine gun fire on a frozen piece of artificial land during an ice storm. Helpless American oil workers appeared to have been murdered in cold blood by American soldiers. An unarmed man with his hands in the air appeared to have been shot and killed by American commandos, and then one of the commandos, apparently the one in charge, started to laugh and joke about it.

The cherry on top of this stinking, rotten fish cake was that it was now clear to everyone on the planet that the Americans were drilling for oil in their own Arctic Wildlife Refuge, which was supposedly off-limits to drilling for oil.

And hints were starting to arise that the small company doing the drilling had on its payroll, or as major investors, several prominent members of American society. This included at least one member of the United States Senate, the esteemed member from Kansas, Senator Edward Graves.

"We have a bit of a public relations debacle," said the White House press secretary, a middle-aged, glass-jawed lightweight named Allen Forbes.

Clement Dixon looked at him.

Remind me to fire you when I have some time.

"I guess I'm already aware of that, Allen. What I'd like to know is how this video came to be, how much of it is true, how far it's gotten, and what we can do about it. I'd also like to know the identity of the grinning lunatic in the last frame there."

"Wasn't there supposed to be some kind of civilian oversight of this operation?" Vice President Thomas Hayes said to the room.

Dixon nodded. "Good point. Where was the civilian oversight we requested?"

"We didn't request it," Hayes said. "We demanded it."

Dixon looked at Thomas Hayes now. Thomas looked well-rested. He looked excited and in his element. He was clean-shaven and well-dressed in a beautifully tailored pinstripe suit. He looked like he might have gotten a massage before coming in this morning. He probably had. Also, his nose could put someone's eye out.

Dixon liked Thomas, he really did. They were on the same page about a lot of things. That's why he had chosen him as Vice President over the hordes of glomming nincompoops who wanted the job. But Thomas's eagerness to become President himself was so palpable that it had taken on a reality all its own. It was a physical presence in the room, with the texture of an undercooked steak. It was raw, bloody, and it didn't smell quite right.

Meanwhile, the corpse in the driver's seat wasn't even cold yet.

Dixon raised a hand. "Okay, Thomas. They know what I mean."

General Richard Stark was here from the Joint Chiefs of Staff. His body, a lean strand of beef jerky, was positioned in the chair across from Dixon. There wasn't a single wrinkle in his green uniform. His eyes were like hawk's eyes. The crow's feet around his eyes were as narrow and as deep as slot canyons.

Clement Dixon did not like Richard Stark. He had been circling that realization for a few weeks, and now he landed smack dead in the center of it. But maybe Stark had some answers. Hell, maybe he even knew a way out of this mess. Even a broken clock was right two times a day.

"General, what's your assessment of the situation? What, if anything, in that video is actually true?"

The general didn't hesitate. He didn't glance at a sheet of paper, or look to an aide staring at information on a tiny computer screen.

"Mr. President, the entire video is basically a lie, made for propaganda purposes. I've spoken with front line troops who were on the ground during this operation. I've spoken with commanders in the field, and I've spoken with Don Morris, head of the FBI Special Response Team, which provided civilian oversight."

Dixon nodded. "Okay. And?"

"If you look closely, and we are working to clean up the video on this, the men killed on the waterfront were heavily armed and firing into the water. They were not environmentalists, but appear to have been affiliated with a Serbian paramilitary group, who attacked us in revenge for the NATO bombing of Serbia. They had been alerted to the approach of the Navy SEALs, and ambushed them. Three SEALs died during the ambush. The terrorists were killed in turn when a member of the civilian oversight team, himself a former elite soldier, took them by surprise in an amphibious assault vehicle."

Dixon stared at him. "And you can confirm this? The cleaned up video will bear all of it out?"

Stark nodded. "We are confident of that, yes sir. Also, the men who committed the massacre inside the oil rig were wearing counterfeit uniforms based on US Army combat fatigues. Insignia on the uniforms identify those men as members of 1st Special Forces. No members of 1st Special Forces, or of any US Army unit, were involved in this operation. It was carried out entirely by the United States Navy, in combination with officers from Joint Special Operations Command, and agents from the FBI Special Response Team. We believe that the Serbians simply put on fake American uniforms to carry out the massacre, and filmed it."

"Jesus," Thomas Hayes said. "The cold-bloodedness..."

The general nodded. "Yes sir."

"And the man in the final scene?" Clement Dixon said. "Who is he?"

General Stark shrugged. "Well sir, he was part of your civilian oversight. As far as we can tell, he's Agent Luke Stone, who was the officer in command of the Special Response Team contingent. By all accounts, the man who was shot had a grenade or a bomb attached to his coat, and was reaching for it. He had been told to keep his hands in the air. That isn't clear in the video. And the agent in question may have laughed in relief. What many people don't always understand is that men and women who have seen a great deal of combat often respond to death differently from civilians."

"Has the man seen a great deal of combat?"

"Sir, he is a former member of Delta Force, with multiple combat tours in Afghanistan, Iraq, and in other, classified theaters."

"Would you say he's expendable?" a voice said.

Everyone turned to look. It was Allen Forbes again. He was standing at the edge of the circle. He wore tan dress pants, a white shirt open at the throat and rolled to the forearms, and frameless glasses.

Forbes shrugged at the fact that everyone was staring at him.

"The damage is done. There are a lot of people in this world, even in this country, who aren't going to believe what we say, even if we give them incontrovertible proof. But if a head rolls... say, a commando who did something inappropriate... that's a beginning. And if certain nameless members of Congress who pulled strings to allow drilling in a wildlife preserve are outed and censured by their peers... Maybe you see where I'm going. Right now, it looks like anything goes. I don't think we can afford to give that impression."

There was nothing Clement Dixon would like more than to see Edward Graves's head rolling down the center aisle of the Senate Chamber. But that was unlikely to happen. Graves was too powerful. He had too many friends.

Not that anyone had mentioned it, but war with Serbia was probably off the table, too. The US had already won that war. And when push came to shove, these terrorists were likely to be well-camouflaged and isolated from the decision makers. Even so...

"I'd like to see us pursue ties between the terrorists and anyone in the government in Belgrade," Dixon said. "I don't want to write that off. I also want to see if they had ties to Russian intelligence. And I want it publicized, beginning as soon as this meeting is over, that US troops had nothing to do with that massacre, and that it happened before any of our men appeared on the scene."

"And the commando?" Forbes said. For some reason, he was bent on seeing someone swing from the neck. "Agent Stone?"

"As a sacrificial lamb?" Dixon said.

"Yes. The people are going to want one. A disaster like this cries out for blood. An excision, of sorts. A pound of flesh."

Dixon looked at General Stark. Stark raised his hands.

"It's a difficult judgment call. Personally, I like Agent Stone."

"Someone should talk to his boss," Thomas Hayes said. "And get a look at his military record. With that amount of combat, there may be a record of PTSD or other troubles. The man in those images seems unstable, at best. Maybe what he needs is a long vacation."

Dixon looked around the room. The faces stared back at him. Nothing about those faces suggested that he was the boss and they were the underlings.

Every single one of them reminded him of a voracious meat-eating predator. They were looking at the President of the United States as though he was an aging antelope, unable to outrun them any longer.

"Okay, good," Dixon said. "I like that. It's what this man Stone needs. Give him a nice long vacation. Call it a suspension, and say the decision came down from the highest levels of government. It'll make it look like we're actually doing something around here."

Chapter Fourteen

10:05 p.m. Moscow Daylight Time (2:05 p.m. Eastern Daylight Time)
Bolshoy Moskvoretsky Bridge
Near the Kremlin and Red Square
Moscow, Russia

"How is the work progressing?"

Oleg Marmilov stood on the sidewalk at the center of the old concrete bridge over the Moskva River. It was a stately bridge, finished in pink granite slabs that gave the illusion the bridge was a feat of stonework. But that part was impossible to see at the moment.

Marmilov had already put the events of the day behind him. Results of the operation in Alaska were mixed, as far as he was concerned. He would have greatly preferred a massacre of elite American commandos, but he had settled for one of hapless civilians instead. The fiction that Serbian environmentalists had seized the oil rig would not last, but events were moving quickly and soon it wouldn't matter anyway.

Best to focus on the present.

It was a strange evening. A type of smog obscured everything. For one, the weather had changed since yesterday, and now it was unseasonably warm, foggy, and damp. For another, wildfires in the ancient forests outside of Moscow had raged again all summer, and the smoke had settled on the city like a blanket.

The fires were Putin's fault. Was the climate changing? Marmilov supposed so. Did this make wildfires larger, more intense, and more dangerous? Marmilov was willing to accept this possibility.

But you couldn't blame the fires for not putting themselves out. You couldn't blame the climate for mismanaging the budgets and handing over important revenue bases to criminals and cronies.

There were no firemen to fight the fires because there was no money to pay them. There was also no equipment for the nonexistent firemen. There were no modern firefighting trucks. There were no airplanes carrying flame retardant. There were no spotter planes or advanced computer mapping of the fires (as they had in the West), determining the places where fires were most likely to start, the direction in which the wind was likely to push them, and the speed with which it would happen.

It was a joke, and it had reached this sorry state of affairs under Putin's watch. Now they faced the humiliating spectacle of people strolling in the evening hours in Moscow, with masks covering their faces because the air was so difficult to breathe. And that was only the most visible part.

People with asthma and lung conditions were trapped inside their homes. And people in the rural areas—thousands of people, if you could believe the confidential reports coming across Marmilov's desk—were being burned out of their homes. It aggravated him, not least because at the current rate, his own country estate, where his wife lived, would one day find itself in the crosshairs of these fires.

He looked downriver toward Central Moscow, but there wasn't much to see. A few dim lights shone in the gloom, but most everything was shrouded in mystery. Saint Basil's Cathedral, close to the bridge on the Red Square side, was completely invisible. Behind Marmilov, a bus rumbled by on the bridge, nearly unseen.

For many years, Marmilov had used this bridge, and others like it, as an office of sorts. It was a good place for meetings, especially at night. It would be difficult for anyone to record a conversation taking place on this bridge. There would be no paper or computer record of it, and no call log.

If information from a private, intimate discussion were to somehow leak out, then Marmilov would immediately know the source of the leak—the person with whom he had been sharing privileged information. This had happened a few times over the decades, with unfortunate consequences for the leakers.

Marmilov enjoyed his bridge chats, as he thought of them, and he liked to play them for theatrical effect. After the military, he had begun his professional life as a spy, and he missed those days. His bridge chats reminded him of nighttime meetings with people in East Berlin. Friends? Foes? A little bit of both? Sometimes it was impossible to say.

This accursed smog carried him back to those days like woodland mists in a children's fantasy story. One moment, the child is walking through a small copse of trees near an industrial park, the next, he is in a time of knights and dragons.

And magic.

"The work is coming along," said the man standing next to him at the rail. Marmilov could barely see the man, but he knew well who he was. His name was Tomasz Chevsky. He was very tall and slim. He wore a long coat and a bowler hat that obscured his face. He carried a knobby walking stick, like an English gentleman might do when out for a stroll in London. He couldn't know how much these affectations pleased Marmilov.

"Are we playing riddles?" Marmilov said. "I ask you how the work is coming along, and you tell me the work is coming along? Have you heard that I am renowned for my sense of humor?"

"I haven't heard that," Chevsky said. Chevsky was a bright young man, well educated, and with a day job at the Academy of Sciences.

At night, however, he worked for Marmilov. In fact, his dreary office work at the Academy was the least of his responsibilities. There were quite a few Moskviches who moonlighted in this manner.

"That's because it isn't true," Marmilov said. "I'm renowned for the shortness of my temper, and my unwillingness to suffer fools. So tell me, please, without my having to beg, what is happening with the important work I've entrusted to you."

"It is going well," Chevsky said. "I'm pleased to report that it's almost operational. As you know, there were a number of challenges to solve, in terms of location of the work, water depth and pressure, functionality in cold weather, transport…"

"Yes, yes, yes," Marmilov said. "I know all that."

Of course Marmilov well knew the challenges. It had been his idea to devise a nuclear bomb that could be detonated beneath the ice of the Arctic. He had talked to the engineers at the very beginning, years ago, and he knew that building such a bomb, one that could resist freezing water, submerged deep in the ocean, which could be transported there secretly, and which could be detonated and at the same time be plausibly denied … it was a tall order. This young man was the third liaison to the project Marmilov had assigned. The work had taken a long time.

"It appears the final challenges have been overcome," Chevsky said.

"So the project is ready for deployment?"

The man seemed hesitant. "Yes."

Marmilov did not like hesitancy. You might say he had a policy against hesitancy. A thing was a thing. A was not B. Say clearly what a thing was. Say it unequivocally. The Americans had a phrase that fit the philosophy well: *Say it like you mean it.*

"Is it ready, or isn't it?"

"Yes. It is."

That was more like it.

Even so, Marmilov almost couldn't believe what he was hearing. It was a project years in the making, with countless delays, a boondoggle even. A white whale of a project, and Marmilov sometimes seemed like its obsessed Ahab, following it to the bottom of the sea.

"When will it be ready?"

"It's ready now."

"It's ready to be deployed? At this moment?"

The young man Chevsky chose his words carefully. "As I indicated, all of the engineering challenges have been overcome. The weapon has never been deployed, and circumstances make an overall test impossible. So something unforeseen could still happen. There are no one hundred percent guarantees, which I believe you must already know."

Chevsky paused again.

"All aspects of the weapon have been tested separately, with complete success. Detonation potential has been proven, and digital and analog mechanisms have withstood Arctic environmental demands in laboratory settings, as have all moving parts. Items of similar size and weight, giving off similar radiological signals, have been transported by both air and sea to the target area and submerged without being detected by the military or intelligence agencies of any world power, including our own."

"Sum it up for me in one short sentence," Marmilov said.

As he waited for the man's answer, it seemed almost as if Marmilov's breath caught in his throat.

"The weapon is ready," Chevsky said.

Marmilov nodded. He had been at this a long time, but the job still had the ability to excite him, and in some cases, delight him. This was one of those cases. He was a very lucky man. He smiled.

"Then what are we waiting for?" he said. "Let's deploy it, shall we?"

CHAPTER FIFTEEN

3:45 p.m. Eastern Daylight Time
Queen Anne's County, Maryland
Eastern Shore of Chesapeake Bay

"Stone!"

Luke's eyes popped open. For a moment, he had trouble focusing. It was daytime. He was sprawled sideways on the couch. He took a deep breath. It seemed like someone had just spoken his name. He pushed himself to a sitting position.

Wow. He was tired.

"Okay. Nobody said anything."

He looked out the window at a lovely late summer day fading into a cloudy afternoon. The old cabin—in Becca's family for over a hundred years—stood on a bluff overlooking Chesapeake Bay. There was plenty of wind out there today. Luke could count probably a dozen sailboats across the broad sweep of water.

He sighed. The surroundings here were beautiful.

The place was two floors, wooden everything, with creaks and squeaks everywhere you stepped. The kitchen door was spring-loaded, and tended to slam itself shut with enthusiasm. There was a screened-in porch facing the water, and a newer stone patio with commanding views right on the bluff.

He and Becca had lived here for more than six months when he started the job, while she was pregnant, and after the baby was born. They had only just moved out a few weeks ago. Luke would almost take this rustic place, with all its quirks, over their new house. He missed this cabin, he missed the views, he missed the expansive wide-openness of the property and the bay. He just didn't miss the commute to work.

If he wasn't working, though…

It was a moot point. He was working. And they were living in Fairfax now, a ten-minute drive from SRT headquarters.

True enough, except that he was out here right now. He wasn't in Fairfax because Becca didn't want him. And that was because in her mind he was a cold-blooded killer. He had tried to call her when he arrived here at the cabin. She had picked up on the third ring, heard his voice, and immediately hung up again.

He should really go upstairs to bed, just sleep the whole thing off, the mission, the videotape, everything. It was all going to blow over. The truth was going to come out. The world was going to realize the Serbians were terrorists and not environmentalists. Becca was going to get over this and invite him home.

Maybe.

The cordless telephone was on the table in front of him. He picked it up and dialed a number from memory.

On the third ring, she answered.

"Trudy Wellington." Her voice was businesslike, professional. Luke still hadn't figured out how to put that office worker tone into his own voice when he answered his work telephone.

"Trudy, it's Luke. What are you still doing there?"

"I slept on the plane ride," she said. "Luke, I was going to call you, but Don said you would be asleep, probably until tomorrow."

Luke shook his head. "I can't sleep. Or, you know, I fell asleep, but then…"

"I get it," she said. "Listen, Swann put that laptop through a workout. Here's the short version. He thinks he managed to pinpoint an IP address where the video footage ended up. He says it's not a hundred percent, but…"

"How did he manage to do that?"

"He's got friends, apparently. He doesn't share that kind of information with me. He just says, 'I have friends.' After that I don't ask."

This was something. It was a breakthrough. If they could figure out who got the footage first, maybe they could figure out who edited it. Maybe the people who received the footage, and the people who edited it, were the same people.

"Where?" Luke said.

"Guess."

His shoulders slumped. "Trudy…"

"The IP address is in Russia. Moscow, to be precise."

Luke gritted his teeth. "The Russians. I knew it!"

Did he really know it? He wasn't sure. Certainly, he suspected it. Where there were Serbs, there were often Russians loitering somewhere nearby.

"The computer the video went to was in the offices of an internet media company called the New Times."

"Who is that?" Luke said.

"It's nobody. As far as we can tell, the New Times doesn't publish anything, and never has. It's housed in offices that also house media companies like New World Marketing, Public Interest Research, Public Opinion Limited, New World Times, Fast Forward Fashion, and about a dozen others."

Luke rubbed his forehead. He was just starting to wake up. He stood, brought the phone into the kitchen, and put the coffee pot on the stove. It was an old-school percolator, the kind he loved. He reached into the cabinet and found some coffee they had left behind when they moved.

"So the Serbians sent footage of the operation, including footage of them committing a massacre and pretending we did it, to some kind of email spam factory in Russia?"

"Luke, Swann and I went through a game of nesting Russian dolls, to figure out who the actual owner of these companies is. It was one shell company after another. Finally, we figured it out. The New Times is owned by Chekhov Media Worldwide."

Luke smiled. He was dumping coffee into the perk.

"And? What does that mean?"

"Chekhov Media is a front organization run by the Main Intelligence Directorate, otherwise known as the GRU. Chekhov Media also owns fifty-one percent of the Russia Now TV network, which was one of the first networks to air the doctored video."

"Russia Now is owned by the GRU?" Luke said.

Talk about propaganda. It would be like the CIA owning its own second-rate cable TV station, then broadcasting its contents all over the world. Come to think of it, the CIA probably did do something like that.

"Partly, yes. They own it in partnership with a group of private investors, including a handful of the oligarchs. They do a reasonably good job of airing things that at first glance, don't seem ridiculously slanted. Mostly it's gossip about Russian celebrities and athletes. They've even got game shows, variety shows, and stand-up comedians."

Luke was putting the pieces together, but it was coming slow. He was still overtired. His brain was not quite firing. Maybe an hour from now, after two cups of coffee, he would get it. But he suspected that Trudy had already done all the mental heavy lifting anyway. No need for him to burn out his wires.

"What are we saying here, Trudy?"

"We're saying the entire thing was a Russian black op. They selected and trained a group of Serbian nationalists, who were angry about the war with NATO. The Serbians were expendables, and the Russians sent them on a suicide mission to take over an American oil rig in the Arctic. The Serbians fed video footage of the events back to a front company controlled by the GRU, to be doctored however the Russians wanted. Within hours, that footage was on Al Jazeera, then Russia Now, then everywhere. Luke, we were never supposed to recover that laptop. That last Serbian was supposed to blow himself up, destroying the laptop, and all the evidence, in the process."

"But why do all this?" Luke said. "Why kill all those men? Why risk open war with the United States? To give us a public relations black eye? They have to know that we would see right through this."

"The only way to find out is to ask," Trudy said.

Luke nearly laughed. "The last time I checked, the GRU weren't the most eager people to share their motives."

"Right. But there's an actual man affiliated with these media front companies. His name appears on much of the paperwork. He's the president of this or that media company, the associate vice president of another. Chief Operations Officer. Government Relations Officer. He's listed as the director of a couple of low bud- get movies, and the producer of probably a dozen TV documenta- ries. He seems to be a real person, and potentially a true civilian, not a spook. His name is Lenny Zelazny, and the storage account the video was sent to is controlled by him. It's possible that he's even the one who edited the footage."

"Great. And all we need to do is ..." Luke began.

He was going to be sarcastic, but he stopped halfway through the sentence.

"He's alive?" he said.

"Yes, it appears so. Very much so. Or he was recently. He really does produce TV shows. Garbage for the most part, but I imagine it's a living. He lives in Moscow, not far from the New Times offices."

"I need to talk to him," Luke said.

"I figured you were going to say that. We know exactly where he lives, where he works, and what kind of car he drives. We have pho- tos taken of him within the past six months. If they haven't killed him today, and they don't kill him tomorrow, he shouldn't be that hard to find."

The man was a loose end. It probably wouldn't be long before they decided to tie him off. That meant Luke needed to get in touch with the man, in person, sooner rather than later. Meanwhile, the Russians knew who Luke Stone was. In all likelihood, he was wanted there because of the Sochi fiasco.

They'd probably love to get their hands on him.

Even so . . .

"I need to go to Moscow," Luke said.

"I think you probably need to talk to Don about that," Trudy said.

"No way, son. It's out of the question."

"Don, just please listen to me for a second."

Don sighed heavily over the phone. "Luke, I will listen to you. I will hear out everything you have to say, and I will give it deep consideration. But I want you to listen to me first. How does that sound?"

Luke felt like a little kid, jumping, excited, trying to convince his dad to let him have a pet giraffe. Don was more than his commanding officer in Delta, his civilian boss, or his mentor. He was a lot more. But this father and son game they were playing was beyond the pale sometimes.

"Okay," Luke said. "Hit me."

"Are you sitting down?"

The question gave Luke the sudden urge to jump up off the couch. Was he sitting down? What kind of way was that to start?

Out the bay window, a giant catamaran yacht with a blue and white sail, the mast probably ten stories high, crossed his field of vision from right to left, headed south toward the open ocean. Luke was momentarily distracted by it. It was a thing of beauty. He couldn't imagine what such a thing might cost.

"Yes. I'm sitting."

"Luke, in the past hour I've been contacted by both personnel from the White House, and by the Director of the Bureau. That video has made a real mess, and the brass have been looking for a way to clean it up. Meanwhile, the mess is spreading all over the world. There are anti-American protests taking place in the Middle East, Eastern Europe, South America, Africa, and Asia. There are candlelight vigils scheduled for tonight all over the United States and Canada. There are talking heads screaming on the TV set. Someone needs to be slaughtered for this, probably more than one someone, and the brass want to make you the first sacrificial lamb."

Luke's shoulders slumped. He felt the breath going out of him. *Here it comes again.* He had just been suspended, unsuspended, investigated, and finally cleared, not even two months ago. How could they keep doing this?

He couldn't find a word to say.

"You with me?" Don said.

"Yeah. I'm with you."

"I told them no. Not on my watch. I told them that in no uncertain terms. I've spent my entire adult life in and around combat. I know what happens. And I know that the looks on men's faces often don't mean anything. The processing happens later. Also, that video is a shuck. A con job. And the truth about it will come out."

Luke felt numb. His hands were tingling the slightest amount.

"What did they say?"

"We negotiated," Don said. "That's half the game around here. We settled on a paid leave of absence, what they're going to call a suspension, pending the outcome of the investigation. I told them I'm confident that when all the testimony is given, your description of the event will be consistent with that of the soldiers and other personnel on the scene."

Luke nodded. He knew what had happened. Murphy shot the guy because he was reaching for a grenade. Ed was there. There were four or five SEALs in the room at that moment. They all saw it.

"Absolutely true," he said. "But will it matter?"

"It'll matter," Don said. "I'll make it matter."

"So I'm out," Luke said.

He didn't know what to make of that prospect. His reputation was in tatters, again. He remembered when he was a little kid, and how the schoolteachers would say, "This is going on your permanent record."

It was a scary thought. But now it was real. Luke's permanent record included two Purple Hearts, a Bronze Star with V device, a Global War on Terrorism Expeditionary Medal, Afghanistan Campaign Medal, Iraq Campaign Medal, and so many combat badges, marksmanship badges and clasps that he'd lost track of them all. He had passed airborne training, Special Forces training, had been recruited into the elite Delta Force, and served with distinction.

His permanent record also included a botched special operation where only three men survived, one of whom committed suicide soon afterward. It included an inpatient stay at a psychiatric hospital. Somewhere, there might be a diagnosis of post-traumatic stress disorder, though if there was, he hadn't heard of it. He had already been suspended from his civilian job once before, under suspicion of committing an atrocity.

And now?

"Why am I suspended?" he said. "Officially?"

"You're suspended pending the outcome of an investigation into your actions, and the possible summary execution of an enemy prisoner or prisoners, during the Martin Frobisher incident. That's what it is. That's how it's worded."

It was baloney.

"What am I supposed to do in the meantime?"

To Luke's mind, there was a lot to do. There was a chance of pinpointing the culprits behind the oil rig attack, and he felt they should take that chance. This was personal to him. He was there. He saw what those men had done. The people who masterminded it should pay. And they should be stopped before they did anything else.

Don paused. The moment stretched out between them.

"Well, to be honest, there's not much for you to do. You're out of the game. I'd say go and enjoy yourself, if you can."

Enjoy himself? "Enjoy myself doing what?"

"You play golf?"

Luke grunted. He almost laughed. "No."

Luke could almost hear Don smile over the phone. "Uh, in that case, I'd say take a trip to Europe. Why not? Rome is great this time of year. I hear your friend Big Daddy Cronin is in town. His doctor told him he has high blood pressure and should take some time off. Hell, son, why don't you take your friend Ed Newsam with you? He's requested some personal time, to rest up and recuperate after the recent operation, and I told him to take what he needs. Why don't you both make a little holiday of it? Some time away wouldn't hurt you."

"Let me get this straight," Luke said. "You think I should go to Rome on vacation? Meet Bill Cronin there? And take Ed Newsam with me?"

"That's what I think, yes. You're all on the sidelines for the time being, so you might as well make something of it. Put this whole oil rig thing, and this Russia fascination, right out of your head. I can tell you, when Big Daddy has a few drinks, he's one heck of a storyteller. He'll curl your nose hairs."

Luke let the weight of these words sink in.

"I'll bet," Luke said. He'd never had a drink with Bill Cronin before.

"I shouldn't do this," Don said, "but I'll even sweeten the deal for you. I'll have someone here arrange the travel. We'll pay for it out of the petty cash drawer. You can reimburse us later."

"That's really generous of you, Don."

"Go," Don said. "Have a good time. And don't say I never did anything for you."

CHAPTER SIXTEEN

4:50 p.m. Eastern Daylight Time
Best Western Hotel
King's Dominion
Doswell, Virginia

Kevin Murphy was long gone.

He was in a strange hotel or motel next to a large amusement park somewhere off Interstate 95, maybe a hundred miles south of Washington, DC, and just north of Richmond. The place had an onsite pizzeria that doubled as a bar, and also a Denny's restaurant, apparently open twenty-four hours a day. There was a small outside swimming pool.

On the near horizon was the amusement park. The roller coaster was visible from Murphy's window. He watched it in a state of near hypnosis, again and again.

At the beginning, the cars would slowly climb up a circular track, up up up to the sky, reach the camel hump at the top, seemingly pause to give the riders a terrifying view of what was in store for them, then whoooosh! Down and around and upside down. He could hear the screams from here.

Murphy had trouble peeling his eyes away from it. He was *that* tired.

He had decided to run. The trip to the Arctic had convinced him. If he hung around Luke Stone and the SRT much longer, he was going to get killed. The assault by boat was bad enough. The grenade bouncing around in the bow like a pinball was worse.

But if Murphy had donned that underwater space suit, and climbed through that gravesite in the ice…

He didn't like to think about it. Probably, they all would have died.

Stone was everybody's bad luck charm.

Not to mention the little fact that Don Morris wanted Murphy to spend some time in Leavenworth. Not to mention that Wallace Speck was floating out there, a loose end certainly, but more like a ghoul from a bad nightmare. It was all too much.

So Murphy was leaving.

He had a late flight booked tomorrow night out of Fort Lauderdale, under the name of one of his aliases. Florida to Grand Cayman, direct. His money was in a numbered account at Royal Heritage Bank, which was in a small, very tidy, very well-kept building right in the middle of George Town.

The bank manager was Mr. Johnson. Johnson was a polite, well-educated black man, short, balding, always impeccably dressed, who knew his business backwards and forwards. He treated clients like long-lost family. He took you into his office and served you strong tea in little ornate teacups. It was all very civilized, and Murphy looked forward to seeing Mr. Johnson again.

Murphy had been depositing bits of money at Royal Heritage Bank for years. But he had never made a deposit like the one that had come from the Montreal Score.

That's how he thought of it—the Montreal Score.

With the $2.5 million that Wallace Speck had transferred in, Murphy's account at the bank now stood at a little over $2.8 mil. Speck hadn't sent the second payment. But that was to be expected, since the events in Montreal didn't go Speck's way. Speck was currently languishing in federal prison, preparing for a date with the needle still some years in the future.

Murphy noticed his cell phone was ringing.

The ringer itself was off, but the silent phone was lighting up. He looked at the phone there on the scuffed motel coffee table. It rang for a while, and then stopped.

There were a bunch of brochures for nearby tourist attractions on the table with the phone. There was a brochure for the pizza place downstairs—you could call and they would bring the food up to your room. Murphy's fake passport was also on the table, along with his real passport.

They were both American passports, and they were basically identical. Once in a while, Murphy spent some time trying to notice any discrepancy between them. Other than the name, date, and place of birth, and the passport number, there didn't seem to be any. It was a very clever forgery. He'd gotten it in Colombia.

The Colombians were known for their devotion to quality. Cocaine. Marijuana. Cut roses. Counterfeit American money. Forged documents. If Colombians were doing it, they were generally doing a good job. Murphy had also gotten his fake Irish passport in Colombia, and his British one.

He had credit cards under several different names. He had small piles of cash in several different currencies. He was good to go. A gun in his luggage might throw red flags, so he didn't have one. He could pick up a weapon during his travels, if he felt the need for one. Which he probably wouldn't. When dealing with normals in the regular world, he didn't usually feel that need.

He had driven south out of the DC area, and within a short time, the exhaustion hit him. He could barely stay awake at the wheel. So he stopped here—wherever here was.

The place was comfortable enough. The screams from the far-away roller coaster were oddly relaxing, like waves crashing on the beach. The carpet smelled a little funny, like they had treated it with disinfectant. But the king-sized bed was just what the doctor ordered. In a little while, he was going to crash out and he wasn't going to wake up until tomorrow morning. Then he was going to drive like the devil to Fort Lauderdale.

The phone started ringing again. He glanced at it. Okay, it was her.

He picked it up. "Hi."

Trudy Wellington's musical voice. "Murph?"

It hurt to leave someone as beautiful as Trudy behind, but she hadn't shown the slightest interest in him, so . . .

"Yeah. Hi, Trudy. What's up?"

"Did I wake you? You sound tired."

"Uh . . . no, you didn't wake me. I've been sleeping all day, but I got up a little while ago to make a bite to eat."

"Listen, I wanted to catch you," she said. "I know Don gave you a few days off."

"Yeah, he did."

"I wonder if you want to spend those days in Europe."

Europe? The question gave him pause. Did he want to go to Europe? There was a catch here, and Murphy treaded lightly.

"Just me and you?"

"Ah . . . ha, ha, no. Sorry. Luke and Ed are going to Rome later tonight. Luke's been suspended again—well, actually he's on a leave of absence. And Ed asked for some recuperation time, which Don greenlighted. If you want to go with them, SRT would pay your travel expenses."

Murphy let the silence draw out. What were they doing?

It wasn't a vacation. It couldn't be. Stone and Newsam weren't vacation types, and if they were, it wouldn't be to a tourist trap like Rome. What were they going to do, visit museums? Buy a bobble-head doll of the Pope? The idea was ridiculous. Stone and Newsam didn't even seem to like each other that much. But if they did go on a vacation together, they'd probably go fall off a mountain some-where, or get eaten by crocodiles.

"Stone and Newsam are going on vacation to Rome?" he said.

"Yes."

"Together?"

He could almost hear her smiling. "Yes."

"And they want me to come with them?"

She didn't say anything.

"Someone else wants me to go with them? On vacation?"

Her voice sounded the slightest bit peevish. "Murph, you don't have to question every little thing, do you? You're not even a full employee here, and yet the SRT wants to give you a trip to Europe. Don thought it would be a nice gesture, after the operation you guys just went on. Call it a team-building trip. Can you live with that?"

This was no vacation. It was a clandestine mission, right on the heels of one that nearly ended in disaster.

Murphy scanned the money and the passports again. There was no way he was going to Rome with Stone and Newsam, or wherever they were really going. He was done. He was going to Grand Cayman, and then he was going wherever the winds, and his whimsy, took him. Stone and Newsam would have to live or die on their own.

"Do I have to go?" he said.

"Of course not. It's a vacation."

"Then I think I'm going to pass this time. It's a generous offer, but I'm completely wiped out. I think I'm going to just chill out here at my apartment, and sleep for the next three days."

He smiled to himself as the next thought occurred to him.

"You're welcome to come over here and help me, if you're tired. I have a very big, very comfortable bed. California king-sized."

"Murphy!"

A long moment passed. Was she thinking about it? If she was, Murphy might turn around and go back for that.

"Call me if you change your mind in the next half an hour. They're leaving tonight."

Then she hung up.

Murphy stared at the room around him. It was growing later in the day, the shadows were growing longer, and the place seemed a little bleaker than when he arrived. But that was the exhaustion talking. In a little while, he would be sound asleep, and it wasn't going to matter what the place looked like.

"They think of me as part of the team," he said out loud.

He wasn't expecting to say that. But of course it was true. Why wouldn't it be? He was a cynical bastard, and he always had been. But he'd also been on the team.

He'd been a starting wide receiver for the football team in high school. He'd been part of the elite United States Army Rangers—Rangers Lead The Way—and he'd been all the way on the team then. He'd even gotten *RLTW* tattooed on his right bicep.

In Delta, he'd been on the team, but things had gone sideways. And when he was on loan to JSOC and the CIA, he had started to work solo. The strange experiences began to pile up. He started to feel alone, like he was different, like there was no way he could explain any of this to anyone. Then Afghanistan happened, he was out of the military, and he was all the way out there on the edge by himself.

Stone had sensed this, and thrown him a lifeline. *Come back onto the team.* But now the Montreal Score had happened. And this new team—the Special Response Team … Murphy wasn't sure about it.

Maybe he was better off alone. Maybe the best thing to do was to fall asleep on this big hotel bed and forget all about Luke Stone and the SRT. Then wake up in the morning and put as much distance between himself and them as possible.

He lay down on the bed, put his head on the pillows, and closed his eyes. Within seconds, he had already started to drift.

CHAPTER SEVENTEEN

10:15 p.m. Eastern Daylight Time
The Situation Room
The White House
Washington, DC

The meeting was running long.

"Just a few more things to address, Mr. President."

It was crowded in here, so crowded that it was hard to tell the shape of the room anymore. Clement Dixon knew that it was an oblong egg shape, but only from memory. And its space-age features were obscured by the press of bodies.

The sheer number of breathers in here was robbing the room of oxygen. The body heat had raised the room temperature to an uncomfortable place. Dixon, hale and hearty for so many years, a firebrand for so long, almost felt like he was gasping for air. Would he pass out?

That would make for some headlines. None that he might want to read.

This was not a classified meeting, hence the throngs. This was a meeting to let the President know about all the things that he wasn't currently dealing with.

"Okay," he said. "But let's try to move it along. It's getting late."

He paused.

"I don't like to miss *Letterman*."

The joke went flat. There were a few snickers here and there. They were embarrassed for him—he could see it in their eyes. Was

Letterman even still on the air? It didn't matter. No one in here believed that an old man like Clement Dixon stayed up late to watch David Letterman on TV.

No. The people in this room pictured their President in slippers and jammies at 11 p.m., enjoying a nice cup of warm milk before taking his teeth out and calling it a night.

He wanted to pound the conference table and scream at them all.

"It isn't true!"

He looked around the room. No one was even looking at him. Everyone was going through their own paperwork, whispering to aides and assistants, the young people typing with one flying finger into their infernal Crackberries.

There were a lot of military men here tonight. They were all the same. They were clones of one another. Men in their forties and fifties, thin, very fit, impeccably clean shaven even though it was the middle of the night, with buzz cuts and dress greens without a single wrinkle. Did they notice they were all the same, or were they so indoctrinated into a way of thinking and being that something like that was invisible to them?

Did wildebeests know they were all the same? What about goldfish? He should commission a study on this. He was the President, after all.

"So let's do it, Richard."

At the other end of the room, General Richard Stark nodded.

"As we all know, there's some ongoing fallout from the events in the Arctic. Protests are being held in at least a dozen cities about the drilling in the ANWR. None of these protestors seem to realize that what was being done was not illegal. It was a case of horizontal drilling from out at sea, which was having no impact on animals in the refuge. Would you say that's accurate, Allen?"

Allen Forbes, the press secretary and alleged media wizard, was here, sitting at the table. Dixon was almost relieved to look at him. Nothing much was disciplined or upright about Allen Forbes. He looked tired, slouched over, and had a pronounced five o'clock shadow. His suit jacket was hanging on the chair behind him, and his tie was loosened. Allen wanted to go home.

"That's correct, General. It's a technical issue, and one that a certain segment of the public isn't likely to embrace. We can try to educate on it going forward, but at the moment, a lot of people are not buying it. A better tack might be a hard wrist slap on the offenders, along with messaging from our environmentalist President that he's as shocked as we are, and we all need to do better."

The general shrugged. "The law's the law. But I'll leave that to civilian minds to grapple with. In any event, protests against the drilling are happening, as well as candlelight vigils for the murdered oil workers. In several places, the two groups have come into contact with each other, and there have been clashes at a result. We've learned that about an hour ago, a twenty-four-year-old woman died during one such clash in Seattle."

"A twenty-four-year-old *woman*?" Dixon said.

The general nodded. "Yes sir. Nowadays women take part in these street battles along with the men. It's a time of liberation."

"How did she die?" Dixon said.

"She was hit by a car, sir. It may have been intentional, and the driver may have been using the car as a weapon."

Dixon was tired. Tragedy was piling on top of tragedy. What in God's name were people doing out there, and how did he become the ineffectual ringmaster of this 900-ring circus?

He supposed he shouldn't be surprised. In his day, young women were out in the streets with the men, fighting for the things they believed in.

He ran a hand through his hair and sighed heavily.

"Allen?"

Allen Forbes's eyes came alive. For a split second, he looked like a deer caught in the high beams of an onrushing Mack truck.

"Yes, sir?"

"What am I doing about the dead girl? And the unrest in general?"

"Well sir, we could do an early morning taping, just yourself in the Oval Office, calling for calm until all the facts are in, and offering condolences to the family of the young woman. Something we can release to the early morning shows. It'll probably play all day. I wouldn't want you to face the press on it, though. There are just too many uncomfortable questions floating around right now."

Dixon nodded. "Sounds good. Set up the taping. I'll be in the office by seven a.m."

A military man at the table, a colonel, raised his hand. Dixon had no idea who he was and didn't really care. The guy had eyes like laser beams. He was smiling and confident, glad to be here.

General Stark acknowledged him. "Mike?"

"Excuse me, sir. But if you offer condolences about the dead girl, won't that appear you're taking sides on this issue?"

Dixon stared at him. "I am taking sides, Colonel. I'm on the side of young women who care so much about the state of their world, who feel so strongly about it, they go out and get themselves killed. And I'm on the side of families bereft at that loss."

The colonel's smile died on the vine. His eyes became downcast, no longer sharp. He regretted speaking. That much was clear. The guy had gone from a silverback gorilla to an organ grinder monkey in seconds flat.

Dixon liked to see that sort of thing. There should be more of it.

On the screen behind General Stark, an image of the world appeared. It was round, a globe, but from a perspective Dixon was not used to seeing.

"Mr. President," Stark said. "With your permission, I'd like to steer this meeting back to the elephant in the room."

"What is that elephant, General?"

"Sir, the elephant is the relative states of preparedness in the Arctic between ourselves and the Russians. I imagine I'm beginning to sound like a broken record to you, but something needs to be done, and this incident points at that need."

"The attack was committed by Serbians, General."

Stark looked at another military man at the table. "Jeff, can you illuminate this situation for us?"

The man had papers in front of him. He nodded.

Stark looked at Dixon. "Sir, Colonel Woods and his people have..."

Dixon nodded and waved his hand. These Pentagon guys with their papers and their reports and their people. Holy moly. "Yeah. Go ahead."

"Sir," the colonel said. "The Serbian government has denied any ties to, and any knowledge of the activities of, the men involved in the oil rig attack. NSA data confirm that there was no apparent contact between the men and any agency of the Serbian government during the crisis. CIA has been slow to declassify its data on this. But what we have so far from them suggests there was no discussion of an impending attack within Serbian military, government, or elite circles in the weeks leading up to the attack. They seem to have been as surprised as we were."

"So who were the attackers?" Dixon said.

"By working with Interpol and Scotland Yard, we've used fingerprints, DNA, and body markings such as scars and tattoos to identify eight of the men involved so far. Five of the men were legitimately members of disbanded Serbian paramilitary organizations, and veterans of the Yugoslav Civil Wars. All eight of the men had ties to Eastern European criminal networks, including mafias operating in Russia and Ukraine, but also with tentacles in Poland, Romania, Hungary, and the United Kingdom. Taken together, the eight men have a record of over ninety arrests in various countries, and have spent a total of forty-six years in jail. We suspect at least two of the men were assets of the Russian FSB or GRU, or both, but details of that have not yet been declassified."

Dixon nodded. "So they were Serbians, but they weren't *the* Serbians."

"Correct, sir. We believe it was the Russians. As you know, Russian intelligence makes widespread use of criminal networks to do their dirty work."

Dixon nodded again. He bit his tongue. There was no sense getting started on …

"We've never been known to do that, have we?"

Vice President Thomas Hayes had just spoken. Dixon glanced at him. Thomas was still fresh, his eyes alert and aware. He was eating from a plastic yogurt cup. Dixon was either going to have to put a muzzle on Thomas, or send him on a baby-kissing tour of American Samoa.

He looked at Richard Stark. "I get it. Russians. Please continue."

"Sir, if you look behind me, you will see a map of the top of the world. There is no land at the top of the world. There is the Arctic Ocean, and the countries ringing it. Now, throughout recorded human history, the Arctic Ocean has been frozen nearly solid. It has long been one of the most impassable, forbidding places on earth. But a joint study by Swedish and German climate scientists, due to be released next week, strongly suggests that within twenty-five years, 2030, many parts of the Arctic will be wide open for shipping and resource exploitation. Indeed, based on computer modeling, in one scenario, by that time there will be no summer ice in the Arctic left at all."

Clement Dixon didn't say a word. He grunted. Of course he had known this was coming. He had known it for a long time. But it was a shocking assessment, and one that he didn't enjoy hearing spoken out loud.

Hopefully, the world was not ending. But it was definitely changing, and very rapidly. And apparently, the natural Pentagon response to this was not, "How do we stop it?" Instead, it was, "How do we take advantage of it?"

The general went on.

"Sir, Russian preparedness in the Arctic dwarfs ours, to put it mildly. I'm afraid the Soviets anticipated this thawing, and if we don't act quickly, the Russians are going to reap the benefits of that foresight."

He used a wooden pointer to indicate a long, swirling mark on the map.

"They have good reason to be ahead of us, because they will be the major beneficiary of a warming Arctic. Within the next several years, the so-called Northeast Passage, which skirts Russian territory in Siberia, is going to be passable for shipping. Once fully open, it will be the shortest, least expensive ocean route between manufacturers in Asia and markets in Western Europe. Less than half the distance for ships circumnavigating the globe, and about one-third shorter for ships taking the Suez Canal. And the Russians will control it. They are already plowing billions of dollars into upgrading seven old Cold War military bases along the route, with advanced radar and missile systems designed to withstand extreme cold. They are planning to become the world's wealthiest tolling authority."

He paused.

"That doesn't even take into account… well sir, it doesn't take into account anything at all. The Arctic is thought to harbor thirteen percent of the world's undiscovered oil, thirty percent of its undiscovered natural gas, an abundance of uranium, rare earth minerals, gold, diamonds, and millions of square miles of untapped natural resources, including fisheries galore. By controlling vast regions of the Arctic, the Russians are planning to catapult themselves back into relevance again. It's clear they are going to challenge us for dominance of the Arctic, and if they win, they're going to be challenging us everywhere."

Clement Dixon could see where this was going. He'd been around Washington long enough to know when the pitch was coming. And the generals were always making the pitch. Dixon had heard it said that some companies out there trained their sales forces in the somewhat unscrupulous ABC rule—Always Be Closing.

He was beginning to wonder if the Pentagon did the same.

"I'm not the Congress, General. I'm not even in Congress anymore. What you're saying makes sense, but I don't hold the purse strings around here, and you know that."

Stark raised a hand. A new image appeared. It was of a red and white ship in drydock—the size of the ship compared to the buildings and vehicles around it made the thing seem enormous.

"Mr. President, just one example should make this clear to you. The Russians have more than forty icebreaker ships deployed in the Arctic, not including three new Ural class icebreakers due to come online in the next two years. The Ural class ships are gigantic, the largest, most powerful ships to ever operate in that region, and are each powered by two small onboard nuclear reactors. The Russians are not going to wait to let nature take its course. They are going to force the issue and clear the ice themselves."

Dixon stared at him. He had no reason to disbelieve the general. The military was not Clement Dixon's favorite organization. If Stark were to come in here and lie to him, there would be a new Stark the next day. Stark knew that.

It was clearly madness, what the Russians were doing.

Stark went on: "Sir, the United States Navy currently has zero icebreaker ship. The Coast Guard has three icebreakers, two of which were built in the late 1970s. One of these, the USCGC *Polar Sea*, is out of commission because three of its six engines have failed. There is no firm date for redeployment. Both of these ships are nearing the end of their effective thirty-year lifespan. Soon, we will have one icebreaker available, USCGC *Healey*, which was completed in 1999. The state of readiness aboard this ship became clear last year when two Coast Guard divers died in a mishap during a routine cold-water training mission, after which the captain was relieved of his duties."

Dixon nodded. The general had made his point. Dixon didn't love that fact, but he had to admit it was true.

"How many, and how much do they cost?" he said.

"Sir, with modern icebreakers, ones that can compete with the Russians, we are talking about one billion dollars for one. But if we build seven of them, we will realize economies of scale, which should bring the price down to about seven hundred million dollars each."

Clement Dixon ignored the economies of scale. He'd been around government spending long enough to know it was a joke.

"So between seven and ten billion dollars, you'd say?"

"Yes sir, just for the icebreakers. After that, the Russian icebreakers would still outnumber ours four or five to one. And we haven't even touched upon the cold-weather battle tanks the Russians are already deploying."

"Richard, did I mention I'm not the Congress?"

"Mr. President, the oil rig attack was a provocation. It was designed to test our readiness. We failed that test. It was also designed to humiliate us and give us a black eye publicly. Mission accomplished. The Russians are going to seize control of the Arctic, and it's going to happen sooner than anyone thinks."

General Stark paused and looked around the room. Clement Dixon almost laughed at the bush league theatrics of the gesture.

"Mr. President, please don't let it happen on your watch."

"General," Dixon said. "It's not going to happen on my watch. You know why? Because I'll probably be asleep. I'm going upstairs to bed."

Chapter Eighteen

September 6, 2005
1:05 p.m. Central European Summer Time (7:05 a.m.
Eastern Daylight Time)
La Scalinata Ristorante
Piazza di Spagna
Rome, Italy

"You guys look like something the cat dragged home."

Big Daddy Bill Cronin, deeply tan and wearing shorts and a Polo shirt, relaxed, well-rested, looked at them both with the eyes of a bird of prey. Neither Luke nor Ed took the bait. They'd come in on the overnight flight, and they were tired. They'd barely said a word to each other since they arrived, never mind to Bill.

Luke had called Becca one more time, last night, just before he and Ed left the United States. This call had actually gone a little better than the previous one. She didn't hang up right away.

"Hi, Luke."

"Hi, babe," he said. "Listen, I really need to talk to ..."

"I don't think we have anything to talk about."

He paused, shaking his head in frustration. "I'm going out of the country for a couple of days."

"Of course you are. I don't even want to think about that."

"Becca ..."

"Have a nice trip."

Click. The phone went dead.

See? You could almost call that progress.

Now he, Ed, and Big Daddy sat in the small outdoor dining area of a restaurant just off a crowded plaza. Their seats were cordoned off from the street with a red velvet rope. It was a hot day with bright sun, but they were under the restaurant's canopy. The sounds of silverware and plates, people chatting and laughing—lunchtime eating sounds—came from inside the restaurant. It was loud and echoey in there.

Outside, all over the plaza, the voices of the picture-taking tourists made a low, steady hum. There was a lot of ambient sound here, hard to edit it out, hard to differentiate individual voices. It was a good place to talk.

From where Luke was sitting, he could look directly at a fountain, the famous Fontana della Barcaccia, which dated from the 1600s. He had the tour book open to it. The stone fountain was sculpted to look like a half-sunken ship with water overflowing its sides. Two human faces were embedded in the inner walls of the boat. The water was a light blue-green.

Beyond the fountain, a wide steep set of stairs ascended straight up to a whitewashed church at the top. The church had what appeared to be two bell towers, each with a crucifix carved in the front. People milled everywhere. People stood all around the fountain. People sat on the far edges of the staircase. A throng of at least forty people stood at the top of the steps near the church. They must be a tour of some kind.

"Here's what the guidebook won't tell you," Big Daddy said. "That fountain? It's fed, to this day, by an aqueduct built by the Romans before the time of Christ. Talk about built to last. Those people were ahead of the curve, all right. After Rome fell, a thousand years passed before anybody in the west was even attempting similar engineering feats."

Luke stared at Big Daddy. Big Daddy was annihilating a chicken dish with pasta as he talked. He was on his second glass of red wine.

Luke had almost nothing in front of him. Just a cup of coffee that was already going cold. He was so tired, he felt physically sick.

He sipped the coffee. Tepid at best. He watched Ed pick at a thin slice of veal.

Big Daddy gestured with his head.

"See the house on the right at the bottom of the steps? That's where the English poet John Keats lived at the end of his life. He died in that house in, I'm gonna say … 1821."

There was a long pause at the table.

"You missed your calling, Bill," Luke said finally. "You could have led package tours of retired ladies from Ohio."

Big Daddy smiled. "I heard you guys nearly ate a shit sandwich in the Arctic the other night. I'm glad to see you bounced right back."

Now Ed smiled. "What are we doing here, Big Daddy?"

Big Daddy shrugged. "Well, I'm supposedly on a break for my health. Much-needed, and well-deserved. Really, I'm under investigation. Nothing new there. You have to crack open a few eggs to make an omelet. But this isn't cooking class. You guys, so I understand, are on your way to another destination. And if that's true, I've got some things for you."

He reached down into a backpack at his feet. He came out with a book, another Rome guidebook, this one by a different company, and placed it on the table.

"Don't open that," he said. "When you get up to leave, take it with you. It's not what it looks like. Inside are some documents."

He gestured up the wide stairs, indicating the church—just a guy from America pointing something out to a couple of friends. He spoke quietly.

"Here's something you should know. You guys are businessmen from the United States, in Moscow to look at possible investment properties. Nothing huge, maybe a couple of high-end apartments you can rent to visiting bigshots. Your names, ages, places of birth, backgrounds, families, it's all in the documents. Passports are in there. Carte Blanche. Diner's Club. Impressive. You guys are music producers, got lucky with a couple of rap and dance hits."

Ed shook his head. "Of course. That explains the rich black guy."

"Relatively obscure songs, nothing in the Top 40, but they made you a lot of money. The songs were actually produced by an Agency front company. You guys were involved. The names of the songs and artists are in the documents. You should memorize that stuff in case it comes up. It won't, but you never know."

"Produced by the Agency?"' Ed said. He smiled. He seemed to be perking up. Maybe Luke shook have eaten something.

Bill nodded. He coughed, his hand covering his mouth. "We've got our little fingers in just about every pie you can imagine. Sometimes the best way to get a message out there is through music. Or in a movie. Or on TV."

"Okay," Luke said. "And?"

"Don't check out of your hotel here. We've got a couple of doppelgangers who are going to play you for a few days. Wander around Rome, enjoy the sights, turn up here and there, have a nice time."

"How do they look?" Ed said.

Big Daddy shrugged. "Big black guy. Not as big white guy with blond hair. Not necessarily handsome, but not as ugly as you two. They'll do."

He took a sip of his wine.

"There are clothes and luggage being placed in your hotel room as we speak. Take that stuff with you. Wear the clothes. The suits, the watches, the shoes, everything. Dress the part, okay? Because you guys…" Big Daddy gave them both the once-over, smiled and shook his head. "You don't look like high rollers right now."

Ed was wearing jeans short and a tight, dark blue T-shirt. His sunglasses were perched on his head. Luke was wearing jeans, sneakers and a green Boston Celtics replica basketball jersey.

"I mean, look at the state of you both."

Big Daddy burst out laughing. He laughed so long that his face started to turn red.

"Don't give yourself a stroke," Luke said. "I hear you're a ticking time bomb."

It took Big Daddy a moment to stop. He took a deep breath, and his broad smile started to fade.

"When you touch ground, you'll be contacted by a real estate agent. Albert Strela. He's going to show you the properties. It wouldn't kill you to actually go look at a few of them. But Albert's really your translator. He's also the one who does your surveillance. You guys are going to stick out like a couple of giant sore thumbs, so let him do his work, and don't step all over it. When he says go, you go. When he says sit tight, you sit tight."

Big Daddy took another long sip of wine.

"He knows what you're looking for, and he's already found it. That's the good news. But you have to tread carefully, because Uncle Joe is always watching. All these people are connected, and the connections go up and down, high and low. Everybody knows everybody, it's a spider web, and our friends over there routinely drop people in the Roman aqueduct, if you know what I'm trying to say."

Luke did, without even having to be told. The Russian government was all-knowing and all-seeing. Its reach extended to the streets, the hotel suites, and everywhere else. The most untouchable mobsters, and the most savage street thugs, were all on the payroll. Clandestine murder in Moscow was barely even a crime.

"Which leads me to my next point," Big Daddy said. "When you're over there, you're on your own. I know you guys are on the friends and family plan, and you like to keep in touch with the folks back home. In most cases I'd say that's a good idea. But the walls have ears, and every call you make goes through the hotel switchboard, if you know what I'm trying to say."

Luke nodded. It wasn't what he wanted to hear. He often relied on Swann and Trudy when he was on a mission, and tried to stay in touch with them. Swann was able to encrypt calls and bounce them from satellite to satellite across the world, baffling attempts to track them or listen in.

Big Daddy was saying that wasn't going to work this time. It made sense. They were going to Moscow. It was one of the most closely watched places on Earth.

"Yeah, sometimes it's just nice to get away from everybody," Ed said.

Big Daddy looked at Luke. "What do you think about that?"

Luke nodded. "It's okay."

What else was it going to be? A deal breaker?

"Let me ask you a question," Big Daddy said. "Totally off topic. How come your friend Murphy's not here? This seems like a trip he might enjoy. Or at least one you might enjoy having him on."

Luke shrugged. "He got some time off. And he deserves every minute of it. Decided to take that time and lay low, I suppose."

Big Daddy nodded. "Yeah? What's he doing?"

"I don't know."

"That's what I figured. I'll tell you what he's doing. He booked himself a flight to the Cayman Islands under a pen name. He's headed down there later today. Then he's got a flight to the Bahamas tomorrow night. Nassau. He's an interesting guy."

Luke wasn't sure he liked where this was going. Special operators were unusual people. Getting a few days off, then suddenly jumping on a plane to the Caribbean under a false identity was hardly out of character. Luke wouldn't have raised an eyebrow if Big Daddy had said Murphy left on a flight to Zimbabwe.

"I guess he likes to travel."

Big Daddy shrugged. "Yeah."

Ed was still tucking into the tortured remains of his veal. "Why are you keeping tabs on Murphy, man? He do something to you?"

Big Daddy smiled. "I keep tabs on everybody. It's a little hobby of mine. And Murphy's been a friend of the Agency before."

"Haven't we all?" Luke said.

There was mirth in Big Daddy's eyes. "Some better than others."

Luke decided the strain really was getting to Big Daddy. He had tossed out that he was under investigation like it was nothing. It was never nothing. Luke hadn't been around nearly as long as Big Daddy, and already he knew that. If you overstepped, if you made them look bad, they would eat you for lunch.

Now he was letting it slip that Murphy was under surveillance. That wasn't the kind of thing you shared around. If Murphy was a threat of some kind, Big Daddy should tell them that. Otherwise, he was just spreading gossip and sowing division, like an old washerwoman leaning over the back fence.

"Is that everything?" Luke said. "Are we done here?"

Big Daddy shook his head. "No, there's one more thing. When you get where you're going, say hi to Albert for me. Also, don't get him killed. I like him."

CHAPTER NINETEEN

8:15 p.m. Moscow Daylight Time (12:15 p.m. Eastern Daylight Time)
Hotel Baltschug Kempinski Moscow
Zamoskvorechye District
Moscow, Russia

"We should have come here for vacation."

Ed Newsam had spoken.

They were walking into the lobby of the hotel, a grand old palace right on the boulevard that ran along the Moskva River. Red Square and the Kremlin were across a wide thoroughfare from here, and lit up for the night in spectacular fashion.

The lobby was wide, gleaming, with two-story ceilings. It had white marble floors and walls, fresh cut flowers in stone vases on the tables, and a hallway lined with expensive boutique shops. A white-gloved man in a red top hat and tails pushed their luggage on a rolling cart.

It took every ounce of Luke's will to allow it to happen. He preferred to carry his own bags.

He glanced at big Ed. The man was in his glory playing music producer. Ed wore a form fitting gray pinstriped vest and matching pants, with a black dress shirt under the vest. His shoes alone must have cost $500. His watch was big and garish. He wore a gold chain around his neck, with a crucifix dangling from it. To complete the look, he wore sunglasses, indoors, at night.

Ed followed the man pushing the cart, big jaw thrust out, massive arms swinging. He was strutting like a peacock. His legs in the pinstriped dress pants looked like overpacked sausages about to burst from their casings.

"Maybe you missed your calling," Luke said. "Maybe you really should have been a rap mogul."

Ed shrugged. "I am a rap mogul."

Luke wore a blue pinstriped three-piece suit, with a white shirt and red tie. The suit was perfectly tailored to his body, but he had to admit he didn't own the look. Not like Ed. Luke felt awkward, almost apologetic, in these clothes.

Check-in was effortless. The man at the desk was small, skinny, dressed in a starched white shirt that fit him like a circus tent. He was smoking a cigarette. The haze of gray smoke rose toward the ceiling high above them.

His English was very good, with a slight evil Russian villain accent that Luke remembered from cartoons during childhood.

"Hello, Mr. Simmons. How was your flight from ... America?"

Luke was Rob Simmons on this trip. Ed had the improbable name Max Funk. Luke nearly laughed. Big Daddy had a sense of humor—you had to give him that.

They had pushed on from Rome, with just enough time to stop back at their hotel rooms and pick up the clothes and the documents Big Daddy had left for them. Luke had been so exhausted he slept the entire flight here. He'd popped a low-dose Dexie right before the plane landed and drunk a cup of coffee. Other than the clothes he was wearing, he felt pretty good.

"Very nice, thank you."

The man glanced from Luke to Ed.

"Will you gentlemen be looking for companionship this evening?"

"Companionship?"

"Yes, sir." The man stared into his computer terminal. He didn't look up from whatever he was doing. He shrugged. "Ladies ... to accompany you. Out to the nightlife. Who know all the places to go. Bars. Shows. Clubbing. You understand. *Companions.*"

There was a young woman nearby, blonde, very pretty, wearing a blue hotel uniform. She stood at a long table, collating papers and stapling them together. Luke looked at her, and she at him. She smiled, and blushed just a bit.

This must be a normal question.

"Uh … no thanks. We're here on business."

The man smiled. "Of course."

He handed digital room key cards to Luke and Ed.

"Enjoy your stay."

They rode the elevator upstairs to their rooms. They weren't speaking. The man with the luggage cart had gone on ahead of them, and for Luke, it didn't seem quite safe to speak. There was no doubt in his mind that this elevator was bugged.

Then again, if there were bugs, it wouldn't be natural to act like mutes.

"Quite a night, huh?" Luke said.

Ed nodded. "Yeah."

"Can't wait to get out there and just … you know."

"Check it all out," Ed said.

"That's right."

"High rollers," Ed said. "Watch out Moscow, because here we come."

Luke smiled. "Young and dumb and full of …"

Ding!

The elevator arrived at their floor.

Their rooms were about twenty meters apart. Luke let himself into his room. His bags were here, near the bed. The room was nice, but he barely glanced at it. There was a long picture window, with the heavy curtains and drapes pulled wide. It gave him a panoramic view of Red Square. St. Basil's Cathedral with all its minarets, and painted like candy canes, was closest to him.

Incredible. It didn't look real.

Big Daddy said the real estate agent would contact them. So they would have to wait for that. In the meantime, they should probably go out and soak up the local color. Maybe he would wash up a touch first.

He turned to look for the bathroom.

A man stood there, across the bed from him. The first thing Luke noticed about him was the silenced gun in his hand, pointed directly Luke's way. The barrel was like the beginning of a tunnel under a mountain.

The second thing Luke noticed about him was he kept his distance. The man was just far enough away that if Luke made a move, he wouldn't get there in time.

Luke felt very little about the gun—no fear, certainly. Just curiosity. This man was good. But would he be good the whole time?

"Stone?" the man said.

There didn't seem to be any point in denying it. "Yes."

"You were in disastrous mission in Afghanistan. What was commanding officer's name?"

Luke didn't hesitate. He would never forget the name, if he lived to be a hundred.

"Morgan Heath."

"Rank?"

"Lieutenant Colonel."

The man didn't lower the gun. His eyes were serious. "Your baby. When born?"

"May ninth," Luke said.

"Name?"

"Luke Stone, Jr. We call him Gunner."

"In Iraq, you were undercover as mujahid. You killed entire death squad, and saved man and his children. A doctor. Name of man?"

Luke smiled. Very few people on the planet knew about that. Big Daddy Cronin was one of them. This man was the contact—the Moscow real estate agent.

"Ashwal Nadoori," Luke said.

The man lowered the gun. He was a sandy-haired guy, short but broad, like he spent his free time lifting weights. Luke noticed, for the first time, that this was the man who had taken their luggage on the rolling cart. He had put the hat and gloves aside, but he was still wearing the coat with long tails.

"Man at desk, he offered you girls?"

Luke shrugged. "Yes, he did."

"But you declined?"

"Yes."

The man shook his head. "You don't decline girls in Moscow. It looks wrong. People talk."

Luke held up his hand with the wedding ring. "I'm married."

The man shrugged. "No matter. We fix. You bring girl home tonight. Front desk man sees, everything is normal."

"I can't do that."

The man smiled. "Girl works for us. It's just for show. She sleeps on floor." Now his smile broadened into a grin. "Or you do."

"Albert?" Luke said finally.

The man nodded. "Come on, Stone. It's Moscow. Welcome. We go out and have good time. Meet your TV producer friend."

CHAPTER TWENTY

9:45 p.m. Moscow Daylight Time (1:45 p.m. Eastern Daylight Time)
Noor Bar
Tverskaya Street
Moscow, Russia

"Do not drink beer here," Albert said. "This is not American bar."

The bar had bright yellow walls with a turquoise ceiling. Glowing pinwheel chandeliers hung from the ceiling like alien spaceships. Strange purple light appeared to come from somewhere above their heads. They were sitting at a small, round glass table, in tall leather-back chairs.

This was Moscow nightlife.

The place was crowded, packed with young Muscovites, and some not so young. The beautiful people. Dance music pounded through the speaker system. Outside of the thumping bass, Luke could barely hear it.

"Martinis," said Albert. "The best. Bartender? The best in Russia. Famous bartender. Famous bar, all over the world. Drink wine here? Okay, if you must. But Russians will drink real alcohol."

Albert smiled.

"Including me."

Albert had told them to walk here, then had turned up moments later wearing a blue tracksuit. It was as if he had never been a luggage handler at the hotel at all.

"Are we working?" Luke said. He had to shout over the noise.

Albert nodded. He gestured with his head to the left.

Sitting two tables away was a thin man with a dark black goatee, greased black hair swooped back from his forehead, and round-rimmed glasses. He wore a pale blue dress shirt with a very wide collar, open three buttons down. Tufts of chest hair poked out at the top. He was sitting with two young blonde women.

They were all huddled together and laughing.

"That's him?" Ed said.

The guy looked maybe thirty, at the most. Around Luke's age. Luke wasn't sure what he was expecting, but this wasn't it. TV producer sounded like a job that older, more accomplished people had.

This guy seemed like a bit of a clown. He was on the payroll of the intelligence networks, had just been involved in a very sensitive misinformation operation, and he was in here, apparently drunk, laughing it up.

"Loose lips," Luke said.

Albert shook his head. "Don't misunderstand. In Moscow, everybody drinks. Everybody talks. Everybody lies. No one believes a thing."

"That's him?" Ed said again. Albert hadn't answered him the first time.

Albert looked at Ed. He stifled a yawn with his hand. It was the move of a working man who just got free from his job after a long day, and had pushed through his tiredness to get out and sample some nightlife. It also served to cover his mouth in case any lip readers were around.

"Zelazny? Of course. That's him. That's why we come here."

"What's your plan?" Luke said.

Albert shrugged. "He likes to drink. He likes the girls. He likes to talk. I know his car. Very nice, new Mercedes. Parked two blocks from here. He is drunk by now. In a little while, one more drink, we go out, wait by car. He comes. We all go for ride. He tells us what he knows."

"What if the girls come to the car with him?" Ed said.

Albert shook his head. "They won't."

Ed and Luke exchanged a glance. They weren't here to get young women involved in this. Anyone who got sucked in was liable to get killed.

"How do you know that?"

"Our friend? Secretly gay. Dangerous business in Russia. Talks to girls for cover story. Gets drunk here, works up courage, goes to underground nightclub in other part of town. How do you call it in English? *Speakeasy*. Apartment in run-down building. Knock knock. What's the password?"

Luke thought about it. The heavy music washed over him. The laughing faces seemed almost surreal. Zelazny was living a double life, even a triple life. He appeared to be a low-budget TV producer, and perhaps he was. But he dressed expensively, and spent freely, because he was on the government's secret payroll. He also lived an underground life as a gay man in a city, and a country, that disapproved of homosexuality. Strenuously.

If Zelazny's bosses found out about his proclivities…

Luke didn't care to pursue that thought.

Apparently, Albert was watching the wheels turn in Luke's head.

"Yes, easy man to blackmail. Put gun to his head? Scary, and maybe he lies to you anyway. But secret police learns that he likes men?"

Albert grimaced and shook his head.

"He will tell us the names of his mother's secret lovers."

He gestured for a refill to the passing waitress, a brunette in a very tight skirt. The skirt was so tight she could barely walk.

"He will tell us everything."

It was easy to capture Zelazny.

When he left the bar, he could still walk. But not well. He came reeling down the street like a cartoon drunk man. He didn't seem to notice Luke and Ed standing near his car, in the shadows against a brick wall.

The car was a blue Mercedes sedan, M series. Albert was right. It was an expensive car, late model, probably imported from Germany. With the exchange rate between rubles and euros what it was, it wouldn't make sense that Zelazny could afford this thing, TV producer or not. His extracurricular activities were what bought the car.

Luke had a slight buzz from the martini. But Zelazny was clearly bombed.

He pressed a button on his key fob. The car's headlights came on and the doors unlocked. The car made a loud chirping sound.

Luke stepped out of the shadows. *"Da svadanya?"*

It was Russian for goodbye. He said it like he was asking a question. It was all he could think of.

Zelazny turned to look at him. He saw Luke there. He didn't know what to make of him. Behind his thin glasses, his eyes seemed to squint.

Albert appeared next to him and pressed the barrel of the gun to his head. He barked something quickly in Russian.

Zelazny raised his hands. He said something to Albert in return. He didn't try to do anything. He didn't even seem particularly worried. Maybe it was the booze. Or maybe this happened to him all the time and he was used to it by now.

Albert handed Luke the gun. Luke felt the heft of it. Rare for him, he didn't know the make. It almost seemed homemade. Stapled together sheet metal. It had a long sound suppressor attached to the barrel.

"Sit in back with him," Albert said. "He tries something, shoot him in the head."

Albert turned to Zelazny and said something in rapid-fire Russian. He indicated Luke. Zelazny nodded without saying a word.

Albert turned back to Luke and Ed.

"I'll drive," he said. "This guy is too drunk."

They headed north along a wide, nearly empty boulevard.

A few expensive cars zoomed by them in both directions. Luke spotted a Lamborghini, a Rolls Royce Silver Shadow, and an old Lotus Elite, without even trying. The big money was going straight up the ladder. Most Muscovites apparently still took public transportation.

Albert drove at a sedate pace. Cars passed them. Luke kept the gun low, out of sight, but pointed directly at Zelazny. Luke wondered what Albert planned to tell the cops if they happened to pull this car over. He supposed he'd let Albert worry about that.

Grim, nine-story Stalinesque towers flanked the roadway, yellow lights on in hundreds of windows. It was public housing. It was the worker's paradise. A dense fog appeared and disappeared as they drove.

Zelazny looked at Luke. He squinted again, as if seeing better might help him understand.

"American?"

Luke nodded.

"I can tell," Zelazny said.

"Leonard Zelazny?" Luke said.

The man shrugged and sighed. "Of course." He couldn't be sobering up yet, but his eyes were more alert than before. They were the eyes of a prey animal, like a bunny rabbit. Fear was starting to appear in those eyes. Being carjacked by three men would do that to a person.

"I will tell you nothing," he said.

Luke smiled. He almost laughed. "We know about your sex life."

Zelazny stared straight ahead. He did not respond.

"We know you like men."

Luke spotted Albert looking at Zelazny in the rearview mirror. Albert's eyes were as sharp as knives. He blurted something in Russian. It sounded like a question. Zelazny shook his head but didn't speak. Albert smiled.

"He will talk," Albert said. "He will sing an aria, if we want."

They passed out of the city. The towers began to give way to open land. The traffic, never busy to begin with, dropped away to nothing. The fog was thicker out here. The smell of it began to permeate the car. It was not fog. Albert adjusted a couple of dials and cranked the air conditioning.

"Is it smoke?" Luke said.

Albert nodded. "Big fires now. Out of control."

"Where are we going?" Zelazny said. His English was very good, better than Albert's. His voice shook a tiny amount.

"Shut up," Albert said.

After a time, they left the highway. Albert made several turns, and then they were driving down a narrow back road. The road was cracked and pitted. Zelazny made a pained face every time Albert lurched the car over a pothole. After one very hard BANG, and then a scraping sound, Zelazny blurted out several angry words in Russian.

He turned to Luke. "He is ruining my car."

Albert glanced at Luke in the rearview mirror and shrugged.

"I wouldn't worry about it," Luke said.

Albert pulled over in a dirt parking lot. He put the car in park and turned it off. The smoke was everywhere around them. It was hard to see what this place was.

"Dock by the River Moskva," Albert said. "Let's go."

They climbed out and walked Zelazny down to the dock. There were no lights, except for a glow in the sky off to the south. You almost needed an oxygen mask to stand out here. Luke could feel the smoke getting deep into his lungs.

They walked out on the dock. It was about fifty meters long, made of wood, and was old, creaky, and unstable. The four men stood near the end of it. The river was all around them now. Luke could almost feel its rapid flow beneath his feet. The air was a little better out here—you could still smell it, but there was less actual smoke.

"Gun, please," Albert said and extended his hand to Luke.

Luke gave Albert his gun back. A second later, Albert pointed it at Zelazny's chest.

"Tell us."

Zelazny shook his head. "If I tell you anything..."

"If you don't tell us everything," big Ed said, "we're going to kill you."

That was it. Ed had hardly spoken before now. Somehow, having this giant, silent black man threaten death so matter-of-factly was the breaking point. Suddenly Zelazny was crying.

"I don't want to die now."

"You don't have to," Luke said. "You just have to tell us what happened, and who was involved."

He felt something for the man. It wasn't pity. It wasn't even sympathy. After all, if the intelligence was correct, this was the guy who received the video feed from the Serbians, then doctored it to make it appear that the Americans were butchers. Then he sent it out to news media worldwide.

Luke didn't sympathize with him. But he could see where the guy had painted himself into a very bad corner. It was awkward. Luke almost felt embarrassed for him.

"The Serbians sent you the video feed?" he said.

Zelazny said nothing. He seemed to have a lump in his throat.

"We could kill you right now," Ed said. "But that would be too easy. We could also let the FSB and the GRU know what a bad boy you've been. I think that would be the harder way to go."

Albert stepped up and pressed the silenced gun to Zelazny's head. He barked something in Russian.

Zelazny raised his hands. "Okay. Okay. I will tell you. I got the video. I edited it. I sent it to the media. I did that. But I had no choice."

He looked at Luke. "You think they will kill me because I'm gay? They don't need a reason to kill me. I'm still alive because I am useful. Maybe I can be useful to you."

"Who are you working for?" Luke said.

Zelazny shook his head and laughed. "You have no idea..."

Luke shrugged. He looked at Albert. "Oh well. I'm done. Kill him."

"Wait!"

Albert pulled the trigger without hesitating.

Zelazny's entire body convulsed.

Click.

Nothing happened. Nothing came from the gun. There was almost no sound.

But the trigger pull alone sent a shock wave through Zelazny. A split second later, he dropped to the ground. Then he was on his hands and knees. He seemed to be choking on something lodged in his throat, like he would vomit it up. Then he was hyperventilating. His face turned bright red. He went on coughing and gagging for several moments. He gasped for air, taking giant gulps.

It was a mock execution. Mock executions were against all the laws of war. Luke knew that. But then again, no one had declared war.

Slowly, Zelazny's breathing began to return to something like normal.

"The next one is real," Luke said.

Zelazny coughed again.

Luke crouched on his haunches next to him.

"Did you hear me, Lenny? I'm going to ask that man to put a bullet in your brain, and he's going to do it. He doesn't care about you. I don't care about you. Like you said yourself, the only thing that keeps you alive is how useful you are. Nothing else."

Zelazny took a deep breath. He was starting to cry again.

"I am afraid to say the man's name."

Luke shrugged. "Then you're going to die right here. It's your choice."

A long moment passed, Zelazny on all fours like a dog, Luke crouched beside him. Ed loomed nearby. Alfred pointed the gun at Zelazny's head.

Luke sighed. "Lenny? I'm going to count to three."

Zelazny didn't wait that long. "Marmilov," he said. "Oleg Marmilov. You won't know who he is. He is the secret power behind many things. I believe he was KGB before the collapse. Now he is GRU. But where his state salary comes from is no matter. He runs things, but he is invisible, layers and layers deep. You will never get to him. You will never meet him. It's impossible."

"What is he doing?" Luke said.

"I don't know."

Luke shook his head. He looked up at Albert.

Albert came closer with the gun. He placed the muzzle against the back of Zelazny's head again. Albert was calm. Luke was calm. Zelazny's squeezed his eyes shut.

"Lenny," Luke said.

"I can't tell you."

"You can't tell us or you don't know?"

Zelazny was crying now, all the way. It was a quiet, gentle sobbing. His shoulders shook with it. Luke watched as tears dropped from Zelazny's eyes onto the dock.

"If I tell you, my life is over. You might as well kill me now. Go ahead."

Luke took a breath.

"Can you get us near him?" he said.

Zelazny shook his head. "I don't deal with him. I have never met him. I am a small man, and he is a big man. Bigger than you can know. Great things are afoot, but they would never entrust that knowledge to me. I deal with an engineer. A young man. Tomasz Chevsky. He works for the Academy of Sciences."

"It is big organization," Albert said. "Which branch?"

Zelazny shook his head again, more forcefully this time. He kept shaking it and shaking it. He was like a head shaking machine.

"Chevsky has special clearances. He works across branches, has no permanent mandate. Everything is secret. He keeps an office near the Kremlin, in the Special Annex. The building they call the Breadbox. He meets directly with Marmilov, God help him. They are working on a project. I do not know what it is. I do not want to know. This attack by the Serbs was part of it. What part, I cannot say. Misinformation, maybe. Fear. Terror. Confusion."

Zelazny fell to his elbows. His body made a forty-five-degree angle to the dock now. He was still on his knees, with his butt in the air. His hands balled into fists. His back extended and lengthened, as if he were going through a muscle spasm. His eyes squeezed shut and his mouth opened wide in a silent scream. He looked like a man in agony.

"Oh my God," he whispered. "I know I'm going to die."

Luke looked at Albert and Ed.

"Do we believe any of this?"

Albert shook his head. "No."

"It's true!" Zelazny said. "Please. Look in my phone. You will see Chevsky's nickname—frog."

"Why do you call him frog?" Albert said.

"Like the scorpion and the frog. He is the frog. Marmilov is the scorpion. Look! He is in my contacts. Maybe there are still texts. I often delete them, but I forget sometimes."

"You forget to delete dangerous messages?"

Albert looked at Luke and Ed. He shook his head.

Ed shrugged. "We use burner phones for that. Use them once, then toss them."

"They are not dangerous messages," Zelazny said. "*Meet me nine p.m. How are things coming? Good. Coming along.* We never say anything important, or even interesting. We meet in person for that."

"Where do you meet?" Albert said.

Zelazny's shoulders slumped. "If I tell you, I am dead."

Albert shoved the barrel of the gun against Zelazny's head. Hard. Luke could hear the soft THUNK it made, metal against skull bone.

"If you don't tell me now, you are also dead."

Luke shook his head. This was a sad display, but he almost smiled at it. It was play acting at this point, that's all it was. Zelazny was going to tell them everything, just as Albert had said. He would be relieved to get it over with. But he needed to feel like all choice had been taken from him.

"Three seconds," Luke said.

"Two," Ed said.

"One," Albert said.

Zelazny's hands shook. "Okay. Okay. Okay."

166

"Talk," Luke said. "Or we're done here."

"We meet different places," Zelazny said. "Always at night. Sometimes Gorky Park, where we walk and talk. But more often a small footbridge over the Moskva, not far from Red Square. You can see Moskvoretsky Bridge from there. But this bridge is a bit to the south. It is old, and closed, in an area overgrown with bushes and weeds, and with concrete barriers at each end. Perhaps the bridge is condemned, I don't know. Grass grows down the middle of it. It is nearby to his office and convenient for him. He works night and day. He seems to feel safest on this bridge."

"How do you communicate these places?" Albert said.

Zelazny shrugged. "Simple. One word. Gorky or Moskva. But it is reversed. If we say Gorky, it means Moskva. If we say Moskva, it means Gorky. That's how we fool them, the ones who are watching."

He looked up at them and tried to smile, but his face broke and he only started crying again.

"Give me the telephone," Albert said.

Zelazny handed it up without hesitating. The light from the phone's screen shone in the darkness. Luke spotted a blur of Cyrillic words. Albert clicked his way through screens. He looked up at Luke and smiled.

"You met him most recently, code word Moskva, when?"

"A week ago," Zelazny said.

"This means Gorky Park?"

Zelazny nodded.

"Why did you meet?"

"He gave me the update on the Alaska project. He told me it was about to go forward, and to be prepared to receive and edit content to his specifications."

"And code word Gorky, when was last time?"

"Two days ago. The content was coming, and he told me how he wanted it, and what to do with it. It was a very brief meeting."

"It's all here," Albert said. He gazed down at Zelazny. "You've been cooperative witness. A very good boy. But you were stupid to leave messages undeleted. This is very dangerous."

Zelazny kneeled with his head bowed. "You don't know what's coming now. You don't know anything."

"What's coming?" Albert said.

Zelazny shook his head. "I don't know. Something terrible. There is always something terrible coming. Men like you. You will never understand how terrible everything is."

He seemed completely spent.

Luke would love to hang around here and explore Zelazny's ideas about terrible things, but they should probably save the philosophical discussions for another time. It was getting late, and the sooner they could find out what they needed, and get out of this country, the better Luke would feel.

It occurred to him, not for the first time, how exposed he felt when he was out of contact with the SRT. Swann and Trudy were his lifelines, and they couldn't play any part in this. It was just he and Ed, in a long tunnel.

Albert shook his head. He looked at Luke. "It's okay? Enough?"

Luke nodded. "Good."

Luke and Ed turned to go back to the car. They moved along the creaky dock in the silent darkness.

"What do you think?" Luke said quietly.

Ed shrugged his big shoulders. "I don't know, man. It's dicey. They probably watch this guy. Maybe not twenty-four/seven, but enough. If we talk to his friend, afterwards I think we better be ready to get right back on that…"

CLACK!

The sound was barely a sound. It could have been a heavy branch snapping.

Luke and Ed stopped and looked back.

Zelazny was dead at the end of the dock. Luke couldn't see the details, but he knew what he was looking at. Albert reached out with his foot and pushed Zelazny's corpse into the river. There was a small splash. Then the dark water and the smoke took him. And just like that, he was gone.

Albert came up the dock. He looked at them both. His face was blank. "He will arrive Moscow tomorrow or next day. Always they find bodies like this."

Luke's mouth hung open. He found himself in an odd place— he could not think of a single thing to say. A phrase occurred to him, something Trudy Wellington sometimes said in jest: *Words fail me.*

"What did you do that for?" Ed said.

Albert blinked. A sound escaped him, almost like a laugh, but there was no humor in it. "This is Russia. I don't kill him, he talks to the next ones who find him. Week later, I'm dead."

He shook his head. "Americans can go home after this. I must live here."

CHAPTER TWENTY ONE

11:20 p.m. Moscow Daylight Time (3:20 p.m. Eastern Daylight Time)
The New Stage
Bolshoi Ballet
Tverskoy District
Moscow, Russia

The show was almost over.

Oleg Marmilov sat in the darkness of his private balcony two stories above the main seating area and the orchestra pit. His view was splendid. To his left, the white balustrade disappeared into the dark. On stage, there was an explosion of lights and sound, beautiful young dancers leaping and frolicking. The Bolshoi Ballet was putting on *Le Corsaire*, the story of Byron's pirate Conrad, the production faithful to Marius Petipa's 1899 revival in Saint Petersburg.

It was an astonishing spectacle, a display of technical prowess from the dancers, as well as lights, staging, and set design, not to mention exquisite music from the live orchestra. It was the kind of thing Marmilov loved—a return to greatness for Russia.

Nothing in the West could match the grandeur of Russian theatre at its finest. The only shame was that this production had been relegated to the New Stage, a lovely venue in its own right, but nothing compared to the original theatre.

Unfortunately, the Bolshoi Theatre proper was closed for repairs. Over time, it had succumbed to wear and tear, and the Soviets had repeatedly delayed maintenance on it. Soviet society was certainly an accomplishment in itself, but its rejection of the great cultural triumphs of previous eras was a disgrace. Thankfully, they hadn't quite seen fit to tear the Bolshoi down. In the meantime, no one yet knew the extent of the damage or when the theatre might open again.

Marmilov glanced to his left.

Sitting with him was a twenty-three-year-old painted whore named Tamara. She was beautiful, slim, with dyed blonde hair and ruby painted lips and black cat's eyes makeup. She wore a $6,000 Oscar de la Renta gold leaf cocktail dress Marmilov had provided her for the occasion. A $700 brown raccoon fur jacket from Elena Furs was draped over her chair. Together with the pocketbook and the shoes, she was wearing nearly $10,000 worth of clothes and accessories, while watching the best ballet company in the world stage a legendary ballet from Russia's proud past.

And of course, she looked like she would prefer to be nearly anywhere else. He could see it in her eyes. She was bored out of her mind. Should this go on much longer, she was prepared to become petulant.

If Marmilov told her she could go back to the hotel suite to watch overwrought romantic dramas on TV and gossip with her other young whore friends on the telephone, she would leave at once, and be relieved to do so.

He shook his head at the thought of it. The so-called young women these days behaved like small children.

Marmilov didn't blame her. The collapse of the Soviet Union had destroyed the education system and poisoned the minds of the young people. They had become untethered from their history, and infected by the degeneracy beamed in by satellite from the decadent West.

But all of this would be fixed, and soon. Marmilov would see to it.

A shadow appeared on his right, and Marmilov nearly flinched. He was ever mindful of how things were done in Soviet times, and often enough, how they were still done today. Nothing was guaranteed—not one more moment of life, not one more breath.

An image flashed in his mind of the unfortunate Mr. Lincoln, the American president, at Ford's Theatre, wasting his last moments watching a bit of mindless slapstick called *Our American Cousin*.

Marmilov was wiser than that. His own personal gunmen, vetted by him, with loyalty sworn to him, and whose private lives were under constant surveillance, protected this balcony. Marmilov and his young date were safe.

He turned to the man hovering over him.

"What?"

"Sir, everything is ready," the man whispered. He glanced down at the stage, mindful that his voice not disrupt the proceedings.

"TV is ready?"

The man nodded. "Yes. Except…"

"What is it? Simply tell me."

"The producer seems unavailable."

Marmilov nodded. He let out a breath. It was a frustration, but frustrations were inevitable. Marmilov's life was a minefield of frustrations, from slaughtered Serbian commandos, to poor maintenance on landmark theatres, to young whores who would prefer to eat pastries and watch television than spend a night at the ballet.

The producer was Leonard Zelazny, of course. Marmilov knew right away what his being unavailable meant. He had gone missing, and not for the first time. He was drunk, and in all likelihood, engaging in immoral acts with other men of his ilk. Zelazny was a valuable asset—creative, intelligent, highly skilled, and obedient. But he was living on borrowed time.

"He has completed his task?"

The messenger nodded. "Yes."

"And do we need more from him?"

The messenger shrugged. "He has always been available before, to facilitate should there be technical concerns."

"Have there ever been any?"

The man shook his head. "No."

Marmilov nodded. "Good. Send someone to find him, in the usual dens of corruption that he frequents. When he is found, bring him to me. I want to speak with him. In the meantime, move forward as planned."

The man nodded. "As you wish." He turned to go.

Marmilov grabbed the man's shirt sleeve.

"As soon as the video emerges," he said. "Mere moments later, you leak the intelligence document. Moments. One-two punch. No time to respond. Is that understood?"

The man's eyes were hard now. "Of course."

He disappeared as abruptly as he had come.

Marmilov made no sign, but inwardly he smiled. His heart skipped a beat. It was an exciting and terrifying night. Putin would be scandalized in front of the world tonight, and perhaps he would be arrested.

He was the most powerful man on Earth, but tonight—within the hour—they would begin to see exactly how far that power extended. Who were his friends? Who would leap to defend him? The Americans, to preserve the world order? Maybe. But that didn't matter. Who inside Russia? Would no one step up for the Russian President?

This was a mad gamble, Marmilov recognized that. But now was the time for such gambles. Putin had been a phase, perhaps even an era. It had been a time of resurrection and reconstruction. But it was moving too slow. It was not restoring old glories. And it had put into place a corrupt cabal—cronies, Mafiosi, capitalists, who would stymie further progress in the name of lining their own pockets.

It could be that the time of Vladimir Putin was at its end. The end couldn't come quickly enough for Oleg Marmilov.

He turned to the beautiful Tamara once more. Later tonight, if all went according to plan, he would celebrate by helping himself to her ripe young body.

"How are you enjoying the show, my dear?"

She gave him a pained smile. "Very nice."

"Wonderful dancers, eh? A beautiful reminder of Russian greatness."

She nodded. "Yes. Beautiful."

Chapter Twenty Two

3:55 p.m. Eastern Daylight Time (11:55 p.m. Moscow Daylight Time)
Headquarters of the Special Response Team
McLean, Virginia

"Something's happening in Russia," Trudy Wellington said.

Swann didn't look up from his computer screen.

"Yeah?" he said. "What's that?"

They were sitting in the conference room. Swann had a bank of three laptops laid out in front of him on the table. Across from him, and a little bit down, Trudy had one. Swann was monitoring the tiny GPS units embedded into the heels of both Luke's and Ed's shoes. He had the signals superimposed on a digital map of Moscow.

Luke and Ed were still together, and had just moved back into the city center, at the pace of a car on a highway—maybe sixty miles an hour.

It was a boring assignment, and Swann was tired. He had slept more than ten hours last night, and still hadn't shaken off the trip to Alaska and back. It was hard for him to believe that Ed and Luke had gone to Rome, and then on to Moscow, almost immediately after coming back from Alaska. They were like supermen.

He looked up at Trudy. She looked as tired as Swann felt. She was a beautiful woman on most days. Today she was a beautiful woman with her hair tied up in a bun, her mouth hanging slack, and puffy dark pouches under her eyes. She was watching something on her screen.

"There's another video," she said. "Same deal as before, Al Jazeera is playing it on TV in Middle Eastern countries. It looks like it's already been picked up by other news outlets. Here's a right-wing Ukrainian TV channel showing the same video."

Swann glanced across at her. He hoped that Trudy wasn't going to make him play a game of twenty questions.

"What is it a video of?"

She shook her head. "I don't know yet. It shows Vladimir Putin sitting at a wide desk, talking and joking with someone off screen. It's kind of a worm's eye view, as though someone was holding the camera below his line of sight, and filming him without his knowledge. The conversation is in Russian, and so far the subtitles are in Arabic. But there's a graphic headline embedded on the video, and I know enough Russian to know what it says."

"And?" Swann said.

"It says, *Putin ordered attack on America?* Phrased like a statement, but with a question mark at the end, probably just to give journalistic cover."

Swann reached to his right and pulled up an internet browser on one of his other laptops. Instantly his fingers were flying across the keyboard, operating with a mind of their own. One of his eyes watched what the fingers were doing. The other eye watched Luke and Ed's GPS blips. Now they were in Moscow, not far from Red Square, and no longer moving at all.

"Should we talk to Don?" he said. "I was never in favor of this communication blackout. I think we should take a chance and try to get in touch with them."

"And tell them what?" Trudy said.

"I don't know yet," Swann said. "But the Russians aren't all-knowing. I think I can sneak a call in there without them seeing it, if we do it fast enough."

"And as long as Albert Strela even has his cell phone on," Trudy said.

Swann shrugged. "Naturally."

He didn't like being out of contact. He didn't like having to make contact through Albert Strela, supposedly a valuable CIA asset, but a compete unknown to the SRT. Really, what did anyone know about Strela?

Swann had seen a bare-bones dossier—aside from hearsay and maybes, there was almost nothing in it. No background, no place or date of birth, no education, no military record. Just: former pimp, former murderer-for-hire, turned American informant.

It was likely that Albert Strela was not really his name. It was possible he had killed a dozen or more people. It was possible he had spent five years in a high-security prison in Siberia, sentenced to an unknown number of years for unknown crimes, and then had been released suddenly and without explanation.

This was the guy Bill Cronin had given them? This was the guy Ed and Luke were wandering around Moscow with, looking for a TV producer whose name might be an alias and who might not even be real, and also checking out…rental apartments?

Swann shook his head. This stuff was weird sometimes.

No, scratch that. It was *always* weird.

His fingers found what they were looking for. Al Jazeera had a TV channel they broadcast to American servicemen in Doha and in the Green Zone in Baghdad. It was like a reverse Radio Free Europe. They were showing the Putin footage.

"I have it with English subtitles," Swann said.

Trudy got up and came around the table. She hovered just behind Swann's right shoulder.

On the screen, the man himself was there, Vladimir Putin, the star of a grainy, poorly lit video. But it was definitely him. He sat at his desk wearing a tan sport coat over a shirt and tie. The tie was pulled loose. He was sipping something amber in a glass, with ice. He laughed and said a few words.

"Serbs are built for combat," said a subtitle across the bottom.

Unseen people in the room with him laughed.

"They are harsh people, designed by God for harsh environments. They are perfectly adapted, and this little disaster will play well on American TV."

An unseen person, a man, spoke.

"They are our friends," said the subtitle.

Putin spoke and raised his glass. A hand came in from the right, also raising a glass.

"They are great friends," said the subtitle at the bottom. "Centuries of friendship. We drink to them."

Trudy pointed to the screen. "The video is time and date stamped. September fifth, the day after the initial attack. With the time zone difference, this would have been just hours later, and before our counterattack. Would he really be this foolish? We need to get this video analyzed, and find out if Putin is even saying these things. I mean ... I don't think this can be real."

Swann shrugged. "Thousands of American personnel are probably watching this across the Middle East right now, and working up a nice, murderous rage about it. I'm sure NSA, CIA, DIA, and the rest of the alphabet soup will all be analyzing it in the next ten minutes, if they aren't already."

"What does it mean, if it's true?" Trudy said.

Swann shook his head. Did it mean war was imminent between the United States and Russia? Did it mean someone was trying to take Putin out? Clearly, the video was designed to make him look bad. The President of Russia certainly *seemed* to be laughing about Serbs invading Alaska and carrying out a massacre against American civilians.

"It means Stone and Newsam should probably get out of there," he said. "They went in to find out who ordered the attack, and why. If this is real, then that mystery is solved. So there's no longer any reason for them to be in Moscow. The situation could go south in a hurry."

"Do you think they're not aware of this video?" Trudy said.

Swann shrugged. "I have no idea what they're aware of. We haven't spoken to them since they left. But I do think it's probably a good time to launch their exit plan."

Trudy nodded.

"I'll talk to Don."

CHAPTER TWENTY THREE

**September 7
12:05 a.m. Moscow Daylight Time
(4:05 p.m. Eastern Daylight Time, September 6)
Unnamed footbridge over the Moskva River
Near the Kremlin and Red Square
Moscow, Russia**

Tomasz Chevsky was coming to meet Zelazny. Focus on that. Not this:

"Once, there was a serial killer."

Albert's voice floated to them like a disembodied spirit at a seance.

They stood in fog and smoke on the pedestrian bridge over the Moskva River. A thin line of tall grass grew in the center of the bridge like a Mohawk haircut. It was dark here, the mists so dense it was almost impossible to see the man standing next to you. Three hundred meters away, there was movement in Red Square.

From here, it was hard to tell what was happening. Trucks rumbling in. Siren lights flashing. A crowd seemed to be gathering. Luke could hear the low murmuring of a crowd. In his mind, he associated the sound with groups of people hanging around, talking, waiting for something to happen.

A serial killer.

It was an odd thing for Albert to talk about. Something was happening over there, and he didn't seem to care. He was focused on a mass murderer instead.

"His name is Andrei Chikatilo," Albert said. "They call him the Rostov Ripper. Horrible man. He kills more than fifty women and children. A madman. When they capture him, they put him on trial. They keep him in cage in the courtroom. He makes foul outbursts during proceedings. Saying obscene words. Cackling laughter. Exposes himself. The judge cautions him, but he does not stop. They put the dog muzzle on him so he cannot speak—like the cannibal man in your American movies. He is found guilty, of course. After trial ends, short time passes. One day guards walk him out of cell, take him down hall to soundproof room. Turn him around, put bullet behind his right ear."

Albert clapped his hands once, to mimic a single gunshot.

There was a pause in the darkness. Luke could almost hear Albert shrug.

"Russian justice."

In the gloom, two cars with flashing sirens went by over on the main bridge to Red Square. The sound was muffled, and the red lights of the sirens were muted by the dense mists. The cars themselves were invisible. A few seconds later, a truck rumbled by unseen. The sound of it reminded Luke of a heavy lorry, like a troop transport.

Suddenly, Luke understood.

Albert was still trying to justify the killing of the TV producer. Was he trying to justify it to Luke and Ed, or was he just trying to convince himself?

That wasn't clear. But what Albert needed to know was Luke, and in all likelihood Ed, had already moved on. There was so much death in this underworld where they lived. There was no sense trying to justify any of it. There was no sense trying to make sense of it.

Zelazny had participated in a project that led to the massacre of nearly a hundred civilians. He had probably known about it beforehand. He had done his best to make it look like the work of American soldiers. He had lied to the world about it.

Maybe Zelazny had not killed anyone himself. Maybe he had never killed a living thing in his entire life. Maybe he had never eaten a piece of meat or even stepped on a spider. But to Luke's mind, the man had signed his own death warrant just the same.

If Luke were killed in battle, in his final moments he might be disappointed and sad. He would be heartbroken for Becca and Gunner. He might even be afraid. But would he find it unfair, or unjustified? No. He had also signed his own death warrant, a hundred times over.

Luke had been surprised that Albert killed Zelazny. That's all it was: surprise. Luke had thought they might keep Zelazny around in case any other questions came up. But did the TV producer deserve to die? You bet he did.

A silent moment passed.

Suddenly, Albert whispered something in Russian. He did it forcefully, a stage whisper, designed to be heard.

On the walkway, the silhouette of a figure appeared. It was a man, and he was tall and thin. He seemed to stretch toward the sky. In the dark, he almost didn't seem human, like a stick bug or a praying mantis.

"Zelazny?" the man hissed.

Ed stepped back, into deep shadow, and away from the figure. No sense spooking him right away.

Could the man see Luke here? Impossible to tell.

Albert grunted, a sound like, "Mmmm."

The slender man barked something in Russian, barely above a whisper. Luke caught the gist of it. "Where have you been? People are searching."

Albert said something in return. Luke couldn't grasp it.

This was going to have to happen fast. Albert looked nothing like Zelazny, and he sounded almost nothing like him as well. Zelazny had a guttural voice, raspy with cigarettes and alcohol. Albert had a deep and clear voice.

The clouds parted briefly, and the approaching man stepped into a yellow circle of light from the moon.

"Zelazny?" he said again.

He was a young man, maybe early thirties. And he was big. He must be six and a half feet tall. He wore a long leather overcoat and an old-style hat, like a bowler. He carried a white, knobby walking stick. He looked like an advertisement for the 1890s.

He saw Luke there with Albert, and his eyes went wide with surprise. But he didn't turn to run. Not yet. Although he was thin, and seemingly all limbs, his shoulders were broad. He did not look weak.

His eyes recovered quickly from their initial surprise. They said he was not afraid.

He barked something at Luke now.

Luke shrugged. "*No hablo*," he said.

The man looked from Luke to Albert. Albert pulled the gun he had used to kill Zelazny. The silencer stuck out, long and mean. Then Ed stepped out of the shadows.

A new light dawned in the man's eyes.

"Americans?" he said in a thick accent.

Luke didn't answer.

Ed quickly slipped along the other side of the tall grass, past the man and to his rear. The man's escape back toward Red Square and the Kremlin was now cut off. He had allowed it to happen as if he had momentarily been taken by a dream.

"Chevsky," Luke said. It wasn't a question.

"*Da. Kto ty?*"

It was a simple phrase, and Chevsky spoke it slowly, as if to a small child. Luke translated the man's Russian easily.

Yes. Who are you?

"*Druz'ya*," Luke said.

Friends.

Wrong answer.

Instantly, Chevsky stepped forward and swung his walking stick at Luke's head. Luke slipped the blow and slapped the stick away. But he didn't grab the stick, and he didn't get in his own shot. Chevsky moved too fast.

Chevsky spun past Luke, his bowler hat flying off. Now Ed was no longer behind him. He brought a fist around backhand to the side of Albert's head. It connected perfectly. Albert's face squinched and he stepped sideways, off balance. He went down to the pavement and didn't move.

Knockout—one shot.

Luke sent his own jab, but the man was tall, and his reach was long. He blocked the punch and sent a crazy elongated front kick Luke's way. Luke sidestepped and Chevsky jumped backwards like some kind of oversized crab.

An image flashed through Luke's mind: old video footage of the basketball great Kareem Abdul-Jabbar sparring with Bruce Lee.

An instant later, a whistle appeared in Chevsky's mouth.

The guy was good.

SCREEEEEEEEEEE! SCREEEEEEEEEEE!

He blew the whistle frantically, like a referee calling a penalty. At other times, the sound could have been loud, but now it was muffled by the thick fog and smoke.

Ed moved up and stood next to Luke. They were both on the Red Square side of the bridge now. Chevsky backed away from them. He moved along the bridge, keeping to the right side of the tall grass. Luke felt like he had seen this movie before—in another second, the man was going to turn and run.

Luke and Ed both took steps forward.

"High low," Luke said. "I'm high, you're low." He almost couldn't believe what he was saying. He had just suggested they resort to the old schoolyard trick.

"Okay," Ed said. "Watch that stick, though."

"You want high instead?" Luke said.

Ed shook his head. "No. You got a harder head than me."

Luke smiled. "On my go?"

Ed shrugged.

"Sure."

Luke took a breath.

"Go!"

They both jumped forward, moving in sync. Chevsky swung the cane. Luke blocked it with his forearm. The cane connected hard, wood on bone.

Thokk!

That hurt.

Ed went low and got Chevsky around the legs.

SCREEEEEEEEE!

He lifted Chevsky in the air and they both went down to the ground, Chevsky on his back, Ed on top. The walking stick went flying.

Amazingly, the man wrestled Ed.

Ed was stronger, but Chevsky's arms were lightning fast tentacles. They punched and slapped at Ed, Ed trying to subdue them. Luke moved in close. This couldn't last long. No man could survive Ed Newsam on top of him.

SCREEEEEEEE!

The whistle was still in Chevsky's mouth.

Like a magic trick, a snubnose gun, a .38, appeared in Chevsky's hand. He tried to point it at Ed's head. Ed shoved it away. They both gripped it, fighting for control. They grunted like pigs.

Now it was real. Luke rolled to the ground next to them. He had to get that gun away before…

CLACK!

In the fog, the gunshot was even quieter than it would otherwise be. A stifled cough. Someone punching holes in a stack of paper.

Chevsky's head cracked apart, and a jet of blood and bone and gore splattered backward across the ground in a fan shape, surrounding his head like a halo.

A fountain of blood sprayed upward, hitting Ed's dress shirt in the chest, splashing a Rorschach pattern across the front of it.

Luke looked behind them.

Albert stood there. His eyes were half open. He blinked like a man awakening from a twenty-year nap. He gripped the gun in two hands, the silencer sticking out like a long, accusing finger.

Luke and Ed turned to each other. Ed was sprayed with blood, but nothing else seemed to have hit him. No bone, no bullet. He wasn't dead. He wasn't even hurt. Albert had threaded the needle, shooting Chevsky without hitting Ed.

"You okay?" Luke said.

Ed nodded. "I think so. I don't know how that bullet went past me, though."

They both stared at Albert.

He stared back at them quizzically.

"I cannot let him kill you, can I?"

"YOU could have killed me," Ed said. He gazed down at his own blood-spattered chest. "Look at my shirt."

Albert shrugged.

"I got some on you," he said. "Sorry."

They were looting the man's pockets when Albert's phone started ringing. He glanced at the screen, and ignored the call.

He shrugged.

"Junk call. Number from outside country. Scam artists from Poland or Hungary, probably."

The three of them were crouched near a concrete barrier, low and out of sight. The barrier reminded Luke of the highway barriers put up around roadwork sites in the United States. It had no business being here. It was as if a giant had dragged the thing out onto this bridge and dropped it, leaving it slightly askew.

Luke felt the press of urgency. They'd been lucky so far, and it felt like it couldn't last. They had to get rid of this body.

They took the man's gun, his wallet and state ID, and his money. They took his cell phone. He had an Academy of Sciences badge around his neck on a long tether.

"Electronic," Albert said, holding up the badge. "Will open door to office building. Might also open office door. Files, computer…"

He shook his head and sighed.

Luke looked at him.

"Very dangerous. Cameras everywhere. I cannot go in building. If I am filmed, I will die."

Sirens seemed to be all around them now, converging on Red Square. Police cars roared past on the other bridge.

After a few moments, they had searched the guy thoroughly, all the way down to his underwear and his shoes. They seemed to have everything they were going to get. Albert sat propped against the concrete barrier, scrolling through Chevsky's telephone. Luke and Ed kneeled beside the body, feeling for anything else it might offer.

Albert shook his head, the phone still in his hand. "Nothing here. Nothing we need. Friends. Family. Wife and child. It is no good. We must get his computer."

Luke's shoulders slumped. An image of Becca and Gunner flashed through his mind. This guy Albert was cold-hearted to an extreme.

"What do we do with the body?" he said to Albert, although he already knew the answer. "We can't leave it here."

Albert shrugged and gestured at the river with his head. "Moskva, like before. In Russia we have saying. *The river is hungry.* So feed it."

Luke looked at Ed.

Ed gestured at the articles of clothing they had gathered around the body. "Let's keep the hat and coat. And the stick. If we play it right…"

Luke raised his eyebrows, but he already knew what Ed was thinking.

"We need to get into his office," Ed said. "Otherwise, what are we doing here?"

Luke nodded. "My thoughts exactly."

Together, they lifted Chevsky's body and dumped it over the railing. The body was heavy. Not for the first time, or the tenth, it occurred to Luke how much heavier people were dead than alive.

At the sound of the splash, Albert looked up from scrolling through Chevsky's text messages and photos.

He nodded. "Good. Now you go in his office."

CHAPTER TWENTY FOUR

4:30 p.m. Eastern Daylight Time (12:30 a.m. Moscow Daylight Time)
The Oval Office
The White House
Washington, DC

"Aw hell. This just keeps getting better and better."

The room was full of aides, assistants, and even senior advisors, but Clement Dixon had never felt more alone. No one had a reasonable explanation for what was going on, and no one seemed to know what was coming next.

Dixon glanced outside the tall windows at the Rose Garden. It was happening again. A lovely, late summer day was passing into oblivion.

Tomorrow morning, he would be attending, and giving remarks, at a prayer service for the fallen, to be held at the National Cathedral. It was almost more than he could bear. The final count was eighty-seven oil workers dead, along with five men missing, and three dead Navy SEALs.

Five missing—that number seemed to stick in his craw. Where were they? Were they drifting south on prevailing ocean currents? Had they run out for sandwiches? Where did the missing go?

Of course they were dead. He knew that. Everybody knew that. If they were alive, they would have turned up by now.

In his mind, Dixon could already see the families of the dead— the widows, the aging parents, *the children.*

It was going to take an immense effort to keep his composure. The oil industry was not his favorite American industry. That much was true. But these were workingmen. They were not part of any fight. They hadn't asked for this. Their families hadn't asked for it, either.

Dixon sighed heavily. That was only the beginning.

In the Arctic, every country with any sort of claim to anything, no matter how paltry, was racing to prepare for war. It was absurd on its face.

Iceland, a country of 300,000 people—less than the number of people waiting in line for ice cream on the boardwalk in Virginia Beach any summer afternoon—had sent its one naval destroyer on patrol to protect its interests 200 miles into the Arctic Circle.

Iceland! Iceland was a nice place to visit, but it didn't have "interests." It couldn't afford them. A gang of thirteen-year-old juvenile delinquents from Baltimore would make short work of the entire Icelandic military.

The Canadian government had just released an advisory, complete with aerial maps, demonstrating that the Northwest Passage was their sovereign territory, in case anyone needed reminding of that.

Norway, Sweden, and Denmark were all issuing random threats, designed to intimidate whom, exactly? Each other? Finland was a little more cautious—they shared a common border with Russia, and knew better than to stir up trouble.

But none of that was the worst. The worst was Russia. The situation there was like a forty-ton tractor trailer, rumbling downhill with no brakes. Right now, Russia was all over the news.

On the Oval Office's flat-screen TV, a handsome young news reporter Dixon had never seen before was reading from the teleprompter. His short hair was blond, his eyes were blue, and his face was broad and angular and perfectly symmetrical. You could draw a vertical line down the middle of his face, and each side would be a mirror image of the other.

The newscaster's expression tried to suggest he was knowledgeable and serious, but Dixon wasn't buying any of it. He would bet a dollar the man couldn't point to Russia on a map of the world.

Dixon shook his head. Everyone on TV seemed to be thirty years old nowadays. What had happened to all the deep-voiced, stoic men from Dixon's generation? Could they not see the print anymore? Were the home health aides feeding them pureed carrots?

Frankly, it would give him a profound sense of reassurance if Walter Cronkite suddenly rose from his nursing home bed (or wherever the hell he was), tottered into a news studio somewhere, and started reading from a stack of papers in his hand. Seeing these kids on TV made Dixon feel as if all the adults were gone, and no one was in charge anymore. The fact that Dixon himself was supposedly the one in charge made the feeling even worse. He was manifestly, unequivocally, *not* in charge.

The young newsman spoke:

"While American intelligence and defense agencies are analyzing the videotape to determine if it's a forgery or not, President Putin was hit with more bad news. Moments after the video surfaced of him seeming to celebrate the Serbian terrorist attack in Alaska, there was an intelligence leak, apparently from within the Kremlin itself.

"We are told that the leak suggests the order for the attack on American oil infrastructure was given at the highest levels of Russian government, possibly from within the office of the President himself. Further, that the attack was carried out at the behest of Russian oligarchs who control the former Soviet oil monopoly, now privatized under the name Yukos, and the former Soviet natural gas monopoly, operated as a public, shareholder-controlled company under the name Gazprom. Gazprom is now the largest oil and gas producing company in the world, and the majority of its shares are thought to be in the hands of six individuals, or their proxies.

"Already, a dozen members of the Russian state Duma, and two members of the Federation Council, have called for an investigation into these allegations of corruption. At this time, CNN does not have access to the documents in the intelligence leak, though the network has made Freedom of Information Act requests to the

Joint Chiefs of Staff, the Central Intelligence Agency, the National Security Agency, and the Defense Intelligence Agency. Each of those organizations has officially claimed to have no access to the documents, or knowledge of their contents."

The man stared directly into the camera. He put a hand to one ear.

"Yes? Yes. We have more information coming in now. Apparently, some sort of event is taking place in Red Square, outside the Kremlin, which houses both President Putin's offices and his official address. It is late at night there, after midnight, and the Square is filling up with police, as well as crowds of people. There are rumors of military troop transports entering the Square as well. I'm told we have live footage of the events taking place."

The image on the screen changed to an outdoor night shot. It was hard to make out what was happening. There were people milling around, and red sirens flashing. Someone picked up a smoke canister and threw it at a line of cops.

"Why are we watching this on the news?" Dixon said. "Don't we have experts who can tell us what's going on? Couldn't we have known yesterday that this was coming? I'm the President, and I'm seeing this at the same time as everyone else on Earth. Does that seem right to you?"

He looked around the room at the faces gathered there. They all seemed blank-eyed, like young, confused deer standing astride a railroad track, about to be crushed by a slow-moving, but immensely heavy freight train.

He noticed that there were no military men or women in the room. Why was that? General Richard Stark seemed to be a permanent fixture around here, but now that the President of the United States needed clarity on an issue of importance, he was somewhere else.

Right now, the clever monkeys in the Pentagon were probably drawing up plans for a nuclear first strike which Stark would then come here and pitch (with 100% confidence and not a hint of irony) as a way to wipe out the Russians, cause a toxic radiological cloud to settle in the Chinese heartland, and leave Uncle Sam astride the world as an unchallenged global colossus.

"Let me put it another way," Dixon said. "Did Putin authorize the attack, or didn't he? Obviously, we're not morons, so we can't go by what we see on the television. And hopefully, we don't have to put in a Freedom of Information Act request to the CIA or the Pentagon ourselves. But if Putin did authorize the attack, I need to know that."

A young woman's voice spoke, light and musical. "Why don't we let the Russian investigation into his actions play itself out?" she said.

Clement Dixon stared at her. She was pretty, and dressed smartly in a gray skirt suit. Her hair was short, cut in a conservative but perky bob. Her eyes showed a bright self-assuredness all out of proportion to her apparent intelligence. She held her hand up as though she was in school.

"What's your name?" Dixon said.

"Tracey Reynolds," she said. She said it eagerly and proudly, as though President Clement Dixon would remember it five minutes from now. Clement Dixon couldn't remember what he had for breakfast this morning.

But here was something he could remember:

"Ms. Reynolds, the Russians lie about almost everything. Almost every official word that comes from their government, and reaches our shores, is a lie. This has been true for at least sixty years. Are you aware of that?"

Her confidence faltered the tiniest amount. A look of uncertainty crossed her face, but then quickly disappeared.

She nodded and smiled. "Yes."

Boy, these kids were raised on a steady diet of self-esteem, weren't they? They seemed to believe in the inherent rightness of everything they did and said. She was being admonished by the *President of the United States,* and somehow she didn't realize that yet.

"So then, if we know that all they're going to do is lie, why would we wait for the outcome of their investigation?"

Her big eyes looked up toward the ceiling. Amazingly, Tracey Reynolds was trying to think of an answer. If she could, she would continue pursuing this doomed line of reasoning, out loud, in front of a room full of White House staffers, supposedly the best and brightest that the country could muster.

Behind her, an older woman reached out, put a hand on her shoulder, and whispered something into her ear. Tracey Reynolds nodded and clammed up. Her mouth closed with such a snap it was audible from where Clement Dixon was sitting. A flush crept up from her neckline and turned her face red.

"Anyone else?" Dixon said.

Another hand went up. This one belonged to a man, maybe in his late twenties, maybe in his early thirties. His hand was soft and somewhat bulbous, like the hand of the Pillsbury dough boy. Dixon recognized him—he was an aide to … someone. He had something to do with intelligence sharing between the White House and the spy agencies. He was blonde with thinning hair, overweight, in a suit that did not fit his pear shape well. It was too big at the shoulders and too small around the midsection.

The man's eyes were large and earnest. He could be a baby seal about to be struck down by a heavy club.

"Mr. President?"

"Yes, Mr.…"

"Jepsum, sir."

"Yes, Jepsum. Of course. Okay, give it to me straight, Jepsum. I can take it."

Jepsum was hesitant. He was older than Tracey Reynolds, and given his body type and his face, he probably hadn't been nearly as popular in high school. His parents probably hadn't loved him as unconditionally. All of these things were good. At least he knew enough to be cautious about sticking his neck out.

"Well, sir …"

Dixon made a spinning wheel motion with his hand.

"Out with it. I'm an old man. I could be dead before morning."

Jepsum cleared his throat. "Okay. I was thinking that after the smoke clears, it might be a good idea if you publicly embrace the next person who comes out on top over there. Not right away, but soon after. If Putin goes down, the intelligence my office has gathered suggests the winner is likely to be Dmitri Gagarin, the current Prime Minister. He's less bellicose than Putin, and he's not as smart. He's a political operator, a bit of a team player and not anything like tyrant material. He could be much easier to deal with in the long run."

Dixon wasn't sure how he felt about that. But at least this man was thinking.

"And if it turns out that the Russians really were behind the attack?"

Jepsum shrugged. It was an awkward gesture. His small shoulders nearly touched his ears on either side of his head. Dixon liked him already. Jepsum was clearly an underdog.

"That's Putin," Jepsum said. "Putin and his people. He has a close-knit circle, and he keeps a tight grip on information. Since the action was carried out by a Serbian paramilitary, it's possible this was a Putin in-house operation. The Russian military, intelligence agencies, and the larger government might not have been involved at all."

"It would be nice to think that, Jepsum."

"Yes, sir. And potentially a helpful way to look at it. As tragic as it was, the attack in Alaska could be an opportunity for us. It's an idea for bigger brains than mine to think about, sir, but if Gagarin comes in, and we support his ascension, we might be able to help him purge Putin's people right out of the government. It might be nice to go back to the kind of friendly relations with Russia that we enjoyed in the 1990s."

"You mean when Boris Yeltsin was our lap dog?" Clement Dixon said.

Jepsum raised his hands in the *don't shoot* gesture. "You said it, sir. Not me."

Dixon looked at Allen Forbes, the press secretary. Forbes was busy trying to blend in with the crowd.

"Allen, what do you think of that?"

Forbes appeared to give it some thought, and then deftly avoided answering the question. "Well, Mr. President, I think we would need to get a group of foreign policy experts together and brainstorm the pros and cons of taking an action like that. It might have a lot of upside, but it also might leave us exposed."

Dixon looked back at Jepsum.

"We do things by committee around here, Jepsum. But keep plugging away. I like your initiative, and it doesn't hurt to have at least one person on board with measurable electrical activity in their brain."

Jepsum stifled a smile. "Yes sir."

Dixon looked around the office again.

"Any more?"

Now everyone just stared. No one said a word. Dixon realized his sarcasm was starting to hurt him with these people.

"All right, then let's break this thing up. Thanks, everybody."

They hated him. He could tell. He had been around long enough to know when he was buying someone's back, but not their heart.

They hated him, for sure.

But you know what? He hated them, too.

CHAPTER TWENTY FIVE

12:45 a.m. Moscow Daylight Time (4:45 p.m. Eastern Daylight Time)
Special Ministries Annex
Red Square
Moscow, Russia

R ed Square was filling with people, more coming all the time. Luke and Ed stayed to the far edge of the gathering. The growing masses were held back by lines of police. Large armored vehicles, similar to American SWAT Bearcats, were parked nearly nose to tail, like a fence. The Kremlin building itself was in the distance, more than a quarter of a mile away.

There was a commotion going on over there.

Lights flashed. Choppers passed overhead, including the heavy WHUMP of helicopter gunships. News trucks from at least a dozen countries were parked fifty meters from the armored vehicles. Reporters stood with cameramen, surveying the scene, and broadcasting to their legions back home. Whatever was going on, at least there hadn't been a crackdown on freedom of expression.

Yet.

Luke and Ed detached from the crowd, and walked away across empty paving stones toward the Special Ministries Annex. The building was a bleak Soviet-era box, gray, three stories high and a city block long, tucked away behind Saint Basil's Cathedral, in a distant corner of the Square.

A distant corner was a good place for it, as far as Luke was concerned. It was quiet over here. There didn't seem to be anybody around.

"I hope this key card works," he said.

Ed nodded. "Amen, brother."

"In and out, just that easy," Luke said.

He felt a trickle of something—it wasn't fear. He didn't like what was happening behind them. Gatherings of chanting people became riots sometimes, and riots got ugly. Governments cracked down on rioting. Movement became restricted.

Two dead men were floating in the Moskva River. They were important men, involved in a terrorist attack against the United States, but also something else, something that was still coming, something that few people knew about. Those bodies were going to turn up at some point, and when they did...

Luke wanted to get out of the country before that happened.

The Special Ministries Annex was close enough to their hotel that they could easily leave the office building, sprint through Red Square, cross the river and then a wide boulevard, run down the block, and straight into the lobby. But it would never do. There was too much surveillance. They were going to have to walk out of the office building, through the crowds, across the footbridge, and then find Albert waiting in the car.

Then he was going to have to drive them out around the city and back to the hotel. During that time they would transform themselves from spies out stealing secrets and dumping bodies in the river, into rich American tourists coming home from a night of drinking in the famous Moscow bars. All of this assumed they didn't get caught inside the building, or get videotaped in the street and turn up on some advanced facial recognition database that no one knew the Russians had.

"What have we learned so far?" Luke said.

"Oleg Marmilov," Ed said.

"The puppet master. GRU, probably."

"Right," Ed said. "He organized the attack on the oil rig. It was either his call to kill the hostages, or somebody went crazy and it just happened. Either way, he had Zelazny edit the videotape to make it look like we did it, and send it out to the world. Zelazny used to meet in secret with Tomasz Chevsky to get his marching orders."

"Chevsky was an engineer for the Ministry of Sciences," Luke said.

Ed nodded "But he really worked for Marmilov."

"The attack was the start of something bigger that they're planning."

"And so here we are," Ed said.

They approached the building. Ed wore the engineer's long coat and bowler hat. He also carried the engineer's walking stick. Ed was black. The engineer was white. Ed was as broad as a mountain range. The engineer was as thin as a wraith.

They were both tall. That's where the similarities ended. If Ed kept his head tilted down, there was the barest chance that someone looking at a security camera would mistake him for the engineer.

Luke came as he was. No one was going to mistake him for anything. Maybe an invited guest coming in to … what? Go over some files late at night?

They skirted the double glass doors of the wide front entrance and went around to the right side of the building. There was a single door here, made of heavy steel with reinforced glass. There was a black electronic lockbox mounted at its side.

Ed took the ID card tethered around his thick neck and swiped it at the box.

The LED light went from red to green. Luke heard an audible click as the door unlocked. And just like that, they were in.

"Voila," Ed said, as Luke pulled the door open.

"I'm not going to lie. This one looks bad for him."

Sergei Abramoff was watching the Putin fiasco unfold on TV. He sat at his desk in the security office of the building the government officially called Special Ministries Annex, but everyone else called The Breadbox. Spare, utilitarian, and Soviet in every possible way, it was an unsightly carbuncle added to the baroque grandeur of Red Square during the Stalin years.

The place was drawn with a cookie cutter. In the beginning, the offices were, quite literally, all the same. That had changed somewhat over the years, with walls being torn down and added, bathrooms upgraded, security features installed ... but even so, it was as drab as a building could possibly be.

It was slated to be removed at some point, and Sergei himself would happily bulldoze it for them. The sticking point was the more than two hundred officials, aides, minor governmental organizations, office workers, and miscellaneous others who were warehoused here and needed to be close to the Kremlin to carry out their daily duties. You couldn't simply tear down a building and leave all these people with nowhere to go in the morning, could you?

Sergei sometimes entertained fantasies of getting this same job—night watchman—at the Kremlin, where he could wander the grand marble halls, his footsteps echoing in the shadows, as he absorbed the wonders of times long past. The time of the tsars, and the time of vision, and imagination, and possibility.

But he knew it wasn't to be. Jobs like that ... they came to those who were well-connected. The men who had those jobs guarded them more jealously than they guarded the Kremlin itself, as if the fate of the world hung in the balance.

No. Sergei would work here until they tore the old place down, and then probably he'd be transferred to somewhere equally dispiriting.

He stared at the television. There were no windows in this room, but just outside this building, in Red Square, the largest commotion in fourteen years was unfolding. The Square, so many times the site of Russian history, was filling with policemen, soldiers, protestors, and counter-protestors.

Putin was being credibly accused of corruption, and possible treason. He had risked the Apocalypse by sanctioning a Serbian attack on American interests, all to benefit his gangster friends in the oil and gas industries. There was the question of his removal from office, and even his arrest. It could happen as soon as tonight.

And Sergei was trapped inside here, with history happening not even a kilometer away.

"Putin will fall," he said, while on the silent TV, a swarm of people behind pro-Putin banners chanted and raised their fists. "And I will miss the whole thing."

He took a deep drag of his cigarette. He sipped his cold black coffee, which was spiked with two shots of cheap vodka. He had been nipping at the bottle since the shift started. And he had been nipping at it before he came in, if he was being honest.

It didn't matter. Nothing ever happened in this building. Here he was, in his dungeon lair, with about six hours to go, the world standing on its head outside these walls, and he was a little bit drunk. He almost felt like he could take a nap.

"This is my fate."

He glanced at the bank of security screens. Five screens high, eight screens across. The security cameras shot video that was as drab as the building itself. Black and white, grainy, snowy, poorly lit, with everything seeming to take place in the shadows. Watching these videos was like an exercise in contemplating post-modern abstraction. What was happening in there? People were moving around, but what were they doing? Did it even matter? These people were functionaries, at best.

"Let them stay home after all," Sergei said.

At the bottom of the screen a message was blinking. *EAST DOOR: 12:57 a.m. ID: CHEVSKY, T. 8675309.*

Hmmm. Tomasz Chevsky had come into the building…just a few moments ago. That figured. He was always creeping around. After years on this job, Sergei knew the office tenants by heart.

Chevsky was a young guy in his thirties. He was tall to an extreme, and thin. He resembled a piece of taffy that had been pulled too far. He supposedly worked for the Academy of Sciences, overseeing research funding in various corners—universities, government labs, private think tanks. He traveled a bit, both abroad and across Russia. Sergei suspected he was FSB, with some minor role peering over the shoulders (and policing the thoughts) of scientists and professors. Why else would they put someone from the Academy of Sciences, all by himself, in this building?

And why would he creep around the way that he did? For example, now. Chevsky knew that standard protocol when coming in after hours was to access the main entrance, and give a wave and a hello to the night watchman. He hadn't done that. Of course, this was because he was FSB and above the law.

If the protocols were to make any sense, then the side entrances would be inaccessible during night hours. The ID cards simply wouldn't work. Naturally, that wasn't the case, or how could FSB men come and go as they pleased?

Sergei smiled. He enjoyed theorizing as to what the denizens of this Breadbox actually did for a living. Of course, most of them probably did what they claimed to do, but that was boring, wasn't it? Might as well liven things up a bit.

He watched the screens that monitored the third floor. There was Chevsky now, the international man of mystery, wearing his long coat and his hat pulled down over his face. He moved down the narrow hall toward his office, 313. Sergei couldn't see Chevsky that clearly—the footage on the third floor was the worst of anywhere—but he *could* see that Chevsky wasn't alone.

There was a second man with Chevsky. He was tall with light hair, pale-skinned—his skin color contrasted starkly in the image, between its whiteness and the poorly lit darkness of his surroundings. He was somewhat smaller than Chevsky, and less broad.

Sergei took a drag from his cigarette. He took another long sip of his spiked coffee. Tomasz Chevsky had come into the building in the middle of the night, with an unauthorized and unannounced visitor.

There was a reasonable explanation, as there always was. They had gone to witness the protests, of course. And they had come in to use the men's room. Or Chevsky had forgotten a file and dashed in to retrieve it. Or he decided to take this opportunity to show his friend his office. Chevsky's office could not be much to be proud of, but people in this world took what small victories they could get.

Even so, the rules were the rules. Chevsky ignoring them and pushing them aside could one day get Sergei in trouble.

Sergei sighed. He took another sip of coffee. He picked up his nightstick. His gun was where it always was—strapped to his right thigh.

"Let's go talk with these gentlemen," he said.

The door to the office wouldn't open.

Luke watched Ed try every permutation of swiping the ID card against, or near, or along the side of, or over, the electronic lockbox. Every time he did anything, a small red LED light would flash. And the door wouldn't unlock.

The door itself was heavy steel, out of sync with most of the doors on this hallway, which were primarily thick wood and smoked glass. It was obvious that whatever was going on inside this Academy of Sciences office, Room 313 of the Special Ministries Annex, was not for public consumption.

"Ah, man," Ed said under his breath. "This thing…"

"It doesn't look good," Luke said. "Standing around like this *does not* look good. We are on camera."

"I'm aware of that," Ed said.

There was a small black video camera mounted on the ceiling at the end of the hall. They kept their backs to it. Somewhere, someone might be watching that video feed. And the longer Luke and Ed stood here, the more likely that someone was going to start paying attention to them.

"We're just going to have to blow it," Luke said.

Ed shrugged. "Yeah, how do we do that?"

"The tall guy's gun," Luke said. "I have it in my pocket."

Ed shook his head and sighed. "Look at the lock. It's steel reinforced. You'll need to shoot it two or three times at least, and even then…"

"We have to get in there somehow," Luke said.

"It's going to be loud," Ed said.

"Yeah, I know. But at this point it's either that, or go right back out the way we came in. We could be an inch away from knowing everything. If we're going to find out, it's on the other side of this door."

Ed's big shoulders slumped inside the engineer's coat.

"All right, well…"

Just down the hall, the ancient elevator groaned into life. The sound of gears cranking was loud in the silent tomb of the building. Someone was downstairs, and had just called the elevator. The elevator's pulley system sounded like it hadn't seen an ounce of lubrication in decades.

Luke pulled the gun, keeping it low and against his body, out of sight of the camera.

"Stone…" Ed said.

"Don't worry. I'm not going to do anything hasty."

This was some Keystone Kops right here. Albert had declined to come into the building. Luke could understand that. If Albert got picked up on camera during a break-in at a dead GRU agent's office… forget it.

Okay, so they were without Albert. They had the electronic door card, but it wasn't working, and for reasons they didn't understand. Maybe there was a button to push somewhere? Maybe a sequence to type in? There was no way to know.

And now the elevator…

Luke couldn't move toward it. If he did, and anyone was monitoring the video camera, then they would see his face clearly, and they might alert whoever was in the elevator that Luke was approaching it. Instead, he had to stand here and wait, pretend the elevator didn't bother him, pretend that he barely noticed it.

Ding!

The elevator passed the second floor and kept creaking along. It was coming.

"Your call," Ed said, his head still down, his body still facing the lockbox.

"I'm not going to have a lot of choice," Luke said.

"I know it."

Ding!

The elevator was here. It stopped. Luke took a breath.

He held the gun pointed down, ready to swing it around.

The elevator door slid open. It sounded like an asthmatic gasping for air. Luke turned his head to see what came out.

A man in a blue uniform stepped from the elevator. He was bulbous, and the uniform fit him too tightly. He was smoking a cigarette—it dangled from his mouth. He turned, and the first thing Luke noticed was the gun strapped to his meaty thigh. The next thing Luke noticed was the nightstick in the man's left hand. The man smiled and said something in Russian.

Luke raised the gun, holding it in a two-handed shooter's stance. He moved quickly down the hall toward the man.

"*Ne dvigaysya!*" he said.

Don't move.

"*Politsiya!*"

Police.

The cigarette dropped from the man's mouth. If the situation hadn't been so dire, Luke would have laughed.

At the last second, the man must have caught the accent—Luke sounded like a first-year exchange student. The man's eyes widened, and he went for his own gun. But Luke was already on top of him.

Luke grabbed the man by the hair and pulled him backward, off balance. He spun Chevsky's gun around, raised it, and brought it down grip first on the man's head.

Then again.

And again.

The guard's eyes went blank. He swooned. His head hit the floor with an audible THUNK. It sounded like someone had just thumped a cantaloupe, checking for ripeness. The man's eyes rolled back into his head, showing the whites. His mouth hung open.

The camera was still there on the ceiling, and Luke felt its eye upon him. He was painfully aware that he had just assaulted a night security guard, in full view of that camera, in a Russian office building near the Kremlin.

Okay, never mind that. Think fast.

The man had a tether around his neck, with a white electronic key card, very similar to the one Ed had.

Luke snatched it and pulled hard. The tether snapped and the card came free. Luke walked back to Ed with it and handed it to him.

"Here, try this. With a little luck, this guy can open any door in the building."

Ed swiped it. The green light on the lockbox lit up. Luke heard the lock disengage. Ed turned the metal handle and pushed the door open.

He gave Luke a sidelong glance and grinned.

They were in.

Ed led the way inside. The room was in shadow, with red and blue lights flashing in the windows from Red Square. There was a voice out there, booming through a megaphone.

There wasn't much in here. Near the window was a floor lamp, but they ignored it. There was a desk with a computer screen on top and a tower CPU underneath it. There was a rolling office chair that went with the desk—the chair looked like something a middle school vice principal would have sat in when Luke was a kid. He ran his hand over its leather seat—sure enough, here and there were cracks in the leather, patched with heavy tape.

There was no filing cabinet anywhere. There was a small refrigerator, like a kid might take to college. Luke opened it and pawed around inside—a half-eaten sandwich, a couple of plastic tubs with leftovers of some kind, a few bottles of beer on a shelf built into the door, and a can of Coke.

Besides the fridge, there was nothing—just this desk with a computer. Luke opened the desk drawers—barely anything in there, either. Here was a roll of heavy masking tape, probably the same tape Chevsky had used to patch his chair. There were some pencils and pens in the desk, a stack of lined paper, and a scientific calculator. There were no computer disks of any kind.

On top of the desk, next to the computer monitor, was an old abacus.

Ed reached out and touched the beads.

"No way," he said under his breath.

He moved a few beads along a metal rail, from one side to the other. "When I was a kid, there was this old, old guy who owned a candy store. Him and his wife. White couple, they were from … somewhere. Eastern Europe, maybe even Russia. I used to watch the old man counting his cash sometimes, going over his receipts. He had one of these things. His fingers moved so fast, it was like …"

"Ed," Luke said, breaking the reverie. "We have to get out of here. I need you to bring that guard inside this room. We can use this tape to tie him up and gag him. I don't want to kill him. If we're lucky, nobody finds him until morning."

Ed nodded. "Yeah, all right."

Luke sat at the computer. He ran his hand along the CPU, looking for an On button. He found it in seconds. A round light appeared on the screen, went to black, then the screen came on. It was very bright in the darkness of the room.

A login page appeared, with a box to enter numbers and letters. There was a blinking cursor inside the box. Words in Cyrillic instructed the user what to do. Luke couldn't read words written in the Cyrillic alphabet.

"Of course," he said. "What else did I think was going to happen?"

With nothing to go on, he tried a few easy password guesses.

1111. He hit the button that would normally be the Return key.

The numbers disappeared. The blinking cursor reappeared.

0000.

No good.

1234.

Negative.

This was ridiculous. Luke didn't even know how many characters there were supposed to be. Considering a guy like Chevsky—
who carried a walking stick he used as a bludgeon, a .38 inside his
coat, a rape whistle in his pocket, and who showed a surprising ability with the fighting arts for someone who looked like Big Bird…

His password was bound to be complicated.

Ed came back in, dragging the guard along the floor. He flipped
the man over onto his face.

"He's heavier than he looks. Toss me that tape, will you?"

Luke gave Ed the tape. Immediately, Ed pulled a long strip of
it, pulled the guard's arms behind his back, and wrapped the tape
around his wrists. He pulled another strip, and did it again, doubling the tape up. Then he did it again.

Luke turned back to the computer. Ed knew what he was doing.

He looked down at the CPU. It was a black rectangle, maybe two
feet high. At the bottom, it was hooked to two metal clasps built into
the floor. So much for taking the entire box with him. But that was
probably a good thing—all he needed was the hard drive. Someone
back home would be able to access it and read the contents.

He hit the power button. The screen went dark, and returned to
a white dot in the middle. After a few seconds, that faded and went
out. Luke stood.

He glanced down at Ed. Ed had already finished taping the guy's
wrists and mouth. Now he was taping the man's ankles together.

Luke lined up the computer tower, and gave it a heavy kick with
the heel of his foot. The shoe connected, but the casing didn't break.
He kicked it again. And again. At each kick, the tower wanted to
slide across the floor, but it couldn't—the clasps anchored it to the
spot.

Luke kicked it again. The hard plastic casing cracked apart.
He kneeled, put his fingers inside the crack, and wrenched it open
further.

"You want me to do that?" Ed said. "You seem to be having some
trouble."

Luke smiled and shook his head. He took a breath, then pulled the two halves of the tower away from each other. He snaked an arm inside and found the hard drive. It was mounted inside the box with tiny screws. With no screwdriver, it could take all night to get those things open. He yanked on the drive and broke the plastic mounts. Then he unplugged the drive from the motherboard.

He pulled it out and looked at it—just a silver metal box. Okay. He slipped it into his pocket, then reached inside the tower again on the off chance there was another one. His fingers moved along the board, then behind it, then along the top and bottom—nothing. Satisfied, Luke stood.

Ed was already standing. The guard was hogtied on the ground, snoring deeply, the air being sucked through his nose. His mouth was sealed shut. Luke had clocked the guy three good ones—he was going to wake up with a whale of headache tomorrow.

"You ready?" Ed said.

Luke shrugged. "Born ready."

There was chaos in Red Square.

Someone was shouting through a speaker system. The sound was loud. The cops were driving the people out. They were firing tear gas shells from the tops of the armored trucks. A massive crowd was surging. People were running, falling, crying.

Luke and Ed barely looked at it. They walked briskly along its edge. People ran past them, trying to get away.

"We should probably find out what's going on," Ed said.

Luke shook his head. "That's their problem. I think we just need to leave."

They walked to the narrow overgrown area along the river. They crossed the condemned pedestrian bridge. A handful of protestors lurked here in the semi-darkness, hiding from the cops. Luke stepped over the mess where Chevsky's ruined head had once been—no one seemed to notice it.

On the far end of the bridge, a car was parked. It was the only car parked on the boulevard. Its engine was idling, steam rising from its tailpipe. Crowds of people streamed past it.

BMW M-Series. It was Zelazny's car.

They opened the rear doors and climbed in. Albert looked back at them from the driver's seat.

"Good?"

Luke nodded. "I think so."

"Did you find something?"

"Hard drive," Luke said. "Not sure what's in it."

"I can open for you," Albert said. "I can translate."

Luke shook his head. "Thanks. We have people for that."

Albert shrugged. He handed Luke an open bottle of vodka.

"Drink. Spill some on yourselves. Checkpoints everywhere now. Putin is arrested. Government? Maybe collapse. Maybe not. I don't know. You are Americans, out drinking. You care nothing of politics. I am taxi driver for you."

Luke stared at him. *Putin was arrested?* That raised some questions, but now was not the time. He took a swig of the vodka. He felt the heat in his mouth, down his throat, and in his belly. It tasted good. He poured a bit down the front of his shirt.

"More," Albert said. "Drink up."

He held his hand out to Ed. There was a box cutter in his palm. He pushed the lever forward and the razor blade extended outward.

"What do I need that for?" Ed said.

Albert gestured with his chin at Ed's shirt. Then he made a slicing gesture with his finger. "Blood all over you. You cut your lip. Somebody punched you in bar."

He shrugged as if to say: *That's the best I can do.*

Ed looked at Luke. Now Luke shrugged. He handed Ed the vodka bottle and Ed took a swig. He swallowed the fire water and took a breath.

He grimaced and dragged the blade across his bottom lip. The slice was deep, and the blood started flowing instantly.

Albert nodded and smiled. "Good. It will swell up. Will need stitches."

He put his thick hand out again.

"What now?" Ed said.

"Knife. Please."

Ed handed him back his box cutter. "I wasn't gonna keep it."

Albert winked. "I know Americans. Never steal anything. Just forget to return."

Ed and Luke both laughed.

Albert looked at Luke. "Man has called me three times. Call I thought was Hungary before? No. Friend of yours. Now I must destroy phone. Please talk to him first."

He handed Luke a flip cell phone. Luke opened the last call and pressed the green button. There was a long silence. The phone beeped … and beeped … and beeped.

"Hello?" a reedy male voice said. "Don Wellington."

Don … Wellington? Luke nearly laughed.

Swann.

Luke immediately assumed his alias. "Hi. This is Rob Simmons with Worldstar Entertainment. I'm in Moscow. My driver told me I got a call from this number."

"Yes, Mr. Simmons. This is Don Wellington with the State Department, sir. We've got a unique opportunity for you, which we think you will enjoy. It's an invitation for you and your associate, Mr.… ah …"

Luke looked at Ed. "Max Funk."

"That's right, Mr. Funk. Long story short, we've got a delegation headed from Moscow to Athens in a couple of hours, a State Department plane, and we'd like you both to join that delegation as cultural attaches. The plane is leaving early because there's a whole slate of activities scheduled for tomorrow with the Greek Ministry of Education. I think it will be a wonderful …"

Luke smiled. "We'll take it."

He listened while Swann gave him the details. A driver from the US embassy would meet them at the hotel. Once the driver got them, they'd be inside the protected womb of American diplomacy. Luke breathed deeply. It was good.

Luke thought of the hard drive in his pocket.

"Let me ask you a question, Mr. Wellington. I have something I would love to get your opinion about. But it's on a computer file that I can't seem to open at the moment. Would there be someone on the plane who can handle the technical details for me, and perhaps send you the material?"

"Of course there would," Swann said. "Consider it done."

Luke handed Albert the phone back. Albert drove away from Red Square and through the wide streets, looping out, and then back toward the hotel.

"It will help me," Albert said, "to know contents of hard drive."

Luke wasn't sure how to answer that. Whatever turned out to be on that hard drive, it was bound to become classified.

"Information. It is like money here. It keeps me alive."

"I will do my best," Luke said.

Up ahead, lights were flashing. They were about to hit a police checkpoint. Half a dozen cops stood by two cruisers, their roof lights spinning, throwing shadows across the roadway.

Albert slowed to a stop and opened his window. He handed the cop an ID card. Luke noticed the folded American dollar bills he slipped into the cop's hand along with the card.

The cop probed the car with a flashlight. He shined it on Ed and Luke. He said something in Russian. The words went by too fast. Luke didn't catch what he said.

Albert gestured back at Ed and Luke with his head.

"*Amerikantsov.*"

Yankees.

"*P'yanitsy.*"

Drunks.

The cop laughed and shook his head. He waved them through.

"Yes," Albert said as he brought the car up to speed again. "Do your best. I do my best for you."

CHAPTER TWENTY SIX

1:30 a.m. Moscow Daylight Time (5:30 p.m. Eastern Daylight Time)
Premier Suite
The Ritz-Carlton Moscow
Tverskaya Street
Moscow, Russia

Oleg Marmilov waited for a knock at his door.

The night was quiet. He wore a rich brown robe, and sat in the semi-darkness of the living room in his suite on the top floor of the Ritz-Carlton. He breathed deeply the smoke from his cigarette and let out a long exhale. He held a glass of red wine in his other hand.

He regarded the cigarette. The hotel was no-smoking now, taking its cue from the West. Of course Marmilov smoked anyway—who would question him? The odd thing, though, altogether the strangest thing...

...was how they made you feel guilty about it.

In the course of his long career, Marmilov had been responsible for the deaths of thousands of people. It didn't bother him in the least. Yet somehow he felt guilty about smoking in his own hotel suite—a place he had lived for more than two years—because it was against the rules.

"It's going to kill me one day and I know that," he said to himself now. "But in the meantime, they would also guilt me, and deny me its pleasures."

Across the living room from him, a giant flat-screen television silently showed news footage of Red Square, empty now except for some soldiers and policemen patrolling near the Kremlin. The crowds from earlier had been dispersed.

It had been an incredible night, and Putin must be reeling.

The footage of him had gone around the world. The tape was ten years old, of course, and showed a younger, ambitious, but not yet in power Putin toasting the Serbs and their resistance to the Americans and NATO. The tape was also doctored—courtesy of Leonard Zelazny—with a fake timestamp and just enough haziness to mask Putin's age. But it would take several days for anyone to realize these things.

Meanwhile, the very real GRU assessment that Putin was enriching himself and his friends in the oil and gas industries had been released—along with a forged document suggesting the Alaska attack had been the result of these relationships.

A rumor had gone around that Putin was arrested. This was not true, unfortunately. He had been questioned by FSB agents at his official residence in the Kremlin. Afterward, his own supporters had taken him to an undisclosed location—likely his Black Sea dacha—for fear that if he stayed in Moscow he might be arrested, or that a coup might kill him.

But first impressions were best impressions, and they lasted the longest. Millions of people, across the whole world, and even in Russia, right now believed that Putin was under arrest. Many probably believed he was being tortured.

Marmilov smiled at the thought.

Putin was on the defensive now. He had abandoned the city. Already, three dozen GRU-friendly lawmakers in the Duma had demanded his resignation. There would be more tomorrow. Also tomorrow, a group of five members of the upper house, the Federation Council, would stand together and suggest that Dmitri Gagarin, the current Prime Minister, be sworn in as acting President until the crisis was past.

Marmilov's smile broadened.

The office of Prime Minister, in the current era, was a toothless position with no real mandate. The Prime Minister spent a great deal of time cutting ribbons of various kinds, meeting with delegations of middling diplomats from other countries, and smiling on the TV. Gagarin was perfect for this role.

He was tall and handsome and athletic, with a bright white smile. He was a veteran of the Soviet war in Afghanistan (who seemed to have suffered no adverse psychological effects from it), and an upstanding family man with a wife and three grown children. He was quite charming and pleasant in public. But privately, he was a weakling with a penchant for young girls—*very young* girls. Unfortunately for him, there was no longer any such thing as privacy.

In the past, Marmilov had procured lost souls to feed Gagarin's unhealthy lusts, and of course Marmilov owned footage of some of these encounters. Naturally, Gagarin was well aware of this fact. Not to put too fine a point on it, Gagarin was Marmilov's marionette. He would dance to whatever tune Marmilov chose to call.

Marmilov took a sip of his wine. Yes, Dmitri Gagarin would make an exceptional acting President. How nice it would be if the Russian people in their wisdom decided that Gagarin should take on the role more permanently.

A strange feeling began to come over Marmilov—he was very close to seizing control of this country. It was a heady, breathless feeling, and he must remind himself not to let it carry him away.

A quiet knock came at the door to the suite.

This was the knock Marmilov was waiting for. He insisted his visitor knock instead of ringing the doorbell because beautiful young Tamara was asleep in the bedroom after a celebratory lovemaking session, and Marmilov did not want to wake her.

He padded across the carpeting to the door. When he opened it, the young man from the balcony at the Bolshoi was there. Marmilov silently waved him in.

They stood perhaps two meters apart, near the unlit stone fireplace. The man was several inches taller than Marmilov. He looked tired, but he stood at attention.

Marmilov had trouble understanding why anyone ever got tired. He had always been tireless, needing little sleep, and this had barely changed as he aged. Sleep? His work excited him, and kept him awake well into the night. Many mornings, he could not bear to stay in bed a moment longer than necessary.

He spoke to his visitor in a low voice.

"Excellent work tonight," Marmilov said.

"Thank you, sir."

"Everything went as well as could possibly be expected. Now, what news of the TV producer?"

"None, I'm afraid."

Marmilov didn't like to hear that. His men always knew where to encounter Leonard Zelazny. Zelazny was fooling no one with his cover stories and his alleged girlfriends. The underground world he frequented was an open book to men like Marmilov.

"None?" he said.

"Sir, plainclothes agents entered the places he frequently haunts, but found no sign of him. He was last seen, very drunk, leaving the Noor Bar between ten and ten thirty p.m. He is not at his flat, and his car is not there. Neither is he at his office."

Marmilov thought about it for a long moment. Zelazny's personal habits were an irritant. Marmilov should not, at a crucial juncture such as this, spend even a moment wondering about Zelazny's whereabouts.

"The engineer Chevsky is in frequent contact with him. Have you spoken with Chevsky?"

"Chevsky does not answer his telephone, sir."

Marmilov shook his head and sighed. It was late and the men wanted to respect Chevsky's privacy. He was a family man, after all. And he was a well-respected cog in this machine. But he was of the machine, and not above it. In earlier times, an agent like this would have known to simply go and knock on his door. If the door didn't open, then the agent would kick it in.

"Go to Chevsky's home and wake him. This is important."

"Of course, sir."

After the agent left, Marmilov went back to his sofa. Zelazny bore thinking about. When he disappeared like this, the issues only became clearer. He was very skilled at his work, but it was dangerous to have him running around in the streets. He drank too much alcohol. He consorted with degenerates too much. He was deeply involved in Marmilov's projects, and he knew too much about them.

If he were to speak to someone, spill his secrets, perhaps during a tryst...

It could lead to problems.

Marmilov had kept him around all this time because his work was excellent and he delivered it quickly. But there were other TV producers in this world. Perhaps this was the right time to snip off a troublesome loose end.

They just needed to find him first.

Marmilov's free hand clenched into a fist. Can you imagine? On a night like this, worrying about an expendable like Leonard Zelazny. No. Marmilov wouldn't allow it. In a sense, this was a good thing. Zelazny had shown his true colors.

And as a result, he would be dead before morning.

"Chevsky will know how to find him," Marmilov said, his voice quiet in the darkness. "A quick message from Chevsky, and then..."

Marmilov smiled. And then right back to the business at hand.

CHAPTER TWENTY SEVEN

7:15 p.m. Eastern Daylight Time (3:15 a.m. Moscow Daylight Time)
The West Wing
The White House
Washington, DC

"Why are you calling me? Do you have any idea where I am right now?"

Robert Jepsum was in his tiny closet of an office, tucked behind a wide pillar about a hundred steps down a stately marble hallway from the Oval Office. The office was barely 250 square feet, and was packed with office equipment—there was hardly any room to move.

His desk, his chair, his computer, three filing cabinets, a combination printer and fax machine, a large floor-mounted globe of the world that was nearly up to the minute in terms of the ever-shifting boundaries between countries, a small office refrigerator... these were just the big things that took up the most amount of space.

There was also a hotplate where he made his Ramen noodles and his macaroni and cheese. He didn't eat cheap food because it was cheap—he made very nice money, thank you—he ate it because it was fast, and he didn't like to waste time. Also there was a coffee maker, a small microwave oven, several baseballs mounted on pedestals and signed by entire major league teams—one day he would collect them all—a giant wall calendar with big day squares where he could scribble his scheduling notes (his handwriting looked like hieroglyphics), and a framed photograph of his parents. Yellow manila folders were piled high on top of a folding card table.

This place was beyond cluttered. It was practically a fire hazard.

He was almost surprised that they let him keep it like this. Then again, he was a hard worker who produced results and kept to himself most of the time. He was willing to bet that most people didn't even know what this office was like. Jepsum didn't know what their offices were like.

He held the cell phone to his ear. This was very, very dangerous, calling him while he was at work. His heart skipped a beat, and a moment later, as the fact of it began to sink in, his pulse began to race. He ran a hand through his thinning hair.

"We must talk," the voice said. The man spoke English perfectly well, but his Russian accent was all too apparent.

"I'll have to call you back."

"When?" said the voice.

"Five minutes."

Jepsum got up from his desk, went out in the hall, and locked his door. The wide hallways were quiet. A handful of people—the usual suspects—were still here working after hours, but a lot of people had already gone home. In the White House, you could tell who the people with real ambition were very easily—just look to see who was here in the middle of the night. Jepsum was always one of them.

He walked down the hall toward the security checkpoint, his footfalls echoing off the stone floor. Two uniformed guards stood chatting by the metal detector and the X-ray machine. They were older men, clock punchers who worked eight hour shifts, and wouldn't dream of doing anything else. To each their own.

"Calling it a night?" one of them said as Jepsum passed.

Jepsum smiled and shook his head. "Are you kidding? I'm just going out to catch a little fresh air and grab a snack out of my car. I'll be back before you blink."

"That's the spirit, kid."

Jepsum walked across the grounds to the parking lot. He reached his car, a late-model Toyota Camry, slid inside, pulled the door shut, and took a deep breath.

Okay. This was the best he was going to do.

He wasn't going to drive off the grounds, make this phone call, and then come right back again. That would raise more suspicions than if he just sat here, and appeared to eat a candy bar while chatting with someone from his personal life.

He opened the last call he had received and pressed SEND.

The man answered right away. "Hello, my friend."

Jepsum shook his head. "Talk, but make it quick."

"A man is missing," the voice said. "We cannot find him. He was crucial to the effort, and now he is gone. We don't think we are going to find him. Another man is also missing. He was involved as well. In a certain sense, he was even more important. We may find him, we may not. We are still hopeful at this moment, but…"

As far as Jepsum was concerned, that was just Russia. These people killed each other all the time.

"I'm sorry," he said. "What does this have to do with…"

"Everything. Concern is starting to rise. If someone took these men, it is not a coincidence. It would have to be someone…"

"Who knows," Jepsum said.

"Yes," the voice said. "Someone who knows. Can you think of anyone like that?"

"On my side?"

"Of course," the voice said. "Do you suppose we would ask you about this side?"

No. They wouldn't do that.

Jepsum thought about it. There was one thing about all this that had quietly eaten at him. During the raid on the oil rig, a man had taken a laptop used by the Serbs. That was widely known. Several Navy SEALs had seen it happen. Heck, it was captured on video.

The man was Luke Stone, the lead agent for the FBI Special Response Team, the one who had been suspended afterwards. As far as Jepsum knew, the SRT still had the laptop, and no one else had gotten a peek at it.

Jepsum was walking on eggshells right now, but he couldn't think of a way to ask the right question in code. Could White House security pull these cell phone signals out of the air? Of course they could. But why would they? No one had any reason to suspect him.

He plunged ahead.

"Just speaking hypothetically here. Theories, you understand? Guessing about how things work. If someone discovered a laptop that had once been used to send pictures somewhere, or maybe a home movie from years ago, or grandma's recipes from the old country, could things be traced from there? Could secrets be revealed?"

The voice was silent for a long moment.

"Possible."

"Well," Jepsum said. "In that case, I guess we better find out."

"Good idea," the voice said. "Update me on the progress."

The phone went dead. Jepsum stared at it.

He was all the way in now.

How it had come to this? People on the outside would be baffled if it ever came out. Why would a guy risk his job, his freedom, his very life? Why would he betray his country and the things he claimed to believe in?

For the money? No. Money was nice, but Jepsum had never wanted for anything, not in his entire life.

For the ego? For the excitement?

For the camaraderie? Definitely not that. He didn't even like these people.

If he was honest with himself, it was because at first, it made him feel like he was finally on the inside. He had been on the outside his entire life, trying hard to fit in, trying hard to be as good as other people, working his butt off to achieve things.

A lot of people didn't have to try—it all just came to them. But not Jepsum. He was constantly spinning his wheels, getting somewhere, yes, but not nearly as fast as the others. Tall people, good-looking people, people from rich families. It was like they knew something he didn't know. They just showed up and it all happened for them.

When this started, it had seemed like he knew something they didn't know.

Of course, it was an illusion. The Russians played him for a fool, and now it was too late to stop. There was no way out. The only way was forward. At this point, the Russians had so much compromising material on him—they called it *kompromat*—they could pull the plug on his entire life at any moment they chose.

Jepsum walked back to the West Wing main entrance, went through security, and walked straight to the Oval Office. The door was open. The Secret Service men at the door let him in without bothering to check him. They knew him well enough.

President Clement Dixon was in the sitting area with the Vice President. A handful of aides and assistants orbited nearby. Dixon looked old and unkempt. He had a bushy mustache and untamed white hair that looked like a stormy sea. He reminded Jepsum of a cartoon version of Mark Twain.

But his eyes were sharp and aware.

"Hello, Jepsum," he said. "What can we do for you?"

He remembered my name this time.

God. If Jepsum had any future to speak of, that would be a beautiful thing. This new President had already remembered his name. That meant Jepsum was making himself useful. The things he said were worth hearing.

Well, he had no future, so it didn't matter. His career, his freedom, his escapade as a double agent, possibly his very life—the clock was winding down on all of it. So he might as well forget about the future, and throw caution to the winds.

Jepsum's grandmother used to have a saying:

In for a penny, in for a pound.

"Sir, Mr. President, I'm sorry to bother you. But as I think you might be aware, during the raid…the rescue attempt…on the Martin Frobisher oil rig, the FBI Special Response Team confiscated a laptop used by the terrorists. I don't believe anyone outside of the Special Response Team has seen the contents of that laptop. Not the CIA, not the NSA, not us, and maybe not even the FBI proper. Frankly, my office has made three requests through channels to inspect the laptop, and we've been stonewalled so far. I suspect the contents might be important, though I can't say that for sure. I'm a little concerned that this late in the game..."

Dixon held up his hand in a STOP gesture.

Jepsum stopped speaking immediately.

Dixon looked at the small crowd of people.

"Get Jepsum the laptop, somebody. Please? Even if we need to seize it from our own people. No more requests. We've asked for it, and they've dragged their feet. So just go in and take it. Now. Tonight. While we're waiting for the Pentagon to pull their heads from their collective fundaments, maybe we can come up with some answers around here ourselves."

Instantly, two aides moved to the corner of the room and were on their phones.

Dixon looked at Jepsum and smiled. "Satisfied, Jepsum?"

Jepsum returned the smile.

"Very much so, sir. Thank you."

CHAPTER TWENTY EIGHT

8:01 p.m. Eastern Daylight Time (4:01 a.m. Moscow Daylight Time)
Headquarters of the Special Response Team
McLean, Virginia

"Yes, sweetheart," Don Morris said. "Yep. Got it."

Don sat behind the wide expanse of his desk, talking with his wife, Margaret. His blue dress shirt was open at the collar, and his sleeves were rolled to three-quarters length on his forearms. He was leaning back, one hand on the desk, scribbling the items from his wife's "honey-do" list on a small notepad.

Nearly touching the notepad was the Serbian laptop Stone had brought back from the Alaska operation. It was closed. Mark Swann thought he had obtained everything from it that he was going to get. Now came the decision about what to do with the infernal thing. NSA had requested it, CIA had requested it, and some kid from the White House had called about it three times. Don was toying with the idea of destroying it, and claiming that it had never been worth a damn to begin with.

That laptop had sent Stone and Newsam to Moscow. Stone was supposed to be suspended, pending an investigation. If the bureaucrats and desk jockeys found out about the little mission he was currently...

"Don, are you listening?"

"Of course I am."

He smiled, putting the computer out of his mind, and tuning back in to Margaret. They'd been together over thirty years now, and she'd put up with a lot of his shenanigans over the years— the long deployments, the classified operations where he basically disappeared for periods of time, the combat missions, the night drops into hostile territory, the early mornings and the late nights, along with the boys-will-be-boys dalliances that she might not know about, but probably suspected.

She was a good woman, a great partner, and the love of his life. The least he could do is pick up some groceries on his way home.

"I love you, too," he said and hung up the phone.

Trudy Wellington stood there in the doorway to his office. Her big eyes stared at Don. Trudy should be a poker player on the professional tour. Few people were harder to read. If she had thoughts about the conversation Don was just having with his wife, those thoughts weren't apparent on her face.

She glanced down at the notebook in her hand, all business. Don wanted to go to her then, take her beautiful face in his hands, and talk to her, and tell her everything. But this was the office, and some things were not appropriate here.

He sighed. Growing old was a funny thing, and not in a good way. He still felt like a young man. Hell, he felt like a bull in a field. Even so, Trudy was younger than both of his daughters. It was a melancholy thought. She had her life ahead of her, and he …

… did not.

"Don," she said. "Stone and Newsam are on the State Department plane in Moscow. They are safe and sound, uninjured, a little tired, but none the worse for wear. There don't seem to be any red flags about their presence, and the plane is scheduled for takeoff in the next few minutes."

He nodded. "Okay. Good. Did they get anything?"

"They have a computer hard drive with them. Luke isn't saying much about where it came from. Swann thinks he wants to get off the ground and out of Russian airspace before he reveals anything. There's a tech guy on the plane who's going to break the encryption, copy the whole thing to another computer, and send it here during the flight."

Don raised a hand. "That's fine, but as soon as he's done, we want the hard drive back, and we want the computer he used to transmit the information. Whatever Stone has, if it's important, we don't want every Tom, Dick, and Harry making copies of it. Make sure people know that. That comes straight from me. All right?"

Trudy nodded. "Okay. I'll do that. Now the flight is going to Athens. If we're keeping up the fiction that Luke and Ed are music producers as long as possible, then we need to make it look real. So I've booked them both suites at the ..."

Suddenly Swann was standing behind Trudy. He was easily a foot taller than her. He was scrawny in his black t-shirt, yellow aviator glasses, and hair pulled back into a ponytail. He didn't even look real.

"We've got a problem," he said.

Don raised his hands. "What?"

"We're being raided."

Don's shoulders slumped. "Raided? Who's raiding us?"

"The FBI."

"Son, *we are* the FBI."

Swann shrugged. "Tell that to *them*. In the meantime, I have some things to take care of." A second later, he had disappeared down the hall.

For a moment, Don and Trudy were alone again. Their eyes met.

"Lose your cell phone for the time being," he said in a low voice. "If anyone asks, you're not sure where you left it. Then break it into pieces and dump it. Down the toilet, into the river, anywhere. If no one asks, fine. Keep it. But we need to think about all these text messages going forward."

She nodded. She looked like she was about to say something.

A man tall man appeared behind her. Unlike Swann, this one had short hair and the generic, chiseled, clean-shaven face of a federal agent. He wore a suit. His hair was dark and short, and swept back from his forehead. His eyes were hard, like the eyes of a man on a hunt.

"Excuse me," he said to Trudy.

Behind him, another man just like him appeared.

Don looked at Trudy again. "Ms. Wellington, if you'll give me a moment with these gentlemen."

Trudy nodded. "Of course." Then she was gone like Swann before her.

Don looked at the men.

"Director Morris?"

Don rubbed his face. He nearly laughed. "Yeah."

He had seen combat, or been on clandestine black operations, in Africa, Asia, the Middle East, the Caribbean, Central America, and Eastern Europe. He had parachuted blind into the central African jungle under cover of darkness and landed smack in the Congo River. He had ridden horseback into battle with Afghan tribesmen, and had the horse shot out from under him. He once saw a jihadi running with an AK-47, lose a sandal, trip over his own two feet, and somehow manage to shoot himself under the jaw, blowing his own brains out the top of his head. Don had seen a lot of circle jerks in his time, but this one surely took the cake.

"How can I help you fellows?"

Both men already had their badges out. Behind them more G-men went by in the hallway.

"Sir, I'm Agent Randolph from Bureau headquarters."

"Sir, I'm Agent Garrett with the Secret Service."

Don shrugged. "Terrific. And as I guess you know, I'm Don Morris of the Special Response Team. Now that we've made our introductions..."

"Sir," Agent Randolph said, "we're here to acquire a laptop computer that Agent Stone confiscated from the Serbians during your recent Alaska operation. We understand that the White House intelligence office has repeatedly requested..."

Don gestured at the laptop. He supposed he wouldn't be destroying it after all.

"It's right there. You can have it. I was about to have it couriered up to the White House before I left for the night."

"This?" the agent said. He touched the laptop. It was a bit of an unsightly thing, that computer. Bulky, battered, gray in color. It looked like it had been to hell and back. Everything about it screamed Iron Curtain. It was nothing like the pretty, fragile, streamlined little slivers of plastic they kept around the office here.

Don nodded. "Yeah. Take it."

"Sir," the agent said. "You should know that we're mandated to collect any other technology, weaponry, or evidence that your team seized or amassed during that raid. We also need any correspondence related to the mission, including emails, voicemails, text messages, memos or other printed material. And we need an account of any further plans or actions your team has either developed or carried out as a result of…"

Don shook his head. "Take the laptop, son. That's all you're getting from us. That's all we have."

This was not good. Someone had gotten wind of… something. Now was not the time for Don to rack his brains, looking for the leak. It could be anywhere.

It could be the fact that Stone and Newsam had just boarded a State Department plane. It could be they had stepped on some toes over in Russia, and it had gotten back to the White House. It could be Big Daddy Bill Cronin was being surveilled, and someone saw him with Stone and Newsam in Rome. It could be Big Bill turned them in himself, for his own reasons. There were any number of possibilities here.

"I'm sorry to hear you say that," Agent Randolph said. "In that case, it looks like we're going to be here awhile."

Chapter Twenty Nine

7:05 a.m. Moscow Daylight Time (11:05 p.m. Eastern Daylight Time)
The "Aquarium"
Headquarters of the Main Intelligence Directorate (GRU)
Khodynka Airfield
Moscow, Russia

"Tell me everything," Marmilov said. "Leave nothing out."

He sat at his desk in a windowless basement office, smoking his first cigarette of the morning. The ceramic ashtray was in its customary place on the green steel desk in front of him. It was clean and empty, waiting to receive its first dead soldier. His first cup of coffee (with two shots of whiskey this morning) was also on the desk.

Marmilov was tired. It should be a triumphant morning, a heroic morning, but it did not feel that way. Putin's location had been pinpointed to his Black Sea dacha, yes, and he was there with his wife and a handful of advisors, in seclusion and isolation.

Perhaps he was plotting his next political move, and his return to the Kremlin. Perhaps he was plotting to flee the country—he could be in Turkey by helicopter in thirty minutes. But it didn't matter what Putin was doing at this moment. Marmilov would move against him—maybe with an indictment, maybe with a bullet—as soon as it made sense to do so.

But there were more pressing matters to worry about.

The young man stood in front of Marmilov, his back straight, his thick legs planted, his chin high, his hands folded in front of him. He wore another cheap suit, but he could be at parade rest on a military proving ground.

"Yes, sir. Is it wise to speak here?"

Marmilov's office was soundproof. It was swept for listening devices every other day. There were better times and places to speak, but those were not available at this moment.

Marmilov nodded. "Speak."

"There is unfortunate news," the young man said.

Marmilov waited, and said nothing.

"The engineer has not been found. His office was entered last night, his computer was broken open, and the hard drive was stolen."

"How was his office entered?" Marmilov said. The question alone gave him a sinking feeling.

"Two men entered the Breadbox through a side entrance using the engineer's digital key card. Security cameras at the Breadbox captured them on the third floor of the building, trying to enter the office with no success. One of them was wearing the engineer's signature long coat and hat. They must not have known that the engineer's office door required a code be entered from his telephone in addition to the use of the card. The night watchman on duty noticed the men on video, and went to investigate. They subdued him and used his access card to enter the office."

"The night watchman's card does not require a telephone code?" Marmilov said.

"In case of emergencies, the watchman's card overrides all other programming, sir. Of course."

Marmilov nodded. "Of course."

He paused. He took a deep drag of his cigarette. He had enjoyed Chevsky, to be honest. Chevsky was an intelligent young man, hardworking, ambitious. He had a quirky and independent sense of personal style. He was a bit daring and courageous. At times, Marmilov had even entertained the notion that he and Chevsky were in a mentoring relationship.

"We are assuming the engineer is dead?"

The young man before him nodded. "I think we are, sir."

"Yes, I suppose," Marmilov said.

People died. It was that simple. In this line of work, they died all the time. The missing hard drive was very problematic, though. If Chevsky was going to die anyway, he should have given his life to protect the information entrusted to him.

Worst of all, Chevsky was Marmilov's primary contact with the project. Now that link was broken. For many reasons, Marmilov preferred not to communicate with the participants directly. He was going to have to find a replacement for Chevsky, and right away.

"Was the night watchman in on it?" Marmilov said.

"He was questioned thoroughly. He denies knowing anything. The video footage suggests that he was pistol-whipped severely by one of the intruders. They bound him hand and foot with electrical tape. Medical tests indicate a concussion."

Marmilov shrugged. "Beatings don't mean anything. Keep him for another twenty-four hours and really press him."

"Yes, sir."

"What else?" Marmilov said.

"The TV producer is still missing, and now presumed dead."

Marmilov nodded. "Of course."

"We have been in touch with our friend in America," the young man said.

Marmilov didn't like where any of this was going. But he supposed the disappearances of Zelazny and Chevsky, and the theft of the hard drive, could only have been leading to one place.

"And?"

"He was able to seize the laptop computer that was taken during the Serbian raid. His technical experts have analyzed the contents and concluded that the video shot during the raid was uploaded to an anonymous satellite, then forwarded to a private media company based in Moscow. The contact person associated with that company was a man named Leonard Zelazny. It is likely that the FBI Special Response Team, the agency which originally confiscated the laptop, was able to determine these things on their own, but did not share the information with their superiors in the FBI or at the White House."

Marmilov had an odd sensation—something that would not normally occur to him. He felt that he wanted to place his head on the desk and close his eyes.

"Likely because they planned to send covert operatives here?" he said.

The young man nodded. "Yes, sir. And they didn't want their mission compromised by potential leaks at other agencies."

The sand had shifted under Marmilov's feet. It had happened with little or no warning. The Americans now knew, beyond any shadow of a doubt, that the Serbian attack originated in Russia. They knew the name Leonard Zelazny. They sent enforcers here, to Moscow, to question him. At the very least, Zelazny gave them the name Tomasz Chevsky. Chevsky gave them the clothes off his back, and access to his office. He gave them the hard drive to his computer. Did Chevsky, or Zelazny, also give them the name Oleg Marmilov? He had to assume they did.

This placed him in an awkward position.

"Do we know who they are?" he said.

The man shook his head. "We don't know for sure. But our intelligence suggests that the Special Response Team is the same agency responsible for the rampage outside Sochi some months ago, when an American submarine crew was rescued, and war between Russian and America was nearly instigated. The video footage at the Breadbox appears to show a very large black man and a tall white man. Both of these men can be seen during the last moments of the video taken at the oil rig. Both of these men are thought to have been present at the Sochi operation."

"Get me the dossiers on these men," Marmilov said.

The man nodded. "Of course."

Marmilov's mind began to leap forward, examining the moves ahead. He'd been a fair chess player in his youth. He'd lost the flavor of it when he first joined the military, but he had never lost its lessons.

"When they analyze the contents of the hard drive, they will learn of the Beirut project," he said. "So they will go to Beirut."

"Yes, sir."

Marmilov looked at the young man. He recalled how he had given this man the order to kill the oil workers. He had hesitated for a few seconds, and then had done exactly what he was told.

"With Chevsky gone," Marmilov said, "I need someone who can take over his duties. Specifically, I need someone to immediately handle the details of the Beirut project, at least in the short term. You seem a capable man. Tell me…"

"Babayev, sir. Victor."

"Yes, Babayev. Tell me, do you have any experience in the sciences?"

"I attended two years of technical school, sir, before I joined the military."

"And what was your field?"

"I studied electrical and chemical engineering, sir. Primarily chain reactions, explosions, detonators, things of that nature. My ambition was to be soldier, and I thought it would…"

"You're hired," Marmilov said.

The young man Babayev smiled. "Thank you, sir."

Marmilov shrugged. "Of course. You've earned it. Now, your first task is to eliminate everyone associated with the Beirut project. Everyone currently in that facility. To a man."

"Sir?"

It must seem a harsh decision to a person as young as this. But sometimes harsh decisions were the only ones available.

"You heard me."

The man nodded. "Yes, sir."

"If the Americans approach the project—*when* they approach it—allow them to enter unmolested. Allow them all the way inside. Then don't let them out."

Marmilov was reminded of the Old Testament story of the great warrior Samson.

"When our enemies enter the temple, we will pull it down on top of them."

The man nodded again, and turned to leave. "Of course, sir. As you command."

As you command.

It was exactly the correct phrasing.

CHAPTER THIRTY

8:35 a.m. Eastern European Daylight Time (1:35 a.m. Eastern Daylight Time)
The Coral Hotel
Palaio Faliro Municipality
Athens, Greece

The phone was ringing.
Luke opened his eyes.
It was the room phone, not his personal cell or satellite phone. He was half asleep, still in the middle of a dream that was fading away fast. It took him a moment to remember he had left both of his phones with Big Daddy in Rome.

His first thought was of Becca. Maybe she was calling him here. No. That wasn't possible. She didn't even know where he was.

And it wasn't going to be possible to call her. For the time being, he had to give up that idea. It was too dangerous—what if the house was bugged, or her cell phone was? A call could let someone know where he was, and what he planned to do. A simple call home could compromise everything.

But all that said, the phone was still ringing.

It was on the night table to his left. A big blue button on the phone flashed, and the phone itself made an obnoxious buzzing sound. He stared at it. He didn't want to pick it up. He let it ring until it stopped.

It was probably just the front desk, asking him if he wanted room service, or his sheets turned down, or asking whether he'd like to apply for the rewards card.

Luke was on a big king bed. He looked across the room. There were floor to ceiling windows over there, giving him a wide open, room-width view of a beautiful green and blue sea. He hadn't bothered to pull the curtains before going to sleep this morning. He didn't even remember there being curtains. That's how tired he had been.

A sliding glass door opened onto a balcony outside the windows.

Luke thought back to the five-star hotel in Moscow, with its views of Red Square and Saint Basil's Cathedral. He was starting to get used to this whole music mogul gig.

The phone started ringing again.

He picked it up this time.

"Rob Simmons," he said, his voice still thick with sleep.

"Mr. Simmons," the voice said. "It's Don Wellington."

Luke shook his head. Swann.

Who else would call him at…was it 1:30 in the morning where Swann was? Luke thought yes. The guy never stopped. It felt like Luke had just closed his eyes a few moments ago.

"Wellington, hi."

"How are the accommodations?" Swann said.

"Great. But listen I'm kind of tired, so let's just dispense with the small talk, okay?"

Swann paused. You never could tell if you were offending him or not. Usually, he seemed to have skin as thick as a special operator's. But sometimes…

"Of course. I just wanted to let you know that we looked at the information you sent. There is a great deal for us to talk about. But given contractual obligations, non-disclosure clauses, and the like…"

Luke got it. He was holding a hotel room phone in his hand—hardly encrypted communications.

"This probably isn't the best venue," he said.

"Exactly."

"What do you recommend?" Luke said.

"I will arrange a venue for later today. What you should know right now is that we see more travel in your future."

Terrific. At the moment, the travel he was most looking forward to was back to the United States. Even if Becca wouldn't have him back, she hadn't tried to kick him out of the cabin yet.

"Is it going to be hot, where I'm going?" he said.

"Unfortunately, it seems like it's going to be very hot. Historically, it's been one of the hotter places that we know of."

Of course it was going to be hot. What else would it be?

"Are you in your office right now?" Luke said. "It seems to me it must be late at night over there."

"Uh...the office is closed until further notice," Swann said. "There's been some trouble with the parent company."

Swann was mixing his metaphors. Didn't he used to work for the State Department? Now there was trouble with the parent company. Either way, that didn't sound good.

"This is likely to be a solo project," Swann said.

Luke didn't speak for a long moment. He and Ed had just gone on a solo project, and it had gone okay, but he didn't want to start making a habit of it.

"How do you suggest I..."

"Well, Mr. Simmons...Rob...can I call you Rob?"

Luke nearly laughed. "Call me whatever you like."

"I've sent a courier to you with some details of the project. I put them together with uh...Mr. Leishman and Ms...."

Luke was still smiling. Where was Swann going to go with this now that he had appropriated Trudy's last name for himself?

"...Ms. Morris. You should get a knock on your door any moment. Please read the notes over thoroughly. I think the whole package will give you a sense of what we're looking at. When you're done, please commit them to memory and observe all local recycling laws when discarding them."

Read and Destroy.

"Got it," Luke said. "Anything else?"

"Yes," Swann said. "One more thing. There's a soloist I think you should consider bringing in. The guy is practically a virtuoso. You may know who I'm talking about."

Luke nodded. "I think I do."

"I don't think he'll come on board this project unless he speaks with you personally. He's got one of these creative temperaments. The last time anyone on this end invited him to play, he declined."

"Okay," Luke said. "But I don't have my contact book with me. I seem to have forgotten…"

"Oh, his contact information is in the package I've sent you."

"Great. So I'll look forward to…"

A soft knock came at the hotel room door.

"Don?" Luke said. "I think the courier is here now."

"Good," Swann said. "In that case, I'll leave you to it. Happy reading."

Luke got up and padded across the deep pile carpet to the door. He checked the peephole, but didn't see anyone out there.

He put his ear to the door. Somewhere in the hotel, far away, there was a faint rumble of machinery. Other than that, there was no sound.

Luke shrugged. He'd given Chevsky's gun to Albert Strela before leaving Russia. Not because they wouldn't let him on the State Department plane with it—because it was clearly not a service weapon and he didn't want to have to explain where he got it.

Luke was unarmed. If someone out there wanted trouble, they were going to face Luke's bare hands.

He opened the door and a thick manila envelope fell into the room. It had been standing tall and leaning against the door.

Luke looked up and down the long hall. There was no one here.

He picked up the envelope and brought it inside.

The envelope gave Luke more questions than answers.

He sat out on his balcony with a cup of coffee from the room coffee maker. The view was stunning, facing southwest into the Saronic Gulf, with the city of Athens proper spread out to the north, on his right.

This early in the morning, the sun was still behind the hotel. From here, Luke could see a sweep of golden beaches and calm sea. Ferry and tanker traffic passed by out in the gulf, coming and going from the large commercial port facilities in Athens. Far in the distance, Luke thought he could make out a white blur that might be the island of Aegina.

The envelope had contained a small stack of printouts. It had also contained a very small handheld satellite phone, with two numbers preprogrammed into it. One of the numbers said WELLINGTON. The other said VIRTUOSO.

Wellington was Swann, of course. And if Luke understood their conversation correctly, Virtuoso was Murphy.

A cursory look at the documents indicated they were going to need Murphy, or someone just like him.

There was a map of a neighborhood in south Beirut, Lebanon. A small block of text made it clear that the neighborhood had been controlled by Hezbollah militants since the Israelis pulled out of the city in the year 2000.

A spot was marked on the map, which appeared to be at the top of a hill overlooking the city and the waterfront. Superimposed aerial photos showed it was a mosque. The words *al-Khattab Mosque* appeared in a box near the mosque itself. The mosque was a small, seemingly old, sand-colored building with a silver dome and a single blue minaret.

Here was a page with a list of specs that Swann or Ed Newsam would understand better than Luke. The numbers were like a blur to Luke. He stared at them for a moment, until he noticed a single word at the top of the column: *Yield.*

Yield was a word Luke associated with explosives, in equivalent units of TNT. When people like Swann or Trudy or Ed mentioned yield, they were most often talking about nuclear weapons.

Here was a line drawing of what certainly looked like a missile or a bomb. It was bullet shaped, with no obvious means of propulsion at either end. A line cut across it vertically—along the line, it said 10.2 meters. To Luke, that drawing suggested that it was a bomb, and it was more than 30 feet long. Another line was drawn across the bomb. Along this line, it said, 2.5 meters. That meant it was about 8 or 10 feet wide.

If it really was a bomb, it was a big one.

Luke turned to the last couple of pages. Here was a map of the Arctic Circle. A red spot was marked on it, way out on the ice of the Arctic Ocean, hundreds of miles from land. Aerial imagery showed an endless field of white, disappearing into the vast distance. A tighter shot seemed to show a small encampment on the ice, maybe a few temporary structures and paths between them. A little bit away from the camp was a long scratch, which could be a landing strip.

An even tighter shot showed a large grayish dome against all the white. A couple of all-terrain vehicles were parked outside of it. The vehicles gave a sense of the size of the dome—it was big, like a tennis bubble with a dozen courts inside of it.

What did all this mean?

Were the Russians planning to position some sort of military base or missile battery in the middle of the Arctic Ocean? Were they building a weapons lab out there? Were they hoping to be able to launch nukes from the North Pole? Why would they do that, when everyone seemed to agree that the Arctic was melting?

Heck, it wasn't very Christmasy, was it? Santa Claus lived at the North Pole.

Luke picked up the satellite phone. It was bright blue and friendly-looking. He looked at the number for VIRTUOSO.

He felt odd calling Murphy, truth be told. Big Daddy had inserted the smallest germ of doubt in Luke's mind. Murphy had gotten a few days off and had immediately gone to the Caribbean. He did it under an assumed identity.

Luke had to admit that every time he said goodbye to Murphy, it seemed like it was for the last time. Murphy was not on salary. He was a consultant, paid by the day. He was a tremendous asset on missions. Murphy was hell in a firefight. Few were better than he was. But he was not a company man. There were some days—days when it would mean just sitting around the office—when he didn't come in at all.

To put a phrase on it, Murphy was marginally attached. At best. He seemed to have one foot out the door.

Well, if Murphy was going to come in on this job, Luke had better call him now. He glanced at his watch. Just after ten a.m. here in Greece. That suggested wherever Murphy was, it was probably late at night.

He hesitated. Luke couldn't call his own wife, just to see how she and his son were doing, but he could call Murphy. There was something not quite right about that.

He looked at the word VIRTUOSO again.

He pressed the CALL button.

CHAPTER THIRTY ONE

3:10 a.m. Eastern Daylight Time (10:10 a.m. Eastern European Daylight Time)
Bahia Vista Casino Hotel
Nassau
The Bahamas

This life wasn't real.

It couldn't be.

Kevin Murphy stood at the bar inside his hotel suite, making himself a gin and tonic, on the rocks, with lime. He was barefoot, in jeans, and wearing a NYPD T-shirt, dark blue with white lettering. The gin and tonic struck him as a girly drink, but he didn't care. He was in the mood for one, so he was going to make one.

The hotel suite in question wasn't a suite at all—it was a stadium. Two stories high, curved outward, with at least twenty giant windows overlooking the ocean. One entire wall was a fish tank, backlit and full of colorful exotic fish. There were a couple of small sharks in there, reef sharks, maybe four feet long.

A staircase led to a bedroom that seemed to float in outer space. Right now, a sexy young blonde named Stacey was asleep in that bed, worn out after a night that had done nothing but get Murphy's motor running even harder.

He had showed up here in the early afternoon with a single suitcase, and a Nike gym bag stuffed with $200,000 in cash. He had them count the money and put it in the hotel vault. Instantly, they knew what he was here for. A manager came out in a suit, very friendly, and shook his hand.

Suddenly, he had this … suite. Complimentary.

He ate lunch and had some drinks in one of the hotel restaurants—signed it to the free room. In the casino world, they called it a "comp."

He was a player, and the whole stay was comped.

Soon he was in the casino. He played Texas Hold'em for a while. Drank some more—the girl kept bringing them. The cards were ice cold, and he must have dropped twenty grand before dinnertime. That's okay, he was just getting warmed up.

Stacey came out of nowhere and inserted herself onto his arm. She looked great—big hair, tight sequined dress, a lot of body packed inside that thing, dressed up for the town in the middle of the afternoon. Blue eyes. Perky nose. She smelled nice, too. She smiled and laughed a lot—she had perfect teeth.

"How much do you cost?" he said to her at one point.

She leaned in seductively, close to his ear. "I'm a comp."

He looked at her. Her eyes were on fire. His game was in free fall.

"My job is to make sure you keep losing," she said, putting the facts of the matter right out there.

Murphy laughed. "Honey, you have the easiest job in the world. All I ever do is lose."

They had dinner together. Comped. It was fun. They ordered four entrees and six desserts. They sampled everything. Murphy was roaring drunk by then, not that anyone could tell. One thing about being Irish—you seem the same, drunk or sober. No one can see the difference.

They caught a show. Cirque du Soleil. Comped. Murphy couldn't follow the story, if there was one, but he liked watching people in purple and yellow skinsuits flying through the air. After a while, he glanced at Stacey. Her eyes had glazed over. She looked like a clothing store mannequin. She was bored—of course she was. She worked here. She had probably seen the show thirty times.

They left halfway through. Went back to the casino. Roulette now. He was too drunk to focus on cards. He dropped … a lot.

They came here to the room. Did they do the deed? You bet they did.

Comped.

Now she was sleeping, and he was here at the bar, making a drink. The suite was mostly dark. Most of the light came from the fish tank. "Kind of Blue" by Miles Davis played low through the speaker system everywhere.

Murphy had sobered up quite a bit. He was thinking back through the day and night, trying to calculate … make a rough estimate … of the money he had lost. He thought it was probably between $50,000 and $60,000.

That really was a lot.

But come to think of it, he had put one last $10,000 chip on black right before he and Stacey walked out of the casino and came upstairs. It was a grandstand play, designed to please the crowd around the table. Murphy hated when he did stuff like that.

The silver ball came down, bounced around, everybody holding their breath … and landed … on red. Stacey was doing her job, all right.

And Murphy's number was closer to $70,000 than $60,000.

He sighed and took a sip of his drink. He'd been here just about fourteen hours so far.

"Good Lord," he said. "I need to slow down."

His cell phone started ringing.

The ringer was off, but the phone itself was set to vibrate. It was perched on a granite countertop over in the kitchen.

That kitchen was another thing. It was a wide open TV show, restaurant-style kitchen, with islands for cooking and food prep, and heavy pots hanging down from overhead. A small catering staff could come in there and prepare dinner for fifteen people.

The phone made that buzzing sound phones made when they vibrated.

Murphy walked over and looked down at it. He had no idea who would be calling him now. It was after three in the morning. He didn't recognize the number. He picked it up anyway.

Maybe it was good luck calling.

"Hello?"

He kept his voice low. He didn't want to wake Stacey.

"Murph?"

"Yeah."

The voice was familiar, but Murphy's mind was a little slow right now.

"Stone," the voice said.

Of course. Murphy smiled and shook his head. He had been trying to get as far from this guy as possible. The man was a menace. So Murphy had run away. And he had run right into his own arms, and the arms of his apparent demons. He realized now that he could run to the other side of the world, and the only person he would find there was . . . himself.

It was hard to say who the bigger menace was.

Stone was just going to get Murphy killed.

"What's up?" Murphy said.

There was a delay before Stone answered. It occurred to Murphy that it was because Stone had called on a satellite phone—the signal had to beam up into low-Earth orbit, around the world, and back again.

"I need you, buddy," Stone said. "I've got some things to do, and I'm pretty sure they're not going to get done without you."

"Where are you?" Murphy said.

"I couldn't say. But if you call some friends of ours, they'll buy you a ticket."

Murphy shook his head.

"Not good enough, my friend. If I'm going to die, I at least need to know where it's going to happen."

The pause was longer this time. Stone didn't want to reveal much over the phone. Murphy understood that. But Stone owed him something. Murphy was gone. He had already embarked on his new life, such as it was. Stone probably understood that intuitively. That's why he hadn't asked Murphy how his days off were going. Days off were a thing of the past.

If Stone wanted to pull Murphy back in, he was going to have to...

"Lebanon," Stone said.

Murphy smiled, and this time the grin was nearly ear to ear. Where else?

Everybody went to Lebanon to die. The place was a black hole that sucked random lives into its event horizon—US Marines, religious fanatics of all stripes, Syrian spies, college professors, newspaper reporters, Palestinian refugees, young Israeli foot soldiers—Lebanon did not discriminate.

Murphy looked around the epic hotel suite. It seemed garish all of a sudden, like something out of a nightmare.

He had dreamed all this—the money, the hotel, the gambling, the girl. None of it could be real. Murphy pictured himself staying here another night. He would lose another $70,000 easy, maybe another $100,000. He would have the hotel send him up another girl. Oh, he would keep Stacey on—she was doing a good job. But if they were going to bleed him dry, he might as well enjoy a Stacey #2.

Before it was over, he'd probably get irritated at himself, or the situation, and throw a chair through the fish tank. Poor fish. He wouldn't wish that on them.

With the shattered fish tank figured in, and the flooded carpet, and all the exotic fish flopping around on the floor gasping their last breaths, he'd go well over $200,000. His gym bag would be empty, and as he walked out the door the friendly hotel manager from yesterday would hand him a bill.

Frankly, desperate gunfights in Lebanon against chanting Islamic militiamen sounded like a much better deal.

None of this even took into account the fact that there was no running away from the United States government. Murphy had been kidding himself the whole time, and deep down, he was well aware of that. Someone—the CIA, the FBI proper, the NSA, the

DIA—knew where he was. They knew what he was doing. They knew everything. They always did.

But maybe Stone didn't know these things. Maybe if Murphy was on the team, the team would protect its own.

He sighed.

Wouldn't it be nice if he and Stacey were boyfriend and girlfriend, and they could take the day off from the casino, and just have a nice breakfast, and go to the beach? Maybe do a little snorkeling. Hire a dive charter tomorrow.

He shook his head. Stacey came with the casino. The suite came with the casino. He had come here as a player. If he stayed, he was locked in. You don't switch from this suite *to a room*. And you sure don't bring Stacey with you.

"Lebanon, huh?"

"Greece first," Stone said. "We need to chat about the trip a little."

Murphy stared around at the massive suite for a long moment.

"Okay," he said. "I'm on my way."

CHAPTER THIRTY TWO

9:55 p.m. Eastern European Daylight Time (2:55 p.m. Eastern Daylight Time)
A Safe House
Makrygianni District
Athens, Greece

"How you doing, Murph?" Luke said. "Thanks for coming out."

Murphy had just walked in the door of the apartment. The instant he did, Big Daddy had handed him a can of beer from the refrigerator.

Murphy cracked it open and took a slug. "Wouldn't miss it."

They were in a yellow, five-story walkup building on a narrow, leafy, tree-lined street in the Makrygianni District, just south of the Acropolis. There was a porch off the kitchen, and the land behind the building dropped away, giving a view of the city spread out to the north and west.

In the middle distance, the Acropolis was lit up in the night. The Parthenon was clearly visible from here, surrounded by construction scaffolding. Closer still were the ruins of the Theatre of Dionysus amphitheater. According to their host, the famous European tour guide Big Daddy Cronin, it was thought to be the oldest surviving theatre in the history of Western civilization.

"What is this place?" Murphy said, sipping the beer. Murphy had just flown across the Western hemisphere, but he looked none the worse for wear.

"It's an apartment I use sometimes," Bill Cronin said. Big Daddy himself had flown in from Rome for the occasion. He was a little bit sunburned. He wore a floral pattern shirt, khaki pants, and he carried a Glock nine-millimeter on his hip. He didn't look nearly as relaxed or well-rested as he had in Rome.

"It's a good place to talk," he said. "Between Mark Swann's satellite encryption and the sanctity of this apartment, we should be able to have a candid discussion."

Ed Newsam came in from the porch. It was almost time for the call. Ed was unusually quiet—he had been ever since he looked at the bomb specs in the materials Swann had sent Luke. Ed was drinking a beer—also not like him.

Ed had shaken his head when he saw the specs.

"That can't be right," was all he had said about them.

There was a satellite phone on the kitchen table. Big Daddy had plugged it into a black spider-like speakerphone device that sat next to it. A red light on the device came on and the device began to hum.

"Okay," Big Daddy said. "Here we go."

He tapped a button on the phone. There was a moment of open air.

"Hello?" a female voice said. Trudy Wellington.

"Hi, Trudy," Big Daddy said. "Who's there?"

"Well, I'm with Don Morris and Mark Swann," she said. Luke could hear the two men talking in the background. "Who's with you?"

"I've got Stone, Newsam, and Murphy," Big Daddy said. "Plus myself. Don, how do you want to do this?"

Don came on. "How's the security?"

Big Daddy shrugged. "This place is airtight. I control it, and my own people—people I trust—sweep it every couple of days. When I acquired the place, I had the walls stripped out and redone with soundproofing insulation throughout. I don't think the Agency even knows I have this place, so if they suddenly find out, I'll know who told them. Anyway, no worries on this end. How about you?"

Swann's deep, reedy voice came on. "We're at my apartment. I'm paranoid, and I sweep it almost constantly. We are in my little home office, and I soundproofed the walls myself. The encryption on this call is state-of-the-art. We are bouncing from black satellite to black satellite, all over the world. No one can trace us, no one can decrypt us. I'm sure of that."

Luke stared at the spider contraption on the table. He had trouble imagining the legendary Don Morris, a man with shoulders the size of Chicago, crouched in the little home office at Swann's apartment.

"Can I ask an obvious question?" he said.

"You don't even need to ask," Don said. "We're at Swann's because we're in the middle of a lockout. The first thing you guys need to know, at this moment, is the SRT is one hundred percent SNAFU. We were raided by the Bureau proper and the Secret Service last night. I was called on the carpet today at the situation room in the White House. They still haven't given me back the keys to the hotrod, and they're crawling all over headquarters like a hive of termites on a shit mound."

Luke sighed. "Is it me?"

"It's not just you, son. Don't take that on. They're angry that we held the Serbian laptop as long as we did. They're angry we traced the video signals to Russia and didn't tell anybody. And yes, they're angry we put together an infiltration, especially one that included … yeah, an agent under suspension. Okay, it is you."

"Great," Luke said.

"My point being that whatever we put together here is going to be just us, total secrecy, using whatever resources we can muster among ourselves, or with the help of very close associates. With that, I'll put Trudy on. Let her tell her tale, and then we'll figure out what to do about it."

Trudy came on.

"I'm going to assume no one on this call has prior knowledge of the events taking place, or the intel we've acquired. Sound okay?"

Everyone murmured their agreement.

"The documents you've all seen by now are the contents of the hard drive that Luke and Ed took when they were in Moscow. There were many more files on that drive at one time, but it appears they were deliberately corrupted and deleted. Swann?"

"Yeah," Swann said. "We can probably resurrect those files at some point, if we have a few people working on it, and we have access to the SRT offices. We could also farm the drive out to NSA, or DIA, or CIA, but I'm assuming we don't want to do that."

"Absolutely not," Don said. "Something is going on that I don't like. The White House and the FBI just landed on us with both feet. We are all the way on the outs, and being marginalized."

"In that case, what you see is what you're gonna get," Swann said.

Luke looked around the kitchen at Murphy, Ed, and Big Daddy. They were all drinking beer. That, combined with the things being said, gave Luke the urge to drink a beer. He went to the refrigerator, opened it, and pulled one out.

Big Daddy looked at him. "Good man."

He mouthed the words without saying them.

"So what we have is a mystery," Trudy said. "Luke and Ed, where did you say this hard drive came from?"

This was the part of these meetings that often frustrated Luke—bringing everybody up to speed and on the same page. But he saw the value in it.

Luke looked at Ed. Ed made a hand wave gesture: *The floor is yours.*

"The drive was on the computer of a man named Tomasz Chevsky. He was an engineer working for the Russian Academy of Sciences. But that was his cover story. He actually worked for a GRU spymaster named Oleg Marmilov, and was the go-between for Marmilov and the TV producer who doctored the video taken at the oil rig. Marmilov is operating some sort of clandestine project, but no one could or would say what it is. The oil rig attack was part of it."

"You said *was*," Don said. "Is Chevsky dead?"

"Yes."

"So what we have in front of us are three things," Trudy said. "The first is a mosque in Beirut. The second are drawings and what appear to be size and yield specs for an enormous nuclear weapon, though the true details of it are spotty, and there's no way to know if it really exists. The third is what appears to be a Russian military outpost on the ice near the North Pole, in a remote area of the Arctic Ocean often referred to as the *donut hole*."

She paused. "With me so far?"

People mumbled various versions of yes. Murphy gave her the Ranger *hoo-ah*.

"The mosque is known as the Al-Khattab Mosque. It sits on a hillside above a residential neighborhood in south Beirut. It was built in 1890, and is in a serious state of disrepair. Shelling in that area during the Lebanese Civil War and the Israeli Occupation are thought to have undermined its structure. There was some talk of saving it, but it's been closed to the public since 1994, and nothing appears to have been done about it since then."

"Why would the Russians be interested in this mosque?" Ed Newsam said.

"It may be a safe and convenient cover for them," Trudy said. "The Israeli pullout five years ago was seen as a major victory for the Shiite terrorist group Hezbollah. South Beirut is a Hezbollah stronghold. Hezbollah's major sponsors are Syria and Iran, who are close allies with Russia, or if you prefer, Russian client states. If you ever want to find out who is really pulling Hezbollah's strings, you need to look to Moscow.

"Since 2000, Hezbollah has been consolidating its stranglehold on Beirut, and Lebanese society for that matter. Hezbollah's military wing is considered more powerful than the Lebanese military, by a lot. And the Hezbollah religious leadership is seen as more legitimate in many people's eyes than the elected politicians of Lebanon.

"This year in Lebanon has been the year of the car bomb, and the truck bomb. Former Lebanese Prime Minister Rafiq Hariri was assassinated by a massive truck bomb back in February, an attack that killed twenty-two people. Hariri was a prominent critic of Syria, and an opponent of Hezbollah. Since then, it's been a sort of open season. At least fourteen more car and trucks bombs have gone off, mostly in Beirut, but also in other parts of the country. The security situation in Beirut right now is bad. The Russians could be exploiting this to run a secret operation out of a condemned mosque."

"A little paint," Luke said. "A few boards and some nails."

"Sure," Trudy said. "It doesn't have to be anything fancy. You know how special ops people are. They don't really shop at Pier One Imports."

"But you do," Swann said.

"Keep it rolling, kids," Don said. "Every second of banter is a second wasted."

Don was irritated. Luke could hear it in his voice. His overseers had come in and taken his toys away. Luke felt that. He also recognized the respect he had for Don.

A lot of people would lie down in this situation. Don doubled down instead. His bosses didn't like him organizing clandestine missions? Okay, he would organize another one.

"That's most of what I have on the mosque," Trudy said. "Swann has pulled down satellite imagery of it, and there doesn't seem to have been any activity there in months. There is an old overgrown parking lot at the top of the hill, with a couple of junked cars sitting there. It looks like a perfect spot to touch down a helicopter, and if it were up to me, I'd suggest going in there and checking the place out. You guys are already in Greece, and Lebanon is just across from you. You could launch a chopper out of Cyprus, pop in, and pop right back out again."

"Pop in and pop out," Murphy said. "I like the ring of that. Unfortunately, it so rarely works that way in real life."

"Agreed," Trudy said. "And I'll leave that to the military minds here and the people who would actually have their skin in the game. Next up is the nuclear weapon."

"It's big," Ed Newsam said.

"If real, it would be the biggest nuclear weapon ever built, and probably ever conceived. We know that the Soviets detonated the largest weapon in a test during the fall of 1961. That one is often called the Tsar Bomba, a hydrogen bomb that was exploded in the air over a distant part of the Russian Arctic. It delivered a blast equivalent to just over fifty megatons of TNT, about thirty-five hundred times the size of the Hiroshima blast. The specs of the bomb in the drawing suggest a potential yield of nearly a hundred twenty megatons. My calculations suggest that if it were a ground burst, it would be enough to wipe out an area twice the size of Texas."

"Do you believe this thing exists?" Ed Newsam said.

Ed was a weapons expert. He seemed disturbed by the very idea of that bomb.

"I don't have enough information to form an opinion," Trudy said. "It's a drawing with some specs. There's no delivery system indicated. Is it a warhead that mounts atop a cruise missile? It seems too large for that, given current technology. Is it a bomb that drops out of an airplane? If so, then a bomber would have to be specifically built or retrofitted to carry it. Some of the giant cargo planes could carry it, but I doubt they could drop it, or get a safe distance away before it detonated.

"The truth is, any overheated nineteen-year-old physics student could dream up specs like the ones we're looking at. But could someone build it? Would a government have the will to do it, or set aside the funding? Or could someone—this Oleg Marmilov, for example—have the pull to make something like this in secret? I just can't say. But my experience in this business does suggest that if someone can find a way to do something, they will do it."

She paused.

"That's all I know."

"Next," Luke said. He took a long sip of his beer. He found himself impatient to get underway.

"There appears to be a small Russian base or outpost in the far Arctic. There's an airfield, a cluster of temporary buildings. There's also a dome of some kind. This post, if it still exists, is on the ice over wide-open ocean. As far as we know, the images we have of it are the only ones that exist. Swann?"

"Yeah," Swann said. "They've got some sort of clever jamming setup going on. The place is so small, blends in with its surroundings so well, and is so remote, that unless you knew where to look, you would never stumble across it."

"But you did know where to look," Murphy said.

"Exactly. So I commandeered a satellite going that way and tried to get a couple of snaps. As the satellite passed the area, there was a short burst of microwave interference, just enough that by the time the camera came back online, the chance to take the imagery was gone. I thought that was strange, but maybe it was just a coincidence. So I waited a couple of hours and tried again. Oops. Same thing happened. That's good enough to tell me they don't want anybody taking pictures. I didn't want to alert them to my presence, so I stopped trying."

"It's the kind of thing no one would ever notice," Trudy said.

"Right," Swann said. "Satellites are cataloguing the entire surface of the Earth, but they go down all the time, for one reason or another. Then they come back on. There are glitches. No one has any reason to look in that corner of the Arctic. It's a blank white canvas up there. Your mind fills the emptiness in by itself."

"Don?" Big Daddy said. "What are your thoughts?"

"I think Trudy's right," Don said. "If you boys are up for it, I think we go to Beirut first. It's close. We go in there tonight, before dawn, and see if we can scare up some clues. Maybe it'll explain everything. Maybe it won't explain anything. As a backup, we prepare to go to the Arctic."

Luke looked at Murphy. Murphy's eyes gave away nothing. He took a long slurp from his beer.

"I love the Arctic," he said. "I want to live there."

"Can you put together the resources for this?" Don said.

Big Daddy nodded at the spider. "I can get you some gear, a chopper, and a couple of crack pilots to put you on top of that mosque. If need be, I can get you a plane to the Arctic, and maybe even some guys to fall out of it."

"What's the Agency going to say about all this?" Don said. "Because I've got a problem here with information sharing."

"Describe it," Big Daddy said.

"As soon as Luke and Ed grabbed that hard drive, I found my offices full of G-men. They knew we had a Serbian laptop. That's okay. But they didn't just come for the laptop. They came for every-thing—all of our communications. To me, that stinks like a rot-ten fish. It smells like there's a mole somewhere, directing things behind the scenes. Is it a Russian mole? I don't know, but I don't like it. We need to have our ducks in a row before we talk to anyone about this. I hate to say it, but I suspect if we talk to our own people, the Russians will be tipped off. So we're trying to keep this under our hats, as much as we can."

"Well, you're in luck," Big Daddy said. "The CIA and I are not on speaking terms at this moment. I'm not even sure if I have a job anymore. The only resources I can offer are my own."

Luke smiled. "Big Daddy, you are a country all to yourself."

Big Daddy shook his head. "To be honest, it's a lonely feeling."

In the corner, Murphy tilted his head back, downed his entire beer, and then crushed the can in one hand. He didn't even seem to be listening to the conversation.

"I'm ready," he said.

CHAPTER THIRTY THREE

11:50 p.m. Moscow Daylight Time (3:50 p.m. Eastern Daylight Time)
Premier Suite
The Ritz-Carlton Moscow
Tverskaya Street
Moscow, Russia

Babayev was here again, standing at something close to attention.

His knock had been quiet, as all knocks must be, but tonight it didn't matter. Tamara was no longer here. Marmilov had sent her back to her agency. He had given up on her as hopeless case. Some of these young people were too far gone already. Marmilov could be of no further service to them.

Marmilov wore his brown robe, as always, and sat in the semi-darkness of the living room in his suite on the top floor of the Ritz-Carlton. He had been drinking since early evening, and was a bit drunk.

"So Babayev, give me the news," he said. "Leave nothing out, please."

"Everything was done to your specifications, sir," Babayev said. "The weapon reached its destination two days ago, and has been mounted in its proper place. We ordered the initiation sequence launched, and it was done as ordered. Immediately afterwards, everyone associated with the research and development phase of the project was eliminated."

Marmilov was enjoying the matter-of-factness of Babayev's delivery. Babayev was proving to be an exceptional liaison to the project. He had brought himself up to speed quickly, and he carried out orders with no hesitation. Given time, he might turn out to be as cold-blooded and ruthless as Marmilov himself."

"When was the initiation sequence launched?" Marmilov said.

"Just less than four hours ago, sir."

"Which means the weapon will detonate in eight hours from now?" Marmilov said.

Babayev nodded. "Yes. Give or take a few moments."

The scientists who had worked on the project insisted that the initiation include a twelve-hour countdown. Their reasons for this were several. It would give any personnel near the weapon ample time to leave the area. It would give anyone deploying the weapon ample time to change their mind and put a stop to it. It would give the Russian government time to anticipate and respond to the fallout from the project—this last was not a valid reason, since the Russian government knew nothing about the weapon.

Most of all, the twelve-hour mandatory delay protected against a mistaken or hasty deployment. It protected against the weapon being seized and deployed by rogue elements.

Marmilov sighed. He supposed the delay would give him time to prepare himself for the next steps. He could even sleep a bit, and wake refreshed and ready to tackle the unfolding crisis.

During the design phase, the delay was considered not to have a downside, since enemies were unlikely to know about the weapon, find it, and stop its detonation. That had proven false—enemies had probably discovered the existence of the weapon, and they might be able to reach the detonation site in time. But it was very, very unlikely. They didn't know if the weapon was real or not. They didn't know the launch sequence had been initiated.

"Tell me more," Marmilov said.

"Sir, I have deployed a squad of seasoned militiamen to protect the mosque in case there should be any attempt at infiltration. These men are religious fanatics. They do not fear death, and in fact welcome it. Should such an infiltration occur, the militiamen will allow the enemy to enter the mosque before attacking them and trapping them inside.

"A young mujahid has been selected for a martyrdom operation. With the opponents inside the mosque and pinned down, he will drive a truck laden with explosives to the mosque site, and detonate. This will take down the mosque itself, and may collapse the underground levels, obscuring any evidence of activity that has taken place there."

Marmilov nodded. "Very good. What else?"

"Three platoons of highly trained Spetsnaz troops have been deployed to the Arctic base to protect it. They understand that they are involved in a highly classified operation, and are sworn to secrecy. They will defend the base with their lives."

"They are willing to defend the base despite knowing of the weapon?" Marmilov said.

"Sir, the men do not know the weapon is there. They know only that the base may be attacked, and it is their mandate to defend it at all costs. I removed all the men who knew of the weapon."

Marmilov thought about a group of soldiers, standing atop the largest nuclear weapon ever detonated as its timer counts down to zero, defending it against all comers, and not even knowing it is there.

"They will all be killed," Marmilov said, testing his new associate.

Babayev nodded. "I am afraid so, sir. I could not think of another way to deploy a squad of non-Muslim men for a suicide mission. I think it must be for the best."

Marmilov smiled. Babayev had passed the test with flying colors. The soldiers, as elite and highly trained as they might be, were also but so many pawns in a chess match.

"Excellent, Babayev," he said. "I am very pleased with your work. And I look forward to watching the fireworks."

CHAPTER THIRTY FOUR

11:30 p.m. Eastern European Daylight Time (4:30 p.m. Eastern Daylight Time)
Royal Air Force Station Akrotiri
Akrotiri, British Overseas Territory
Cyprus

"What are you planning to do with all that?" Luke said.

Ed Newsam looked like he was preparing for World War III. For starters, he had an M79 grenade launcher—it resembled a sawed-off shotgun with a wooden stock, but packed a lot more punch—and three boxes of grenades to go with it, four to a box.

He also had an MP5 machine pistol and two ammo belts looped over his shoulders. He had two Glock nine-millimeters, matte black, strapped around his waist. He had a curved and serrated six-inch dagger.

Newsam shrugged. "You know, man? The last few days have been kind of unpleasant. I'm hoping if I can stay alive one more day, this will all be over."

"Keep dreaming," Murphy said. "It's never over."

The helipad was a concrete platform on a rocky bluff away from, and overlooking the rest of the installation. Below them, the low-slung buildings of the Royal Air Force station and the larger flight control tower squatted in the night.

In the daytime, the chopper pad probably gave views of the surrounding mountains. Right now, there was very little out there but shadow, with a few lights dotting the hillsides. The warm wind was swirling, the windsocks on the pad shifting directions every few minutes.

An RAF fighter jet took off a half mile away, its engine noise a shriek that seemed to rip open the night. A moment later, the jet reached the sound barrier. If the takeoff was loud, the roar of the sonic boom was nearly deafening. Luke, Ed, and Murphy all covered their ears as one.

The three men stood in a rough semicircle among a small pile of duffel bags and rucksacks full of weapons. Murphy was pawing through the weapons. He came out with an Uzi submachine gun and a couple of long magazines for it. His other hand came out with a night-vision headset.

"It's like a Christmas grab bag in here," he said. "You're not quite sure what you're going to find."

Luke smiled. He felt pretty good. Truth be told, this was the best he had felt in a long while. He had spent most of the day relaxing at the hotel in Athens. He had taken a swim in the rooftop pool. He had dozed on and off. He had eaten a couple of real meals. He had even caught a few winks on the plane ride over here from Greece.

Even better, he, Murphy and Ed had each dropped a Dexie a few minutes ago.

That was going to do the trick.

He gave his men the once-over. Ed looked fine. Ed rarely changed. He was big, broad and physically imposing, but his body always seemed fluid and relaxed.

"Ed? How you doing, man?"

Ed looked at Luke. He flashed a smile—bright white, perfect teeth. "Ready to rock. Naturally."

"Murph?" Luke said.

Murphy looked a little tired, but he had been traveling all day. He gestured at Ed with his chin. "What he said."

Luke shrugged into his heavy tactical vest. The weight settled onto him. He fastened the vest's waistband, taking a little of the weight off his shoulders. His cargo pants were lined with lightweight Dragon Skin armor.

On the ground at his feet was a combat helmet with facemask attached. Also there was a Remington pump shotgun and an Uzi to match Murphy's. Luke picked up the guns. He felt the heft of them. They were heavy. The weight was reassuring.

The Uzi had armor-piercing rounds. If there were bad guys at the mosque—and Luke hoped three weren't—the rounds should punch through any body armor they might be wearing. He had half a dozen magazines loaded, just in case he needed them.

Luke put his helmet on. Instantly, a voice was speaking in his ear.

"Test, test…Luke Stone is in the zone, why he never answers phone?"

Swann.

Luke nearly laughed. He began to stuff the extra mags into his vest pockets.

"Stone? Do you read? Luke Stone." There was a muffled knocking sound, like a Master of Ceremonies on stage, tapping the microphone. "Hey! Is this thing on?"

"I hear you, Swann."

"Why were you ignoring me?"

"I wasn't. I just put the helmet on now."

"How do I sound?" Swann said.

Luke thought about it for a second. "Like Sinatra."

Swann was operating a high-altitude drone that was going to shadow the chopper. As was often the case, Luke and Swann would be in communication throughout the mission. For Luke, it made more than just operational sense. It was like having an umbilical cord, connecting him back to the real world.

Home and hearth—there was something very appealing in that.

"You want me to sing?" Swann said.

"Nah, your speaking voice is good enough for me," Luke said. "Thanks, Swann. Keep in touch. Keep us alive."

"Will do," Swann said.

Luke took a deep breath. It wasn't a full one—the air caught at the top of his lungs. He looked at Murphy and Ed. "Ready, boys?"

He picked up his rucksack, and the other men followed suit. The Black Hawk helicopter was on the pad fifty feet away. The chopper's engines whined into life as they approached. The four rotor blades began to turn, slowly at first, then with increasing speed. Luke reached the cabin and climbed on board.

Murphy and Ed were right behind him.

A moment later, they were off the ground.

The chopper flew low and fast.

Luke went up front to the cockpit. A man and a woman in visor helmets and green camouflage flight suits sat facing dark sky through the cockpit windows, and a bewildering array of glowing controls and displays practically against their knees.

These were Luke's favorite two pilots, Rachel and Jacob.

They were old friends of his, and they'd flown together for years. Both of them were former U.S. Army 160th Special Operations Aviation Regiment. The 160th SOAR were the Delta Force of helicopter pilots.

They made an odd-looking team.

Rachel had dark auburn hair. She was brawny like the old Rosie the Riveter posters. Big arms, big legs, big all over, and barely an ounce of it fat. She was tough, like most women in professions that were once thought to be man-only. She was funny. She could even be a little bit lewd.

Physically, Jacob was nearly the opposite of Rachel. He was thin and reedy. He looked nothing like your typical elite soldier. He didn't joke much as much as Rachel, and his jokes had a tendency to fall flat. But his calm under fire was legendary, almost surreal. He was probably one of the ten best helicopter pilots alive on Earth.

"What's up, kiddies?" Luke said. "You guys working for Big Daddy these days?"

"We're working for you," Rachel said. "Big Daddy said Stone was headed out on another suicide mission. We wouldn't miss that for the world."

Luke laughed. "Nah. Didn't you hear? We're just going to pop into a mosque, pay our respects to Allah, and pop right back out again."

"Beirut's the place to do it," Rachel said. "Lovely this time of year. The explosions really light up the sky."

"And the screams of the maimed and the dying?" Jacob said. "Like a symphony."

Luke didn't know what to do with that one.

"Let me know when we're getting close," he said.

He went into the back, sat down, and strapped himself in.

They were flying low to avoid radar. The Mediterranean buzzed by below them, maybe fifty meters down, almost close enough to touch. Luke watched its inky darkness zipping past. He guessed they were moving at over a hundred miles per hour.

An image came to him—his son, Gunner, sitting in Becca's lap. They were at the country house, and Becca was smiling. In an instant, the image changed. Becca, all in black, a young widow, at Luke's funeral. Gunner, growing up, growing older, all without a father in his life.

Luke hadn't called her from Greece. He hadn't called her from Cyprus, either. The security of the mission was everything now.

It was for the best anyway. He had come back from one mission, and was going right back out on another. There was no sense worrying her. There was no sense finding out that Zelazny's or Chevsky's body had turned up somewhere, and the TV was somehow implicating him.

There was no sense having her hang up the phone on him again.

He took a deep breath.

Despite the Dexie kicking in, and the excitement that always brought him, he found himself drifting. It was hard, he supposed. Being married to him must be hard. When he got back to the States, if it was possible, he would try to fix that.

The flight passed quickly. He was still lost in a dream when Rachel's voice jerked him back to reality.

"Stone?"

Luke grunted. "Yeah, baby?"

She laughed. Somehow her laugh was like piano keys tinkling. Luke smiled at that.

"We're going to be there in ten minutes. We'll come in over the beachfront, pass low over the city, and after that, we're going to be at that mosque in no time. If it all looks clear, we'll touch down in the parking lot to let you out. If it's hot, you're gonna have to rope. Either way, I suggest you guys start thinking about getting ready."

Luke stared out the window at the lights of the approaching city. From here, you'd never guess it had been an active war zone—sometimes hot as hell, sometimes a little less so—since the late 1970s.

It could be the beachfront of Miami up ahead.

He glanced at Ed and Murphy. They were both waking up from their own reveries. This was often when Luke gave his team a pep talk, or their marching orders.

This time he didn't bother. These guys knew exactly what to do.

"We're ready," he said.

Chapter Thirty Five

September 8
12:15 a.m. Lebanon Daylight Time
(5:15 p.m. Eastern Daylight Time—September 7)
Near Al-Khattab Mosque
South Beirut
Lebanon

Ali Barbir sat in the truck, saying his prayers.
"The Prophet Muhammad—peace be upon him—said, 'By the One Whose Hand is my soul, no one is injured in the path of Allah, except that he comes with his wound on the Day of Resurrection, its color the color of blood, and its scent that of musk.'"

He paused, thinking briefly of the many wounds he had suffered in his short time on this Earth. Allah had given him this life as a test of faith. He understood that now. All of his days had been leading to this moment.

He took a deep breath and glanced around.

The truck was small, more a delivery van than a truck. It was in the parking lot of a large bakery, surrounded by trucks of a similar type. Every morning, very early, these trucks and vans emerged from this lot, delivering fresh bread throughout the city and even into the countryside.

Indeed, the night-shift workers were inside the cinderblock building right now, baking the bread, pastries, and other delights. In a few hours, the drivers would begin to appear here, and start loading their deliveries. Ali could smell the bread baking—the scent was strong enough to almost make him faint with desire.

Ali was going to make a delivery of a different kind.

Up the steep hill from here, at the top of a narrow, winding street, was the old Al-Khattab Mosque. The mosque was a phantom. Ali had attended services there as a child, and he remembered these, but he remembered them as part of a vague time, long ago. Al-Khattab was legendary for its age, and for the famous sheikhs who had shared their wisdom there over many years. But the truth was, the place had been closed as a house of worship for a long time.

Something else had been happening there in the recent past, but either no one knew what that was, or no one was willing to say.

It did not matter now. There would be infidels there tonight. If not tonight, then tomorrow, or the next. Ali's prayers had been answered. He was finally selected for martyrdom. He had been waiting in this van for the past two nights, and he would wait as many nights as it took. He would wait years.

For a long time, this life had seemed to him a curse. He was born with a facial deformity that could not be fixed—at least, not in Lebanon. His skull was misshapen, and this pulled his face badly out of alignment. His mouth and nose were too far to the right. His left eye seemed stretched and was bigger than his right. His teeth were a disgrace.

He could not bear to look at himself in a mirror. He was twenty-one years old, and no girl or woman had ever looked at him with love, or attraction. Almost none were willing to speak to him. His own parents, as much as they did love him, seemed ashamed.

He would never marry, he would never be blessed with children, he would never be a householder and have standing in his community. He would not pass on his name, nor his blood line. He was a dead end.

For years, he had cried himself to sleep at night, alone in his room, silently weeping. He stayed silent to spare his parents the worst of this ordeal.

Why? Why would the Merciful One curse him in this way? Why even give him life, if this was the life he must endure?

Only gradually did he come to understand what his purpose was.

His purpose was to be strong, stand tall, and sacrifice himself. He was not a man who Allah called to martyrdom. Allah had sent him here as a martyr. Ali had been marked at birth—before birth—to be one who sacrifices everything in the struggle.

Already, this knowledge had brought him the camaraderie of the mujahideen.

Soon, it would bring honor to his name.

It would bring his parents redemption.

It was Allah's plan for him, and as always, Allah's plan was perfect.

As he waited, he heard the chop of a helicopter passing overhead somewhere nearby. Was it the helicopter of invading infidels? Perhaps he would know soon. Of course, many helicopters passed overhead in Beirut.

But he prayed that this would be the one.

Next to him, on the passenger seat, a radio set squawked into life. "Ali? Brother?"

He picked up the radio. "Yes."

"Are you ready?"

He nodded. He took one last deep breath, nearly rolling in ecstasy at the smell of the bread. Everything was perfect. Everything was beautiful and nothing hurt.

"Yes. I am."

"Good. Because it's time now. You know what to do?"

"Yes."

"May the Peace and the Passion of Allah be upon you."

"Thank you, my brother."

Ali switched off the radio, turned the key in the ignition of the delivery truck, and put it in gear. He rumbled out of the parking lot, moving slowly. The truck was heavy—much, much heavier than it would be if it were loaded with bread. He must be careful driving on the pitted roads up to the mosque.

He smiled to himself, and tears began to stream down his cheeks.

"May all my sins be forgiven, may the Mighty One accept my sacrifice as jihad, and may I see His palace in Paradise this very night."

It was what they called a "touch and go."

The chopper touched down, Luke, Ed, and Murphy scrambled out in three seconds, then the chopper lifted off and was gone again.

Luke watched it for a couple of seconds, flying without lights, rising over the city and disappearing out toward the sea. Soon it was just a shadow, a dark smudge against the night.

The drop off had gone well. They had flown in here and no one had fired a shot.

"That was easy," he said.

The three men moved quickly across the weed-choked lot, submachine guns out and ready. The blacked-out mosque loomed just ahead—its dome and single minaret reaching toward the sky. Luke's night vision was on, showing him a glowing, surreal world. Murphy and Ed were on either side, and just behind, a wedge formation. They both seemed simultaneously relaxed and on hyper-alert.

"Status?" Swann said in his ear. Swann was in an office somewhere on the outskirts of Metro DC, piloting a gossamer drone at high altitude, far above the reach of any ground-based anti-aircraft guns.

"We are on the ground. How's the sky look?"

"All clear…for now."

At the front of the mosque, Murphy darted up the low stone steps and tried the front doors. The doors were ten feet tall, made of wood, with long iron handles. They were old and probably rotting, but there appeared to be new locks on them.

"Locked," Murphy said.

"Blow them?" Ed said.

Luke shook his head. The building would be oriented toward Mecca. He moved around to the right of the building, a south and west facing exposure, guessing at what he would likely find here—windows.

Sure enough, here they were. A line of tall plywood sheets covered what must have once been two-story-high stained glass, designed to capture and play with the light of the sun. He reached for the first plywood sheet and pulled it.

It came out easily—it was still firmly attached at the top, but loose and bent at the bottom, where many hands had apparently lifted it over a long period of time. The plywood sheet was practically a door now.

Luke looked back at Ed and Murphy. Ed was watching the right flank. Murphy had his eyes on the rear.

"Watch for vagrants," Luke said. "Squatters. Campers. We don't want to make any mistakes in there."

He slid underneath the plywood, carefully spun his legs over the windowsill, and then gingerly stepped on the floor of the mosque. He was in. He took one slow step, then another. The floor felt like wood. Luke guessed it had been laid down at some point over the original stonework.

The floor had a soft, squishy quality. It was old. A wrong step could push through it to whatever was underneath. It would be the easiest thing in the world to sprain or break an ankle if that happened.

He scanned the wide open interior of the mosque. The domed ceiling was high above his head. His entrance had disturbed some birds roosting up there. A couple of them flew back and forth.

The empty space was lined with two rows of tall stone pillars. A few of them had started to tilt at cock-eyed angles—the leaning Towers of Pisa, as mosque pillars went. That was a bad sign for the building. Structural integrity was gone. The substructure was giving way. At some point, those weakened pillars would fall. Then the roof would cave in. The place was a tear down, not a renovation.

Oh well.

He sensed Murphy and Ed behind him.

"Swann, what are we looking for?"

"I don't know, man. I just work here. What do you see?"

Luke shook his head. "Nothing. An old, empty mosque. It's in bad shape. Looks like it's still up because it can't decide which way to fall."

There was a brief commotion inside the headset.

"Luke? It's Trudy."

"Hi, Trudy."

"Luke, I would look for an office area, maybe in a basement or on a second floor. Somewhere records might be kept."

"All right."

He walked through the open space toward the area on the north side, away from the tall windows. There was a lot of junk on the ground. Some overturned tables and chairs. A couple of old filing cabinets—these must have been dragged here from somewhere.

He crossed the mosque and reached the far wall. There were three doors here, locked he imagined. He pulled the first door and it opened easily—it led to a large kitchen. He glanced in there, but it was as dark and wrecked as the worship space itself—probably not what they were looking for.

Next to him, Ed opened a door. Inside was a shattered wooden staircase, probably leading up to a loft space of some kind. This was more promising, but the stairs were basically gone. It looked like some kind of water infiltration had eaten away at them.

Luke opened the third door.

A modern, rectangular iron stairwell spiraled down into the bowels of the Earth. There was a light on down there, maybe two stories below them. Another light was on two stories below that. It was a spare, utilitarian kind of staircase, nothing like the century-old mosque it was part of. It was more like something a person might find in a university building, or...

...a technology lab.

The mosque is on top of a hill.

"Oh my God," Luke said under his breath.

He looked back at Murphy. Murphy was near one of the crazily leaning pillars, staring up at it.

"Murph, hold the fort."

Murphy waved. "Aye, aye, captain."

Luke gestured at the stairwell with his head. "Ed, come with me."

Luke folded his night vision up. He and Ed plunged down the stairs, light on their feet, moving fast, but keeping sound to a minimum. The stairwell was four stories high. There were no doors on any of the floors. It seemed to take just a few seconds to reach the bottom. Here was the only door.

It was a heavy metal door with multiple plated locks. Luke reached out and pulled the handle. Unlocked.

He opened the door.

And found the secret.

In front of them was a vast cavernous space. It was made of solid concrete—concrete floors and walls. The ceiling was at least two stories above their heads.

A bank of overhead fluorescents hung down, the lights twitching and flickering. The light was almost too bright. Rows of computer consoles were in the near foreground. The consoles had small video screens with keyboard embedded in the desks in front of them. Above the space were four modern video screens.

A row of tall black computer servers stood on racks, lights blinking. It was cold in here, noticeably colder than upstairs—a large industrial air conditioning unit was embedded in the wall to the right. Luke could hear it running.

Everything was still on.

At the far side of the space was a giant clear window—it went from the floor to the ceiling. On the far side was another huge space. It was empty but for a platform and some kind of scaffolding.

"What the..." Ed said, barely above a whisper.

He pointed, his arm scanning from left to right. Luke followed his finger. He hadn't seen it at first. His mind was so busy processing the strangeness of a modern research facility hidden beneath a decrepit religious building from a previous century, that he didn't notice the more shocking thing, the thing right in front of his eyes.

There were at least a dozen corpses on the floor.

They were bloody, strewn here and there. The floor itself was red and tacky with their blood. Luke didn't need to look too closely to see what had happened. The skulls were shattered, broken, with gaping exit wounds. Most of these people—possibly all of them—had been shot, execution-style, in the head.

In the midst of it a small, middle-aged man sat at a workstation. A pair of reading glasses was perched on top of his balding head.

He watched Luke and Ed approach him.

He did not try to run. He did not raise his hands in surrender. He didn't move at all. His eyes said he was not afraid. They said he was not anything. He was empty. He was done. A null. A zero. Finished. Luke didn't think he'd seen a man more resigned to his fate in his life.

He looked up at Luke and spoke in Russian.

"*Pozhaluysta ubey menya,*" he said, very slowly.

Please kill me.

"Do you speak English?" Luke said.

The man's eyes opened wide, and then wider still. A light began to dawn there. He looked from Luke to Ed, and back to Luke. He stared at the uniforms they wore. The helmets, the weapons, they carried.

"You are Americans?" he said.

Luke nodded. "Yes."

The man took several deep breaths in a row. His eyes closed. Suddenly, his head fell back. His body went limp and rolled onto the floor. A few seconds later, a loud snoring sound came from him. He had fainted—that's all it was.

"You know, man," Ed said, "that's how I've always wanted girls to look at me."

"What happened here?" Luke said.

The man was sitting up, back in the same chair as before. They had found a bottle of water for him, in a glass-faced refrigerator filled with water, soda and beer. Ed had poured some on his face, reviving him. Now he was slowly sipping it. He had been under for maybe three minutes.

"They came and killed us," the man said. He shrugged. He had the hint of a Russian accent, but he spoke English more or less perfectly. "No hesitation. No human feelings. No recognition of the work we had done, or what we had all been through. They just came in, rounded everyone up, and shot them all."

"Who did this?" Ed said.

The man shook his head. "I don't know. Masked men. Local religious militants, I suppose. They weren't Russians. They killed everyone, then left as quickly as they arrived."

"How did *you* survive?"

"I was in my office when the killing started. We are supposed to keep to a strict clean desk, clean office policy here. But I am not what you Americans would call a neat freak. So I have a closet in my office, piled high with my things. Much of it is on the floor— books, files, many clothes, personal items. They are hidden away. At the first gunshot, at the first shouts, I stepped inside and crawled beneath everything. No one found me in there."

He sighed. "I suppose I knew it would come to this from the beginning."

Luke glanced around the lab. This was the sole survivor of another bloodbath—a man who had crawled inside a closet. Luke found that he believed the story without reservation. This man was clearly not a killer.

"What were you doing here?"

The man shrugged. "My name is Yakov Trutnev. I am a physicist. My family was taken by the Russian secret police. I was told they would be killed if I did not cooperate. I was brought here with a group of other men. We designed and built the bomb. The one I imagine you are looking for."

Jackpot.

"We have to get this guy out of here," Ed said.

Luke nodded. That was true.

Trutnev gestured at the dead men on the floor. Luke noted now that they were all men. "Myself, and this team of eminent scientists and engineers you see around me. I suppose now that we were lied to from the very start. I no longer believe my family is alive."

"What kind of bomb is it?"

The man looked at him quizzically. His mouth hung half open. "Don't you know?"

"If I knew, I wouldn't have asked."

"It is the most powerful nuclear weapon in the history of the world. It is also perhaps one of the most advanced. Its creation has solved numerous design challenges. It should unfailingly deliver a blast equivalent to one hundred twenty megatons. Nothing like that has ever happened before. The device is impervious to extremes of cold, and to water infiltration, and its systems will continue to operate in the harshest environment at the very top of the world."

"The Arctic," Luke said. "Is that where it is now?"

The man nodded. "Yes. They moved it from here in recent days. The thing to know is it is a shaped charge, similar to the more advanced roadside bombs you see in this guerrilla combat happening everywhere these days. When it detonates, its force will be directed outward in a fan shape, not in a circle."

"What's the point of that?"

Trutnev shook his head. "You are just foot soldiers, then? You know nothing about this? I should be speaking to your superiors, not to you."

Luke sighed. He pressed the muzzle of his Uzi to the man's forehead.

"Just tell me."

The man closed his eyes and breathed deeply. It was more of a gasp than a breath.

"Don't faint again," Luke said.

"The bomb is deployed beneath the ice. Its explosion will tear up the permanent frozen ice cap. The North Pole will be completely

272

free of ice for the first time in perhaps one hundred twenty-five thousand years. By destroying the ice now, in the northern autumn, it will undermine the freezing effects of the winter. Ice reflects sunlight, cooling the planet. Dark water absorbs sunlight, trapping more heat. We have computer programs that can calculate these things easily. Our models suggest that nearly the entire Arctic will be ice-free next summer, and will be subject to greenhouse feedback loops that mean the ice will never recover."

Ed grunted. "Is that all?"

Trutnev opened his eyes. "No. Unfortunately, it is not all. An enormous surge of water will be forced through the Canadian islands of the Arctic, and down between Greenland and North America. There will be a funnel effect as the water rushes through those narrow corridors. Such is the added benefit of a directed burst.

"For a period of time, the surge will drastically increase sea levels throughout the Western Hemisphere, completely swamping low-lying areas. Lower Manhattan will be underwater, and perhaps be rendered uninhabitable. Miami, Key West, and much of south Florida. New Orleans, of course. Certain smaller island nations in the Caribbean will completely disappear. Much of the Netherlands will be inundated. Venice, in Italy, will cease to exist."

He paused. "Perhaps the worst of it is from an environmental point of view. The Arctic fisheries will be utterly destroyed for a thousand years. No one wants the fisheries—they want the oil and gas. They want the shipping lanes. But the knock-on effects are hard to predict. We know the polar bears will become extinct, but as much as they fascinate humans, large apex predators are not that important. More important will be the migratory bird species who make their home in the Arctic summer. Before they die off, they will travel the world, seeding it with contamination. Contaminated water will circulate through every ocean. The plants and insects..."

He trailed off and looked at the floor.

"Why did you do it?" Ed said.

The man didn't look up. "I already told you. To save my family."

"Is there a time frame for when the bomb will be detonated?"

The man glanced over at a digital clock on a computer panel. Numbers shone red on the panel. 07:53:48.

The seconds were running down.

Now it was 07:53:39.

07:53:35.

"In a little less than eight hours," Trutnev said.

Luke looked at Ed. Their eyes met.

"I think we better go."

"Stone! Stone! Wake up! Incoming!"

The voice shouted through Murphy's headset. He recognized Swann instantly.

"What's up, Swann?"

"Murphy! Where's Stone?"

Murphy shrugged. "He and Newsam went downstairs. He's underground. His radio must not work down there. There's some kind of facility…"

"Never mind that, Murph. You've got unfriendlies coming in fast. A swarm of them. They just came out of the woods at the end of the parking lot. Five seconds ago. I'm calling back the chopper."

Murphy shook his head. Of course. It was a trap. Somehow, the bad guys knew they were coming, let them get all the way inside, and now planned to pin them down and wipe them out. The mosque was a moldy piece of Swiss cheese at this point. Maybe the baddies would just knock it down on top of them.

Clever.

Well, this is what he was here for.

"Where are they?"

"Coming right at you. Any second. Oh, Murph. Watch it! RPG!"

Instantly, Murphy hit the deck behind one of the wide stone pillars.

BOOOOM!

The big front doors of the mosque blew inward. Smoke and debris hung in the air.

Murphy rolled over. The pillar had protected him. He wasn't hit at all. Moreover, he felt calm. He was surprised, but not in shock. He had done this many times.

He rolled to his side, the Uzi pointed at the ragged hole where the doors had just been. Good news—his night-vision gear was working fine. Better news—the chumps out there didn't have night vision. They were coming with flashlights, probably mounted on the barrels of their guns. Their lights crisscrossed, throwing strange shadows.

"Come on in," Murphy said.

Three men darted through the open hole.

Murphy mowed them down with a burst of automatic fire.

Duh-duh-duh-duh-duh.

He breathed and waited a beat. He knew what came next. He always seemed to know. Because people were predictable.

Two more men dashed through the hole.

Murphy killed them, same way as before.

Good grief.

It wasn't even fair sometimes. The guys were not smart. The training wasn't there. Murphy didn't know what the problem was.

"Murphy! More trouble. You got guys working their way around to the right side. Also, there's a truck coming up the hill toward the mosque. It's moving slow. Given the fact that it's Beirut, I think it might be..."

Murphy's head was on a swivel, watching the front door, and now the plywood coverings where the windows used to be. Dammit! Where were Stone and Ed?

"Can you take it out?" Murphy said. "Drone strike. Just get rid of it."

"Negative. It's rolling through a residential neighborhood. There's houses and small buildings. If I take it out..."

BOOOOM!

The explosion came without warning.

Murphy crawled into a ball, letting his Dragon Skin armor protect him. He knew what had happened without having to think about it. They had blown out one of the plywood coverings. He was pelted with little jagged pieces of burning wood.

The bad guys had two ways in now.

Soon they would open another.

"Swann, we got problems in here."

"Chopper's incoming, Murph! Hold the fort."

Murphy shook his head. That was the second time someone told him to hold the fort in one night. Didn't these guys have anything better than that? Hold the fort, Murph!

With what?

He rolled over again. In one fluid motion, he jumped to a kneeling position.

A man was climbing through the window where the plywood had been. Murphy ripped him up with a quick burst. The guy fell back out and disappeared.

He turned to the front doors—more coming that way.

Duh-duh-duh-duh-duh.

A couple went down, one made it. Now there was someone inside.

This wasn't going to work.

"Murph! The van is near the top!"

"Kill it, man! Kill it! Kill the houses!"

A man poked his head over the rim of the window.

A head shot—that was hard. Murphy waited.

Two more came in through the front doors.

The man at the window had a shoulder fired weapon. Grenade launcher. Murphy had to kill him. He gave him a burst, one second before the man fired his weapon.

The man fell backward. The grenade shot upward, no arch, just a flat trajectory headed straight toward the roof. Murphy watched it go, its tail sizzling behind it, like some kind of firework on the Fourth of July.

BANG.

It hit the ceiling, right where the pillar connected. Heavy masonry fell, landing on the floor with a thud, then shattering into pieces. Debris showered down.

The front door was wide open now. Three more charged through. Murphy clipped the last one.

There was a pile of bodies in front of those doors.

Suddenly, Murphy realized something. The pillar was coming down. It happened slowly at first, but then with increasing speed. He was using it for cover. By now there must be at least three guys with guns trained on him. He couldn't get out of its way—he'd be dead the instant he revealed himself.

For a second, he tried to hold it up. It was way too heavy.

He slowed its progress as much he could.

Heavy?

That wasn't the right word. He couldn't control it. It was coming down.

"Oh, no."

It came down, an immense weight, and pushed him into the floor.

The steel door was open a sliver.

Murphy was getting overrun out there. There was nothing Luke could do about that at this moment.

A voice crackled in Luke's head. "Stone! Stone?"

It was Swann.

Luke ignored him for the moment. He looked at the scientist. They were at the top of the stairwell. The scientist's eyes no longer looked resigned. They were wide open and terrified.

Luke pointed at Ed. "You stay close to this man at all times. When he tells you to do something, you do it. You don't think. You don't question. The only way out of here is to do exactly what he says, as soon as he says it. Do you understand me?"

The man's mouth opened slowly. "I think it is a mistake to ..."

Luke slapped him across the face. Hard. The man's head wrenched around to his right. A red welt appeared on his cheek.

"You don't think. You do what this man tells you. You follow him wherever he goes. That's all you do. Otherwise, you're going to die. And I need you alive."

He stared at the man. "Do. You. Understand?"

The man nodded. "Yes."

"Good."

Swann again, crackling in the headset: "Luke, the chopper's there. Rachel's got the heavy guns on the guys in front of the doors. She can clear that out for you."

Luke looked at Ed. "Did you hear that?"

Ed nodded.

"Do it," Luke said into his mouthpiece.

Somewhere outside, the brutal sound of a mini-gun ripped up the night.

"I gotta relieve Murphy," Luke said. "Sounds like the front door is open. I'll draw their attention and take out as many as I can, but I think you and the mad scientist are going to be running through a ring of fire."

Ed shook his head. "Don't worry, man. Grab Murph. I'll meet you at the chopper."

"Good luck," Luke said. "I'll see you."

He burst through the doorway. He ran along the wall, between the columns. Two of them were down, massive stone pillars, lying on the floor. There was junk all over the ground now. The roof was bound to cave in. When that dome came down…

Not good.

Two men were running toward the front doors, maybe to help the men who had been killed by the chopper. Luke slid behind a downed pillar, sighted, and gunned them both down. Gunfire ripped chunks out of the pillar. Sharp pieces of it sprayed him.

Across the open mosque, a man was sighting on Luke, but hitting the pillar instead.

Luke let him have a burst of automatic fire. The man did a jig and went down, dead before he landed.

To his right, Luke saw Ed running for the front doors, dragging the scientist along with him.

"Stone?" a voice said. "Is that you?"

Luke looked down, at the other side of the pillar. Murphy was there, underneath it. Somehow, he was under a thick stone column. He seemed to be embedded in the floor. His face was there, and his left arm stuck out. He still had his Uzi in his hand.

It didn't seem like it could be real.

"Luke," Swann's voice crackled. "It's definitely a truck bomb. It's got to be. He's in between some houses, and backed into a tree covered area. He's at the top of the hill now. I think he's going to make a run for the mosque."

"Can you hit him?" Luke said.

"I can't, Luke. There's civilian housing right there. He's going to make the hundred-yard dash right through the middle of it. If I hit him ..."

"I understand," Luke said.

"The chopper's calling. They've been hit. They lost their guns. They're taking heavy fire from the trees at the end of the parking lot. The scientist is hit. Ed is treating him. They're on board and ready. You have to get out of there."

Luke looked at Murphy.

"How you doing, Murph?"

Murph shook his head. "I'm not in any pain. It's the funniest thing. These floorboards were so rotten, I think the pillar just pushed me right through them. There's some space under here. I might even be able to walk. I don't know. If only I could slip out from under."

Luke stared at him. That couldn't be true. The pillar must weigh thousands of pounds. Murphy wasn't in pain, probably because he couldn't feel anything at all.

"Oh Murph, I'm sorry."

"Nah," Murphy said. "I wouldn't worry about it. This was bound to happen sooner or later. I don't even blame you. You called me, but I'm the one who came. Not for you. For me."

Swann's voice crackled.

"Stone, that truck is moving. I'm gonna try to hit, but you have to get out of there. You have to go right now. He's gaining speed. Get out!"

"I think you better get going," Murphy said.

He started to do something underneath the pillar. He made a squirming, snakelike movement. He was undulating madly, violently. Luke watched him in a sort of dream. Murphy could move. He whipsawed, faster and faster.

Swann, screaming:

"GET OUT! STONE!"

"Go!" Murphy said. "Listen to the man!" He didn't even look at Luke. He was doing some sort of crazy desperate dance under there, rhythmic, insane.

"STONE!"

Luke turned and ran for the front doors.

Outside, the headlights of the van were approaching.

Luke was forced to run toward them. He blew through the doors, leapt down the steps, and ran for the chopper. He turned and trained his gun on the van as he ran.

"Dud-duh-duh-duh-duh!"

The windshield shattered. The driver's side window shattered.

A line of explosions rained down from the sky. Drone strike.

The earth shook. The van was on fire, still hurtling toward the mosque. The driver was on fire. It didn't matter. Those guys wedged bricks on the gas pedal.

Luke ran for the chopper. It hovered three feet above the ground. Luke dove, hit the bottom rails, and hung on as the chopper lifted off. He clambered up and into the cabin. Ed was strapping the scientist into a seat. The man was covered in blood and crying.

Luke looked back. They were already a hundred feet in the air and climbing fast.

The van was like a flaming skull. It hit the stairs at the front, went airborne and flew like a rocket into the mosque. The explosion was immense, a giant fireball launched into the dark night.

Luke grabbed his head.

Murphy!

"Hang on!" Rachel shouted from the cockpit.

The shockwave hit the chopper and Luke was knocked off his feet. He hit the floor at the same time as Ed. The helicopter shuddered, whipsawed, and rode along on its side. The turbulence pushed it along.

For a split second, it seemed like the chopper would flip upside down. Then it found some calm air, leveled out, and surged forward. Luke felt it gaining more altitude.

He looked back.

They were already over the ocean. Behind the high rises of the Beirut beachfront, on a hillside overlooking the city, an enormous fire burned.

Ed put a big hand on his shoulder.

"I'm sorry, man."

Luke nodded. It was too horrible to think about at this moment. "Yeah. Me, too."

He looked up at the scientist, strapped into his seat. The guy was a bloody mess. Luke couldn't remember his name. He gestured at him with his head.

"That guy gonna live?"

Ed nodded. "Yeah."

The image of that doomsday clock flashed through Luke's mind. The bomb was deployed, and there was less than eight hours until it exploded.

"What's your name again?" Luke shouted.

A window was shattered, and wind howled through the cabin.

The man stared at Luke. He was frowning so hard he almost seemed like a circus clown. His eyes were watering, as if he might cry. He looked unutterably sad.

"Trutnev," he shouted.

"Well Trutnev, do you know how to turn off the bomb that you made?"

"Very difficult," Trutnev said. "It would require you to go beneath the ice. The mechanism is in a steel box that must be cut open. There is a sequence. I must probably be there to oversee, but I am not a diver."

"But it is technically possible to do it, and you know how."

Trutnev stared at him. Outside, the dark night raced by. For the first time, Luke noticed that the helicopter had been shot full of holes.

"Yes," Trutnev said. "I know how."

Luke looked at Ed. Ed's face was smeared with blood. It looked like war paint.

"Then we've got more to do."

CHAPTER THIRTY SIX

07:04:58 until detonation
Royal Air Force Station Akrotiri
Akrotiri, British Overseas Territory
Cyprus

"May I try to contact my family?" Yakov Trutnev said.

"Yes, you may," Big Daddy Cronin said. "As soon as you tell us everything you know, and answer every question we have."

Images of Murphy scrolled through Luke's mind. He tried to focus on Trutnev instead.

The scientist had gone back to looking resigned. He was wearing a T-shirt, and his right arm was bandaged where a bullet had gone clean through it. His right cheek was bandaged where a flying chunk of debris had carved a deep, bloody scar. There was another, smaller bandage on top of balding head.

"Of course," he said. "I am accustomed to the inhumanity of dealing with government and its soldiers."

"This ain't about you," Ed Newsam said. "Or what you're accustomed to."

Trutnev nodded, but the nod didn't seem like agreement.

"Talk," Luke said.

They were in a drab office inside a one-story building on the British Royal Air Force base. Big Daddy knew these people and had some arrangement with them. The office itself had brown paneling, with fading landscape paintings in glass frames on the walls. The place looked like it hadn't been updated since the 1970s. There was no telling how many listening devices were in here.

Luke didn't even bother asking Big Daddy if this room was secure.

He, Ed and Big Daddy stood in various corners of the room. They were big men, and the office was small. Trutnev sat in a rolling desk chair at a table. On the table was another one of those spider-like speaker phone gadgets. Don Morris, Trudy, and Swann were at the other end.

Luke had no idea what time it was in Washington, DC. The time on the clock didn't matter anymore. All that mattered was the countdown.

"The bomb," Trutnev said. "As I indicated to you earlier, it is likely the most powerful nuclear weapon ever devised. It was the subject of decades of research during the time of the Soviet Union, the results of which were resurrected in recent years. I will describe it as simply as I can, in layman's terms. It is what you Americans sometimes refer to as a layer-cake. The Russians are great bakers, as you know."

Luke resisted the urge to punch the man in the mouth.

"There is a large sealed compartment embedded within the device. This compartment is the detonator. It is under great pressure, and contains a fissile mass of uranium and plutonium surrounded by a layer of lithium deuteride. Wires run from a battery pack to the detonator, and at the appointed time, a brief, high-power electrical charge will be delivered. The energy from the charge will cause the compressed fissile material to detonate. That small, but very intense, explosion will then be accelerated by the presence of the lithium. The accelerated explosion will, in turn, cause the nuclear material in the bomb itself to detonate. This is known as a chain reaction."

He paused.

"The layer-cake was first designed because it can create a devastating explosion from a small amount of enriched materials. At one time, a great deal of thought was put into the idea of fitting atomic

weapons in suitcases, or the trunks of cars. The innovation here—
one of several—is to use that same basic arrangement to detonate
a much larger weapon."

Trutnev sighed heavily. He put his head in one hand.

"I cannot believe I participated in this."

His body began to shake.

"How do we stop it?" Luke said.

Trutnev looked at his wrist. When the bomb was initiated, he
had synchronized the timer on his watch to the countdown. Since
they had arrived here in Cyprus, Luke and Ed had done the same
thing on their watches.

"Less than seven hours to go. The base where it is deployed is in
the Arctic. It is almost certainly well defended by Russian troops. I
do not know their numbers, or their training, but I would imagine
they are among the elite."

He looked at Luke with baleful eyes.

"Probably, you cannot stop the explosion."

The speakerphone squawked.

"Can we bomb it?" Don Morris said. "Could we just fly over the
base with overwhelming force and drop bombs on it? I know you
can bomb ICBMs in missile silos, and unless the missiles are already
activated…"

Trutnev shook his head. "Unfortunately, this is what you call
comparing apples and oranges. This bomb is always activated.
Nuclear keys are not necessary. Yes, I know this does not conform
to the laws of war, but you are not dealing with rational men. The
purpose of this weapon was never deterrence. It was designed to be
used. If a bomb hits the detonator on this weapon, the most likely
result is it will cause the compressed fissile material to detonate. It
is a clever self-defense mechanism."

He took another breath. A tear rolled down his cheek.

"Even if a bomb dropped did not detonate the weapon, please
understand that the weapon is deployed beneath the ice sheet,
clinging to it from the underside, and held in place by a carriage
and scaffolding. The second most likely result of any bombing from

above is that the scaffolding will be damaged or destroyed, and the bomb will be dislodged. Then it will simply sink to the bottom of the ocean. The Arctic Ocean is approximately three hundred meters deep at that location.

"The weapon is designed to withstand the high pressures of deep ocean water—another innovation, I'm afraid. Obviously, it takes proper equipment, and weeks or months of planning to retrieve items from that depth. Meanwhile, the countdown will continue, and the weapon will detonate at the appointed time. I have not seen the results of any modeling done about a detonation at the seafloor, but I imagine it would still be quite bad."

"In layman's terms," Don said, "don't bomb it."

Trutnev nodded. "Yes. Don't bomb it."

"How do we stop this?" Trudy Wellington said over the squawk-box. "Assume that a way exists, and describe that."

Trutnev looked positively despondent.

"The only way that I know of is to disable the detonator itself. This will require diving under the ice, locating the detonator along the side of the weapon, and cutting into the steel box around it with some cutting rod or other underwater welding device. Once open, it will reveal a small numeric pad. A code must be input."

"The code turns off the detonator?" Luke said.

"No," Trutnev said. "It disables the electrical field created when the wiring from the battery pack to the detonator is cut. In an underwater environment, the field will fatally electrocute any person or animal within … 30 meters, let's say. Once the electrical field is disabled, you may cut the wiring."

He raised his hands as if to say, "See? Simple enough."

"Does the countdown stop when the code is input?"

Trutnev shook his head. "No," he said, a little too emphatically. "The countdown stops when the time runs out. When time runs out, if the wires are cut, the batteries cannot deliver the charge that initiates the chain reaction. That's all. The bomb is still operational. The charge was just never delivered."

"It sounds like a tall order," Swann said over the speaker.

Luke thought about it. He knew welding. He could cut and weld underwater. He could imagine a scenario where he cut open the box. Ed could input the numbers. Then either one of them could cut the wires—likely Ed, whose hands would be free.

It would require that they get to the location in the next six hours or so.

It would require someone who knew their stuff to operate the power supply from on top of dry land.

It would also require that they overcome the resistance of the troops guarding the place, then find the exact spot where the bomb was deployed, suit up and dive down.

Okay, first things first.

"Do you know where the bomb is?"

Trutnev nodded. "There is a dome on the base. It creates a somewhat hospitable environment. A large hole was cut through the ice inside the dome. The bomb was lowered through the hole and deployed on the underside of the ice near that spot. The hole may have frozen over again, or it may still be open. I don't know. But once inside the dome, it should be easy enough to see."

"How thick is the ice there?" Luke said.

Trutnev shrugged. "Twelve meters, maybe fifteen."

"So about forty or fifty feet?"

Now Trutnev smirked. "Americans with their feet. No one uses this system. But yes, maybe forty or fifty feet deep."

"And the code?" Ed Newsam said. "Do you know it?"

Ed saw where Luke was going. And he was going to the same place.

"It is the easiest thing about this," Trutnev said. "18-12-18-78. It is a shorthand for December 18, 1878. Josef Stalin's birth date. The weapon is nicknamed Uncle Joe. You see, even scientists are not without humor."

"We've got nothing," Luke said. "Is that what you're telling me?"

It was getting late. He checked his watch.

06:37:19.

Some British MPs had removed Trutnev from the room. Where they planned to put him was anyone's guess. Luke didn't care if they covered him in syrup and tied him to an anthill.

Everyone else was still here.

Don Morris was talking. "The entire SRT is under suspension. The accounts are frozen. I told them you had captured a Russian scientist with knowledge of a secret nuclear weapon, and they were irate that I still had agents operating in the field. I didn't even mention that we lost Murphy—that's going to have to wait. I did tell them the nuclear weapon was in a terminal countdown, and you know what they said? They said bring the scientist in and they'd interview him.

"I called a friend of mine at Joint Special Operations Command, looking to see if he could lend me some resources under the table. He told me the word is out that I have leprosy. Nobody who wants to keep their career better touch me. It's frustrating, son. I understand that."

"It's a little more than frustrating, Don."

Luke felt like a teenager throwing a hissy fit. He needed to get some control over this situation. To do so, he was going to need to keep his emotions in check. Murphy was dead. It was a complicated issue. They had no resources. They were all about to lose their jobs. And the largest bomb in history was about to go off.

"You've got Bill Cronin standing there, son. You've got the resources he can give you. That's a lot more than nothing."

Luke nodded. "I know. I know that."

It was more than nothing. Big Daddy was a smooth operator, and he always had access to things. But he was under suspension, too. Why was everybody around here always under suspension?

A few of the things they didn't have: advanced fighter planes, supersonic passenger planes, active Navy SEALs or Delta Force or any elite force at all, the logistical support of the vast United States military, NSA, DIA, and CIA surveillance and data collection, open communication with the Russian government (who might suddenly see the error in their ways), state-of-the-art weaponry and equipment, access to the know-how and experience of Arctic allies like Norway and Sweden...

The list could go on and on.

Luke looked at Big Daddy. "What do we got, Bill?"

Big Daddy shrugged. "I pulled together ten guys. They're all guys I've worked with in the past, all of them former military special operators, all of them combat vets, all of them rock stars. They're nihilists like your buddy Murphy, so..."

Luke's patience was gone. He took a step closer.

"What are you trying to say, Bill? Do you know something about Murphy that you want to share, or are you just trying to push my buttons? Because I can promise you that now is not the time to push my buttons."

Ed Newsam casually stepped between them. "All right, man."

Big Daddy nodded. "You're right. Now's not the time. All I meant was they're stone killers, very experienced, and in it for the money and the thrills. I promised them all a big payout if they live. I'm hoping either they all die, or the SRT somehow comes back to life after a successful mission. Because my job is hanging by a thread at the moment, and I don't have a budget for this."

"What else?" Ed said. He glanced at his watch.

"We've got a jump plane and two pilots the English gave me. The plane can land on that ice runway we saw in the pictures, or if things are too hot, everybody can jump. The plane is fast. It'll get to the destination in under six hours. I've got weapons galore, a stockpile, the kind of stuff I know you like. I have scuba gear and underwater welding gear. I've got someone experienced to set up the equipment and operate the console topside."

Luke nodded. It was bare bones as hell, but it didn't sound... terrible.

"Who's the operator?" he said.

"You're looking at him," Big Daddy said.

"Bill, you're coming on this mission? Look, that's a nice offer, but the last thing I need is to ..."

Big Daddy glared at him. "Kid, I was flying combat missions when you were still trying to peak up the girls' skirts in the fifth grade. Also, here's a little-known fact. Before I went airborne, I worked the oil rigs in the Gulf of Mexico. I have a lot of experience with underwater cutting and welding."

They stared at each other from either side of big Ed Newsam.

"These are my guys, my plane, my weapons, my equipment. So get used to the idea. I'm coming."

Luke glanced at his watch again.

06:29:04.

Everything was going too fast. There was too much talking going on, and too much planning. The flight to the Arctic was going to take nearly six hours. They were already cutting it close.

"If that's what you want," Luke said, "fine. But in that case, we better leave right now. We're running out of time."

Chapter Thirty Seven

05:43:22 until detonation
Premier Suite
The Ritz-Carlton Moscow
Tverskaya Street
Moscow, Russia

It was dark. It was the middle of the night.

Everything was quiet outside—the calm before the storm. The lights of Red Square shone into Marmilov's living room.

His suite was beginning to appear run down, unkempt. A few days ago, he had barred the cleaning ladies from entering. Tamara was gone, and Marmilov hadn't ordered another girl—a girl was too distracting at a time like this.

Tonight, he was drinking heavily. He held a glass of vodka on ice.

Putin had disappeared from his Black Sea dacha. There was some indication he might have fled the country. If so, that was good. There were rumors he had returned to Moscow to fight for his political life. If so ... Marmilov wasn't sure.

In any event, Putin dropping out of sight was disconcerting. The man was a scoundrel. He was underhanded. He was dangerous.

Babayev was here. He was giving his report.

"Chemicals in the basement of the mosque appear to have ignited," he said. "The truck bomb caused a firestorm. Indications are that the local fire departments can contain the blaze, but they cannot put it out. It should burn until it dies of its own accord. It is likely to destroy all evidence of whatever was happening in that building."

"This is good," Marmilov said. "Now tell me the bad."

Babayev hesitated. "Why do you believe there is bad?"

Marmilov smiled, but there was no joy in it. "My dear Babayev, you will learn that there is always bad."

Babayev shrugged. "Members of the American assault force survived the truck bombing. Their helicopter was damaged, but they escaped with their lives."

"Keep going," Marmilov said.

"Our friend inside the White House has heard that a scientist was alive inside the mosque. Apparently, he was captured by the Americans. The leader of the Special Response Team espionage agency approached the White House with news of this scientist, and of the weapon deployment. Apparently, he was rebuffed and his funding was cut off. Our friend may have helped this process along."

It was terrible news, of course. Babayev had done his best to sugar-coat it, but no matter—it was a bitter pill to swallow. This American spy agency would not stop. They kept appearing places. They kept discovering things. Supposedly, there was no danger from them, but if so, then why were they still involved?

"They will try to sabotage the weapon."

Babayev was noncommittal. "Maybe they will try."

Marmilov raised his voice, just a small amount. "Of course they will try."

He took a slug of the vodka.

"They will fail," Babayev said. "We are told they have no funding. Their agency may be closed. No one listens to them. Will they go to the Arctic by themselves, and fight through the Spetsnaz? Even if they could, there is almost no time left."

"How much?" Marmilov said.

"By my watch?" Babayev said. "Only a little more than five and a half hours. They were just in Beirut a short time ago. Now they must go to the Arctic? If it is the same ones, they will never make it there in time."

Marmilov smiled and shook his head.

Never. The man had said never.

He had practically cursed the entire operation with that one word.

"Alert the facility," Marmilov said. "Tell them to expect an attack incoming within the next several hours. Assume highest preparation levels. Tell them that once you give them their instructions, they are to cut off all communications with the outside world. They must repulse any attack, and fight to the last man. They must not surrender, and they must not take any prisoners. Any and all invaders are to be killed."

Babayev nodded. "As you wish, sir."

"It is my wish, Babayev. It is my wish that every American who attacks that facility lays dead and frozen on the ice."

CHAPTER THIRTY EIGHT

02:15:38 until detonation
Inside an airplane
The skies over Northern Europe

Luke came alert very gradually.

He glanced around.

The passenger cabin wasn't much to look at. This was a jump plane. There were two benches along either side of the fuselage. There were a bunch of guys sitting on the benches. A couple of guys were stretched out on the floor next to equipment lockers, apparently asleep. The lockers were strapped down, and Luke knew they were full of weapons, scuba gear, the welding gear.

Near the rear of the plane was a jump door. There were overhead lights at the front and back. When those lights went green, that meant:

Go!

It was dark in here, dark and cold. The plane was bouncing along with some turbulence.

There was Ed Newsam in a jumpsuit, sitting with his eyes closed. Maybe he was meditating. Maybe he was dozing.

Ed was a mountain of a man, the biggest one on the plane.

Near him was a guy playing a handheld computer game.

Here was a guy with a little overhead spotlight mounted on his helmet, reading a magazine on his lap, with one leg crossed over the other. He could be waiting in a dentist's office.

Here was a guy compulsively checking and rechecking weapons.

It took all kinds.

Here was the scientist Yakov Trutnev, sitting right next to Luke. If Ed was the biggest, Trutnev was the smallest. He was swimming in his flight suit. He had insisted on coming, and nobody had cared enough to stop him. He said he wanted to see the project through to the end.

"No one is going to be able to protect you," Luke told them before they climbed aboard the airplane. "There's just not going to be time. And saving you is no longer a priority. We got what we needed."

Luke figured he should be honest and get that out there. Maybe the guy would change his mind.

Instead, he just nodded. "I know."

Now Trutnev was awake. His eyes met Luke's.

"Did you try to contact your family?" Luke said.

Trutnev nodded. "Yes."

"Did you reach them?"

"No."

"I'm sorry to hear that," Luke said.

Trutnev sat very still. "I am too."

Luke had tried to call his own family. By the time he called, he had completely lost track of time, so he had no idea whether Becca would be awake, asleep, at her mother's house … he didn't know. And they hadn't spoken in days.

He reached her voice mail.

Her voice was vibrant and bright. He pictured her: beautiful, smiling, optimistic, and energetic. That's how he wanted to think of her, now and forever.

"Hi, this is Becca. I can't answer your call right now. Please leave a message after the tone, and I'll call you back as soon as I can."

"Hi, sweetheart," Luke said. "It's me. I love you. I love Gunner. I love both of you, and I want to be with you."

That was all he could think of to say. So he said it and hung up.

He looked up and down the rattling, shaking plane again. He was tired. He had a Dexedrine in a plastic baggie, all ready to go. But he wasn't ready to take it yet.

He was numb from the fight in Beirut, and Murphy's death. He was numb from the fight in Alaska. He was numb from witnessing the aftermaths of two massacres. He was numb from being suspended from work again, and having his image on TV screens worldwide. He was numb from Becca cutting him out again. And the constant traveling didn't help any.

"It's been a long week," he said.

Chapter Thirty Nine

00:34:56 until detonation
Inside an airplane
The skies over the Arctic Circle

"Stone."

Luke woke with a start.

Big Daddy Bill Cronin was crouched in front of him. His jump-suit was a touch too form-fitting for his bulk. It would almost be funny to see the red-bearded, desk-jockeying, string-pulling torture specialist out here on a suicide mission. But his eyes were serious.

The plane was no longer dark. Natural light was coming through the window on the jump door. It was bright out there.

"What's up?" Luke said.

"Listen, sorry about before. That whole Murphy thing. I've been under a lot of stress lately."

Luke shook his head. "No worries."

But Big Daddy didn't drop it. "Are we cool?"

"We're cool."

Big Daddy nodded. "Good, because we're coming in."

"Now?"

"Soon. Look, these are my guys, but today they're yours, okay? You're the quarterback. I know that. There's nobody like you in the field. You don't know these guys, but some of them know you. Your reputation is way out ahead of you. Okay?"

Luke nodded. "Good. I'll talk to them."

He reached into the breast pocket of his jumpsuit and pulled out the Dexedrine pill. He ripped open the plastic baggie and put the blue and white capsule in his mouth. He gulped it down. These were fast-acting.

He glanced at his watch: 00:33:33

The seconds seemed to run impossibly fast. Not good.

That pill had better act at least as fast.

Big Daddy smiled. "I don't think anybody knows this place is here."

"What do you mean?"

He raised his hands. "We're flying in. This is a secret installation. I talked to the pilots. Nobody approached us all night. Nobody questioned us. No fighter planes buzzed us. Nobody shot us down. Nothing. We were just a plane flying over international waters."

Luke stared at him.

"It's not official. The Russians really don't know about it. That guy Marmilov—it's his thing, and nobody else's. I don't know this for a fact, but I'm beginning to suspect it. When we took off last night, I figured we'd be challenged as soon as we got within five hundred miles of this place. Didn't happen. Still hasn't."

"Does that change anything?" Luke said.

Big Daddy shook his head. "No. Not at the moment. But it might later."

He looked up and down the row of men. They were all coming to life, fiddling with weapons, running through their own mental checklists. They were all freelancers, and that was their problem. They had come here because Big Daddy had promised them money. They didn't act anything like a cohesive unit. They were barely even speaking.

"You ready?" Big Daddy said.

Luke nodded. Already he felt the stir of adrenaline. It couldn't be the pill yet—it was his brain and his body gearing up for action. This was the game. This was the show. His mind started to race, the way it tended to.

"How's the landing going to be?" he said.

Big Daddy shrugged. "Icy. They said they're going to try to spin sideways, with the exit on the back side, and the plane between us and the bad guys."

"Can they do that?"

Big Daddy smiled. "Pilots do it all the time by accident. Who's to say someone can't do it on purpose?"

There was a burst of static and a voice came over the plane's loudspeaker.

"Gentlemen, we are five minutes from the target destination. Prepare for landing and disembark. Repeat, five minutes from target."

Big Daddy gestured at the other men with his head. "Go get 'em, tiger. They know me, and I've got your back."

Luke stood. He looked down the line. It was a motley crew. There was nothing uniform about any of them. Tattoos, beards, scars, bandanas, all manner of weirdness and individualism.

Luke had seen it a lot. Guys got out of the military and they went their own way. When they came back for the payday, or the excitement, or because they just couldn't stop, they were still going their own way.

"Listen up, guys!" he shouted.

All along the line, men turned to look at him.

"I'm Agent Luke Stone of the FBI Special Response Team. I'm your commanding officer on this mission. Thanks for coming out today. Big Daddy Cronin tells me you guys are the best of the best, and I believe him. I'll tell you that I'm former 75th Rangers, and former Delta Force."

"We know who you are," a heavily bearded, thick-bodied man said. He had a pair of Oakley sunglasses perched on his head.

Luke glanced at Ed.

"My partner Ed Newsam is right over there."

Ed raised his hand.

"Ed is former 82nd Airborne and former Delta Force himself. Point being that we both know what you guys are about. We're going in hard today, so be ready for that. There's a bomb under the ice, it's about to go off, and me and Ed have to get down there and defuse it. There's a dome on this base, and the hole we need to go through is inside that dome. But we need you to get us there."

"First things first, mate," a blond-haired guy said. He might have had an Australian accent, it might have been South African. Luke wasn't good with accents. "How we getting back out of here?"

Luke shook his head. "We're not. You bought a one-way ticket, mate. These are Russian Spetsnaz down there, and we have to assume they're going to eat this plane for lunch. That means there's only one way out. We have to get that bomb defused, and we have to win the fight. In that order."

"Kill 'em all," a guy said.

Luke shrugged. "If they want a fight, we give them what they want. If they stand down…"

He let that lie there.

The men laughed. Every single one of them. Not Ed, not the scientist, not Big Daddy. But every one of the mercenaries had a hearty chuckle. These were guys who had stopped taking prisoners a long time ago. There was no nuance with them, no gray area. They were still alive because everything was black and white to them.

The plane lurched and bounced over some turbulence. Luke grabbed an overhead strap. Otherwise he barely noticed.

"I need an A-Team. Four hands."

Six hands went up. Luke picked four.

"Say hello to your best friends. You guys are out that door first. Sorry, you volunteered. The pilots are going to try to slide this thing sideways. If they manage it, it's going to put the plane between us and the bad guys. You're out the door, on the ground, behind the wheels, wherever you can find cover. I need you laying down suppressing fire as soon as you hit the ground. It's going to be wide open out there. Just pick a target and kill it. If you don't see a target, just shoot. Keep them bogged down. Shoot until your gun melts, then grab another one. Got it?"

The men murmured their assent.

"I said GOT IT?" Luke shouted.

"Got it!" one shouted.

"Rock star!" shouted another.

"Hoo-ah!"

The plane lurched again, then banked hard..

A voice came over the loudspeaker.

"Gentlemen, we have enemy contact. I repeat, enemy contact! They are firing surface to air missiles. We are three minutes from the target. Prepare for evasive action. Brace positions for hard landing."

"B-Team, four hands," Luke shouted.

The plane bounced and trembled now.

Exactly four hands went up.

"We've got two belt-fed .50-caliber machine guns on tripods," Luke said. "Tell me if you don't know how to work one of those."

They all looked at him impassively.

"Two guys on each fifty. One guy feeds, one guy shoots. A-Team is going to be suppressing, so you should get a bit of time to set up. But not long. Find some cover, one on each end of the plane. Then tear it up. You guys are our muscle. Rip them a new one. If you see any heavy ordnance, take it out first. But be especially aware—we need to carve a path to that dome. Everybody keep that in your heads. The dome is the target. If we can't get there, this was all for nothing."

"Incoming!" the loudspeaker squawked.

All down the line, guys were belting in.

There were two guys left without an assignment. One was the Australian or South African. Whatever he was, he hadn't been quick to volunteer.

"C-Team, you accompany us to the dome. We're going to be carrying heavy stuff. You guys are our bodyguards. Kill everything that stands in our way."

The plane lurched banking hard to the right. Luke rode the angle, hanging from the strap, his feet barely touching the ground. The plane rode like that for a long moment, then righted.

Somewhere behind them came the distant sound of an explosion.

Missed us.

"A-Team! When those fifties are up and running, your first job is done. Second job is to get us to that dome. If there's resistance there, you have to take it out. Once we get there, you set up and hold those entrances. Make it there, okay?"

He stared up and down the line. Not a single face registered fear.

Luke nodded. "Good. Hit hard fellas, early and often. No slacking, head on a swivel, take care of each other out there. Maybe we'll all come back alive."

The loudspeaker sputtered static.

"Prepare for landing. Hard landing! Crash positions."

Luke sat down and belted in.

This was not going to be pretty.

Trutnev was there beside him. His eyes were wild. They didn't seem able to focus. They found Luke. His mouth hung open. Luke had seen the look before.

It was terror.

"I think I made a mistake coming here," Trutnev said.

Luke nodded. "I think you did, too."

He looked at his watch. 00:27:44.

Oh. My. God.

Suddenly, the plane hit hard and bounced.

Luke got that sickening stomach drop as the plane fell and bounced the second time. His helmet tumbled away from him. Damn! He should have put it on. But you can't rile your people up with your helmet on.

Now the plane was down, skating along the ground. There were no windows. There was no way to see if it was on the runway or not.

Then came the slide. It didn't feel controlled at all. The plane spun, righted, then slid again. It was still moving fast, but beginning to slow. It tilted to the right side, slid, then righted again. That felt like they went off the runway.

The pilots were eerily silent.

Luke got up and stumbled to the jump door. Out the window, he saw a cluster of small buildings ahead. The plane was sliding sideways toward them, but the door was in front. That was not good. Luke spotted men in white jumpsuits. They were running, abandoning shooting positions.

The plane was going to hit the buildings.

He jumped back, lurching to his seat.

"Crash positions!" he shouted.

The plane hit. The rear of the fuselage crumpled and ripped off. The sound of shredding metal was deafening. Blinding white light streamed in.

The plane spun hard to its left. Luke's head hit the wall behind him.

Everything went dark.

He opened his eyes.

It was bright in here again. Too bright.

Ed Newsam was there, right in front of him, crouched at eye level. He was shouting something. No sound came out of his mouth. There was no sound anywhere.

Ed's hand snaked out and slapped Luke across the face.

Now there was ringing in his ears, followed by a rising shriek.

"Stone! Let's go! Move it!"

On his right, Trutnev was pawing at him, desperate. His hands were like claws.

"I can't go out there! I can't go out there!"

Luke shoved him away.

To the right, the rear of the plane was just gone. Black smoke was pouring out of somewhere. Flames licked at the edge of the hole. The plane was on fire.

Nailed the landing.

Luke unclipped and was up. "A-Team! A-Team! Let's go! Out the door!"

Four guys stumbled off the benches, weapons in hand. Luke smacked them as they passed. "Go! Go! Go!"

He didn't have his helmet. Ah, hell.

Across from him, the side of the plane started to crumble. They were hitting it. The Russians were shooting the plane.

Bursts of automatic fire came from outside.

The shooting did not subside. It did not slow down. Whatever was going on out there, A-Team was not achieving suppressing fire.

This whole A-Team, B-Team, C-Team plan was not going to work.

Luke picked up an MP5 that was on the floor. Ed already had one. They were already on to Plan B.

Plan B was improvise.

Luke went to the gaping hole. He peered through the fire. It was fast becoming a wall. They had to get everybody out of here. And the equipment.

A big man with a heavy beard was dead on the ground, ten feet below the hole.

Another man was crawling away, trailing the remains of his legs. They were gone below the thighs. That guy was going to be alive another five seconds.

Luke looked past the dead men. It took him an instant to realize he was starting at the inside of a building. It was some kind of rec center, or mess hall.

A man in a white jumpsuit was across the room, pulling a magazine from his gun. Luke shot him, a center mass burst. The guy fell, but was still alive. Luke gave him another burst, this time in the head. A cloud of red dispersed into the air.

Two guys from A-Team were still in the game. One was on top of a man in white, stabbing him with a knife. Another was crouched by a wrecked doorway.

They'd gotten lucky, maybe. Nobody on the ground had expected the plane to crash into a building. Now Luke's team was inside, and sheltered for the moment.

He turned back into the plane. "Everybody out! Everybody out! Plan B! Plan B!"

A man darted by. "What's Plan B?"

Luke pushed him. "Improvise! Kill Russians! Watch that drop-off!"

The men were filing out, moving fast.

Big Daddy and Ed were loading up the scuba and welding gear. It was a lot of stuff.

"We're gonna have to pass that stuff down. It's a big drop."

Luke went to the cockpit door and opened it.

The pilots were both dead in their seats. The windshield was shattered, gone. Russians were across the way, outside the building, standing on the snow. Luke hit the deck. An instant later, automatic fire ripped through the plane. He slammed the steel cockpit door.

"Pilots are dead."

"Let's go," Big Daddy said. He had a duffel bag in each hand.

Luke grabbed a couple of bags. They moved to the back of the plane. The cabin was filling up with smoke. Everybody was out, except Ed, Luke, and Big Daddy.

And one other. The scientist.

He was still strapped in his seat.

"You have to get out," Luke said. "The plane is on fire."

The man shook his head. "I can't."

"You're going to die if you stay here."

"I know."

Luke looked at his watch.

00:23:10.

There was no more time to worry about the scientist.

Ed unclipped the man's belt, grabbed him by his lapels, and yanked him up out of the seat. He gave him a powerful shove toward the flaming hole.

"Out!" he said.

"Whaddya got?" Luke said.

He was crouched at the doorway of the building. Ed and Bill were with him. Two sentries were at the door. The teams seemed to have fallen apart. But then Luke looked at these guys again. No. They were C-Team. They were the escorts.

Outside, there was gunfire everywhere.

Behind them, the plane was becoming an inferno. The building was catching fire as well. The roof was starting to go.

The guy pointed out and to the left.

"See this alley between buildings? Our guys are holding the corner there. That's fine. Three guys that way. They're taking fire, but holding their own. To the right is where we're going. Three guys are ahead of us. A guy came back and told me it's hot. But they saved a .50 and brought it up. They're trying to clear a path."

Luke glanced at his watch.

00:21:04

It was impossible. Even if they made it to the dome, they still had to put on their wet suits and scuba gear.

"How far is the dome?" he said.

The guy shrugged. "Maybe a hundred yards between these buildings. Then fifty yards wide open no-man's-land."

Luke nodded "All right. Let's hit it."

They ran up the alleyway. The bags were heavy and the two escorts got out ahead of them, guns drawn. It was a short jog, then the men turned left. Luke, Ed, and Bill followed.

Up ahead was an opening between buildings.

Two men were in the opening with the .50 cal tripod. Luke ran, the sound of his own breathing loud in his ears. But louder still was the gun.

The heavy metal of the gunfire came to him, followed by the sweet jingle bells of the spent cartridges hitting the ground.

DUH-DUH-DUH-DUH-DUH.

The gun was coming closer. The shooter sprayed from left to right, found a target, and stayed on it.

A sound rose, a whining scream.

The two men ducked.

SHHHHHHHwwwwww...BOOM!

A rocket hit the side of the building above their heads. Debris blew outward all over them. They barely paused, and were back at it again.

DUH-DUH-DUH-DUH-DUH.

Luke reached the opening a few seconds after his escorts.

The white dome was right across from them, its doorway an open black hole. A man lay dead on the ground between here and there, a spray of blood around him against the white snow.

"What happened to him?" Luke said.

One of the guys shrugged. "He didn't make it."

The feeder was changing out the belt.

Luke, Ed, and Bill leaned against a wall, the escorts just ahead of them.

The shooter was crouched by the corner. "When I start firing again, that's your best chance."

Ed held his watch up in front of Luke's face: 00:18:34.

00:18:33.

32.

31.

"Gun's ready," the shooter said. "Go!"

He was on the trigger.

DUH-DUH-DUH-DUH-DUH.

The first escort ran out, firing. Luke was right behind him. He raced across the gap. Shots kicked up ice around his feet. He was like a mule with this pack on his shoulders. It was too slow!

The black opening was RIGHT THERE.

The escort darted through it.

A rip of gunfire came.

Luke came through, his MP5 in front of him. The escort was down, but still firing. Three Russians were across the way, near what looked like a swimming pool. Luke sprayed them. They all went down. One fell into the icy water. A stain of blood rose there.

The escort was down. He gasped for air.

His teeth were gritted. "Ah, God. That hurts!"

Suddenly his eyes went blank. A second ago, they were looking at Luke. Now they weren't looking at anything.

Six, by Luke's count. Six men left from the original ten.

He looked up and Ed ran in. An instant later, Big Daddy came in, huffing and puffing. His escort was right on his heels.

The belt feeder ran in, carrying the machine gun mount with two belts draped over his shoulder. A second later, the triggerman ran in, carrying the gun.

Instantly, they began to set it up again, near the doorway.

Luke and Ed walked further into the dome. The gaping hole in the ice was right in front of them. It was long and rectangular, blue in color, contrasting with the white of the ice pack all around it.

"Ready to go for a swim?" Ed said.

00:06:13

It took over ten minutes to get the gear on.

The suits were not the state-of-the-art dry suits from the Alaska mission. These were thick neoprene wet suits. They didn't fit perfectly. They were good, but….

Luke sat on the edge of the ice, his legs in the water. He could feel the cold through the suit. It was already uncomfortable. There was no time to think about it.

He dropped into the water. Instantly he surrounded by the dark. He turned his headlamp on.

Something was wrong. The water was getting in somewhere. It was a small amount, but it was too cold.

He popped up again.

Bill Cronin was there, ready to pass him the cutting torch.

"How's the water?" he said.

"It's cold. It's really cold."

Bill nodded. "You'll get used to it."

Luke took the torch. A long black wire depended from it, back to the power source.

Back near the doorway, there was a burst of gunfire.

Luke put his mouthpiece in. Beside him, Ed Newsam dropped into the water.

"Good luck," Big Daddy said.

Luke raised a hand and dropped in again. He dove down, swimming to the bottom of the hole. The ice was incredibly thick, much thicker than the temporary ice they had encountered in Alaska. Twelve or fifteen meters, the scientist had said. This was the permanent ice pack. It had been here for a hundred thousand years.

The sound of his breathing apparatus was loud in Luke's ears.

He reached the bottom of the hole and entered into open ocean. Ed was just ahead, his light cutting through the dark. Luke felt his body shivering, trying to get warm. His body heat should warm up the water that was leaking in, but he had no idea how long that would take. Maybe he would die first.

Maybe the bomb would go off instead.

Up ahead, a large form began to appear out of the gloom. Ed's light shone on it. It was massive, majestic, gray in color. It could be a whale, but it wasn't moving. Luke noticed the scaffolding, almost like a spiderweb around it.

The giant bomb was nestled up against the ice pack.

Luke looked at the watch.

00:03:11

How could that be? How could that be?

Ed moved along the surface of the whale, his hands touching it. He seemed tiny, dwarfed by the thing. He stopped and began to wave crazily. Luke approached, floating weightless, carrying the torch, the wire playing out behind him. Big Daddy was up there somewhere, feeding him slack.

A steel box was mounted there. It was larger than Luke imagined it to be. Ed pointed. Luke nodded.

Luke pressed the button on the torch, requesting power from the surface. A couple of seconds later, the thing came alive in his hands. Big Daddy was on top of it.

Luke let out a big breath. It sounded to him like Darth Vader. Ed held up his watch in front of Luke's eyes.

00:02:04.

It wasn't enough time.

Luke depressed the button and bright red flame fired from the torch. It surprised him, and he turned it off for a moment. He hadn't done this in a while.

Ed's watch was still there. 00:01:51.

Luke turned on the torch again. He cut into the metal. The metal began to glow along the line where he was working. A small scar appeared there, becoming wider. He moved the fire long it, cutting deeper and longer.

The cut was an inch long, glowing like lava.

00:01:29.

He cut. The fire glowed red and hot blinding him, burning his hands through his neoprene gloves. This wasn't the right gear! He breathed heavily.

He was having trouble maintaining his position. The water was moving and he was moving with it.

00:01:16.

The cut was three inches long and glowing like lava.

Four inches long.

Five.

He shut off the torch and tried to wrench the box open. No good with the gloves.

00:00:54.

He lit the torch again. Were they really going to die here? He cut and cut. A piece of silver dropped away. He reached with his left hand, and broke the other piece off. He didn't even turn off the torch. He felt the flame burning through his glove.

Now he cut off the torch.

The keypad was there, the numbers glowing. Running behind it and next to it was a trunk line of black wiring.

00:00:39.

Ed was there, hovering in front of the pad. It was no good with the gloves on. The numbers were too small to press accurately. Ed turned to Luke. His eyes were wide inside his mask.

00:00:32.

His shoulders seemed to drop. He shook his head.

In his left hand, he held the serrated knife he would use to cut the wires. He stabbed the knife through his glove and began to cut it away. Instantly, his body language changed. Water was pouring into his suit, through his hand.

He ripped the glove apart. It was ragged, but still holding on. Luke dropped the welding torch. It floated away and down. He grabbed Ed's glove with body hands, and yanked it off.

Ed's hand was completely exposed. Water was pouring in at his wrist.

He was going to die down here.

He turned back to the keypad. His fingers punched in numbers, moving slowly from one key to the next. Luke watched, but couldn't even remember the code.

Stalin's birthday. Who did that help?

00:00:17.

He turned back to Luke and raised his hands. He had punched in the number. The keypad didn't do anything. The lights didn't change. It gave no indication of anything. Was that it? There was a * button. There was also a # button. Were you supposed to press those at the end? The Russian had never mentioned those buttons.

Ed's eyes began to glaze over. It was the cold. The cold was filling his suit.

00:00:11.

Luke grabbed the knife from Ed's hand. He swam to the box and began to hack at the wires. If this was wrong, an electrical field would enter the water and they would both be friend.

He sliced. He hacked.

A surge of electricity seemed to fill his body.

He was dying. They were both going to die.

He sliced the last wire away. Were these even the right wires? Maybe there were some other wires.

00:00:03.

00:00:02.

00:00:01.

Luke stared at the giant bomb rising above them.

00:00:00

Big Daddy Cronin stood at the edge of the hole in the ice. There was shooting going on behind him, out in the complex somewhere, but he paid no attention to it. The guys had held their own.

The gunfire sounded like finishing shots.

After a time, something began to rise from the bottom of the hole. Shadows appeared, resolving themselves into bodies. A head broke the surface, wearing a diver's cold-water helmet. A second head broke the surface right afterward.

Luke ripped his own helmet off.

"Bill, give me a hand with this guy. He's freezing."

Big Daddy fell to his knees and grabbed Ed by the shoulders. Luke pushed himself up and out. Together, they pulled Ed halfway out of the water. Ed helped a little bit, pressing his hands against the lip. Big Daddy noticed one of Ed's gloves was missing.

He and Luke fell backward, pulling Ed all the way out.

The three of them lay there.

Luke unfastened Ed's helmet and pulled it off.

"How you doing, Ed?" Big Daddy said.

Ed spoke through gritted teeth. "I'm cold, man."

"You dying?"

Ed grunted. Then he laughed. His whole body was shaking, a giant man mountain of quivering flesh. He shook his head.

"I doubt it."

Then the Russian scientist was standing over them, looking down. He pointed up at the giant bubble all around them.

"You know, I've seen pictures of this facility, and I read the plans for it and studied the design schematics, but of course I've never been here before. It's incredible."

Luke shook his head.

"I really want to talk to this Marmilov person."

Now Big Daddy laughed. "Let me handle it," he said.

CHAPTER FORTY

September 10
9:45 a.m. Eastern Daylight Time
The Oval Office
The White House
Washington, DC

A man named Vasil was speaking.
"It was a terrible tragedy, and we are ashamed at the actions of our countryman."

Vasil had a deep, rich voice. He was Vladimir Putin's handpicked translator, and the words he was saying were the English version of Putin's thoughts just a split second after they came out of his mouth.

Clement Dixon sat at the Resolute Desk, the handset of a dark red phone console pressed to his ear. The telephone was old and heavy, a tabletop model much like telephones from when he was young. The major differences were the color of it, and the fact that the dial didn't have any numbers on it. The phone only called one number.

This was the famous "red phone" of legend, the direct line to the Kremlin, in use during crises since the darkest days of the Cold War.

Dixon almost couldn't believe the thing really existed. Sure, he always knew that there must be a way for the White House and the Kremlin to be in contact, but for some reason he had never keyed in on the fact that the red phone was really *the red phone*. He had seen photos of it many times, and he still didn't believe it.

But now he did.

Eisenhower had held this very phone.

Kennedy.

LBJ.

It jazzed him just to touch it. He couldn't explain the feeling. It was like being a part of history, something so much larger than himself that he ...

He shook these thoughts away, and focused on what Vasil was saying. Dixon could hear Putin speaking in the background, just a second or two ahead of Vasil. The two voices in tandem—one in Russian, one in English—made an odd echo effect.

"We know you have made your initial intelligence assessments, and we understand that you have come to conclusions similar to ourselves. The traitor Marmilov acted of his own volition, in concert with a small group of conspirators. Most ground troops and individual scientists associated with the plan did not grasp the nature of the project, nor did they know where their orders were coming from."

Dixon looked around the room. Half a dozen men were listening in on the conversation, holding modern handsets of their own. He imagined there must a hundred or more people listening—here in the White House, at CIA and NSA headquarters, in the Kremlin, the GRU, the FSB, probably even in China.

Two world leaders were having a telephone summit, coming to grips with a violent and unfortunate incident, and trying to find a way to move on from it.

Richard Stark was nodding—what Vasil was saying was consistent with the direction American intelligence officials were leaning. A rogue agent from the GRU had gone all the way off the reservation.

"We want you to know that the Russian government is an open book on this matter. We would like to share with you, in as transparent a way as circumstances will allow, all of the data we have compiled about this incident, and the people who were involved. We have nothing to hide. We look forward to continued good relations with the United States, both in our shared neighborhood of the Arctic Circle, and everywhere on Earth. And we intend to compensate the families of the oil rig workers and the American commandos who died in the attack."

Personally, Dixon was okay with all of this.

Putin hadn't ordered the attack on the oil rig. He hadn't even known about it. Also, his people hadn't known. Dixon wasn't sure what that said about the state of the Russian government, but he did know that revenge was off the table. This was a good thing. Tit for tat attacks between Russia and the United States were a problem for everyone.

The major issue was going to be selling this point of view to the public.

"Well, Mr. President," Dixon said, "I'm pleased by your candor and by your commitment to the victims and their families."

Dixon prattled on for a few moments, mouthing the right platitudes. Before too long, he realized he was starting to bore people, and that it was time to wrap up the conversation.

"Please know that our commitment to partnership runs as deep as yours."

Across from him, the big flat-screen TV was on. CNN was showing a clip of the Russian Prime Minister, Dmitri Gagarin, speaking in front of a group of people. Gagarin was as handsome as people said, but from here he looked like a bit of an empty suit. Vladimir Putin, meanwhile, was the real deal.

Along the bottom of the TV there was a headline: *BREAKING: Russian Prime Minister issues vote of confidence for Putin, calls for unity.*

Dixon scanned the people in the room, hunting for a certain face. In a moment he found it: Jepsum, the young guy who had overstepped and suggested that Dixon step in and support Gagarin as the next Russian President.

It was laughable, and Jepsum looked like a man trying to make himself disappear. He needn't bother. He was going to disappear from the West Wing, whether he wanted to or not.

Dixon glanced at Gagarin on the TV again.

Boy, he was glad he hadn't backed that guy.

A new thought occurred to Dixon. He needed to find a way to get closer to this guy Don Morris, and his team of covert operatives. They had been right all along, and they kept doubling down on their rightness, despite all the obstacles that had been thrown in their way. Dixon could use some people like that in his corner.

There was a pause over the line, and Dixon jumped in to fill the space.

"Yes, Mr. President, I'm glad we had this chance to talk as well. Let's do a better job of making it a regular thing, shall we? I'll have my people get in touch with your people."

When he hung up, Dixon carefully placed the handset back in its cradle. It was such a heavy phone. There was something masculine about it. He almost wished that when his time here was over, he could take the telephone home with him.

Vice President Thomas Hayes had just hung up his own extension. They made eye contact through the crowd of people. Thomas was standing now, and he was taller than most men, by a lot. His overlarge nose suddenly became a symbol of strength, like the woman's bicep in the old Rosie the Riveter posters.

Dixon decided that he and Thomas were going to make a run at this thing. They had weathered a crisis, they had a mandate to govern, and by God, they were going to do so.

"What do you think?" Thomas said.

"Some days," Clement Dixon said, "it's good to be the President."

CHAPTER FORTY ONE

Time Unknown
Place Unknown

"Wake up, miserable dog."

In the first seconds, he didn't remember who he was.

Then the pain came rushing back, and he remembered everything. His name was Oleg Marmilov. They had come for him and taken him out of his hotel suite.

Now he was in total darkness—the darkness that comes when they put a heavy bag over your head and cinch it tight around your neck.

"Marmilov."

"Yes," he said. His voice made a faint whistling sound that he didn't associate with himself at all. He was missing teeth now. His mouth felt strangely empty. He had lost the first couple of teeth in the initial beatings. After that, a man had come in and simply wrenched some of them out with pliers.

They did that to you. They *erased* you. The person you once thought you were was taken away piece by piece. Marmilov was all too familiar with the process.

Perhaps, if he lived long enough, days or weeks from now, they would show him his reflection in a mirror. His body would be half-starved and wasted. His eyes would be sunken, blackened from punches, and ashamed. His teeth would be gone, his skin would hang on bone. His face would look like the skull of a corpse, buried and later exhumed. Maybe they would cut his nose off to complete the effect.

Maybe, after he had told them everything, they would cut his tongue out. And by "everything," he did not mean everything about the conspiracy against Putin, or his dreams of a return to greatness for Russia—but *everything*, every loss, every defeat, his worst, most secret humiliations going all the way back to childhood.

None of this even touched upon what they would do—what they were already doing—to his bones. He had several broken ribs on his left side that made breathing difficult and painful. Most of his fingers were broken. He thought maybe one of the bones in his right forearm was broken—the last time he saw it, the lower arm had swollen up like a sausage about to burst its skin.

And the pain had hardly even begun.

Without warning, someone grabbed him by the neck and roughly pulled the bag from his head.

Marmilov blinked at the light flooding into his eyes. It was not bright in here. He was somewhere underground, in a place without windows. A dim yellow arc lit the room from the ceiling. But after absolute darkness, the bleak light seemed to sear his retinas.

He was bound to a metal chair. The chair was uncomfortable, all hard edges, and bolted to the floor. He had no idea how long he had been sitting here.

"You smell. Do you know that?"

Marmilov nodded. Of course he knew that. He had wet himself, more than once. He hadn't done the other thing yet, and that was a small blessing. But he would, if they held him here long enough.

The man speaking to him had hair the color of sand. He was short and muscular, a sportsman, or someone who spent long hours pushing weights in a gym. His jaw was strong like that of a caveman. There were many such men in Russia.

There were other men in the room, but the sandy-haired man was the one in charge. He wore a tight black shirt, slacks and shiny black shoes. The man stared at Marmilov with the eyes of a hawk.

"I killed Zelazny myself," he said, and smiled.

Around the room, a couple of the other men laughed.

"It's true. I was with our American visitors. Nice guys, they thought I was their tour guide. I put one bullet in Zelazny's brain, then pushed his body into the Moskva with my foot. Do you know that he cried? He was a degenerate, and of course he cried. He cried several times. But at one point, he wept like some grandmother. Why did he weep?"

Marmilov didn't say a word. He just looked at the man. If circumstances had turned out differently, and this tormentor had ended up here in the chair… Marmilov was careful not to smile at the thought.

"Do you know why?" the man said.

Marmilov shook his head. He still didn't speak. He loathed the sound of his voice with the teeth missing.

"He wept when he revealed your name." He looked around the room at the other men. He smiled. "Can you imagine?"

They all laughed.

"He wept because merely uttering the name Oleg Marmilov was so frightening, he could barely make himself do it. The name alone was enough to break the spirit of a grown man. Oleg the Terrible. Oleg the Great."

He shook his head.

"Look at you now."

There was a long moment of quiet. The man appeared to be thinking about something.

"We know everything," he said finally. "We have finally learned all of your reckless, foolish plans. A friend from the other side informed me of them once he was free to do so. Have you no brain, Marmilov? Would you destroy the world to save it? Russia will return to greatness without you. It does not need your help. In fact, Russia will be better off when you are gone."

He paused.

"We've read your diaries, you know? Such grandiosity, such self-regard. Me, me, me, me, me. It reads like the diary, not of a great man, but of a teenage girl. Rest assured we have also looked at all of your files. We have the kompromat on your puppet Gagarin. He's our puppet now, so thank you for that. And we know who your co-conspirators were—all of them, I suppose. Of course, you gave up most of them yourself, didn't you?"

Again, the men around the room laughed.

Marmilov did his best not to cry. So far, he had denied them this. His own end was tragic enough, but this was truly the end of everything. The people who would remove Putin were likely being rounded up at this moment—men in the government, in the military, in business. Marmilov knew who all the players were. If there were any besides these, they were well-hidden and powerless.

Far from overthrowing Putin, the entire exercise had only cemented his rule.

"I also killed Chevsky," the man said. He shrugged, as if he was just bringing up a minor issue he had forgotten to mention earlier.

Chevsky.

Marmilov did cry then, just a few tears running from his eye. Chevsky was a good man, almost like a son to him. If he'd had children, Marmilov would have wanted a son like Chevsky. But Marmilov didn't have children—he had given his life to the country that was now killing him.

"Shot him in the head," the man said. "Threw him in the river, too. What else are you supposed to do with traitors?"

Behind him, a heavy steel door opened.

Another group of men came in. They were tall, very broad, with stern faces. Marmilov recognized them right away for what they were—bodyguards. From behind them a much smaller man emerged. He wore a dark business suit, with no tie, and a white dress shirt open at the collar.

Vladimir Putin.

He looked down at Marmilov—Marmilov sitting in the hard metal chair that had become his home. Putin's eyes said everything. It was business as usual. He wasn't angry. He wasn't amused, either. The state of Marmilov was already past the place where Putin could derive pleasure from it.

Marmilov hated that his old rival would see him like this.

"Marmilov," Putin said.

"Putin."

There was that whistling sound again.

"You were always envious," Putin said. "Even when we were young."

Marmilov shook his head. That was a lie. It was never envy.

"You have not done your job," he said. He ignored the cartoon quality of his own voice. He ignored the humiliation of his defeat. He would say his piece. He must speak the truth of what was happening.

"You promised greatness. But you and your friends will strip us bare, and run us into the Earth." It was all he could muster so far, but there was more to come.

Putin smiled and shook his head. A small breath of air escaped from him.

"I assure you I'm doing my best."

He looked at the man with sandy hair.

"End it. No more of this. However flawed, he was an asset to us at one time."

The sandy-haired man nodded. "Yes, sir. As you wish."

Putin turned to leave. Without a backwards glance at Marmilov, he disappeared behind his wall of bodyguards.

"Putin!" Marmilov said. "Vladimir!"

The heavy black bag came down over his head, and he plunged into darkness again. His throat constricted as they cinched the bag tight around his neck.

Something very hard pressed against his right eye. Marmilov felt a surge of panic rise through his body. The end was coming now. There would be no more statements, and no more truth would be told. The hard object was the barrel of a gun.

This was not right, nor wrong. This was Russian justice.

"Goodbye, Marmilov," a voice said.

CHAPTER FORTY TWO

10:30 a.m. Eastern Daylight Time
Queen Anne's County, Maryland
Eastern Shore of Chesapeake Bay

L uke was cold.

It was a sunny September day, with a stiff breeze that had just a hint of winter's approaching bite hidden within it. There were whitecaps out on the bay. Close to shore, people in black wetsuits raced back and forth on old windsurfing boards, or caught big air hanging from colorful kite surfing rigs.

It looked like fun out there.

But Luke couldn't seem to get the cold out of his bones. He sat at the table out on the patio, with a pair of old, worn jeans on, and a paint-splattered green sweatshirt. He wore a knit wool cap on his head.

He had a cup of black coffee in front of him, along with a peanut butter and jelly sandwich on toast. Not only was he cold, but he couldn't motivate himself to whip up anything more than the world's easiest sandwich. This was his breakfast.

Becca had been calling him all morning, but he couldn't bring himself to answer the telephone. He gathered from her messages that the video which showed he was a monster had been publicly debunked.

It was now widely understood on TV that the raid to take back the oil rig was an act of heroism. Also, rumors of the second Arctic operation were beginning to leak out. Anyone familiar with the

SRT, and who could read between the lines a little bit, would know that they were involved.

So now Luke was her hero again, and she wanted to make up.

She couldn't keep doing this.

She couldn't keep accusing him of being a murderer, only to take it back later.

She couldn't keep forcing him to lie about and cover up his activities.

She couldn't keep withholding her love.

He could make a list of the things that she couldn't keep doing, but he knew that idea was going nowhere. He loved her. They had a child together, and he loved that child more than anything in the world.

He was tired. Physically, emotionally, in every way. He knew there was a compromise here somewhere, he just didn't know where it was, and he didn't know if he had the energy to find it.

There was a thick book open on the table in front of him. This cabin had been in Becca's family for generations, and they were nothing if not highly educated. The living room wall was lined with two floor-to-ceiling bookcases, both of which were chock full of books. The books were old.

It was kind of incredible, given the way the world was going, that bookcases like these still existed. But they did, and Luke had gotten into the habit of reaching in and taking a random book out from time to time. And a couple of months ago, Luke had come across something that seemed to sum up his situation quite well.

That was even truer now than before.

Murphy was dead. That was sad, but Luke was numb to it right now. He imagined he would come face-to-face with that loss repeatedly over the next several months. He might even come to terms with it over time. For the moment, he was rejecting the idea that he had killed Murphy. Yes, Luke had called him, and had asked him to come on the mission. Yes, that happened. But he hadn't tried very hard to convince Murphy of anything. Murphy hadn't needed much convincing.

At the moment, what bothered Luke most about it was what it said about him—he was the last person left alive from the doomed mission in eastern Afghanistan. And Murphy had always accused Luke of being responsible for those deaths. Martinez had done the same, before he killed himself.

There was a lot to think about here. It was a puzzle, and Luke didn't know if he could untangle it by himself.

It would be nice to talk to Becca about Murphy's death. It would be nice to talk to her about what it was like to be the only survivor of an operation that was FUBAR from the beginning, and which he might have been able to stop before it even started.

It would be nice to talk to her about the Russians in the Arctic. Apparently, the soldiers that had fought Luke and company didn't know that the bomb under the ice was set to explode, and that if it did, it would set off a chain reaction of catastrophes that would affect the whole world.

They didn't know that their orders came not from the Russian military itself, but from an espionage agent who had gone rogue and was trying to topple his own government. Those men fought and died in a miserably harsh climate, and had no idea what they were even fighting for.

It would be nice for Luke to hold his son on his lap here, and talk to Becca in a relaxed manner about these things, and about the waves of meaningless that seemed to wash over him every few minutes since he had gotten out of bed this morning.

But that wasn't possible right now because there was a gulf between him and Becca, a gap so cold and vast that it reminded him of the bleak white distances at the top of the world. He could almost see her there, a tiny figure hundreds of miles away.

God, he wanted to fix that, but he didn't know how. He wanted to fix this world, too, and he didn't know how to do that either.

He took a sip of his tepid coffee and picked up the heavy book. It was an anthology of English poetry, from the Middle Ages up until the early twentieth century. He looked down at the page and scanned some lines that he had already read and reread several times in the past hour.

There was nothing new under the sun, and a man named Matthew Arnold seemed to have understood Luke's life perfectly, 150 years before Luke was ever born. Maybe one day Luke would work up the courage to read these lines out loud to his wife:

Ah, love, let us be true
To one another! for the world, which seems
To lie before us like a land of dreams,
So various, so beautiful, so new,
Hath really neither joy, nor love, nor light,
Nor certitude, nor peace, nor help from pain;
And we are here as on a darkling plain
Swept with confused alarms of struggle and flight,
Where ignorant armies clash by night.

CHAPTER FORTY THREE

September 15
6:15 p.m. Lebanon Daylight Time (11:15 a.m. Eastern
Daylight Time)
Spaghetteria Italiana
Beirut, Lebanon

"War is coming."

A man who was not named Kevin Murphy sat at a corner table in a legendary Beirut restaurant, sipping strong espresso. He was tall, with very white skin and short hair. His face was clean shaven. No one in Beirut seemed to look anything like him.

When, in all these years, had war not been coming?

He barely glanced at the person who had spoken—a dark-skinned and heavily bearded young man sitting across from him. Instead, he stared out the open air window, at the stunning seafront promenade, mostly empty as the light faded this early evening, its palm trees pockmarked with bullet holes.

He knew that Beirut had once been considered the jewel of the Mediterranean, a city so beautiful that it brought the jet set—movie stars, musicians, writers, politicians, royalty—from around the globe. He shook his head. Not anymore. It might as well have never happened.

One glance around this famous restaurant was enough to tell you that—there was hardly anyone in the place. Business was bad. Apparently, masked death squads rolling through the streets in pickup trucks, and car bombs going off every few days were enough to keep even the most intrepid foodies at home.

Even so, he had to admit that he liked it here.

"Tell me about it," he said.

The young man's voice dropped to just above a whisper. He leaned in close. "There is going to be a provocation. The Hezbollah scouts have been watching the border patrols for months. They are intercepting radio communications."

The younger man hesitated. He sat up, glanced around the nearly empty restaurant, and lit a cigarette. "Do you even grasp what I'm saying?"

"I guess not. I'm slow. Maybe you should explain it a little more clearly."

The bearded man shook his head. "There is work for someone like you."

The man not named Murphy didn't speak for some time. He looked out at the sea again. Blue sky, blue water. So nice.

Somewhere, not far away, people were looking at this same sky, and this same water, and they were not having this conversation. They were not talking about war. They were not imagining super-sonic jets pounding their cities into dust.

Greece. Italy. Spain. In those places, people were enjoying the beach, and the sun, and good food, and maybe friends and lovers.

But that didn't interest him right now. Maybe it never really had.

He was feeling philosophical these days. Somehow, through some miracle, he had wriggled out from under the stone pillar at that mosque. He didn't like to think of those moments. He had run toward the back wall of the mosque, away from the onrushing truck bomb. Dimly, he noticed he still had an Uzi in his hand.

He fired it at the wall as he ran toward it.

Pure instinct.

There was no rational reason why that would work. Except that the mosque was old and the whole place was falling apart. The pillars had come down, the floor had caved in, the roof was going to collapse. Why wouldn't the walls be compromised, as well?

He didn't think any of this. He just ran toward the wall, as fast as he could, firing an automatic weapon at it. It didn't fall. It didn't budge. But when he hit it, it was weakened so much that he blasted right through it.

And kept running.

When the truck hit, the force of the blast knocked him off his feet and threw him. But it threw him forward, away from the explosion. His body had been on fire, yes, but he had simply hit the ground and rolled around until the fire was out.

The fire in the mosque? It had burned for days.

He had come out of the whole mess alive, and nearly unscathed.

But he was done this time. No person could have lived through that. And yet, here he was. He had some weird bubble around him—call it a cone of invincibility—the same cone that seemed to surround people like Luke Stone and Ed Newsam. But it couldn't last forever. Sooner or later, Stone would get him killed.

Right now, Stone must think Murphy was dead. They all must.

Murphy smiled at that idea. The Special Response Team would never call him again. They couldn't call him. His phone was incinerated, and he was gone. A fire like that? No one would even find his remains.

They'd probably hold a funeral for him and bury him in Arlington National Cemetery. He was a war hero, after all. That was a nice thought. Maybe he would put on a disguise and go.

Nah. Come to think of it, that would never happen. They didn't plant you in Arlington if you had a dishonorable discharge. Hmmm. Maybe Don Morris would finally pull some strings and get that honorable discharge reinstated.

The man who was not Murphy smiled and shook his head.

No funeral. No trip to Leavenworth to fulfill some weird fantasy that Don Morris had. No worries about what Wallace Speck might or might not say when the bright light was shining in his eyes. No more suicidal missions with Luke Stone and Ed Newsam.

None of that stuff.

Instead, this:

More than two million dollars in cash in an anonymous account, a raft of marketable skills during a seller's market for such skills, and total freedom to go wherever he felt like going, and do whatever he wanted.

He looked at the young bearded man again.

"What sort of work are we talking about, and how much does it pay?"

The young man's eyes were earnest. That's what Americans never seemed to get about these Islamic guys. *They meant it.* This wasn't a joke to them. This wasn't something they did while waiting for something else to come along. They weren't hoping to be on a TV show someday, where the host would ask them to describe everything that happened, and how they felt about it.

This *was* the show. They were going to die doing this, all of them, just like the guy who was driving the truck bomb.

"That depends," the guy said. "We know that Americans sometimes have strong ideas about things. We believe these ideas are incorrect. The West is all falsehood. Of course, we know that there are certain actions you will not take—harm women and children, for example. We respect this. But as to the other things, the politics, the philosophy, the belief, each man must decide for himself."

He gave not Murphy a long, serious look.

"Do you care which side you're on?" he said.

Not Murphy thought about it for a long moment, and a realization came to him. He had a sickness, and that's all it was. He didn't have to be here. He didn't need whatever money this kid and his cause could pay him. The kid's religion was a joke. God, if there was such a thing, didn't care if men wore beards. God didn't care if people danced or listened to music. God didn't care if women were wrapped like burritos from head to toe.

God just didn't care.

A jumble of images, like newsreel footage, passed through not Murphy's mind. He had seen, and done, an awful lot. If he was honest with himself, he had done most of it for the adrenaline rush.

There was magic in that, and he smiled.

"No, I don't care. Not really."

Now Available for Pre-Order!

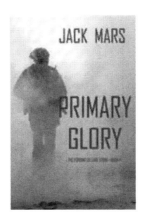

PRIMARY GLORY
(The Forging of Luke Stone—Book #4)

"One of the best thrillers I have read this year."
—Books and Movie Reviews (re Any Means Necessary)

In PRIMARY GLORY (The Forging of Luke Stone—Book #4), a ground-breaking action thriller by #1 bestseller Jack Mars, the President is taken hostage aboard Air Force One. A shocking ride ensues as elite Delta Force veteran Luke Stone, 29 and the FBI's Special Response Team may be the only ones who can bring him back.

But in an action-packed thriller jammed with shocking twists and turns, the destination—and the extraction—may be even more dramatic than the ride itself.

PRIMARY GLORY is a standalone, un-putdownable military thriller, a wild action ride that will leave you turning pages late into the night. The precursor to the #1 bestselling LUKE STONE THRILLER SERIES, this series takes us back to how it all began, a riveting series by bestseller Jack Mars, dubbed "one of the best thriller authors" out there.

"Thriller writing at its best."
—Midwest Book Review (re *Any Means Necessary*)

Also available is Jack Mars' #1 bestselling LUKE STONE THRILLER series (7 books), which begins with Any Means Necessary (Book #1), a free download with over 800 five star reviews!

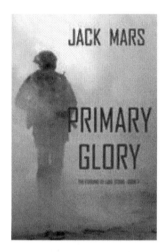

PRIMARY GLORY
(The Forging of Luke Stone—Book #4)

Printed in Great Britain
by Amazon